With One Hand Waving Free

By Connie Kronlokken

The author believes that all quotations in this book have been used under the "commentary and criticism" fair use of copyrighted materials.

Published by

**Lightly
Held
Books**

ISBN-10: 0692517146
ISBN-13: 978-0692517147

DEDICATION

To Jesse, Jessica, Peter, Tara, Andrew, Susannah,
Kimberly, Micah, Isaac and Jonas

With One Hand Waving Free

Paul wasn't home when Foxy, the miniature collie who had been his companion for many years, died. Mother stood in the driveway when Paul and Dad, the Lutheran pastor of a small Iowa town, pulled up with Kristen and Hanna, his sisters, in the back of the station wagon. Dad was exuberant, as always, in the midst of his family flock, but Mother looked sober.

"It's Foxy," she said. "Mr. Brookhaven found her in the road."

Paul knew immediately. Foxy had fallen in with another younger dog and had taken to chasing cars when Paul was at school.

Mother led the little party across the gravel road to where Mr. Brookhaven had dragged her half an hour before, wrapped in a tarpaulin in the ditch against the hot June sun. Mother wanted Paul to collect the little dog himself. If the girls had been smaller, perhaps she wouldn't have brought them, but Kristen, at nine, loved Foxy almost as much as Paul, and Hanna was nearly six, too old not to be included in family sorrow.

Paul felt frozen, his legs walking, his eyes seeing, but his heart stood still. He had been teaching Bible School that morning, wearing a plaid shirt and his school jeans as he did not like to display his skinny polio leg.

Dad knelt down and uncovered the body. Foxy's eyes stared at them, open and glassy. Her pink tongue hung out with dried blood near it, but her long golden and white fur looked untouched.

"I hope she didn't feel anything," said Dad. "Looks like it was quick."

Paul breathed deeply and kneeling down, put his hands in the thick white collar around Foxy's chest. He had felt her little thumping heart so often, but now it was still. The body was warm, but Foxy, Paul's best friend, would not now hear what he said to her.

1

"Can I touch her?" asked Hanna, small and blonde in shorts and a sleeveless shirt, her thin face taking on the solemnity of those around her.

"Sure," said Paul. He took Hanna's hand and led it to where the little heart once beat with life.

Mr. Brookhaven, who had been their neighbor for many years, came out of his house. "I'm sorry I didn't see it happen," he said. "Didn't hear a thing."

"Strange the driver didn't stop," said Dad. "But some of the old geezers around here wouldn't hear a thump on their car anyway."

A tear trickled down Kristen's face and she crossed her arms in front of her stocky little chest. Always blunt as she didn't seem to know what you weren't supposed to say, she asked, "What are you going to do with her?"

"I think we should take her out to the farm where she was born. I'm sure they'll have a place we can bury her," said Dad looking down at Paul.

Paul drew the tarpaulin gently across the lively, sharp-nosed intelligent little face and stood up. "Sure," he said. "That sounds best." He picked up the body, pulling the canvas around it.

"We should do it right away," said Dad low. He waved a hand to Don Brookhaven. "Thanks, Don!"

Paul carried the heavy, limp body back across the road to the parsonage and laid it in the shade of the tall cedars, Dad, Mother and his sisters following.

"I'll call the Odegaards and tell them you are coming," said Mother as she went into the house. "But have some lunch first."

Paul didn't want to leave the little body. Mother excused him to take his sandwich out to sit beside Foxy. He felt bad he hadn't been home. He had just graduated from high school and he wasn't teaching Bible School by choice. He would have been much happier wandering the byways and the rolling hills near town with Foxy.

But Dad needed his broad-shouldered sandy-haired son, and Paul could not refuse. Bible School was only in the mornings, and only for two weeks. Paul's reward would come in a week, when the family went up to their lake cabin in northern Minnesota.

Mother found a soft cotton sheet to wrap Foxy in. She was getting a much-needed rest after a year as a librarian at the high school, helping pay for the college educations of her six children. Dad and Paul wrapped Foxy in the sheet and the tarpaulin too. They drove out to the farm and buried her under an oak as Mr. Odegaard suggested.

Late in the afternoon, Paul still couldn't tell how he felt. He walked out past the Catholic cemetery where a lawnmower buzzed among the gravestones, and down to the creek. No light footsteps were at his side. He and Foxy had walked here almost every day that spring. He remembered the winter day, years ago, when they had been far down the frozen creek and Paul sprained his good leg and could hardly walk. Foxy had sense enough to go get Dad, and Dad had rescued him.

Paul had little experience of death, its silence. But it felt natural. Normal. Foxy was at peace, in dog heaven, perhaps herding the sheep she had never found in life. She was at least seven years old, almost fifty in dog years. She had been a little crazy lately, chasing cars with the Nelson's younger mutt. But she was always calm and attentive with Paul. Kristen loved Foxy too, and Paul had planned that Kristen would take care of her when he left for college in the fall.

But Paul no longer had to worry about his little border collie. He looked around. It was the quiet time while the birds nested. The trees had budded out in May, and their lush canopies also absorbed sound. Willows clumped along the banks of the creek, their long green fronds hanging down on thin golden wands. The creek was full, gurgling over the rocks at his feet. Paul sat in the sand in a thicket of willows, not thinking, feeling the emptiness in his heart. It was a time of change. Without Foxy to talk to, times had changed indeed.

Since his older sisters had left home, Paul spent more time alone. Line, the vibrant leader of the gang, was in Chicago, working in an old people's home. No one heard much from Line, who was always absorbed by the dramas going on around her. Marty, a year younger, was at summer school at Wittenberg College in Cardinal, thirty miles north, and would soon leave for England to spend a year as an au pair in Oxford.

Paul had friends in school, but he never called anyone. The small amount of time he had to spend in the natural world was enough company for him. At the end of summer he would leave too, for a small Lutheran college where the Mikkelson name did not precede him.

At last, when the sun sank behind the willows and Paul got hungry, he walked home. Newly-cut grass lay in fragrant green piles in the cemetery. Maybe there's a baseball game on tonight, Paul thought. He identified with

3

the troubles of the Twins' hitter Harmon Killebrew, who had an injury to his elbow the year before that almost kept him out of the World Series. Killebrew had started the spring season in fine shape, but his home run stats were lower than usual.

* * *

When Marty heard about Foxy, she included condolences to Paul in a letter home. Writing in an old wooden grain mill used by Norwegian pioneers and now on the Wittenberg campus, Marty thought of each member of her family. Summer rain dripped off the pine trees and showered on the roof but didn't touch Marty where she sat on a little ledge just inside the open doorway, a heavy granite millstone at her elbow. Lush green lawn spread down the hill toward the dormitories.

Using a blue cartridge pen on a sheet of thick vellum paper, Marty wore a button-down-the-front shirt that she didn't want to tuck into her shorts and thick-rimmed glasses. With pale skin and dark hair, which she wore short and rolled up in curlers on good days, Marty looked like someone who valued her brains more than her body. She was beginning to notice her body, however, and a few things happened that summer that she couldn't write home about.

For the first time in her life Marty had a room of her own, a spare, light-filled, monastic room with a single bed, a small bookshelf and a lamp, in a house near the edge of campus. The owner, the widowed Mrs. Larsen, had been a missionary to China with her husband and now lived a vigorous life by herself. Wittenberg College felt obliged to keep an eye on her and lodged a student with her. Marty was delighted to be that student for her last summer on campus.

Mrs. Larsen liked Marty. She got up early in the morning and laid out breakfast on the small table in the living room. The room was filled with dark furniture, odd oriental carvings and ancient books. Tall, thin Mrs. Larsen went back and forth to the kitchen, serving Marty, who felt the need to make conversation. It was awkward, as she didn't really know where Mrs. Larsen had been or what she had done.

Not wanting to ask questions, out of courtesy, Marty praised the food. Mrs. Larsen was quite adamant about what one should eat. She served meats and vegetables stewed and sauced, cooked as if for an old person, but some of the vegetables were from her own garden.

"You should feel very lucky to have such a variety of good food in front of you," said Mrs. Larsen. "In China, in 1915, the famine was unimaginable. People were stripping the bark from trees, pounding it into meal and eating it."

Marty did not know how to respond. It didn't fit with the China she knew from the poets, the paintings in the Arthur Waley book. "Famine?" she asked.

"Yes," said Mrs. Larsen. "It was horrible. Babies, little children dying. We were only in China for about fifteen years, but it was heart-wrenching."

Mrs. Larsen didn't talk about the past often. She was interested in what Marty was reading and studying. Marty tried to be a good guest and think of things to tell her, but old people were strange to her. Mrs. Larsen wasn't family and convention stood between them. She asked about the curios in the cabinets and told Mrs. Larsen how much she loved poetry. Marty assumed that Mrs. Larsen would be shocked by her actual thoughts about religion and life which were no longer very Lutheran.

Over the summer, however, Mrs. Larsen told Marty more about the connections between the Norwegian and Danish families who had founded the church and the college, among whom were the Larsens. Marty loved coming home to the ordered little house and garden. In the evenings, before bedtime, she and Mrs. Larsen companionably ate a dish of stewed prunes.

Marty loved the room which she didn't have to share. She washed her clothes and linens in Mrs. Larsen's washer and hung them out on a clothesline to dry, drinking in the smell of fresh sun-dried bedding and clothes. She lay in the long evening light, reading the recently published *Doctor Zhivago* by Pasternak, a translation in a thick book with a red cover. The language, the spacious light on the bare white walls and wooden floor, and her solitude, made Marty achingly happy.

All of this Marty could write home about. She also wrote about her work at the library, where she found supervising other girls her own age wasn't much fun; about her friend Kate, who was preparing to teach in a Christian academy; and about her own travel preparations, getting her birth certificate and applying for a passport. She discussed with Dad the Icelandic Airlines ticket he was buying for her. She tried to thank Mother and Dad for all they had been to her, for her education and for helping her to go to Oxford for the coming year.

But two things happened to grow her up that she couldn't write home about. For one thing, she asked Jack Kjome for a ride to a friend's wedding, because she knew he was going in that direction. It was not something she wanted to do, because Jack ran with the artsy crowd Dad didn't like. He smoked and drank and held free-thinking opinions about religion. Nevertheless, Marty really wanted to go to the wedding. She put a note on Jack's car asking him, and he took her the thirty miles down to Montauk.

Jack brought one of his friends with him and Marty sat in the back seat. They dropped Marty off at the wedding of her friend, which was lovely. On the way back, however, Jack and John decided to drive to Wisconsin where they could get beer. It was Sunday and the "blue laws" prevented the purchase of alcohol of any kind in Iowa.

Marty had no choice but to accompany them. She was scared. She was afraid they would drink while they drove, even have an accident. When they got to the roadhouse in Wisconsin, she refused to go with them into the brightly-lit building. She sat in the back seat and fumed.

When they returned, Jack and John got into the car as if Marty wasn't even there, mild as you please. As they drove back to Cardinal, they talked to each other easily. It was obviously something they often did on weekends. Marty, in the back seat, relaxed. She realized that what they were doing was not something to fear, or fight, and that she was the one who should get over the revulsion towards alcohol built in to her nerves.

When they got to Mrs. Larsen's house, Marty thanked Jack, delighted to be home safe. Jack probably felt a bit sheepish, taking the pastor's daughter off to Wisconsin to drink.

But inside, Marty was happy. She had crossed a barrier that had been in her life since childhood. No one Marty knew drank. Drink was evil. But Marty wanted to open to the world. That night she realized that if she were to move in the world, she would have to see that there was nothing so dread and horrible about drinking. Jack and John had not instantly turned to devils when they came out of the lively Wisconsin roadhouse.

On another night, Josiah Ogude asked Marty to go for a walk with him. There were few students at Wittenberg during the summer and Marty, who was technically already a graduate, was sometimes asked to dinner with young faculty members and other older students. She was as naïve and felt as young as ever, but people had begun to treat her like a grownup.

Josiah was highly respected. He was back in Cardinal for a vacation, though he was getting a doctorate in history in Wisconsin. He and Marty walked around campus, talking about the complicated politics and poetry of Josiah's native Rhodesia. As night fell, they ended up sitting on the bleachers under the sky, kissing and fondling each other in the dark for hours. Neither of them could bear to leave the other, but at the same time, they must. And they did. But Marty certainly wasn't going to write to her parents about this.

To Paul Marty wrote she was sorry Foxy had died and that she was thinking of him. She asked whether anyone had heard from Line. According to the news, there were riots going on in Chicago and Marty wondered whether they might affect Line. Line, as everyone knew, put off writing as long as she could. She was capable of writing a letter, but present moments always took precedence, and she often waited until things resolved themselves. She ought to understand we would be content with developments, thought Marty crossly.

By this time the afternoon shower was over and only a few drops fell out of the wet pine trees high above. Marty packed up the letter, her books, papers and notebooks and carried them home, shielding them from the damp.

* * *

Things were moving too fast for Line to spend any time with pen and paper. The riots didn't affect her. They were around Division Street where the Puerto Ricans lived. When Line took the el south on weekends to help Stephen at the SDS national office on 63rd Street, she went right past it. Line had met Stephen Cohen in Selma the previous year, during the Selma to Montgomery civil rights march.

Militant Afro-Americans, whom Line was learning to call blacks, were becoming increasingly reluctant to include whites in their fight. But Stephen was deeply involved in the programs of Students for a Democratic Society: attempts to organize poor communities in Chicago and protests against the war the United States was waging in a tiny Asian country called Vietnam. He lived in a big, dilapidated house at the edge of the Woodlawn ghetto near the University of Chicago. Many SDS staffers lived and worked there.

One weekend it was terribly hot. Humid heat hung in the air during the day, and it was impossible to be outdoors in the sun. Line hurried down the sidewalk on the shady side of the dingy street and up the stairs of the old wooden building, self-conscious with her pale skin and red-gold hair. She stopped and bought ice cream at the corner store run by someone people called "the Arab." A few black kids were playing ball outside, but mostly the street was empty under the glaring sun.

Line found Stephen making phone calls in the office, oblivious to the dusty stacks of paper around him. Someone else was typing intensely, and from the front room, where the group met for policy discussions, came the sound of a staticky radio playing a Beatles song. She kissed the top of Stephen's damp, curling hair lightly as he talked, and he greeted her by wrapping his free arm around her ample hips.

7

Most mornings the group of eleven or so staffers met to discuss the day's efforts and then fanned out to talk to people in the blocks and pass out leaflets they made up. Stephen stayed in the office, as he was administratively-inclined. Stacks of mail and hundreds of phone calls were coming in as SDS became nationally known as one of the prime sources of information and protest regarding the war, the draft and what the group called "the system."

Line went out to the kitchen and found enough cracked bowls and spoons to distribute the ice cream she had brought to the cadre working in the heavy heat of the office. Line, who had never missed a meal in her life, felt sorry for the austere life the activists led, eating mostly peanut butter sandwiches and beans. It was Saturday, but work in the SDS national office never quit.

Line put down a saucer of milk for the black cat who hung around the back stairs, and watered the dry plants on the back stoop. Long ago, the house had surely held a Victorian household with a hierarchy of servants. The kitchen opened onto a series of steps that led down into the miniscule back yard covered in dry grass where the laundry had once been hung out and the garbage collected.

Stephen slept in a tiny room off the kitchen where a maid must have lived. It was cold in the winter, with its single-paned windows, but Line was comfortable there. During the week, she lived in a converted carriage house on a tree-shaded street in the northern part of the city. Line worked at a Lutheran Home for the Aged, housed in the mansion in front. But on alternate weekends, she was free, and she didn't have to tell anyone where she was going. That was the beauty of the city.

Line stayed with Stephen in his room, sleeping on a thin mattress on the floor. Sometimes she traveled to college campuses with him, if she was sure she could get back for work. There wasn't much privacy. People used the kitchen at all hours of the day and night and didn't mind calling Stephen out for a chat. But Stephen wanted Line with him and she was willing to put up with a lot to be there.

Line's ice cream was greeted with delight, but it was gobbled down and the dish set aside on people's desks. Sarah asked if Line would help her address envelopes, and Line sat down to work, a big stack of paper to fold and stuff in front of her.

Stephen was still smarting from a bout with the University of Chicago over its policy of handing over student rankings to draft boards. For the first time that year, draft boards could call up students. None of them could believe the university was cooperating! A sit-in had been called off when it appeared the faculty would meet. But faculty members upheld the administration's policy and harsh measures against future campus disruption were threatened. Weeks of work had gone down the drain.

The group also argued bitterly about what they should do with their small amount of resources. They had a Jobs or Income Now project going, which engaged poor people who had come up from the South to work in the city, and Economic Research and Action Projects, which organized people to take on local issues. Some thought these projects vied with mobilization against the draft and the war. As a group, SDS tried to take on the system on many fronts, but there was little money and many ideas about what to do with the staff's time.

Line hoped that things would slow down in the evening. And in fact the hot air sat in the rooms so oppressively after the sun went down that everyone in the office went outdoors and wandered over to the lake. At Promontory Point, which stuck out into Lake Michigan, they found thousands of other people driven out of their apartments by the heat, sitting like so many seals or seabirds at the edge of the cooling water.

It was an atmosphere Line loved, celebratory but quiet. Some had brought guitars and banjos. The music moved quietly through the air, modified by the water and the many bodies. In the apartment, Line had felt so sticky she didn't want to touch anyone, but now, in the breeze off the lake, Stephen made a place for Line in the circle of his arms and they sat talking so quietly no one else could understand them.

"Our dog died," Line told Stephen. She wanted him to know that elsewhere, outside the intense political activism around him, people were living ordinary lives. "Well, it was really Paul's dog. It got run over. I got a letter from Marty, telling me about it."

"Sorry," said Stephen, absently. "Will you miss the dog?"

"I haven't been home in so long," said Line. "I miss them all, but not enough to go home, I guess." She looked up and kissed Stephen, getting his attention. "I'd miss you too much if I did that," she smiled.

"I'm glad," said Stephen. "You're grown up now. You get to live your own life."

"Yes," said Line. She had just become 22. It felt good, but she was getting restless. She couldn't be an apprentice social worker much longer.

"I heard from my mother. They want me to take more classes," said Stephen. His parents were in Brooklyn, an educated couple, the children of Russian Jewish immigrants. Stephen was two years older than Line, working on a graduate degree in sociology, but as slowly as possible, to protect his student deferment, which might not be available any longer anyway. "Get that degree." He smiled. "Get a job! I've got a job," he said tentatively, meaning his work at SDS. His parents paid for tuition, but Stephen worked off his board and room at SDS.

Line could feel the irony in Stephen's thin body. But also his determination. Revolutionary rhetoric, served up with coffee every morning, and the daily influx of people wanting to be a part of it, inured him to hardship and stimulated his intellect. Line felt herself to be the soft envelope around the one-pointed hardness in him. She wanted to make a good life for him, as she had seen Kay Freeman do for her husband. But Stephen said he had little to offer Line. The war must end before there could be peace at home.

Stephen stretched and lay down on the sand and Line lay beside him. "I wish we had a blanket," said Stephen.

"Imagine," laughed Line. "That after the heat all day we would want a blanket." But the breeze off the lake was cool. No one was going anywhere. Groups of people sat all around them. They faced south, a string of light stretched out along the city to their right. On the left, the lake was much too large to see anything except the black horizon. Stars in the sky were mere pinpoints, almost impossible to see with the city light all around them.

"We'll keep each other warm," said Stephen. He unbuttoned the buttons on his cotton shirt.

Line lay down next to his chest, listening to his heart pounding and smelling his sweetly acrid sweat. She tried to breathe with Stephen, remembering the first cold night they had lain under the stars at the edge of Montgomery, Alabama, with a rock and roll concert going on nearby.

Dawn was visible when Line woke up shivering a few hours later, the pale sky pinking in the east beyond the lake. She sat up and so did Stephen. Together they stumbled off down the street to sleep a little at the apartment before the heat grew too terrible again.

That morning, Line took a stained and curled postcard with a photograph of Che Guevara off the wall. She didn't feel bad about taking it, because there was another large poster photograph of him nearby. On one of the SDS envelopes, she wrote Paul's name and address and stuffed in a leaflet. On the back of the photograph, in which Che wore a black beret with a star on it, his long dark hair curling around his upturned face, she wrote in an open scrawl:

"Paul, I'm sorry to hear about Foxy. How did she die? It makes me think of you all and wonder how you are doing. Please write!

"It's so hot here that we went out and sat by the lake last night. You would have loved the folk music people were playing on guitars.

"I am doing well. Still working at the Lutheran home, but I'm getting restless. I need to figure out what I'm doing with my life, but the political situation feels so urgent. All of us are putting our lives on hold. I'll let you know if anything changes.

"Please greet everyone and tell them I love them!"

It was the best she could do. Line sealed the envelope and put it into the big batch that would go out in the mail that day. She knew that everyone at home would read it, and she was glad to send Paul the leaflet against the war. She wasn't worried that he would get drafted, as he had had polio and one of his legs was thin and weak. But it didn't hurt for her family to know what the Johnson administration was doing. Line was sure they wouldn't find out on the television news.

2

On a September Sunday afternoon, Line walked through the tiny green space of Hyde Park where many people sat on park benches, having ice cream, talking. Kids played on a little wooden playground. It was still warm, but the nice weather wouldn't last long.

Kay Freeman had invited Line to the home she shared with her husband Bernie, a sociologist who taught at the University of Chicago. The informal apartment, with its big windows looking down into the park, was full of girls. Line sat down on a daybed covered with a colorful collection of pillows.

"Coffee in the kitchen!" crowed Kay, in the low voice Line loved, full of the guttural hints of an older world.

Line followed Ruth out to the kitchen and poured a cup of coffee for herself. She recognized most of the girls: Vivian, with her dark serious looks, Pearl from somewhere in the South, Nancy who was also dark, thin and artistic, and tiny Ruth, who like Line, was some variety of blonde. They wore skirts and cardigans, flat shoes. Some of them were at the university, and some worked at the SDS office.

"I thought some of the guys were cute," Pearl was saying to Vivian. "Texas bandito mustaches and boots!"

Vivian sniffed audibly. "Too much dope smoking, in my opinion. How are we going to get anything done?" She looked very young with her big blue eyes, but staunch. She had been in Mississippi, jailed at 19 for marching for civil rights for Afro-Americans. Everyone now called them blacks, as they sought Black Power and separated from whites, but it still felt funny.

"Did you try it?" asked Pearl. "I thought it was kind of fun. It made everything poetic. All work and no play, Vivian. That might be you!"

Line quickly realized they were talking about the SDS convention in Clear Lake, Iowa. Line hadn't gone because she didn't want to take the week off of work. And anyway, Line thought to herself, if I took a week off it would be to go to Lake Michigami with my folks. A wave of longing washed over her. She hadn't been home since Christmas.

"Balance," said Kay's melodious voice in the background. "Bernie and I have figured it out. All that rhetorical political talk spins you into a whirlwind without some kind of life to balance it out."

Yes, Line said silently. She loved Kay. She followed Kay, who carried a plate of cookies, into the living room.

"Rugelach," said Kay. "The one thing I learned from my mother!"

Line turned them over in her hand and took a bite. Round layered cookies, they were full of walnuts, raisins and cinnamon, and laced with jam.

"Oh God," Nancy exclaimed. "That convention was too much!" She looked at Line, dramatizing for her. "The 'old guard' says we don't know how to write any more! They wanted some kind of new statement about SDS. But the new people just want to decentralize and let each group work things out as they go along."

"And what do you think?" Line asked. She had been hearing some of this from Stephen.

"Oh, I don't know," Nancy said, switching between listless and emphatic. "It's all sort of confusing. And it's run by these guys who don't want to listen to us!"

"You're not a-kidding!" said Pearl. "I got shouted down in a meeting! I couldn't believe it!"

"You didn't tell us," said Vivian. "Why didn't you tell us?"

"Well, if I complain," said Pearl, "they'll take me even less seriously!"

"I know they don't like it when we talk to each other," said Ruth. "I was doing draft counseling in the office, and while I was waiting for a guy to turn up, I talked on the phone to Penny. We were talking about volunteering, and all of a sudden Clark comes into the office and berates me for 'gossiping.'"

"Isn't that weird?" asked Vivian. "Aren't our ideas as important as theirs?"

"They're the ones who will get drafted, though," said Pearl, "as they are constantly reminding me. They want to ditch the ERAP programs because they're more worried about the war."

"I'm worried about the war," said Vivian. "And what I have to say should be treated with at least as much respect as what they say."

"Casey told me that she couldn't cope with organizing women in ERAP who were being beaten up by their husbands," Ruth blurted. "Have any of you read that paper she wrote, something like 'Sex and Caste'?" Casey, Tom Hayden's wife, had worked briefly in the Chicago ERAP projects. She too had worked hard for civil rights.

"I saw it," said Kay. "It's good. She was writing about SNCC, and how women were most often assigned housekeeping and clerical duties, while men made the decisions." She stood with a coffee pot in her hands, pouring into Vivian's cup.

"Exactly," said Vivian. "They want us around, but not to speak! I think they just want us to listen and do the dirty work."

"I had a feeling you girls could talk," said Kay. "That's why I got us all together. Women speak more freely around each other."

Line silently raised her coffee cup to Kay. She was pleased Kay included her in this group. Bernie and Kay were a little older than most of their SDS friends. Kay told Line they didn't connect to the other University of Chicago faculty members, who gave formal dinners served by black servants after which a string quartet would play! "Not our scene," she said.

"Women," said Vivian. "It sounds solid. Like 'black.' I don't think it would hurt one bit for us to organize ourselves, find out how we can work together. The men in SDS are all about intellect."

"That's what I liked about the summer conference," said Pearl, smiling. "Seemed lighter, somehow, that whole intellectual thing looser."

"We need to support each other to work for change," said Vivian. "There's still so much to do, and so much against us."

"Could you find that paper Casey wrote?" Nancy asked Kay. "I'd like to see it."

"I think the guys are threatened by us," said Nancy. "They're afraid of more factions splitting the movement."

"Well, they're right," said Vivian. "That is something to worry about. We all have the same goals. Nothing is more important than getting this country to realize what it is doing to innocent civilians in Asia. And in the name of what?!" Her face expressed the quizzical outrage that animated most of them.

The sun was throwing long shadows into the west-facing room, illuminating the intent faces. Kay gave Line a conspiratorial wink. Line knew Stephen himself was wavering between the two SDS factions. He was part of the generous, all-inclusive philosophy of the old guard and the Port Huron statement, but he was impatient with how little SDS was accomplishing and the new "prairie people" had an appealing energy.

When Stephen talked, Line mostly listened to the logical cast of his mind. He would say, "if A, then B!" as if one thing caused another without fail. Line's mind was nothing like this! She thought of a thousand side issues all the time, most of which Stephen said were irrelevant to the discussion at hand. It was useless to talk politics with him because Line only got lost in the mire and he kept hammering at his point. In any case, she usually agreed with him.

Line found her connection to Stephen didn't involve what he thought or what she thought. It was almost an animal thing. They were a refuge to each other, their relationship a place they had made to rest from their efforts in the world. They did talk, of course, but it was a matter of getting to know each other, their implicit bond unquestioned.

SDS activism came back to the same questions, over and over. The United States, which had suppressed and dis-enfranchised its black citizens, was now dropping bombs on Vietnam, sending in soldiers because it feared the communist influence behind the politics of a country which wanted to govern itself. Line knew no one in the room would defend their country's actions. It was what united them.

"Don't worry girls," said Kay, from her few years of experience more. "Every action you take is having some effect."

"Humpf," said Nancy audibly. "Every day more lives ..."

Line left the meeting all stirred up, as usual. She took the el back to northern Chicago, to the Lutheran home. She sighed. It was clear to her that she couldn't continue there much longer. When she got back to her room in the former carriage house in the back garden, she found Karen ironing a crisp white blouse.

Line lifted her damp hair and twined a rubber band around it into a business-like ponytail to get it off her neck. It was long and curling, fanning around her face, a reddish color. "Strawberry blonde" Karen called it. Sometimes the room Line shared was a refuge from the constant impressions and ideas she received from the city. She just sat on her bed and brooded. But today she was too worked up.

"Come on, Karen," said Line. "I'm so restless. Would you go out to a restaurant with me? I want to try that Japanese restaurant I saw on North Street." Going to restaurants felt daring to Line. She could count the number of times she had been to a restaurant as a child on her fingers. Stephen took it as a matter of course, having grown up in a city. But he had very little money and he and Line usually helped cook and share the communal meals at the SDS office.

Line was often impatient with Karen, who was stodgy and romantic at the same time. Line felt she didn't live in the real world. But Karen listened and made a good sounding board. She wasn't the best person to take on an adventure to a new place, but Line was feeling anxious and wanted to talk.

"Okay," said Karen, in her pliant way. She was nothing like the intelligent, driven women Line had just left in Hyde Park. But they were intimidating and Line didn't know them well enough to talk about her problems.

Line led Karen down a nearby street on which all kinds of storefronts lined the sidewalk. Some of them put their cheap wares right out in front, taking up space. It was a lively scene, but Line didn't like shopping and usually didn't need anything. She had heard about a cheap Japanese restaurant tucked along the street, and, ever interested in the new, she was intrigued. Raw fish? Seaweed? Did people eat those things?

Line had a street number and they looked at the buildings, finding the one before and the one after. "This must be it," said Line low, pushing open the door of an unprepossessing building.

A smiling girl with a mass of shiny black hair put up on her head pointed them to a small formica table. She came over with paper napkins, chopsticks and a couple of menus to place in front of them. "Tea?" she asked. She was wearing a kimono, with a wide band wrapped tightly around her waist.

"Yes, please," nodded Line.

The tea was green and tasted like grain. Line took the lid off the pot and inhaled the sweet fragrance. "I've heard the Japanese eat raw fish," she said. From the menu, she and Karen selected a couple of dishes with foreign names. Translations beside the names gave them some idea of what to order.

"I hope we are doing the right thing," said Line.

"Rice," said Karen. "I'm sure I can eat the rice at least."

The waitress spoke good English with a soft slide on some of the letters. Line loved how she moved in her tight, long kimono. Drinking in the exotic atmosphere, Line relaxed. But as they waited for the waitress to return with the food, Line sighed. "Karen, I just don't think I can stay in this job much longer."

"I know," said Karen. "We need to go back to school so they will let us manage cases instead of driving people around and serving coffee."

Line shook her head. "Even Mr. Welch is getting impatient with my squirrelyness. But I can't go back to school. I just can't do it." Mr. Welch, who administrated the home, was Line's ally. He knew that when Line was on the job there was nothing she wouldn't do for the people in the home. It was like an atmosphere around her. When Line walked into the comfortable old mansion, she knew in her bones what was going on with each person. She didn't have to ask.

"Well?" asked the sensible Karen. "What are you going to do then? I thought you wanted to become a social worker."

"I thought so," said Line. "But I don't want to do management and paperwork. Or theorize about things and discuss reasons and statistics."

Karen sighed. "You just have to get through it. I'm sure I'll go back to school."

"I can't ask Dad and Mom for more money, either," said Line. "Not after I quit Wittenberg. I chose to stay here and now I have to make it work."

"And what about that boyfriend?" asked Karen coyly. She had only seen Stephen once when he stopped by to pick up Line, but she was sure the two of them were headed directly for the altar.

Line poured herself more tea to hide her agitation, but it was too hot and it scalded her tongue. She fanned herself with the napkin and coughed, noting Karen's amusement.

"I love Stephen," Line finally managed to say. "But that doesn't mean we're going to move into a house with a white picket fence and raise 2.5 children. I have to have something to do. And anyway, he's more worried about the draft than taking on any sort of wife!"

"I think it's romantic," said Karen, "the two of you taking on the world."

The waitress came over with two steaming bowls of soup. Line wasn't sure what the bowls were made of, a thin material, not ceramic and not plastic.

"Living on peanut butter sandwiches and coffee isn't romantic," said Line, as she smelled the earthy soup. "And that's all of them! They think only of politics!"

There was no spoon to eat the soup. Line looked over and saw someone else drinking directly from the bowl, so she lifted it to her face, looking into the pale liquid in the black bowl. "Wow," she said. "What a lovely soup!"

"I think there's seaweed in it," said Karen. "And green onions." She had unwrapped the chopsticks, two pieces of blonde wood and was poking around in the soup. "What's this?" She pointed to cubes of soft curd in the bowl.

"Don't act like you've never done this before," said Line low. There was at least one other white couple in the room, enjoying their evening meal, brandishing their chopsticks, but most people looked Asian.

"It's good," said Karen.

The waitress brought little square platters to the table. One was the sushi with flaps of cold raw fish on top of the rice. Line steeled herself to eat it. The other was a plate of rounded balls of rice with seaweed around them. Inside each piece was a hidden bit of what Line thought was cucumber. At least that's what the menu said.

The waitress tittered at them, seeing that they didn't know what to do. She demonstrated, pouring soy sauce into the tiny ceramic dishes at each place. She mimed picking up the sushi in chopsticks and dipping it in the soy sauce.

Line picked up a ball of rice and seaweed awkwardly with her chopsticks. It was difficult, certainly not like the chicken chow mein Mother used to serve out of cans. It fell apart when she tried to dip it in the soy sauce, but she picked out the pieces. "I like it," she said quietly as she rolled the salty tastes on her tongue.

But Karen, stolid and steady, went back to their conversation. "You think of politics too," said Karen. "You're always telling me how SDS is working for the greater good of the country."

"It is," said Line. "I'm just not that good at it. I can stand around and hand out leaflets, and I like talking to people, but I'm never sure I'm saying the right thing. And I can't type. I'm just not what they need."

Line had realized quickly she shouldn't try to work for the movement full time. She stubbornly held on to her slim job at the Lutheran home, which provided shelter, some food and a small bit of income. She felt useful at the home, if not about to change the world. "I balance Stephen out, though," she said, remembering what Kay had told her. "He has no idea what life is like outside the movement by this time!"

"I'm sure you're doing the right thing," said Karen. "But I've noticed you like hands-on work," said Karen. "I've seen it. They always call you when people are sick. You're soothing, somehow. People trust you."

Line nodded. Old Scandinavians didn't really like to be touched. But it couldn't be helped. Growing old, you needed other hands to help you. "I like that kind of work. Intimate work with people's basic, human needs."

Karen grew animated. "I was at Hull House the other day, looking at the flyers on the bulletin board. There was one for Licensed Practical Nursing. It was a program for people who needed to work and study. I was kind of interested, but I think I really want to do social work. I expect to go back to school." Karen's eyes grew soft. "I love Hull House," she said. "The women there are so sweet."

Line's thoughts flickered over what she knew of Hull House. Begun by Jane Addams at the turn of the century, it was created to bring education and culture into the lives of the poverty-stricken immigrants who flocked to Chicago. It was funded by wealthy people and had no particular religious affiliation. Line had been there, but the people seemed persnickety and highly-organized to her. It wasn't a place for her, though she liked the idea.

"There's a bunch of hospitals around there," said Line musingly. "Maybe the nursing school is near there." Everyone in Chicago had heard of Cook County hospital, a huge charity hospital where anyone could come. Line's mind raced. All of a sudden she was in an emergency room, holding syringes and transfusion bottles for dark-eyed men in green masks as they worked with accident victims.

"I'm sorry," said Karen. "I didn't think to take down the phone numbers or anything. But you could probably still find it at Hull House." She kneaded the rice and cucumber wrapped in dried seaweed with her fingers, trying not to let it fall apart as she lifted it to her mouth.

When they had eaten all the nori rolls, Line looked across at Karen. "Well, I guess we can't avoid it," said Line. The plate of cold, raw fish lay in front of them. Line picked up a piece of dark, marbled fish awkwardly between the two sticks of wood. She dipped it in soy sauce and put it in her mouth. The cold fish tasted somewhat pickled, delicious. But all of a sudden, an explosion of heat surprised Line.

"Wow!" said Line. "What was that?!"

Karen balked. "I can't eat them," she said. "I'm just going to have rice." She dug out a bit of rice and put it on her plate, pouring soy sauce over it and eating it as best she could with the chopsticks.

"What about your Norwegian ancestors?" Line said. "They'd eat any kind of fish." Line had not expected much of Karen. But there were still five little slabs of cold fish staring at her. She realized she was on her own. They had ordered it. They couldn't return it without looking stupid. Line picked up another pink slab and dipped it in the soy sauce. The hot explosion mitigated the cold, slimy taste of the fish. Only the first piece was pickled. Line did not like the others, but she ate them, resolutely, one after another.

"I guess I'm still conservative," she said, smiling at Karen. "Can't leave food on my plate."

"It's not just us," said Karen laughing. "My sister was always telling me I must eat the Cheerios that fell on the floor, because kids in China were going hungry!"

At last the square ceramic plate was empty except for mounds of green vegetables and odd thin slices of pink pickle. The green vegetable tasted way too hot and the pickle was also strange. Line drank the green tea to wash the slimy fish tastes away. She smiled as the waitress came to take away the dishes.

"You did well!" said Karen, watching her.

"I like new things," said Line, "as you know." Everything in the Japanese restaurant was new and strange. It smelled strange, an exotic foreign atmosphere. But I could get used to it, thought Line.

"I think you should become a nurse," said Karen. "You'd be good at it."

"You think so?" questioned Line. "I'll think about it. I'll go over to Hull House next weekend and see if I can find that flyer."

When the waitress brought the bill, written in Japanese characters on a small green tablet, the two girls looked at it carefully and split it. Line was glad they had come. She wanted to believe there was nothing she couldn't do.

That week Line listened to her heart, noticing everything, to see what it told her about the future. The city, when you looked carefully, was full of possibilities. And there were many more ways to do things than she had known when she was younger. She laughed when she remembered telling Mr. Hirsch at Wittenberg she wanted to be either a forest ranger or a social worker. In the small town her parents lived in there had been no jobs for her, though she had walked beans and even worked at a coffee shop briefly.

Line had never thought of nursing, perhaps because Mother and Dad were so set on sending their kids to Wittenberg. Aunt Mabel had done some nursing in Alaska, but almost everyone else in Mother's family was a teacher.

At least, thought Line, I don't have the draft hanging over my head, as Stephen does. She went to Hull House in the evening, and on the bulletin board found the flyer advertising a work-study program leading to certification as a Licensed Practical Nurse. She wrote down the telephone number and looked for someone to ask about it.

A middle-aged woman in a stiff suit and blouse smiled at Line as she passed her in the hall.

"May I ask you something?" Line requested politely.

The woman stopped. "Of course," she said. "Come here and sit for a minute." She led Line into a big common room where they both sat in big leather chairs.

"I'm not sure about this program," said the woman when Line described the flyer. "But I do know Licensed Practical Nurses can't do everything nurses do. Hospitals are becoming quite regulated about these things. But LPN's don't have to go to as much school. I would prepare your questions and give them a call."

Line sat up straight, her attention riveted. All of a sudden, she felt that the answer to her heart's desire might be around any corner. "Thank you so much!" Line said as the woman stood up. "I'm grateful for your time!"

The woman took Line's hand somewhat formally. "I wish you the very best, my dear," she said as she took her leave, her shoes clicking as she moved down the hall on the hardwood floors.

When Line got to the SDS national office on Saturday, she was still looking for answers everywhere. She looked at the list of classes for the free university called The School. In The School anyone could teach and anyone could study. It tried to demonstrate what a radical, non-establishment educational experience might be like. There were no grades or exams, but none of the classes led to a degree.

Stephen taught a class called "Neighborhood Organization and Nonviolence." Line attended as often as she could and tried to read the books he suggested. But what she mostly learned about was Stephen.

When the dishes were washed and the kitchen put to rights, Line and Stephen went out on the back steps and sat in the twilight. It was getting cooler, but to Line being outdoors was always preferable to being in the hothouse of the office. A thin sickle moon hung in the clear, pale sky. Line hoped no one would notice that they were gone and leave them alone for a few minutes.

"How are you, Line, my girl?" asked Stephen, putting down his cup of black coffee.

Line shivered and leaned against Stephen, happy to have his attention. "I'm happy," she said. "I think I might finally know what to do with myself. I think I want to be a nurse." At the bottom of the steps, the black cat delicately washed each of his paws in their white socks.

"A nurse?!" said Stephen.

"Yes," said Line. "I don't know why I didn't think of it before. Do you remember when we met in Selma? You said I should go help the Medical Community for Human Rights group? Maybe you knew already!"

"Wow," said Stephen. "I certainly did not. I think you said you were good at listening." He put his nose in her neck, nuzzling. "You are good at listening," he said softly. "My body is talking and yours is listening."

Line sighed. It was so nice to be with Stephen. After a while, she said, "I found a work-study program for people who want to become a Licensed Practical Nurse. I'm going to get my grits together, as Pearl says, and call them this week."

"Good idea," said Stephen. "This is in Chicago?"

"At Cook County Hospital," said Line, seeing in the distance the promise of the new. "I can't wait. I'd like to see what goes on there!"

3

A woman in a sleek blue suit on an Icelandic flight high over the snowy Arctic wastes handed Marty a small, globular glass of cognac. Heading to Dublin, and then London, Marty had resolved to try everything that came her way. The cognac was free and so was conversation with her seatmate, a handsome American student.

"I think Icelandic must have a deal with Courvoisier," said Matthew. He wore a light woolen sweater with a freshly laundered shirt collar visible at the neck and looked to be about the same age as Marty, who was 20.

"It's my first time," said Marty, taking a tiny sip which burned all the way down her throat.

"Cheers then!" and Matthew lifted his glass and touched hers.

"Cheers!" said Marty. "Is this your first time in Oxford?"

"No," said Matthew. "I was there last year. I've just been home for summer holiday. Michaelmas term about to start. And you?"

"It's all new to me," said Marty. "My first time out of the country. The first time on an airplane." She took another sip of the sweet burning liquid. She felt very unkempt next to Matthew.

After traveling for several days in an upright seat on a train from Chicago, Marty had gotten off at New York's Grand Central Station. She was sleepy and things were a blur, but she was young and it didn't matter. Marty took a subway to Central Park, where she sat in the sun all afternoon, suitcase by her side, and then a taxi to John F. Kennedy International Airport.

In all that time, Marty hadn't properly bathed or slept. Washrooms helped, but she knew her hair was greasy, her clothes grimy and her skin must not smell very good.

"What do you want to study?" asked Matthew, affable and listening. He had nothing else to do.

"Literature," said Marty. "I'm staying with an American family, helping with their daughter, but I will go to lectures during the day when she's in school."

"You will love it," said Matthew. "Great libraries and bookstores everywhere."

"Bookstores?" asked Marty.

"Blackwell's Books," said Matthew. "It's in the Broad; been there for almost a hundred years! It's easy to find. Everything's in walking distance."

Marty settled back into her chair. It seemed incredible. Bookshops she could walk to. "Professor Magnusson is going to be at Mansfield College," she ventured. "Which college are you in?"

"I'm at New College," Matthew laughed. "That is 'new' in the sense that it began later than the others. It was founded in 1379!"

"Wow!" said Marty. Everyone knew Oxford University was ancient. "When do you think it all started?"

"I'm not really sure. But apparently, when Henry II wouldn't let students run off to the university at Paris it really got going, like about 1160 something," said Matthew. "The town's really old too. There's an Eleventh Century tower on Cornmarket still standing. Cool stonework. It's part of St. Michael's."

"Oh, it sounds so wonderful!" said Marty. She was so excited, she didn't feel shy about talking. And there was so much she wanted to know! "Are you from New York?"

"Connecticut," said Matthew, casually, self-deprecating, as though it weren't important.

"And what are you studying?"

"Literature," said Matthew. "And history, of course. There's history everywhere."

Marty was astonished at her luck. What were the chances of sitting by a nice-looking guy going to the University to study literature? But she was also careful. It was obvious Matthew was more well-off and sophisticated than she. He was being a gentleman, kind to the new girl. Marty did not want to take advantage.

Stops in Iceland and Dublin were uneventful, though it gave Marty a chance to look out on the landscape as they landed, one grey, one emerald green. A few people got off and on the flight, but Marty did not leave the plane.

The flight down to London was rough. "We'll be hitting some weather, now," came the captain's voice over the loudspeaker in his English accent. "Please return to your seats and fasten your seatbelts." The stewardesses were serving drinks, but the flight got so bumpy they careened down the aisle.

Marty's stomach was queasy. Bubbles of liquid jumped into the air from the plastic glass of water she held and fell back down into the glass.

"Air pockets," said Matthew, calmly. "It's often bad down this corridor to London."

"Nothing unusual?" asked Marty weakly as another jolt shook the plane.

"Well, I must say," Matthew moved his glass to catch the liquid which jumped into the air above it, "I haven't seen liquids jump around like this in some time!"

At last the airplane flew lower, coming in for a landing. Marty thought about asking Matthew's full name, and where to find him in Oxford. As the flight touched down, it seemed that they had talked so much that they were friends. But Matthew didn't offer, and Marty, resolutely, didn't ask. It was her own brand of courtesy.

When the passengers entered the terminal, Marty went straight to the washroom. She washed as best she could and wrapped a thin white scarf around her head, tucking the ends into the collar of a blue, polyester sac coat with white buttons.

The terminal was a huge room, with rows of wooden seats like pews. Marty went over and sat down.

All of a sudden Irene Magnusson rushed up to her. "Marty!" she said. "I'm so glad I found you! You're sitting in the Departures section. We were looking for you in Arrivals!" She looked relieved at not having lost her young charge in the dimly-lit terminal.

Right behind Irene were Dr. Magnusson and their daughter Thea, bright and healthy as if they were right at home. They helped Marty load her suitcase into the black car they had procured and drove off to Oxford on the left hand side of the narrow roads.

It was late when they arrived. Thea showed Marty her room on the second floor, which Irene was in the process of painting pink. A big wardrobe held Thea's things.

"We hope there's no lion or witch at the back of it," laughed Irene. "We're reading a C.S. Lewis book about a wardrobe."

"Count yourself lucky," said Dr. Magnusson to Marty. "Not everyone has central heating. The college realized that American professors would come to expect it. I, for one, plan to enjoy it."

There was a wardrobe in Marty's room also. But for Marty, the most extraordinary thing was the bath. Irene showed her how to put a capful of Badedas into the tub with the hot water tap on.

"We discovered it in Germany," Irene said warmly. "And since then, we haven't been able to do without it! You don't need to rinse it off."

The thick green liquid smelled of pines and foamed up into lovely suds. Marty sank into them. She was sleepy, but she managed to stay awake long enough to feel the lovely tingle on her skin. The pungent woodsy smell followed her to bed like a cloud. She lay in the unfamiliar bed, cleansed and exhilarated after the long trip.

In the morning, from the bay window in her room at the front of the house, Marty looked out over Hayward Road at a row of stone houses with blue trim, chimney pots and gardens in which roses bloomed profusely. She heard Irene picking up the milk, which arrived on the front step in glass bottles, and watched Thea dance out to the car. Rolfe would drive her to school, then go to Mansfield College where he tutored.

Irene called her husband Rolfe, and Marty could not help but do the same. They had lost none of the glamour Marty sensed in them when Dr. Magnusson taught at Wittenberg College, however. The couple was perhaps 15 years older than she, very attractive. Ten-year-old Thea, with long blonde hair and apple-pink cheeks, was the essence of a well-brought-up child.

As soon as she was rested, Marty set off to explore, buying a map of the city. A shiny silver sixpence on a double-decker red bus was all it took to go from the north end of Oxford down into the center of town.

Traffic during the day in the middle of town was horrendous. Marty noticed that many girls, even older women, wore mini-skirts. Boys' hair was often long and unkempt, as if they paid no attention to it at all. Marty found comical the way they had of wearing school uniforms as if they were rags wound around their bodies.

The colleges were ancient stone buildings, graced with beautiful wooden doors, mullioned windows and towers, massed around grassy quadrangles, which looked as if they had been manicured for hundreds of years. Marty looked in at the gates, wishing she were a real student. Black gowns worn over their ordinary clothing gave students admittance to buildings, grounds and lectures. "Commoners" wore short sleeveless ones with streamers at the shoulders, and those on scholarship, "scholars," wore longer ones with short, open sleeves.

Many of the buildings were hidden behind scaffolding. Thick coal dust grimed the stone facades. Now that other forms of heat were used, the colleges were slowly cleaning their ancient buildings. The round, classical Radcliffe Camera, which housed part of the university library, was completely wreathed in pipe and boards for workmen to stand on as they sand-blasted and washed its walls.

Every street and building in Oxford was steeped in lore and legend. Much of it, the beautiful grounds and parks, verdant streets and college chapels in which boys' choirs sang matins and evensong, was available to the public. Christ Church college had a vast expanse of green where students played football (what Marty knew as soccer). It had been the home of Lewis Carroll. Rowing with three young sisters on an Oxford river one summer afternoon, he had come up with the story of *Alice's Adventures in Wonderland*. One of the little girls begged him to write it down.

The walls of St. Johns, which edged the Banbury Road, were topped with the spikes of glass shards to prevent anyone climbing over. Marty didn't try to enter any college gates. She walked the streets and found Blackwell's Books in Broad Street.

Blackwell's was in a beautiful building, painted dark green with casement windows and gold-painted iron letters over the door, displaying in stunning array every book Marty could imagine. Beautifully bound books on several floors, but also paperbacks. No matter that the university buildings and gardens intimidated Marty. Blackwell's welcomed her. Marty had never before seen such a tempting array of her favorite modern authors. She could not afford to buy books, but she could look to her heart's content. No one seemed to mind.

Over the next week, the routine for the term became apparent. Rolfe dropped Thea off at her school and then spent his days at Mansfield College. Irene made an art of homemaking and was often absorbed in projects. Some evenings Rolfe and Irene went out, but in general, they didn't seem to need Marty very much.

From the small allowance Mother and Dad had provided Marty paid a fee of six pounds for the privilege of attending lectures at any college in English Language and Literature for Michaelmas term. From the array of lectures, Marty set about finding the ones that most appealed to her. Now is when my real education begins, she thought.

The main interest in Oxford was in the medieval, perhaps because books and manuscripts from that time were available. Lectures in early English literature abounded. Though J.R.R. Tolkien was no longer lecturing on *Beowulf*, he was becoming famous for publishing his fantasies of Middle-earth, peopled with hobbits, dwarves, wizards and princes. C.S. Lewis also published fantasy literature, and their group of writers, the Inklings, met in an Oxford pub. Many other dons in Oxford were important cultural and literary critics. But Marty found few lectures regarding 20th Century authors. Almost none.

It was October and the days were clear and bright, but darkness came early, the skylight fading by 5 p.m. One evening, Marty hurried up the street to evensong at Magdalen College chapel, whose beautiful tower dominated the High. (Marty learned to pronounce it "maudlin," as others did.) A screen of carved stone apostles and saints covered the wall at the front of the chapel. It was almost empty and Marty sat in the back. A procession of boys in white robes carrying candles entered, their angelic high voices rising into the carved and vaulted ceilings. Marty listened, amazed that this tradition continued, despite the unkempt, iconoclastic students. Afterwards, she rushed out in the darkness and took a bus up the Banbury Road.

Dinner at the Magnussons was festive every night, laid in the dining room and lit by candles. Thea set out the china, napkins and silver, as gently and artfully as her mother dictated, the knife edges directed toward the plates. Marty cored the small green Pippins Irene had bought from the produce truck which arrived every other day in front of the house. She stuffed them with raisins, cinnamon and sugar as Irene directed to be baked and served with crème fraîche as dessert. Marty felt clumsy beside the capable Irene.

Irene loved cooking and homemaking, sewing beautiful things for herself and Thea. "I make still lifes, and Rolfe and Thea inhabit them," she laughingly told Marty, implying that living in them messed them up! She was full of bubbling good cheer, laughing her way through difficulties and making droll jokes. At night, Marty often heard laughter coming from the master bedroom.

Irene was the daughter of a minister, and she took a great interest in Rolfe's work, listening to his ideas, taking notes and critiquing. When Rolfe took his doctorate in Germany and studied with Karl Barth in Switzerland, Irene made a home for him and Thea, who had been a toddler. European culture infused and educated the family.

As an appetizer, the family sat down to a leek soup with a dollop of cream and parsley on top. Marty could hardly believe the wonderful tastes Irene created in the kitchen. The soup was ambrosial.

"But darling," said Rolfe. "You're not thinking of my waistline!"

"Too much milk," laughed Irene. "I'm trying to use it up. I must call them and ask them to deliver less."

When she brought in the main dish, Irene said, "I know you may think of it as Wiener Schnitzel, but tonight, with a lemon caper sauce it is veal scallopini."

"What is the difference?" asked Marty.

"Schnitzel from Vienna," began Rolfe, who loved an opportunity to explain, "is simply a thin breaded cutlet. The cutlet is pounded with a mallet, so it is partially tenderized. And now, I suppose, Irene has prepared a sauce which takes us to Positano. Thea's favorite city." He looked at Thea fondly.

Thea smiled, remembering. "We went there last year. I love the gelato," she said to Marty.

"You are right, Rolfe," said Irene. "When you put in lemon you are actually making a piccata, but the ingredients are used all over Italy. It's hard to know where it is from." She served the dish with a few noodles and a side dish of carrots with herbs.

It was all new to Marty. Everything Irene made was glorious. "It's so good," she said, tucking in.

"Ausgezeichnet," said Thea, emphatically. She had learned the word for 'excellent' in Germany.

The Magnussons were fascinated by cultural differences. Like Marty, they were exploring Oxford's potent mix of ancient wisdom, a certain amount of pretentiousness and the trendiness which seeped up from London's Carnaby Street.

They had found a school for Thea at which students did not wear uniforms and were coaxed along with games, art and drama. Thea didn't need coaxing, but she was happy in the school and met an American friend there, Janet Chertok, the daughter of a visiting fellow in physics. They often played together.

Irene drew everyone out at dinner, but no one mentioned the incident of that morning which mortified Marty. She had shut the heavy front door while Irene stood outside, not realizing it had locked. Neither of them had a key. Marty had rushed to Mansfield College on the red double-decker bus, interrupted Rolfe's tutorial and asked him for a key while Irene shivered near the garage, waiting for Marty to return.

"Did you go hear Tolkien read his story today?" Irene asked Marty.

"I did," said Marty. "But the room was so full of people I couldn't see him. People were backed right up to where I stood against the wall."

"It was at Merton?" questioned Irene. "I thought of going, but then I had lunch with Lidia."

"Yes. He read a story about Tom Bombadil in a tiny room at Merton. He was a professor there once. It was interesting to hear his voice," Marty said.

"The Narnia books were written in Oxford too," said Irene to Thea. "C.S. Lewis was in a group of men, with Tolkien, who wrote fiction and fantasy. Imagine that!" she looked at Rolfe.

Marty wondered what Rolfe and Irene thought of Tolkien. She herself was uninterested in fantasy, though she could now understand the medieval preoccupations behind the creation of Middle-earth and the wealth of names and ideas Tolkien invested in it. She was also resistant to C.S. Lewis' work, though Mother and some of Marty's more devout cousins were deeply interested in the Christian themes of his fantasies.

Perhaps Rolfe and Irene were just surprised that the work of C.S. Lewis and Tolkien should be taken so seriously. Rolfe himself was immersed in Anglican Christianity, and its implications for his own theology. From what Marty had seen of the Magnussons' artistic way of life, and their attention to the possibility of transcendence in the everyday, Marty suspected they had as little use for fantasy, except as child's play, as she did.

Thea's little face had become pensive. "I feel sorry for Prince Caspian," she said.

"Don't worry," said Rolfe, smiling at her. "C.S. Lewis will surely arrange for him to be saved." As in Marty's own household where her little sisters Kristen and Hanna held sway, there was great respect in the Magnusson family for Thea's understanding of life and its wonders. Though values were often discussed, no one indulged in adult skepticism.

Irene stood up and so did Marty, clearing plates. "You are welcome to come to the sherry party at Mansfield on Sunday afternoon," Irene said to Marty as they carried in small plates of salad Irene had prepared in the crowded kitchen. "It's to introduce the foreign fellows."

Michaelmas term was full of sherry parties. Marty found them deeply civilized. In the Mansfield college sitting room, wooden sashes allowed large windows to open to a quadrangle bordered with a garden. Late afternoon sun angled in low across the beds of roses and low shrubs, but the air was crisp with chill. A crush of people, standing about with glasses in one hand, tidbits of fish or cheese on crackers in the other, warmed the room, however.

Marty felt like an outsider, a scarcely couth American in a green woolen sac dress she had made herself. But it was all so beautiful, the golden liquid in the glasses catching the light, the smiling people with their careful pronunciation of the King's English, the green sward outdoors cultivated within an inch of its life.

"I'm attending lectures in Language and Literature," Marty carefully told a young man with longish hair and a green and blue striped tie who questioned her. She could never decide whether it was attractive to be American. Probably not.

"You must go hear Isaiah Berlin," said Seamus. "His lectures are philosophy, literature, Western history, all rolled into one!"

"What college?" asked Marty.

"All Souls," said Seamus enthusiastically. "Thursday mornings. I never miss it."

"It sounds great!" said Marty. "Thank you for telling me."

Seamus bobbed his head and went off to talk to someone else. Marty joined a group around Irene and Thea who were talking about Coventry cathedral.

"Yes, we went last week!" Irene said, all of her feeling audible in her rich, low voice. "So amazing. We knew little of war at the time. We were kids. But Rolfe studied in Heidelberg a few years ago. Heidelberg itself was spared bombing, but the efforts Germany was making to rebuild were impressive."

Marty had gone with the Magnussons to Coventry. As Irene spoke, she felt the hush of space the roofless cathedral opened up. The cathedral, bombed during the Battle of Britain, had been left standing as a monument, with its tall spire. Grass grew at the foot of its stone walls and only the frames remained of the windows. Beside it, a very modern cathedral had recently been consecrated. But the eloquence of the bombed cathedral, left for remembrance, said the most.

Marty had little actual sense of World War II, though it touched down often in her consciousness. She had a vivid sense of Anne Frank's young life in hiding, and later in concentration camps. Virginia Woolf had killed herself in 1941, the war which hung so heavily over Britain bringing on an episode of madness. Joyce had fled the Nazi occupation of France, dying in Zurich in the same year. She also had an uncle, Dad's brother, whom she had never known as he was killed just before the war ended.

The British matron Irene was speaking to said, in the accent Marty had begun to associate with the university, "It isn't surprising to me to see evidence of the war twenty years later. Such a heavy burden it laid on this little island. But now look at these mod kids! They're having such a good time!"

Irene laughed. "Yes, we can't begrudge them. They lived through all that rationing. And now there's plenty of everything. Why not celebrate?"

"The new swinging London," said the woman. "Who'd have thought?"

Thea held on to her mother's arms, looking up. "Can we go, Mother? Please?"

"Soon," said Irene to the little blonde up-turned face.

Thea danced up and down. "I can't wait!"

"You'll find some of that mod atmosphere on Little Clarendon Street," said the woman. "Posh little shops and boutiques, if you're looking for them."

Marty took note. She was always looking around corners, up side streets, as if they were magic. But she was also fearful that her money would run out. Breakfast and dinners at the Magnussons' were so wonderful, and she was eating so much of Irene's tasty food she was putting on weight. Perhaps because her stomach was getting bigger, she was terribly hungry in the middle of the day. Sometimes she had tea and a bun at a tea shop, but she usually made do with a Cadbury's bar, bought for sixpence, for lunch.

Marty also wished she could buy presents for Thea and Irene. Just that week she had bought a pair of scissors for a project she was doing with Thea, and noticed that her sheaf of travelers' checks was very thin. She felt her poverty keenly, but there was nothing she could do about it. It was a new feeling for Marty. She had never felt poor. Growing up there had been nothing to buy!

31

That evening, when Thea was asleep and Rolfe studying, Marty and Irene watched a television show. It was a good way to see what England was like. Irene, whose hands were always busy, hemmed a dress.

When she turned off the television, Irene turned to Marty. "What an interesting time to be in England," she said. "We'll go down to London one of these weekends and look around. Are you finding your classes worthwhile?"

Marty didn't know what to say. "Very," she said. "I love being here."

"Are you finding the areas you are interested in?" asked Irene.

"Yes," said Marty, a little tentatively. "Though there is little emphasis on the Modern era."

"Do you think you want to go on to do more study?"

Marty did not know what to say. She was deeply stirred by her surroundings, but she wasn't preparing for anything. She felt tongue-tied when Irene turned her attention toward her. Was she even allowed to speak? "I don't know," said Marty, softly. "But I so appreciate the opportunity to go to lectures." She was pursuing her own burning interests in modern writers, but she didn't have the words to say what these interests were, especially not to Irene Magnusson, the wife of a dramatic and stimulating professor.

"I think you need a black dress," Irene said, changing tactics. "Every woman needs a nice black dress."

Marty nodded. Irene was always right. But how would she get such a thing?

"Why don't you look around for a pattern, and I'll buy the cloth for you for Christmas." Irene looked pleased with her idea. "I think black wool, with a grey silk lining."

Marty looked at her, mortified. She could hardly do enough for the Magnussons to merit her board and room, let alone their generosity. "Yes," she said, responding to Irene's warmth. "Thank you so much, Irene. I'll look."

4

Paul drove to college, one hundred miles west in the little Studebaker Lark. Mother had leased a new Chrysler to drive to school and no one needed the Lark.

"I hate to see you drive that thing in bad weather," said Dad. "It's really nothing more than a tin can!"

"I'll try not to," Paul smiled at him mischievously. He knew Dad had done his share of driving under hazardous conditions. Paul had come to love and trust the little Lark, knowing it well.

Arriving at the small college was a completely new experience for Paul. He was on his own with no one to show him around or pave the way. No one at Astoria had even heard of the Mikkelsons.

The main building had white fluted classical columns supporting a portico in front. It had been a hotel, built in the center of town in 1903. But when a rival hotel stole all the customers, it became vacant and a Norwegian pastor found the resources to start a two-year college. Conditions in the building were crowded, but a new Campus Center was being built, and students were told they would be using it by Christmas.

Having everything in one place made Astoria feel like a big family. With about 300 other freshmen, Paul found his way from classrooms to dorm to cafeteria. Paul loved the cozy library on an upper floor of the building with its racks of newspapers, magazines and big comfy tables for studying. Delicious food smells wafted up from the cafeteria below while he read *The Brothers Karamazov*. Lines for the cafeteria stretched out into the front lobby and the clanking and roaring of the dishwasher could be heard while the students ate, but it was all close. It felt like home. It was Paul's very own.

A greenhouse attached to the science hall became one of Paul's favorite places. The ancient botany professor, Mr. Johnson, was almost always there, poking about among the flats, tamping down soil around new seedlings, and dripping water on them carefully with a long, dank hose. Sweating pipes knocked and the air hung with steam and the fecund smells of mold and humus. Paul couldn't wait to see what it was like in the winter, with snow lying on its glass roof, moist heat and warmth steaming up the inside.

Paul's joy overflowed in a cappella choir. The director, Oddmar Svendson, a silver-haired older man, couldn't help philosophizing. He was serious and wanted his singers to work hard and memorize the songs he chose, which were often difficult. But he was perfectly happy to be called Oddmar and everyone loved him. His wife Maddie played the piano to get them started, though most of the time they sang without accompaniment.

"Come, come," said Oddmar, lifting them all to a standing position with his arms. "You can't praise the Lord sitting down."

One Thursday Oddmar described a Benjamin Britten choral series they were about to take up as he passed out the music: "Now it personally surprises me that the British have such a strong choral tradition," he said. "Our own Lutheran tradition with all our great German composers is very strong. But the founders of some Oxford and Cambridge colleges provided for the establishment of boys' choirs and the tradition continues to this day."

Paul was entranced. He had gotten a postcard from Marty describing evensong sung by a boys' choir at a chapel in Oxford.

Oddmar went on. "These choirs were formed to celebrate masses. Britten wrote *Rejoice in the Lamb* during the war and it was first performed in 1943. The words come from a much older poem by Christopher Smart who was in an insane asylum when he wrote it. I particularly love it because it is about the worship of God by all created beings, each in its own way."

Oddmar looked to his wife, who began with a few eerie notes. "Now this needs an organ," said Oddmar, "And we'll have one in the spring when we sing this. I just want you to begin thinking about it." He began to go through the piece, singing as he went. "Let Nimrod, the mighty hunter, bind a leopard to the altar and consecrate his spear to the Lord." He continued with the strange words and odd rhythms. Many animals were named. "For the mouse is a creature of great personal valour."

The song of the mouse was an alto solo. "All of the altos should learn it," Oddmar said. There was a treble solo about a cat, and one about flowers. A chorus followed, in which Smart said exactly how he felt. "The watchman smites me with his staff. For the silly fellow, silly fellow, is against me."

The words sent chills down Paul's spine and the rhythms, as Oddmar tapped them out with a stick on his music stand, ricocheted through Paul's brain. "For H is a spirit, and therefore he is God." The strange chords strengthened and then lightened.

"Chaotic and yet, full of genius," said Oddmar. "I'm sure Britten thought the war made England an asylum of some kind."

They struggled through the music. "All right, all right," said Oddmar, finally. "That's enough. Let's get back to something we know."

The choir sank into an old hymn, Paul picking out the tenor part. "When peace like a river attendeth my soul, and sorrows like sea billows roll, whatever my lot, Thou has taught me to say, it is well, it is well with my soul!" The song moved from one voice to another in a round. It rolled into Paul's mind, lodged there, and it was still there when he woke the next morning.

A big wind blew up in the middle of October. Strong winds tossed up the cloud cover and it was extremely warm outside, in the 70's. Thunderstorms followed. Paul wondered how the greenhouse was holding up and went over to see whether Mr. Johnson needed help. The putty that held the glass to the frames was cracked and old. Sure enough, old Mr. Johnson was standing precariously on a ladder, tying boards across places where the glass had broken.

"Let me do that," said Paul. He didn't like seeing Mr. Johnson up on a rickety ladder.

That night Paul heard that the storm had become a tornado which touched down half an hour south of the college. It barreled into the small town of Belmond in the afternoon just as a homecoming parade was finishing. Six people were killed and many injured. Farms were leveled and havoc left a trail across the town.

The college organized buses full of male students to go down and help clean up. There wasn't a great deal they could do. Wrecking balls must topple the damaged brick buildings and bulldozers level the unsafe wooden houses. But Paul and his friends helped people take salvageable furniture and belongings from their homes. Women cried to see boards driven through kitchen cupboards and homemade curtains flapping at broken windows, but the little boys' faces were full of excitement as Paul dragged bicycles and wagons from a garage.

For several weekends after that, the college paid for gas and Paul drove down to help, his car filled with students. Gerald, a big Norwegian farm kid who rode with Paul, talked about hunting deer and wild turkey nearby. Just above Belmond, Gerald showed Paul where two rivers converged. Rivers made Paul think of exploring, in a canoe.

After the excitement of the tornado, Paul tried to settle back down into college life. Snow came, falling gently, softening the hard lines of buildings and laying on the branches of trees like frosting. People threw snowballs at each other as they walked between the buildings.

Paul drowsed in Bible class, where they were studying the Old Testament, book by book. He had never read the Old Testament thoroughly, but learned little in class that he hadn't already taught in Bible school to little kids. Mr. Hanson, an older man who had been a pastor, stuck closely to what was in front of him.

The classes used the Revised Standard Version of the Bible. Paul had no specific problem with the version, which was intended to be easier to read in modern English, but the Bible verses he had learned by heart as a child used the poetic, slightly archaic English of the King James' version. Paul questioned Mr. Hanson about the translations, but he didn't seem to know much about them. "Look it up, Paul," he said, gruffly. "Write a paper on it. Enlighten us!"

The King James version, Paul learned, had been completed in the 1600's. Translators worked from Hebrew and Greek texts, but also from William Tyndale's earlier translation. Tyndale, who was interested in the doctrinal reforms of Luther and used his commentaries, translated words such that they challenged the authority of the Holy Roman church. Like Luther, he felt the Catholic Church need no longer be the intercessor between people and God. He fell afoul of Henry VIII, however, and was tried and executed, his body burnt at the stake.

The international council which developed the Revised Standard Version had also worked from original Greek and Hebrew manuscripts, and, Paul was excited to discover, had used parts of the Dead Sea Scrolls in translating Isaiah. He concluded that the RSV had corrected some inaccuracies in the King James translation, though the language of the King James version was still the most beautiful.

Mr. Hanson's response was noncommittal. "We can't get too involved in this," he told Paul. "If you let people know that texts vary, it undermines their belief in the infallible nature of the doctrines as revealed to the prophets and disciples."

Paul was surprised and frustrated. But Astoria College's original intent had been to educate people in secular fields. If you wanted to be a pastor, you went to Wittenberg, or one of the other colleges set up for pre-seminary training. Paul would have to be patient. He would find more dedicated religious professors when he went to a bigger school in a couple of years.

This made choir, where Oddmar approached old English songs with a great deal of enthusiasm and scholarship, all the more precious. In the language itself, Paul could sense change and history. For Christmas the choir prepared a song called "Adam Lay Ybounden" in which Adam is bound "four thousand winters...And all was for an appil, an appil that he tok." People had once spoken like this. And yet, for all the binding, the medieval songwriter suggested that if Adam hadn't eaten the apple, "Ne had never our lady a been heavene quene." It was so human, and so old.

The fresh snow hastened the feeling it would soon be Christmas. Twilight lowered quickly in the afternoons and grey skies made the world monochromatic except for the evergreens. Lying in bed on a Saturday morning watching the snow fall was delicious. Paul got up and went to the greenhouse. He wanted to know how the snow looked from inside and how the plants were doing with so little light.

Old Mr. Johnson didn't like to use the lamps which hung over the plants. He was a purist, allowing the plants their seasons as much as possible. "They like dormancy as well as the rest of us," he said, shuffling around in an old pair of rubber galoshes.

The soft snow slid off the glasshouse roof, collecting in corners of the panes, but because of the warmth inside, it didn't stay.

"Does the snow ever get too heavy?" asked Paul. "Break the glass?"

Mr. Johnson grabbed one of the columns which held up the steel structure, trying to shake it. "An old greenhouse may be the best," he said. "They built this one strong. You saw how the big winds of the tornado broke glass. The snow's weight might break a pane, but the structure's going to hold."

Mr. Johnson turned back to his geranium cuttings. "If we were a nursery and had to produce flowers for sale, or hot-house vegetables, this could be a real forcing house. It's possible to turn fall into spring by managing the heat and the light. But that's not our purpose."

Paul liked his approach. "I don't feel dormant," Paul said. "It's like hibernation, I guess. My mind is wide awake." He explained the paper he had been writing on Bible translation.

Mr. Johnson took notice, raising his eyebrows behind his glasses. "Don't believe all that stuff about creation happening in six days, do you?"

"Well, no," said Paul. "It's metaphorical. A lot of science shows us otherwise."

"Good!" said Mr. Johnson. "I could tell you had some common sense! Not always easy to come by!"

A picture of Mr. Johnson's life flashed in front of Paul. Mr. Johnson was surely old enough to have been born in the last century. Perhaps, teaching in a Christian college, he had had to keep his mouth shut about what he thought. History right beside me, thought Paul.

"My Dad is a pastor," Paul said. "But he likes science as well as the next person, especially electronics and radio. He's pretty modern. And the way he preaches, I never see a conflict."

"Good for him," said Mr. Johnson. He peered down at the geranium leaves in a large pot. Some of the leaves had been half covered by tinfoil to demonstrate photosynthesis. Mr. Johnson plucked one off and handed it to Paul. "Take a whiff of that," he said.

Paul inhaled the strong, herbaceous scent, turning the hairy little leaf over. He looked hard for the stomata, the cells which allowed for transpiration of water and gases, but he could not see them with his naked eye. He had seen them under a microscope.

"Millions of years," said Mr. Johnson. "And lots of adaptation to environment result in these complex organisms which take in light and give off gases."

"Lots of structure to move water through," said Paul looking at the veins running through the leaf. "It almost mimics a river delta. Or our own veins." He held up his hands, on which could be dimly seen the blue veins below the skin.

"Good point, Paul," said Mr. Johnson. "You have an original mind."

Paul wished Mr. Johnson would talk, wished he knew how to ask him about his life. But Mr. Johnson was taciturn, more in tune with his plants than people.

The night of the Christmas pageant, Oddmar gathered the chorus together in their blue gowns and satin collars to warm up their voices before going out on stage. Paul felt a little strange in a gown, wondering how Dad felt about it. Dad wore them often.

Oddmar wore 'Tillie,' his tuxedo with tails. "She was always unfamiliar," he explained. "So I decided to make a friend of her and give her a name." He smoothed the cummerbund over his ample tummy as he looked fondly at his wife.

Waiting with the chorus was very different from going out on stage with Dennis and the Dots, the folk group Paul had sung with in high school. Dennis was always keyed up, ready to shine out like a flashing jewel, ready for applause to raise him up. He wanted to sing, wanted people to enjoy the music. Paul had admired him for it, liked being in the group. Without Dennis, there was no group.

But Oddmar was completely different. He was one with the choir, encouraging each of them to let the music sing through them, to let it have its way with them as they added to the overall harmonic. "The purpose of music is praise," he said, once they had arranged themselves in their accustomed rows. "And what are humans for, if not to praise?" he told the choir. "Give me an A," he said to Maddie at the piano. "Hmmmmmm. Let it come up from your diaphragm!" They all joined in, going up the scale.

On stage the choir broke out into another Britten carol, the wild olde English "Wolcum Yole!" Voices in the high registers sang out the Welcome. Paul's tenor voice was just able to sing the lower parts of the round. "Wolcum bothe to more and lesse." The basses had to hang out. There was no part for them. What were 'more and lesse,' Paul wondered.

After the pageant, Paul scuffed back through the lightly falling snow with Naomi, a girl who seemed to like him. Under the streetlights the snow's falling mass filled the air with whiteness, blown slightly sideways by the wind.

"Going home soon?" the tall, blonde Naomi asked. She had been born in Madagascar to missionary parents, but now her family lived in Minnesota.

One streetlight, right beside a tree, threw a striking shadow of the delicate tracery of tree branches onto the white ground. Paul was so moved he could hardly answer. "Look," he said, standing beside the tree and sweeping his hands out toward it.

Naomi stopped too. The snow muffled the footsteps and talk of the people near them, hurrying home. "It's beautiful," she said.

Falling snow was so forgiving you didn't have to worry about messing it up. It would quickly fill in your footsteps or refrost the trees. The outline of a bicycle, left out in the bike stand was capped with a thick layer of white crystals. Finally Paul said, "Yes, I'm going on Saturday," but by this time their paths had diverged and Naomi was waving at him, headed in the direction of the girls' dorm.

The Astoria Christmas meal was served in the new Campus Center. It wasn't even open yet, but the college administration was so excited by the building they treated it like a Christmas present for the students. With three floors, the place was spacious, orderly and pleasant after the crowded conditions of the main hall.

A thick, luxurious carpet hushed the students' footsteps in the cafeteria on the top floor. Windows looked out on the snow-covered treetops. One window wall was accordion shaped, with strips of glass floor to ceiling at angles to each other. Christmas carols played over a loudspeaker.

"I can't believe it," said a student who stood near Paul in the line as the dark, unctuous smells of turkey and gravy rose near them. "It just doesn't seem real!"

The rest of the building wasn't open, but it was said there would be a new snack bar, mailbox area, lounges with pool tables, a new bookstore. These floors would be ready when the students came back after Christmas. The fine meal in the wonderful new building did feel like a gift, the new carpet, colors and textures sensuous at Paul's fingertips.

After the meal, Paul got in the Lark and drove home through the snow, the headlights blazing into the white wonderland. At home, things were comfortingly familiar. Standing on a chair, six-year-old Hanna tacked up the Christmas cards which came in the mail from relatives and friends, while Kristen, who was nine, mixed and baked cookies in the kitchen. Christmas music by the Robert Shaw Chorale poured through the house.

The piano was topped with new ceramic figures in a scene of wisemen and shepherds worshipping the Christ Child in the manger. But Kristen and Hanna had put their favorite manger scene on a bookshelf, using the ancient miniature dolls dressed in homemade costumes and scraps. Gathered around a makeshift wooden stable, the little Mary in a blue hood, shepherds and wise men worshiped the tiny rubber baby.

Paul couldn't help missing Foxy, who arrived at Christmas when he was eleven. She had been his closest companion when Line and Marty left home. Marty was in England until spring, but Line was coming home from Chicago for a few days.

On Saturday morning, Paul was dispatched with the old green Country Sedan to pick Line up in Olwein at the train station. Kristen and Hanna tagged at his heels. It was a day of brilliant sun, with the roads clear and the sun warming the remaining snow to an icy crust.

The train station made Paul think of old Mr. Sherwood, who told Paul so many stories about the Rock Island line. He had died that year. His wife, also in her 90's and unable to manage the big garden, sold the property next to the parsonage and moved in with her daughter. Things were changing. Like the snow and the seasons, time could not be stopped.

Line, shiny-faced though she had been up all night, got off the train with her suitcase in one hand and a grocery bag in the other. Putting them down, she lifted both of the little girls off their feet and hugged Paul tight. "It's so good to be home!" she said.

Kristen and Hanna badgered Line about what she had brought.

"I didn't bring presents," said Line. "But I brought something for everyone. You'll see," she said. "Did you already have St. Lucia's?" she asked, looking at Paul.

Paul shrugged his shoulders, driving north. "I wasn't here," he said.

"I was St. Lucia," said Kristen flatly, "since I'm the oldest. I made refrigerator cinnamon buns. I just popped them out of the Pillsbury roll and baked them! Frosted them too. I can make coffee, and orange juice."

"Ummmmm. Coffee!" said Line. "I'm really ready for a cup of coffee! That was a long night. I was too excited to sleep."

Hanna stood behind Line in the passenger seat, playing with the long, curly hair Line had drawn tight into a ponytail. "Do you want to hear my Christmas piece?" she asked. "We already had it, the Christmas program. But I can remember."

"Oh yes, Hanna," said Line. "Please give me your piece."

"It was a Bible verse. We went down the row and each of us told part of the Christmas story. Mine was: "And it came to pass, as the angels were gone away from them into heaven, the shepherds said one to another, Let us now go even unto Bethlehem, and see this thing which is come to pass, which the Lord hath made known unto us."

Every word was precise in Hanna's small voice, just loud enough over the road noise, though Paul had to admit he knew it well.

"They gave her a long one," said Kristen loyally, "because she is good at remembering."

"Dad said he could hear me too," said Hanna. "Not like the other kids."

Paul smiled proudly at Line, as if the kids in the back were their own. "Were you there?" asked Line.

"Nope," said Paul. "I missed that too. I just got home a day ago."

At home, Mother was in the kitchen, waiting for them.

Line took a plastic bag full of round rolls, like doughnuts, from her grocery bag. "These are bagels," she said. "Jewish people eat them. They boil them and then bake them. They're really good toasted, with butter. Or cream cheese. I brought some."

"Hmmmm," said Mother. "Shall we have them for lunch?"

"Sure," said Line.

That was a merry meal. Four kids at home, everyone telling their news, the toaster popping up and down and the smell of browned wheat and melted butter hovering in the warm air. Some of the bagels had poppy and sesame seeds on them, giving the toast a nutty taste. Paul liked the cream cheese, but the bagels were best with butter.

"A package from England arrived at the post office today," Dad said.

"Now Carl, we are not opening that ahead of time," said Mother firmly.

"No, no. But just think. It's been on a ship for two months! Marty sent it at Halloween!"

"There's a package from Italy, too," said Mother, looking conspiratorially at Paul and Line. "But I put it under the tree." Ellie, their eldest sister, was living in Milan with her husband, who worked for the 3M Corporation, and their two little girls. They came home once a year in the summer. "It came by air to 3M in Minneapolis and was forwarded down here."

Two sisters in Europe, thought Paul, bagels for lunch. It felt as if the world were full of bounty and he was partaking of its riches.

The days before Christmas were very full, but the day after, Dad started talking about driving up to Lake Michigami. "We could start a fire in the Ben Franklin, and get it warm enough for a few hours. It's tempting to go look at the ice on the lake and see the woods," he said. "But there wouldn't be any water." The pipes had been drained at the end of the summer to prevent them from breaking. Paul wanted to go as much as Dad did. They had never been up to the lake in the winter.

They planned a very early start. Much of the day would be spent driving. But that morning, after a sheaf of bland, sunny days, a blizzard howled in and Dad called off the trip. According to the television news, it was even worse up north and most of the small county roads wouldn't get plowed that day at all. For Paul, the storm itself became a compensation for not going. Thick snow fell over everything.

Paul got Line to settle down to a game of chess with the carved wooden pieces in Marty's package. While they played, Line explained that she was starting a Licensed Practical Nursing course. In order to pay for her keep, she would work half time at the old people's home. Working shifts at the hospital would pay her tuition. It sounded difficult, but it was only for a year, and Line was thrilled.

"Nursing is just right for me," she told Paul. "I never knew. And I don't have to ask Mom and Dad for much help!" They had paid for her train to come home, but mostly, Line was on her own. "No more weekends with Stephen, though," she said, quietly. "SDS is going to have to get along without me."

"Can they get along without you?" asked Paul. From her stories, and from newspapers, Paul thought of Line as demonstrating in front of police barricades. He thought about telling her about the mouse, the creature of great personal valour, whose solo kept running through his head. But he didn't know the whole thing, and wasn't sure he could do the magnificent song justice by himself.

"There are hundreds, maybe thousands of people like me, Paul," said Line. "Does anyone talk about the war at Astoria College?"

"Not much," Paul had to admit. "It really is a 'junior' college. But I hear of guys getting drafted now and then."

"Humpf," said Line. "Sad state of affairs. Kids being taken in like that."

"I'm not sorry it's a junior college," said Paul. "Great people. My choir director is the best and there's an old botanist I like. I feel really free there, completely at home!"

On New Year's Eve the family sang 'happy birthday' to Marty at 4 p.m., which they had determined would be midnight in England. Mother made a chocolate cake and put a piece away in the freezer for Marty when she came home in the summer. A candlelight supper celebrated the arrival of the New Year.

"Whatever my lot, thou has taught me to say, it is well, it is well with my soul," sang Paul to himself. The world felt very large and very full. Praise was the only response.

5

Line hugged her coat collar around her neck in the bitter wind when she left to go to school. The elevated train was warm. Line looked around. Every face was closed, full of thoughts, worry. Did anyone else look forward to the day as she did? But other than smiling at people, Line didn't speak. She was finally learning that, in the city, it was best not to engage.

Downtown, Line got off the train, turned up her collar with one hand, and walked toward Cook County hospital. The wind was behind her as it blew off the huge icy lake, but she took small breaths, trying to avoid taking in too much cold air. Even in North Dakota as a child Line had not been this cold. Finally she reached the big, blowsy hospital complex which had become her second home.

The small building where classes were held was steamy with heat, puddles dripping on the concrete floors in the hall and moisture coating the peeling paint on the walls. Hurrying through the streets had warmed Line. She burst into the classroom, beaming at her classmates who were taking off coats, scarves and sweaters.

From the desk in front of Line, Doreen turned around. "It's so nice to be warm!" she said in her soft accent. "A lot warmer here than it is at home." She wore a plain shirtwaist belted with a cloth belt of the same material, her hair pulled tight back. Red blotches stained her scrubbed face.

She probably doesn't get to wash her hair very often, Line noted. "How did you study?" Line asked, laying the heavy chemistry text on the arm of her desk. "I hate to study in the cold." She wondered whether Doreen had had anything but potatoes to eat for dinner.

"Under the covers!" said Doreen. "I'll never get used to the winter up here," she sighed. Her family had moved up from the South to work in the mills and factories associated with steel in Chicago.

Line turned to SueAnn, behind her in the row of desks. "How is it at your house?" she asked. SueAnn was a tall wiry black girl, all arms and legs.

"Oh, my mama keeps the stew pot going and we all hang out in the kitchen. We're fine and warm," she smiled. "But this chemistry is going to be the death of me! Are you sure we have to know this stuff?"

The girls looked up to Line because she was older. She didn't tell them she had three years of college under her belt, though she had never taken much chemistry. "I think the idea is that we should know more than we need," Line said. "I'll bet we end up doing baths and bedpans all day anyway." She laughed.

"The aides do that," said SueAnn, emphatically. "I been an aide! That's why I'm in school!"

All of the students were poor, Line had been surprised to discover. All of them worked to pay for classes or contribute to families. All of them were hopeful young women. It was like being in Atlanta, at the girls' college where everyone was working to better themselves, except that these girls, from poor Southern families both black and white, as well as several Filipino immigrants, had no chance to go to college.

Line had never been so acutely conscious of class. As the wife of a pastor and educated herself, Line's Mother had an innate superiority which didn't have much to do with how much money she had. Mother spoke intelligently with perfect diction, dressed as carefully as she could, and subtly required the same of her kids. Living in small towns, Line had always felt equal to anyone.

At the moment Line had no more money than any of these girls, but she knew her worth. She chose to do this nursing program because she loved helping people and found, working at the Lutheran home, that she did it best one to one. Some of that work was patient care. Line worked four evenings a week and Sunday, and still had time to study. And she had good meals and a warm place to live.

When Nurse Arnold walked in, she had a smile on her brown, lined face. "Good morning, students," she said. "This is the day you've been waiting for. I'm going to pass out your name pins and hats, and explain what uniforms you need to get. Next week, we'll tour the hospital and set up clinical practice assignments for each of you. Please come up and get your things when I call your name." Nurse Arnold taught chemistry and anatomy and also took responsibility for the group.

Line liked Nurse Arnold, who had lots of experience and had been on a hardship tour on a navy ship as a young woman during the war. She was reasonable and compassionate toward the students, without letting them off at all. A lot of information was crammed into the classes. Line was a sponge when she wanted to be. She was more stimulated, she thought, than she had ever been at college.

Doreen turned around and gave Line a look as Nurse Arnold called out "Line Mikkelson." Line walked up to the front to receive the small straight pin with the letters of her name on it as well as a brilliant white hat, starched into a graceful curve. She popped it on her head with a smirk and everyone laughed as she went back to her desk and sat down.

"The medical profession is very disciplined, as you know," Nurse Arnold said in mild reproof. "You will find that the people we work with in a functional hierarchy, need to know who is who. It's one of the ways we keep a scientific outlook. So you must wear a white uniform, white stockings and comfortable shoes."

Line imagined each of the girls mentally tabulating how they were going to get these things. They had known it from the beginning, but now it came to the point. Line planned to ask Mother and Dad for the money, as they were proud of her for setting up her program and knew she had little extra.

"White nylon will stand a lot of washings," said Nurse Arnold. "But you will have to be careful of your underthings. No pink slips glowing underneath your white uniform!"

All the girls laughed and Line heard SueAnn whispering under her breath, "White nylon, my eye. That's not goin' to work."

"Now, your school cap comes with your tuition. I'll show you how to wash them, and pin them on next Monday. LPNs don't get stripes on theirs. For regular nurses, colored stripes mean they haven't graduated. A black stripe means they have. Any questions?"

Line sighed, looking around. It seemed to her that the girls had never paid such attention as they did to this question of caps and uniforms. Line thought what was in her head more important than what was on it, but she could see that the other girls couldn't wait to be crowned with white caps.

"All right," said Nurse Arnold. "Enough of all that. Please open your books to page 50."

Line had Saturday free, her only day off. She and Stephen met downtown, at an ice skating rink in Lincoln Park. Neither of them had money to spend on renting skates, but they sat in a shelter with big outdoor heaters blasting at them, watching the skaters and talking.

"It is so good to get out," said Stephen. He had a long muffler wrapped around the collar of a thin coat, his long curling hair tucked under. His hands quickly found Line's body under her coat as they sat tight against each other.

Line knew exactly what he meant. "There is life outside of SDS," she said. "I've been telling you so." Stephen no longer lived at the SDS national office, which had moved to the West Side, on Madison, but he was spending a great deal of time there. He lived in a room in Hyde Park near the University, where he took classes.

"I'm not complaining," said Stephen. "I'm just saying it is nice to be out here, with you." He kissed the end of Line's nose.

"What are you working on?" Line asked.

"Well ...," Stephen took a while to think about it. "Mostly the usual. So much mail. Phone calls. But I've also been helping Greg Calvert write a speech. Shows the difference between a liberal and a radical."

"Which is?" pressed Line. Her toes were cold in her boots. She wished she had worn an extra pair of socks.

"Liberals aren't personally oppressed. They may try to help those who are, but they are usually at least somewhat removed from the problem. We're saying that radical, or revolutionary consciousness sees oneself as oppressed. If you see yourself as radical, you'll join in the struggle with others and share the burden."

"Are you talking about yourself?" asked Line, burrowing her nose into his muffler. Below them, on the ice, a tiny girl practiced jumps at one end. Mostly people were moving in circles around the oval rink, some together, some alone. Over the loudspeaker came the Mamas and the Papas, singing "Monday, Monday." But it was Saturday and she and Stephen had sunk into the familiar, profound place they found themselves when together.

"Actually, yes!" said Stephen. "And you too. The military industrial complex runs roughshod over all of us and doesn't care!"

"Yes," said Line. He was right, but she couldn't think of anything she needed from them, or anyone else.

"You'd really like Greg," said Stephen. "I hope you get to meet him. He grew up in a shack in Washington State with his grandparents. His first language was Finnish!"

"That sounds pretty radical," said Line.

"Actually," said Stephen, "draft dodgers have the most radical problems right now. We're trying to get a group to burn their draft cards at the Moratorium in April. It's no small thing. There could be consequences."

"You too?" asked Line.

"Absolutely," said Stephen, smoothing a curl off Line's forehead and back under her wool hat. "Hell no, I won't go!"

Line giggled. She had no idea what it meant.

"I can't tell other guys not to go if I'm sitting out," said Stephen. "I don't know if I'll get in trouble or not. As far as I know I'm still student-deferred."

"Just so long as you show up and hold me on Saturdays," said Line. "But my toes are awfully cold. Could we go have a cup of coffee?"

There was no sauntering down the street with the wind at your heels. Line and Stephen walked briskly into town and found a drab coffee shop. Sodden people in dark overcoats sat at the tables. Cigarette smoke rose above some as they blew out smoke and flicked their cigarettes into ashtrays. Waitresses in dingy pink dresses with white aprons moved among the tables, pouring coffee out of glass pots with plastic handles.

Line tore the tops off two packets of sugar and poured all the milk left in the small aluminum pitcher into a thick china mug of coffee. Her toes tingled as they got warm.

Stephen sat across the table, watching her, amused. He was thin as a rail and drank his coffee black.

Line looked back at him, wrinkling her nose. "So, Mr. Radical," she said. "It's winter! I can have as much cream as I want!" Around the two of them was a glow of youth, of hope, of love. She could tell that some of the older people watched them enviously.

"So, you're even more beautiful," Stephen said, evenly. "Tell me about school."

Line sighed. How could she tell him everything that had happened that week? "We're going in to the hospital finally," she said. "I'm looking forward to it. Classes are fine." She took a sip of hot liquid. "When I was a kid," she mused, "we had a big medical encyclopedia and in the middle were these transparent plastic pages of the internal organs of a person. Bright colored, red and blue blood. I know I turned over those pages again and again. I never dreamed they would be so important."

"Male or female," asked Stephen.

Line smiled at him, knowing he was hoping to talk about sex. "I'm not sure! Maybe they didn't have the bottom part of the person. But they must have!" She wrinkled her brow, trying to remember. "It was hidden in the closet when I was little," she said. "But then later we used to pull it out and scare each other with the pictures in it. Elephantiasis, now there's a disease you don't want!"

"Mostly in Africa, I think," said Stephen.

"Yes," said Line. "But Stephen," Line's mind leapt. "The girls in my class are oppressed. They are hungry and cold and poor, most of them. They don't have a radical thought in their heads, though."

"Chicago's a big city," said Stephen. "We've been working with some of these people, you know, in the ERAP and JOIN programs. That was in our 'liberal' phase," he said sardonically. "But there are always more."

"And I know even Johnson's poverty programs are supposed to make a dent," said Line. "But it's more than that."

At the mention of Johnson, Stephen looked like he would explode. "Johnson!" he said. "If only he'd stick to domestic affairs! He's making a mess in Vietnam, I'll tell you. Civilians, children, plans to bomb them back into the stone age!"

"I know, I know," said Line, putting her hand on his. She searched earnestly for words to describe how sad it made her to see her new friends scrambling for crumbs beneath the table. "I love the girls in my class," she said. "They're feisty and every one of them is so happy to be in school! But they've had such a hard time. And for every one of them, there are people at home not so lucky." She remembered sharing her tuna-fish sandwich with Doreen, whose bread seemed to be spread with bacon fat and beans.

"You're right," said Stephen, quietly, raising his shoulder in the direction of a middle-aged lady who was whining to her husband. "Look around you. This is America, beaten down, poverty-stricken, lonely." The husband silently shrugged his shoulders.

"But Stephen," said Line, sitting up and brightening even more than usual. "I'm sorry for talking this way. We shouldn't spend our only afternoon trying to solve the world's problems. Let's walk through the Congress hotel on our way to eat." Line had found before Christmas, when the historic, luxury hotel had Christmas displays and music playing, that no one seemed to mind if she walked through the lobby. It was another good way to get in out of the cold.

The two of them walked up the street, the icy wind whipping them as it gathered speed between high-rise buildings. In the lobby of the hotel, people sat on plush couches under the windows overlooking the park along the lake, but most bustled from one place to another down the long hallways.

"The real difference between me and the girls in my class," Line said as she took off her gloves and stuck her nose in a huge bouquet of roses sitting on a table, "is that none of them could walk into a place like this with any confidence." She turned to Stephen.

"I'm imagining you in your new nurse's uniform," he said, his eyes twinkling.

Line sighed. She couldn't wait to get into the hospital.

"I wish I had something to offer you," said Stephen all of a sudden, taking Line's hand, "but all I see in the future is resistance and rebellion!"

"It's okay," said Line softly. "The war won't last forever. We just have to take things as they come." She leaned toward him. "As long as we come from the north and the south, like two magnets meeting in the middle on our free time, I can manage."

Right there, in public, Stephen kissed her, but they could see someone in a dark uniform coming toward them and they melted into a corridor. "Resist, resist," whispered Line, giggling.

"When you say that, it makes me want to fuck you," whispered Stephen. But it was too cold and there was no time or place for it. They had plates of spaghetti at a cheap place Stephen knew about and then went back to their lives, to school and to work.

That week the nursing students toured the huge Cook County hospital complex. When they were given their clinical assignments, Line was surprised to find herself in an obstetrical ward.

"You've got plenty of experience of older people," said Nurse Arnold. "We thought you should see the other end of life! There'll be rotations of course, but you have a lot to get used to. You'll stay on this ward for the next four months."

Three days a week, after that, Line was in the hospital. She put up her hair and pinned on the hat with its little comb and bobby pins. But it bobbled around on her head just when Line was most busy. She hated it. Over her uniform she wore a cotton pinafore.

In the obstetrics group with Line were two Filipino girls and Doreen. The very first day they were on the ward they were drawn into the labor room and watched nurses monitor deliveries. Only when the baby was about to come did the doctor walk into the room and gently assist the baby down the birth canal.

In one case, the mother had had a spinal block, but in the other, things were moving too quickly. It was Ms. Albright's third child. She was so used to labor, she simply turned around in her bare-assed little shift, got on her knees and pushed while the doctor guided the baby.

"He's crowning," said the doctor when the widest part of the head was visible. "Steady, steady, we're almost there."

"That's the biggest the vaginal opening has to get," said the matron quietly describing the procedure to the four girls. "The head has to come through. The shoulders usually rotate a little and come out sideways."

"Does he know it's a boy?" asked Line, in awe.

"Maybe not yet," said the matron. "He's guessing, I think."

At last the whole body of a little boy emerged. A ripple of excitement went through the room as the doctor held up the little boy and spanked his bottom. He started to yell.

"One more push!" said Nurse Jamison. "Just the placenta to come." Mrs. Albright sank onto the mattress. "Come on, darlin'," said the nurse. "You're doing so well!"

Line smiled at Doreen, whose face looked white, and leaned in, as close as she could get, watching.

Everything moved quickly. The doctor clamped off the chord between the baby and the mother in two places and cut it. The mother turned over and lay back to take the tiny red boy in her arms. Her face grew soft and tears flowed down her cheeks. The matron, watching Doreen, motioned for her to sit down in a chair and put her head down so she wouldn't faint.

While the mother and baby were being cleaned up and wrapped in blankets, groans came from the other bed. The limp woman in it was whimpering. The doctor was gone already, but the attending nurse looked at the matron and her four student charges.

"When did she have that block?" asked the matron.

"A couple of hours ago," said Nurse Jamison.

"And nothing's happened?" asked the matron.

They looked at each other ominously. "Could you take Mrs. Albright back to her room," asked Nurse Jamison, going over to check the blood pressure of the limp woman. She looked at the chart at the foot of the bed. "Maybe one of you could stay and bathe Mrs. Simpson's face?"

Line's hand shot up. "I'll do it."

"Wash your hands, there's warm water over there and some towels," said Nurse Jamison.

The matron and the other three girls each took one leg of the rolling bed and rolled the now smiling Mrs. Albright and her baby down the hall. "I'll be right back," said the matron.

Mrs. Simpson looked apathetic, waiting for it to all be over, for someone to take care of her. By the look of her, Line thought, she needed it. Her red face was feverish and wet with moisture.

"Come on, Mrs. Simpson," said Nurse Jamison, trying to open her legs. "I need to see what's going on." To Line she said. "If they have a spinal block they can't feel much below the hips. Less pain, but the baby gets kind of sluggish also."

When she was able to get a look, Nurse Jamison said, "I think we need a doctor here right away." She looked around her. "Go to the nurses' station," she said to Line. "Tell them we need the doctor in Labor Room 5, immediately."

Line raced to the nurses' station, gave the message and went back into the labor room, where the matron, Doreen and the other girls had returned. Mrs. Simpson was starting to yell. "It hurts!" she said. "Can't you give me something?!"

Line washed Mrs. Simpson's face and arms with a wet cloth to take her mind off what was happening below. After watching how simple it had been for Mrs. Albright, Line had little sympathy for this Mrs. Weakfish, but she tried to put her own strength into the young woman, who could not have been older than Line herself.

When the doctor came in, he said, "Mrs. Simpson, your baby wants to come now. We don't have time to give you another spinal block. We need you to push now."

Between contractions Mrs. Simpson sobbed with anger, "You said it wouldn't hurt!"

"Push, Mrs. Simpson, Push!"

Line leaned over, massaging the girl's arms and neck.

"Gentle hands," whimpered Mrs. Simpson, reaching weakly toward Line.

When the next contraction came, Mrs. Simpson screamed. Her whole body convulsed and a little head began to emerge into the waiting doctor's hands. "Good girl!" said the doctor. "Not long now. Relax a minute."

Line whispered in Mrs. Weakfish' ear, "Hush, it's almost over."

With another contraction Mrs. Simpson's face clenched in pain as she yelled. But the baby's body squirted out like a seed from a fruit. It was a little girl, Line could see, an energetic little body come into the world.

"Here you are, Mrs. Simpson," said the doctor. "A lovely little girl child. She's going to make you so happy!" He held the little girl upside down, cut the chord and handed her to the waiting Nurse Jamison, who washed the little girl down and wrapped her in a towel.

But Mrs. Weakfish wouldn't look. She rolled over on her side and lay still. The nurse put the little girl beside her in the bed and Line transferred her attention to the tiny baby.

"Oh, so cute," Line said, stroking the red head, which was downy with black hair. "So soft and so pretty." She looked to see whether Mrs. Weakfish noticed. But the woman's eyes were shut. Line was appalled. What kind of mother would she make?!

The nurses cleaned up the limp Mrs. Simpson and the student nurses wheeled her back to her room. Nurse Jamison took the swaddled baby to the nursery. Line wondered what would happen, but she wasn't allowed to stay. The matron directed them to the nurses' station and began to explain the charting for the two labors they had seen.

"As you can see," the matron said. "Every birth is different. But, in terms of charting, these were two quite normal births. Any questions?"

Line had no questions. She felt silenced, the immensity of the experience washing over her. This was what it meant to be a woman, to have another life grow in you and then emerge. She recalled all the times Mother had gone off to the hospital and come back with a baby. None of them knew what Mother went through for each of her six kids, but Line suspected it must have grown easier with practice. Like Mother, Line herself had big hips, which were supposed to make child-bearing easier.

The nurses were matter-of-fact, clear in their duties. Line's class was advised to be professional, not to involve themselves in the emotional lives of their patients. But how could one keep from doing so? Line's hands tingled with the feel of Mrs. Simpson's skin. After only one day in the hospital, she could see a life of purpose spreading in front of her, full of questions and things to learn.

6

Marty closed the heavy wooden door on the house in Hayward Road with a clunk and headed for the roundabout. She climbed the stairway to the top of a red double-decker bus and sat where tree branches brushed against the windows. She loved the birds' eye view of the houses as the bus trundled through the suburbs of north Oxford.

It was February, a misty day with the sky beginning to separate into actual clouds which might let the sun through. When they got close enough to town, Marty got off the bus and wandered into the university gardens on her way to the Bodleian library. Water drops glistened on leaves and lay in puddles. The smell of the dark wet earth rose up, fecund and enlivening. Marty's shoes crunched on the gravel paths as she walked between hedges and banks of rose bushes pruned back to their bare canes. The benches were too damp to be inviting, but Marty wanted to air out her thoughts as she walked.

"My secrets cry aloud. I have no need for tongue. My heart keeps open house, my doors are widely swung," Marty chanted under her breath her current talisman, a poem by Ted Roethke. He had been her favorite modern poet, the most like herself, she thought. He had grown up in a greenhouse in Michigan.

But there was no evidence of Roethke in Oxford. Marty peered near-sightedly into a rosebush to see whether any little leaves were forming. The light blazed out from behind a cloud above her briefly, dazzling and blinding her, firing the garden with color.

"Silence, exile, cunning," said Marty to herself, moving off down the path. They were the weapons James Joyce allowed himself in his personal fight against country and church. Both of these bits of language, so precious, celebrated silence. Marty herself had need of silence. It protected her still unknown self.

Marty couldn't accept the huge regard for the artist Joyce was trying to fashion for himself. In Joyce' eyes, artists were like God, world creators. Artists were only people, after all. But it did help Marty that Joyce felt he could get along without his Christian faith. Marty was hoping she could too.

In Oxford only one professor lectured in the Twentieth Century literature Marty wanted most to study. Francis Warner was a young, enthusiastic don who took up the challenge offered by the Modern era in which the university as a whole showed little interest. Marty longed to know more about the writers of the current century. She believed that contemporary writers could tell her more about herself and what she was meant to do in the world. The question felt like a dim landscape of confusion in which she was feeling her way. Writers held the lamps by which she might navigate.

At last the sun steadily burned through the clouds. Waterdrops glistened on rosebush canes and the few shrubs which hadn't lost their leaves. The mist thinned. Marty found the world magical. The near trees were hard-edged though the distant ones were still softly enveloped in the watery air. Puddles along the path shined like mirrors, reflecting whatever was above. Color returned to the garden with the sun, laying on gray greens and brighter greens with a palette knife. In the distance, a man brushed up leaves on the path.

Marty thought of the Turners she had seen in London over the holidays. Most of Turner's paintings were much wilder than the placid scene in front of Marty. Turner painted the sky and its reflection on land or sea, a few brief strokes sketching in the horizon. Marty had been lost in the paintings.

But everything Marty knew, she had learned from literature. Not the classical literature which was everywhere available. Modern writers. *The Golden Notebook*, by Doris Lessing, had been most revelatory. The young teachers at Wittenberg College were all reading it. But was it even literature? In it, Anna, the main character, talked realistically about her body in a way Marty never could with her friends, or even her sisters.

Everyone knew Joyce was important. He had been canonized as a Modern, though his book *Ulysses* had once been banned in England. Richard Ellmann's thick biography of him which had just come out graced the windows at Blackwell's Books and stood on a shelf at the Radcliffe Camera where Marty could read it.

Perhaps Joyce was right, artists were gods, geniuses. But Marty doubted it. They were people, pushed to greatness by a combination of the light inside them and the world they were born into. It was wonderful to study them, however. People in whom the light blazed brightly.

Marty headed down the Parks Road, past the wonderful Rhodes House which she could never resist visiting. Rhodes House was built by the diamond miner, Cecil Rhodes. It had beautiful light-colored woodwork and wonderful mullioned windows.

Marty went through the imposing portico and up the steps. She felt comfortable in Oxford now, slipping invisibly into the college quadrangles, through the gardens, into the buildings. Few students actually wore their black gowns and Marty acted like one of them. Rhodes House was not a place she had any business being, but Marty sometimes sat in the library a moment to write in her journal, reminding herself that the beautiful place, the famous American Rhodes scholars, floated on the backs of black men working in dangerous conditions in South Africa, mining diamonds.

Restless, Marty kept moving. Oxford struck Marty as a tame place, the gardens long cultivated, the buildings ancient and beloved. It was beautiful, manicured into smoothness. But Marty couldn't feel at home. She missed the rough fields and wide sky of the upstart country where she lived, with scarcely one hundred years of known history in it. She felt herself rougher, less civilized than the landscape and people of Oxford. It was why she needed silence. You couldn't say such things.

Normally, Marty spent most of her free time in the Radcliffe Camera, a round building hidden behind scaffolding, being cleaned of grime and coal dust. Inside, the big room was quiet, filled with shelves of books in the humanities, and desks where silent people read and wrote under the lovely windows. The Ellmann biography of Joyce sat on an open shelf, as pretty as you please. No one else seemed to use it, so Marty took it down and read it each day, putting it back where she found it.

Today, however, Marty went to the Bodleian, where she was now officially a "reader." She walked through the beautiful vaulted Gothic ceilings of the ancient Divinity School part of the building, now unused, and into a large room where people waited for the books they had ordered. On the far wall was a row of librarians behind a counter as if it were a bank. Books must be used in the big library reading rooms. Marty intended to have a look at the infamous *Ulysses*.

"Oh," said a librarian, when Marty went up with her card and her request. "That book is probably in the protected books section."

"Can I see it?" asked Marty.

The librarian checked the many drawers of cards behind her. "Yes," she said. "Just one moment. I'll take you there."

Marty followed the woman out of the room, her heels clicking as she went down marble steps. Rows of books on shelves ran through this lower room. At the end was a section walled off by a steel cage. High windows lighted disorderly shelves in the cage. The librarian opened the door with a key.

"You may have a look," she said, pointing to a stool. She pulled the book off the untidy shelves. "Just pull the door shut behind you on your way out."

Marty was astonished. But here was *Ulysses*, in her hands. She sat on the stool, light coming from the bright windows above her, and opened the book to the last page. On this page supposedly, were Molly Bloom's long thoughts as she had sex, ending with her orgasm. Marty read: "and then I asked him with my eyes to ask again yes and then he asked me would I yes to say yes my mountain flower and first I put my arms around him yes and drew him down to me so he could feel my breasts all perfume yes and his heart was going like mad and yes I said yes I will Yes."

The word "yes" in Molly's voice had been raised to a hymn. Marty continued, reading backwards in the book to get its flavor. She wouldn't have it in her hands long. Stephen, the main character at the beginning, must be the continuation of the Stephen in *A Portrait of the Artist as a Young Man*, she concluded. Joyce himself.

Soon Marty became aware of time. The light shone down on her. She looked up, put the book back on the shelf and slammed the steel door shut behind her. Joyce's work in a steel mesh cage! It was amazing.

Marty rushed off to Francis Warner's lecture at St. Catherine's, not far away. The light was starting to grow longer each day, even on wet evenings. Grey stone churches and towers stood against the opalescent sky and pavements were wet. Some trees were already budding. At St. Cat's, Marty joined other students in a wood-paneled lecture hall newly-built by a Danish architect. She looked for a blonde head in her peripheral vision.

His name was Glyn, Glyn Pritchard. The two of them had become friends through their dedication to Warner's lectures. Warner was Glyn's tutor at St. Peter's College. Glyn told Marty he couldn't miss one on pain of death. Nor did he want to.

Sure enough, Glyn sat in a row by himself in the sparsely populated room. Marty took a seat beside him. Glyn was short with longish, tousled hair and a scruffy brown corduroy jacket. Marty would never have mistaken him for an American. He was a scholarship student from Sheffield, militantly clear about his future.

"I got a look at *Ulysses*," Marty said quietly. "In a steel cage at the Bodleian! It was so interesting!"

"You can buy it in a bookstore," said Glyn laconically.

"I know," said Marty. "I just wanted to see if I could read it at the Bodleian."

"Apparently, you can!" said Glyn amused. Glyn's major interest was in modern poetry, upon which Francis Warner waxed eloquent. Glyn was especially interested in T.S. Eliot, another safely-canonized literary saint.

Warner dressed impeccably in a navy suit coat, a white shirt, and a wide green and gold tie, which, Glyn pointed out, were the colors of St. Peter's. He took poems line by line, as Marty's teachers at Wittenberg had done, extrapolating and explaining them in dramatic terms, making them live. A large part of the joy of his lectures was his own language, colorful and yet with perfect Oxford diction.

"He's from Yorkshire too," said Glyn, when Marty mentioned his speech after the lecture. "But the university, over the years, knocks it out of you."

Marty wondered what a Yorkshire accent sounded like. Glyn's speech was soft, but he was trying to train it into the regulation university accent. "Why?" Marty wondered.

"Because no one will take you seriously if you don't have upper class diction! Look at Keats, one of our greatest poets! He was labeled 'Cockney school' because he couldn't afford an education. Unimaginable," scoffed Glyn with disdain.

"You're kidding!" said Marty. She had never paid much attention to the romantic Keats. His poems about beauty had never been among her incantatory inner sayings.

"He trained as an apothecary!" said Glyn, putting on his coat and wrapping a scarf around his neck as they left the building.

Marty knew Glyn to be intense and passionate about many things, as he often walked to the bus with her after lectures. He loved jazz and was intent on plying his own poor circumstances into a university career. She still didn't understand how one's birth or diction could affect one's life to such a degree. In her world, nothing held one back if one had a passionate interest and the intelligence to apply oneself.

At the bus, Glyn said, "There's Ibsen tonight at the Playhouse. Do you want to come?"

"Oh, yes!" Marty said. She was worried her American enthusiasm was too much for Glyn. She hardly knew how to tone it down.

"Meet me in front at 7:45," said Glyn. He pulled a crumpled black scholar's gown from the pocket of his corduroy coat. "I have to wear this if I'm going to eat in hall."

Marty giggled, watching him slip his arms into it. "I'll be there," she said. It was twilight. Hopefully the Magnussons wouldn't mind if she ducked out after dinner. She suspected they liked it when she was gone, leaving them to their comfortable three-some at home.

When Marty got back to Hayward Road, Thea was setting the table for dinner. A slender little blonde in a bright woolen jumper over a cotton turtleneck, at ten she was as tall as Marty's shoulder. Blue twilight shone in at the big bay windows in the dining room.

Irene was in the kitchen, absorbed in reading an unfamiliar-looking can. "I bought these escargot from France. We've eaten them before, but

I've never tried to cook them." She held up a two-fold can in which the bottom held the shells and the top vacuum-packed snails. "The instructions are in French! But it can't be too hard," she mused.

When Marty asked her about leaving for the evening, Irene said, "That sounds fine. Ibsen? *Rosmersholm*? I've never seen that. Rolfe and I will go another night."

"Mother said I could light the candles," said Thea, dancing into the room. "Will you help me?"

Marty brought in the matchbox and held it for Thea.

"Oooooh," said Thea, as she drew a match across the flint. "It's so exciting!" She dropped the match when a candlewick wouldn't catch fire. "Help! Help!"

Marty laughed and picked up the match, which had fallen on the wooden table. "Don't cry for help unless you really need it," she admonished. "Remember the little boy who cried wolf!"

Dinner was exciting and delightful as always. Irene had stuffed the escargot, along with garlic and parsley butter, into their shells and baked them. With a bottle of white wine, a baguette of French bread, and a green salad, the meal was simple. The escargot tasted as rich and meaty as they smelled. Like they had come from sea and salt, which of course they had not.

The Magnussons drank whatever wine they thought appropriate to the meal, as Europeans did. Rolfe was the family wine steward, choosing and buying it. When Irene felt sad, Rolfe brought home a steak and a bottle of Sangre de Toro, or Bull's Blood from Spain, to inspirit the family. Marty's glass was never very full. The wine sometimes made her light-headed but didn't affect much else. Before living with the Magnussons, she had only had communion wine.

At dinner Thea played with her snails, eating mostly bread. She was always given what the grownups were eating plus a glass of milk.

"Thea, we'll be able to pick up Bambi this weekend," said Rolfe. Bambi was the family's short-haired toy terrier, who had been in a kennel for the past six months, in quarantine to make sure it was carrying no diseases, as any animal coming into the United Kingdom must be.

"Oh!" Thea clapped her hands. "Poor little Bambi. I can't wait!"

"Neither can she, I'm sure," said Irene, dryly.

Marty mopped the garlicky butter out of her snail shells with a piece of bread, imagining the poor little red-gold dog, which they had visited once in its kennel, its ears, too big for its head, standing straight up.

"Will she remember me?" asked Thea.

"After she's been here a little while, and when she feels at home, I'm sure she will remember you," said Rolfe. "She's been through a lot." He looked across the table at Irene. The Magnussons were planning on staying in Oxford for several more years, and had judged it worth transporting their dog.

Mention of the little dog made Marty's stomach clench. Time for her was short. She must leave at the end of May. Just as she was beginning to get used to things. And Kate was coming!

Kate had quit her teaching job and was on a freighter at this moment, heading to England. Though it would be fun to see Kate, it made Marty miserable. She did not feel she was pulling her own weight at the Magnussons, but here was her friend Kate, coming to stay with them! Marty quaked in her boots. What would she do with Kate? Who had no job or prospects in England!

"Lidia told me she wished she was in the United States," Irene said. "There's going to be a big protest at the Pentagon soon, and she and Boris would like to be there."

"They wouldn't go back just for that, would they?" asked Rolfe.

"No," said Irene. "But Lidia is in touch with an American protest group here. They're quite serious about it!"

Boris Chertok, a physics professor at a California university, had risked his job to protest the Vietnam war. The Chertoks wouldn't pay income taxes because taxes went to support the war. Rolfe and Irene were paying close attention to the Chertoks' stance. Marty wondered whether Line and Stephen, her boyfriend, would go to the demonstration.

Irene teased Marty gently about her 'date.' "Are you going to wear your Carnaby Street dress tonight?" she asked.

"Yes, I guess so," said Marty. Irene had found a brown woolen dress cut like a trapeze and inset with a piece of purple wool. Marty loved it, but it was so short she had been afraid to wear it until she had thick brown tights to cover her legs. "We'll just be in the theatre," she said, indecisively.

"Oh please," said Thea, clapping her hands. "Wear it!"

"Maybe you'll go out to a pub or something afterwards," said Irene.

"Yes," said Marty. "I hate to run out without doing the dishes," she said.

"Don't worry," said Irene. "There's not much. Thea will help me," she said smiling fondly at the little girl.

"Then, please excuse me," said Marty. "I better hurry." Buses were frequent, but she would be cutting it close to get into town by 7:45. "The snails were delicious. Thank you so much!"

"Have a lovely time," said Irene. "I can't wait to hear about the play!"

Marty was late getting to the Oxford Playhouse. Glyn was waiting with a pair of tickets. They quickly climbed to seats in the front of the balcony. The audience was sparse on a Wednesday night.

Marty turned over the thin playbill. "Judi Dench plays Rebecca," she said to Glyn. "She's really good."

Glyn nodded. "I don't know the play," he said. "But I believe Ibsen was an inspiration to your Mr. Joyce."

"Yes," said Marty. "Richard Ellmann writes about this. Just think, a Norwegian at the base of all those obscenity trials!"

"Ibsen caused quite a bit of trouble in his time," said Glyn, taking Marty's hand in his warm, rough one. "Got to watch out for you Norwegians!"

Marty giggled and settled back in her seat as Glyn's other hand strayed across her tummy, setting off the latent inner fires Marty associated with being in love.

The curtain went up. Marty struggled to keep up with what was happening around the two characters, Rosmer and Rebecca. Rosmer, trying to become a political reformer, was overcome by his guilt at his wife's death and the surrounding scandal. Rebecca, a powerful character whose every word Marty could hear clearly in the low, powerful voice of the actress, was also beset by guilt. Society closed in around them and tragedy followed.

To Marty it all felt much less important than what was going on between Glyn and herself. Had she expected it? Marty wasn't sure. As the play progressed, and even between the acts as they sat quietly together, Marty dwelt on the comfort between them. Not since her misguided romance with Glen at Wittenberg had anything felt so right. Here was Glyn, a short, powerful man with both the intellect and the physicality to awaken her. He was bent on an academic career. There was nothing Marty wanted more than to become a partner and helpmate to such a man.

After the play, as they wakened from their private dream, Glyn asked, "Shall we stop by the pub?"

"Sure," said Marty. She did not want the evening to be over.

The night air felt warm as they walked down the street, Glyn's hand wrapped firmly around Marty's. "Spring is coming!" said Marty, her voice full of hope. She was thinking about how glad she would be to get rid of her shabby winter coat. She planned to walk into an Oxfam shop soon and give it to them.

Glyn smiled at her. "After that tragic play?" he said. "That's what you're thinking?"

"It was good," said Marty. "Well done."

"Quite," said Glyn sardonically. "Guilt spread evenly throughout the characters."

Welcoming light and the sounds of conversation spilled out from the windows of a nearby building. Public houses came alive in the evenings and were full of students. But Marty disliked the dark tastes of the drinks she had had in them. "Something light," she said, when Glyn asked what she wanted.

Glyn considered. "I'd get you a pale ale," he said. "But that's actually more full-bodied than bitters sometimes."

Marty waved her hand as if she didn't care. She would try to drink whatever came to her.

"A sherry maybe?" asked Glyn.

"Oh yes!" said Marty. "That would be perfect." She did love the sweet warm taste of sherry. She hoped it wasn't more expensive.

"One bitters, one Harvey's," said Glyn to the bartender, who was hardly visible behind the array of kegs, bottles and glasses. Two glasses, a diminutive one of cream sherry and a tall glass of dark liquid with an impressive head of foam on top appeared in front of them.

Marty took her glass gratefully. "I really don't like the taste of hops," she said apologetically. It was hard to admit. Everyone in Oxford drank ale. "And I tried cider once," Marty said. "But it was so strong I couldn't even finish it!"

"To the evening," said Glyn, raising his glass.

"Yes," said Marty. "To the evening. And to spring coming!" She tipped her glass and the fiery liquid trickled down her throat like sunshine.

"I did think the Rosmer character weaker than Rebecca," said Glyn, as if his opinion mattered.

"It's hard to compete with Judi Dench," said Marty. "She's so memorable. They probably put on that play just for her! I saw her as Julia in *Romeo and Juliet* in the fall."

"Hmmm," said Glyn. "I guess I missed that."

"You've seen Shakespeare so often," said Marty. "You probably didn't want to see it again." In the cacophony around them as they stood at the bar with their heads close enough together so they could hear each other, the conversation felt intimate.

"Probably," said Glyn. "I wish the Playhouse had the guts to take on T.S. Eliot. Like *The Cocktail Party.*"

"It does seem incredible that Ibsen could dramatize inner problems so clearly," Marty said. She mentally added Ibsen to the list of people she knew of who had lost their faith, and survived.

"No shortage of courage there," said Glyn.

"I've never loved theatre much," said Marty. "But of course I've never seen it done so well."

"I think you would like Eliot's plays if you read them," said Glyn. "People think of him as a wrecker, as chronicling a dying culture, but in the end he was quite conservative, trying to put things back together."

"Yes," said Marty. She resolved to have a look at Eliot's plays.

"Francis Warner is writing a verse play," said Glyn.

"Really?" Marty asked. It all felt rather distant, far from the warm sensuality of the smell of bitters, damp wool and people's breath. Light bounced off the rows of glasses and bottles behind the bar. Marty could feel her hair touching Glyn's as they put their heads together.

"Not easy to do," said Glyn. But he must have sensed Marty's attention wandering. He looked at the large gold clock on the wall. "It's late," he said.

Marty's eyes flew to the clock. It would be fine. Buses ran late in Oxford, even to the northern suburbs.

"I'll walk you to the bus," said Glyn.

Waiting, they stood in companionable silence until the big red bus pulled up. "Thank you so much!" said Marty. "It was a wonderful evening!"

"Yes it was," said Glyn. "Goodnight." He didn't kiss Marty. He waved as she stepped into the bus.

Sitting up high, Marty felt blessed, resting her head against the window. Her eyes were heavy and soft in the harsh light. "So this is what starry-eyed means," she said to herself. It was a real thing.

Another thing she didn't want to tell anyone was that she wanted to be Nora Barnacle, Joyce's wife, a model of femininity and the inspiration for wonderful literature. Under the shabby coat, which hid the short Carnaby Street dress, which hid Marty's waistline, thickening from the delicious food the Magnussons served, was a hungry little heart.

7

The Astoria College choir went on tour during spring break, Paul among them. They were headed to Seguin, Texas, where the director, Oddmar Svendson, had friends and where they would put on a major concert. They traveled in a big silver bus with velvet-cushioned seats and all along the way they stopped at churches and sang, staying in people's houses for the night.

Paul kept his face to the window as the big bus traveled south through states he had never seen before. "I've never been anywhere," he told his seatmate Carol when she put *The Hobbit* down for a moment. "I feel like we're off to see the world."

Carol giggled. "You sound like Bilbo Baggins," she said, "who never has any adventures or does anything unexpected. But maybe you want to," she said. Carol pushed her glasses up with a finger and settled back into the comfy seat.

"My sister's in England," said Paul. "She's in Oxford, where Tolkien lives. My other sister's in Chicago. Mikkelsons do go places," he offered.

Carol smiled at him. "I believe you," she said, raising the book to her face.

Paul wondered how Carol could read *The Hobbit* when the adventure was taking place right outside the window. But he had read it over Christmas and had to admit that he did have Hobbit tendencies. He knew Carol sat by him because he wouldn't talk to her and she could become lost in her book.

What Paul loved most was when they turned off the big Interstate and the bus slowed, heading into a small town. Then you could really see what was going on around you.

Maddie, Oddmar's wife, set up the choir tours every year. Pete and Bob, two older men who did maintenance for the college, took turns navigating and driving through the long days. Oddmar carried a black satchel he called Hans packed with a huge bottle of aspirin and all sizes of bandaids. The choir members didn't have to worry about anything. They just had to show up, be on their best behavior, and sing.

In the morning Paul woke to the delicious smell of butter cooking. He was sleeping on a couch in a living room, a pile of blankets on top of him. Patterned curtains hung over the windows. Paul peeked out but it was still dark. Sleepily he gathered up his things, found the bathroom and washed. In the kitchen in bright electric light, a woman about Mother's age was brewing coffee.

"Oh, here's the sleepyhead," she said when Paul entered. "Sit down, let's have breakfast!"

"Sorry," said Paul. He found it exhausting to wake up somewhere different every day. A formica table in the kitchen was laid with place settings and the man of the house, who turned out to be a schoolteacher, smiled as Paul sat down at one of the places. On the other side was Michael, another member of the choir.

"Good morning," nodded the man. "Norwegian, are you, Mr. Mikkelson?"

"Mostly," said Paul.

"Well, my wife makes darned good pancakes, Swedish as the day she was born." The teacher's voice sounded a little softer than the flat voices of the north, Paul thought. His ear was tuned to listen for it, and yes, he sounded a little Southern.

Michael, who had probably been up for hours, spooned sugar into his coffee and grimaced gleefully at Paul. In last night's coin flip, he had gotten the guest room.

The woman set a platter of thin golden pancakes on the table, and then turned to pour coffee for Paul. The coffee smelled great, but it was scalding hot. Paul put in sugar and cream and sipped it.

Michael served himself pancakes and passed them to the man of the house. Paul could not remember his name, or even the name of the town they were in, but Michael could. "Are we close to the Texas border now, Mr. Jackson?" he asked.

"A few miles," said Mr. Jackson, taking three pancakes and spreading jam on them. "You'll cross that border this morning. Lots of history in this area," he said. "Especially Indian history of course. So many Indian nations were funneled into Oklahoma."

Paul's ears pricked up. Fully awake now, he asked, "Into Oklahoma?"

"More than a hundred years ago now," said Mr. Jackson. "Everyone had to fight it out. It's still a poor state. But oil is giving the place some hope these days." He looked significantly at his wife, who looked nervous.

Paul tried to imagine the conversations between them, the reasons they had settled in the state. Neither of them were young. A family photograph in the living room showed sons in military uniform.

The pancakes went around the table followed by a glass jar of jam. "Looks like my wife has brought out the Swedish jam for you boys," said Mr. Jackson. "Lingonberry."

The pancakes were so buttery and delicious Paul didn't want to spoil them with jam, but he politely took some. It tasted sweet and sour at the same time. "These pancakes are great, Mrs. Jackson!" he said gratefully.

"You boys know that the United Nations' purpose is to build a world government, don't you?" said Mr. Jackson.

Paul looked at Michael. "No, sir," said Michael. "Never heard of that."

"Well, pay attention," said Mr. Jackson. "We need less government, not more. You boys aren't voters yet, but you will be."

After breakfast Mrs. Jackson dropped her husband off at school, and drove Paul and Michael to the small Lutheran church where the silver bus was pulled up. "Enjoy your trip, boys!" she said as they got out. "Thank Mr. Svendson for me! Such wonderful music you all brought us."

Paul and Michael thanked her profusely. "The best breakfast we've had yet," said Michael.

Paul laughed as she drove away. "You said that yesterday," he said, elbowing Michael in the ribs.

"It was!" said Michael. "I swear. And you got to watch out for these Birchers."

"Birchers?" asked Paul.

"Dyed in the wool," said Michael. "You heard him. 'Here to save our country from a communistic plot!'" He quoted the Chad Mitchell trio song.

"Wow," said Paul. "Are you sure?"

"Yup," said Michael. "There's a stack of postcards in the den, ready to go out to congressmen from Mr. Ronald Jackson, John Birch Society, etc."

"I never would have thought," said Paul. "They're Lutherans! And he's a science teacher."

"Birchers make darn good pancakes, though." Michael snickered.

The two of them greeted the other choir members waiting in the cold early morning. The choir felt like a big family, with Oddmar and Maddie as the parents. Every day was different.

"Red River coming up!" sang out Bob from the front seat, navigating with a map. "Actually it's kind of looping all around us."

They were headed down Highway 35 straight into Texas and would be in Seguin that night. Paul kept his eyes glued to the window. My Red River is in North Dakota, he thought to himself.

The river was wide but unremarkable from the Interstate. Paul thought Texas would be desert, but what he saw was farms, windmills, homesteads and black fields newly tilled, trees budding out, just like at home, though spring had made more progress here.

When they took a moment for sandwiches and fruit put up by the ladies at the church in Oklahoma, Paul asked Bob, who had lived in Texas, "Where's the desert?"

"Well," said Bob, "there's a line that goes down through Texas, just like it goes down through the Dakotas and Nebraska. On one side, it's green and on the other side its dry. We're not going to get into the desert. We're going straight south, toward the Gulf. Big dry grazing lands to the west of us, farms to the east. You'll see some cotton, soybeans down through here."

"Cotton!" Paul had never seen a cotton plant. Cotton meant they were in the South and no mistake!

"'Course cotton doesn't look like much this time of year. They're just planting it. Pecan trees, now," said Bob. "You'll see some."

Back on the bus, Paul watched out the window and wished he could see cotton bolls erupting on a plant about to be harvested. Some of the pastures were blue with flowers.

"So beautiful," said Carol, looking up from her book.

"Bluebonnets," said Bob, turning around. Drifts of light green Spanish moss hung from big old oak trees.

Paul tried to sit with different people every day. A few boys were starting to pair up with girls, but Paul was certain he would be a bachelor forever. Girls were fun to talk to. He was used to them after so many sisters. But getting involved with someone seemed fraught with problems. Every so often he had to listen to someone going on and on about how they felt about a potential girlfriend, or a boyfriend who was giving them problems, or even a fantasy boyfriend. It all gave Paul a headache.

But he was a sociable creature in his way, interested in everything. "How's old Bilbo doing," he asked Carol.

"They just left the Last Homely House," said Carol, as if Bilbo was a real person. "They're going up into the mountains and Bilbo is looking back longingly at the valley below, where his little hobbit hole is, and thinking gloomy thoughts." She looked sideways at Paul. "I guess this plushy bus doesn't compare."

"Nope," said Paul. He wondered if he should tell Carol about the Birchers, but he decided not to.

That afternoon, when they arrived at Texas Lutheran, the air smelled sweet to Paul. The sun lay on Paul's shoulders like thick warm syrup. It felt so good he didn't want to go indoors! The campus was mostly white-painted brick, small like their own, with beautiful old trees. Everyone was put in dorm rooms where students had left for spring break. Paul relaxed. It was nice to have a bed, and they would be staying in the same place for two nights.

That evening they piled on the bus and went to a church in a nearby town. Outside the church, in big rusty oil drums cut in half in the parking lot, pork and beef and chickens roasted over charcoal, the fragrant smoke drifting through the air. Other food was laid out on picnic tables which looked well-used by the church.

A big old oak just beginning to leaf out shaded the back of the church and the parking lot. Paul was impressed to see some black faces among the crowd, young and old.

Oddmar made the rounds, making sure everyone tried everything. "Real Texas barbecue!" he kept saying. Paul filled his plate with steak and spare ribs basted with a thick, sweet sauce. He took it boldly over to a table where people he didn't know sat. Hands and greetings were extended. Pretty soon Michael followed.

A pretty, blonde girl came over with a sweating glass pitcher filled with ice, lemons and tea. She filled plastic glasses and handed them around. It was sweet and sour, refreshing to Paul's throat.

"Do you barbecue after church every Sunday," Paul asked a black teenager politely.

"Well, in the summer, it's too hot during the middle of the day. We just all lay low," he laughed, his teeth very white in the shade. "But we do it most of the winter."

"Wow," said Paul. "No snow?"

"Nope," said the kid. "But sometimes it rains. Pours, more like."

Paul looked at Michael, who had sunk his teeth into some spare ribs. "Wouldn't work to barbecue most days up north," said Paul. "We'd freeze to death!"

Paul went back to the serving table for red kidney beans and rice. He was stuffed but he wanted to try everything. He noticed David King, the choir chairman for the year, making the rounds of the tables, his hands out and pumping, just like a politician.

"Don't miss the pies," said the black teenager as Paul sat down again. "My mom's sweet potato pie's somewhere in there."

Paul sighed. "It's all so good!" He and Michael got up and stood in the pie line.

Michael sang softly, devilishly, in Paul's ear, "If Mommy is a commie, then you got to turn her in!" Paul was laughing, hoping no one else heard him.

But after the merry meal, the mood grew somber as people filed into the church for the Maundy Thursday evening service. On Thursday night of Holy Week, Christ had washed the feet of his disciples, shared a meal with them and then prayed in the garden at Gethsemane asking his

Father that the cup be removed from him. In the end He said, "Not my will, but Thine be done."

As Paul put a flowing blue choir robe on over his clothes, he wondered what Oddmar would suggest they sing on such a night.

When the choir collected Oddmar said, "I know this evening's mood is one of suffering and sadness, but we can also speak to Christ's acceptance of the Lord's will. We'll start with our Bach chorale, and then let's do 'This Is My Father's World.' Just do it quietly, as if you were both humbly accepting and praising the Lord at the same time."

Paul smiled to himself. It was so like Oddmar. He always told the choir that song was praise. Even during Holy Week as people prepared themselves to contemplate Christ's death, Oddmar insisted on singing the Lord's praises.

The altarpiece of the church was a statue of Christ, arms open and hands outstretched. The pastor warmly welcomed everyone, reading the gospel passages for the evening from Matthew and Luke. Paul noticed that the piano stood idle. Two men with a guitar and a banjo led the congregation in songs so well known no one needed a hymn book. Everyone took up "What a Friend We Have in Jesus." And then a woman came up and sang, "I Come to the Garden Alone" very slowly and soulfully.

When the choir stood up, Paul processed with the group to the front of the church and found his place at the back. The a cappella Bach chorale was the choir's signature, sung without the need for any instrument. They practiced the fugue at every rehearsal, as it was difficult. "All breathing life sing and praise ye the Lord, Alleluia," sang the different voices, the melody taken up by one and then the other in endless runs up and down the scale.

Paul knew the chorale backwards and forwards. It ran in his head while he brushed his teeth in the morning. But tonight it felt like an exercise, an intellectual expression of his Northern heritage, contrasted with the soulful gospel renditions of songs sung by the Southerners.

Oddmar raised his hands again, gathering the choir into one deep harmonic, singing "This is My Father's World." It was Paul's favorite. It spoke to his own feeling that "all nature sings," that "in the rustling grass I hear Him pass." They sang it quietly, gravely, their faces still but full of life. "Why should my heart be sad?" Paul saw tears running down Oddmar's cheeks as they finished.

The pastor thanked the choir and closed his book, walking down the aisle through the church pews to the front. People left quietly, walking out into the warm, fragrant night. In the distance, above some fields, the moon was rising in a clear sky.

That night, as the bus took the choir members back to the dorms at Texas Lutheran, Paul felt quietly uplifted. No one spoke much in the dark bus, illumined only by little lights on the floor. How wonderful it was to meet others in Christian fellowship so far from home.

Paul's thoughts went out to the choir members he was getting to know so well, to Oddmar and Maddie, Pete and Bob. What a great thing it was to travel like a family and to bring praise to the Lord wherever they went, to congregations of people young and old. He didn't think Oddmar was the only one crying during the service that night. Strains of music filled Paul's head. "He speaks to me everywhere."

Paul fell into bed. It had been a wonderful day. Tomorrow was the main concert in the auditorium at the college. And during the day, Bob had promised he would show Paul a cotton field!

But when Paul and some friends entered the cafeteria in the morning for breakfast, something strange seemed to have happened. People were huddled in knots talking. "Oddmar had a heart attack this morning," was the answer they got when they asked what was wrong. Paul was dumbfounded.

Oddmar and Maddie were staying in town with their friends, the Bergquists. Alfred Bergquist, a professor at Texas Lutheran, had gone to school with Oddmar years ago. Apparently, Oddmar had been doubled up in pain that morning at breakfast. An ambulance took him to the hospital. Maddie was with him and she told Pete to alert the students. "Pray for us," she had said.

The students had breakfast quietly. There was nothing they could do but pray. No one went anywhere after breakfast. It seemed best to just stick together and wait in the cafeteria. Paul stood by a window with Naomi, looking out. After a while they saw Pete, walking up the sidewalk. His face was weathered and dark.

When he came into the cafeteria a hush went over the room. Pete said, "Oddmar died this morning at 9:30. Maddie thanks you for your prayers. We'll have the concert tonight, because Oddmar would have wanted us to," he said, his voice breaking. When he mastered himself, he said, "The rest of the tour is cancelled. We'll be leaving tomorrow morning, driving straight home."

Naomi, who was much more expressive than Paul, broke out into tears. But Paul just stood there woodenly, shocked. Oddmar was dead, so far from home, his children far away. So suddenly. Yesterday he had been full of life, touching Paul's elbow as he urged him to enjoy the barbecue and exhorting them all once more to praise the Lord in song.

Paul couldn't help it. He began singing, quietly. "This is my Father's world, O let me not forget, That though the wrong seems oft so strong, God is the ruler yet." Naomi, beside him, sang thru her tears, and soon everyone in the cafeteria was singing with them standing in their places. It seemed the only way to remember Oddmar.

The rest of the day felt unreal. The campus was empty, but the campus pastor, when he heard Oddmar had passed away, called for a small Good Friday service in the afternoon. Maddie came, escorted by Pete, her faced closed. After the service, however, she made the rounds of the students, consoling them and being consoled. She would stay with Oddmar's body, riding home with it to the funeral in Iowa. The students would not see Oddmar until then.

The concert that evening was solemn, conducted by the director of one of the Texas Lutheran choirs, who had been prepped by Maddie. It was an eerie thing. The choir was so used to Oddmar. They sang as they always did, the new director trying to keep up.

The Benjamin Britten piece which the choir had been working on all year, *Rejoice in the Lamb*, fell somewhat flat, Paul thought. To appreciate it you needed to know its history, as he did. The words, written by Christopher Smart while he was in an insane asylum somewhere in the 1700's, showed how each creature worshipped God in its own way. Oddmar had allowed Paul to become the solo voice for the song about the mouse, the "creature of great personal valour," even though it was an alto part. Tall blonde Naomi sang the soprano part about the poet's cat, Jeoffry.

But the music grew on you, transporting Paul beyond the present. The choir had been singing the words with their strange stresses and melodies for months. Maddie played the accompaniment on a small organ, which no one could have done without practicing it. Paul found it poignant on Good Friday. In hushed tones they sang, "For I am under the same accusation with my Saviour." When God plays on his harp in the end, the devils themselves are at peace.

The auditorium was about two thirds full. Maddie stood up to thank people, the director who had stepped in with so little notice, the choir members, their friends the Bergquists who had made the visit possible. When she spoke of Oddmar, many of the choir members wept as if they had lost a father. David King, acting for the choir, went up and embraced her. The audience, who didn't know any of them, wept with them. Paul was glad when it was over.

Early in the grey morning the choir members collected around the big silver bus with their suitcases. It was raining as they boarded the bus. Paul sat first with Naomi, then Carol, who was now in the middle of *The Hobbit*, then Michael. Even the mischievous Michael was subdued. The rain didn't stop all day. The bus itself stopped only for a few rest stops.

Paul said little all day. As the fact of Oddmar's death began to sink in, he realized it felt normal. Bodies were part of Nature and subject to Nature's laws. It was just that it was so sudden. Paul had spent time with Oddmar every day for months. The hole where daily communication with Oddmar happened could not be immediately filled. It was like losing a companion, like losing Foxy.

When he lost his grandparents, Paul accepted death as the end of a full, rich life. He had never spent much time in their presence. But Oddmar was only in his 60's. It was a terrible loss. Paul would not forget Oddmar's vivid personality. He would never cease to think of songs as praise. He would probably never see a mouse without remembering Oddmar's first animated rendition of the part in *Rejoice in the Lamb*.

And he had learned from Oddmar that song, especially song raised together by many people, was the best way to embody and express shared emotion. None better.

8

Marty and Kate hitchhiked to Dover on a grey day in late spring. They stayed in a hostel that night, handing in their yellow membership cards in the International Youth Hostel organization. In the morning they boarded the ferry for Calais, France. The wind whipped across the channel and the chalky cliffs did indeed appear white to Marty as they receded into the distance.

When the ferry docked, they went to a small cafe where Kate tried to order ice cream, for comfort in the strange, foreign place. But nothing Kate said could make the waitress or the proprietor understand. What the waitress brought was hot tea with lemon. Marty and Kate drank it.

When Kate had arrived in England, she found a housekeeping job at Hothorpe Hall, a neglected manor house in Leicestershire bought by the

Lutheran church to provide help for Lutheran refugees. But in the spring she wanted to visit Sam, the American serviceman she was in love with, in Germany, and maybe get as far south as Greece. She convinced Marty to come with her on this continental adventure.

The Magnussons were taking an Easter trip to the continent themselves and didn't need Marty. Marty wrote to Aunt Rose, who sent her $200 for the trip. Kate and Marty had each turned 21 within the year. Kate was prettier, with soft dark curls which framed her face, big bones and wide hips. She wore a short coat over her blouse, a skirt and flats. Marty's hair was a pile of dark thatch unless she rolled it into curls. She was thick in the waist and her face was very round, her eyes bright behind the upturned frames of her glasses. They each carried a small train case with a change of clothes in it.

The hot tea tasted good on the cool, grey day. Marty pulled out *Let's Go: Europe*, a guidebook written by students at Harvard for other students, and spread it out on the table between them. At least it was in English.

"I don't think we can make it to Paris tonight," said Kate. It was late afternoon and neither of them wanted to hitchhike after dark.

Marty traced a route with her finger, peering at it near-sightedly. "There's a hostel in Boulogne-sur-Mer. Do you think we can make it there? It's only a few kilometers."

"Sure," said Kate off-handedly. It was cold, growing dark and raining as they left the little café. "Wait!" said Kate. She stopped at a shop where plastic rain hats were sold. "I'll buy a red one and you can get a white one!" she said. The hats had wide brims which kept the rain off their faces.

That night they stayed in a large rambling dormitory room in what had once been a Norman chateau. Hardly anyone was about and it felt gloomy and strange. In the morning they set off as quickly as possible. When the smell of fresh bread wafted through the air as they walked down the stone street, Marty's heart leapt up. They bought milk and warm croissant, baked that morning, and ate them by the side of the road in the misty rain.

Thumbs out, they quickly got a ride to Paris where they found the student hostel with some difficulty. It was in a large imposing building which must once have been a lovely mansion with beautiful woodwork. People circled about but no one seemed to be running it. Trash lay about in the large rooms. Marty looked for a bathroom she could use and was astonished to find, in the large white-tiled bathrooms, that there was nothing but a hole in the floor. No one had cleaned the toilets and toilet paper and actual human feces lay around them.

"Turkish toilets," sniggered a French student who tried to help her. "Americans? This hostel is full, but maybe you can go to the other one." Marty pulled out her guidebook. On the Paris map, he pointed to a location near the center of the city.

By the time they took the metro to the other hostel it was late afternoon. It was in similar condition, also full. Kate shook her head. What were they going to do? It was raining lightly and they had nowhere to go. "Dinner," she said.

They settled into a warm bistro and ate a good meal of fish and potatoes, taking as much time as they dared. "We're going to have to find a hotel," said Marty. But where would they find one they could afford this late in the evening?

They were near a large open market called Les Halles. Small carts and trucks were parked outside a series of open structures. The wet, fresh scents of flowers enveloped them as they passed. People, mostly men, wandered about, shouting at each other, loading and unloading vegetables, fish, meat. It was noisy and companionable. Seeing the two girls walking in their shapeless coats, men shouted to each other, "Ah, rouge et chapeaux blanc!"

Kate thought it was funny. "I guess we are a novelty," she said.

But it was becoming less funny. They were dropping with tiredness and they had no idea what to do. A handsome young man came up to them and began to speak broken English. "American?" he asked. His head was bare, but his hands were stuffed into the pockets of his woolen pea coat.

"Yes," said Kate, following him and smiling.

"Come," he said, leading them out of the rain and under the vast steel structure which housed the stalls of the produce, meat and flower sellers.

Marty shook the rain off her coat and took off her hat.

"It's okay," said the young man. "Doesn't matter if we don't buy."

"The men laugh at us," said Kate. "The 'rouge et blanc chapeaux!'"

"It's okay. You are students? My name is Pierre." He shook out damp, dark curls. "May I buy you some pommes frites?"

Kate accepted gratefully with her easy sociability.

"Hot food. It is nice," said Pierre. "Where are you going?"

Kate explained that they were too late to find a hotel they could afford.

"Oh, good!" said Pierre. "You will find one in St. Germain tomorrow. Easy. Not dear. Tonight you will walk with me."

There was nothing else to be done. Carrying their train cases, the two girls followed Pierre to a cart which gave off the tantalizing smell of hot oil and potatoes.

"I don't have money, but it makes me feel good to buy you something," he said. "I am looking for work. I will find it soon." He handed paper packets of hot potato fries to Kate and Marty.

Marty liked the romantic name of potatoes in French, pommes des terre, apples of the earth. Coming in out of the cold rain, and eating the hot, salted potatoes, felt delicious. Following Kate and Pierre, Marty walked along the wide aisles, looking at everything through drooping eyes.

Sausages and hams hung from hooks. Crates full of vegetables Marty had never seen before spread all around them. So many colors, peppers in green, yellow and red. Big purple bulbs, piles of apples and onions, oranges and lemons. Heads of lettuce, cabbage and greens, herbs in bunches. Mushrooms and cheeses and fish and shellfish on ice. Smells assailed her and men smiled at her as she straggled behind her friends.

In the flower stalls, branches of blossom alternated with pussywillows, tulips and roses. Lilies stood in pots and small clumps of violets were tied together with twine. Everything Marty saw with sleepy eyes glowed and pulsed with life.

At four a.m. Pierre showed them into a booth, joining some of the produce sellers, making them all safe for each other. Pierre explained that the girls were traveling south, students. Roasted snails reeking of garlic were produced, baguettes of bread and glasses of wine. Kate looked nervous as the dish of snails went around.

"It's okay," Marty nudged Kate. "I've eaten them before. They're delicious," she whispered. Neither of them had much courage alone, but together, using each other's very different gifts, they were fine travelers.

"Vive l'Amerique," sang out an old man in a woolen cap and vest, raising his glass. "Vive la France!"

They all raised their glasses.

"Is the food for restaurants?" Marty asked Pierre.

"For everyone," he said. "Brandy?" he asked. "They want to buy you a brandy."

When they finally left, the sky was much lighter.

"You'll find a hotel," said Pierre. "Merci por la marche avec moi," he said to Marty. "Here is Notre Dame. On the other side of the Seine you will find a place pas trop cher." He pointed south.

"Mille fois merci," said Kate, picking up phrases from him. "We are happy to meet you."

With a small salute, Pierre left. Marty and Kate sat sleepily on the steps of Notre Dame as the full sun lit the front of the cathedral, warming them. When people began to go into the church for mass, Marty and Kate did too, sitting on rickety woven chairs near the front in an almost empty chapel. Sunshine streamed down through the richly-colored medieval windows and organ music rolled out into the space. Marty fell asleep as she sat and Kate had to dig an elbow in her side when they were supposed to stand up.

An hour later they arrived in the office of a small hotel on Rue St-Julien-de-Pauvre. It only cost a few francs, the equivalent of $2. Marty was astounded. The room was white and beautiful with a double bed and beside it what looked like a urinal. "What's this?" asked Kate. Neither of them knew. But the room did have a real bathroom, with a real toilet. The two girls fell asleep and slept until early afternoon.

In the morning they ate croissant and hot chocolate. Wandering the streets, they looked for Shakespeare and Company, the bookshop and lending library Sylvia Beach had established for American expatriates in the 1920's. Hemingway had been a frequent borrower and Beach had published Joyce's books. They found the address Marty had written down from Richard Ellmann's book: 12 Rue de l'Odeon. It was nothing but a nondescript doorway. Nothing showed of its original spirit or the artistic and literary adventures the building had sheltered.

They made no attempt to go to the Louvre, but wandered through the large white rooms of the Jeu de Paume, wonderstruck. Each was dedicated to a different Impressionist artist. On the walls of the Salle Monet shimmered Monet's cathedral paintings, lavender in the light. The unforgettable water lilies hovered in their huge paintings, more about the sky and water than the flowers.

After a few days in Paris they went to Dahn, Germany, where Americans were stationed. Sam Forland, whom Kate had gotten to know at Wittenberg, had given her the address of a room in the village he rented with three other friends in an old-fashioned cottage. Two big double beds were stuffed under the low eaves. The American soldiers took their leave in this room, listening to a record player, smoking and cooking up banana skins, which were rumored to get you high.

Negotiations for the beds were heated. Kate lay in one talking quietly to Sam, and another American soldier kissed and fondled Marty. Marty responded, but she would not take off her clothes. She did not want to become pregnant by someone she didn't even know. It made the soldier angry. Standing up, he left in a huff. Marty could hardly wait to leave herself.

Heading south through Italy they were picked up by a thin woman who drove very fast and ate an enormous meal beginning with a plate of pasta when they stopped at a roadhouse. Even after Irene Magnusson's wonderful cooking, Marty was astonished by the intense tastes of Italian pizza. So simple, but so delicious. They stayed in a wonderful old building which had become the student hostel in Milan.

Kate could not stop talking about Sam. She wanted to go over every detail of their stay in Germany. "I do think he likes me," she said. She had spent every moment of the visit with Sam, while Marty wandered disconsolately through the little German town, climbing the old castle ramparts and walking through damp parks.

Marty sympathized with Kate's need to talk. Her own heart was in Oxford. She described Glyn to Kate, but she had very little to tell. She had only seen Glyn after class and gone once to the theatre with him.

Further south, an older and younger man picked them up. After driving a little, the car turned off onto a side road. The driver stopped, looked back at them and mimed with his hands that he wanted to sleep with the girls. The younger man looked on appreciatively. Kate and Marty grabbed their luggage and jumped out of the car. The driver gunned his motor, driving off. They had to walk back to the highway. Kate was outraged, but Marty was not surprised. What did they expect, anyway?

When they got to Rome, there wasn't a single place to stay. "I'm sorry. It's just not possible," an American told them at the hostel. "It's Easter week and the city is full to the brim!"

They went to the train station and got on a train for Brundisi, where they would catch a ferry to Greece. There was nowhere to sit on the train. It was full of troops. Marty sat on her train case in the corridor for hours. The troops stood all around them in brown uniforms and plastic-brimmed hats, polite and friendly. Marty didn't feel friendly. She was exhausted, once again awake all night.

Early in the morning they transferred to the ferry, and watched the grey-green horizon to the east as they crossed the Mediterranean. Greece began to emerge in the mist. Igoumenitsa, on the Greek shoreline, had white buildings with a forest-covered mountain behind it. They had breakfast in this fishing harbor town at a small white taverna while they waited for the ferry back to the island of Corfu, their destination.

On Corfu, the student hostel was in the country on the other side of the island from Kerkyra harbor. Crowds of children begged to help them at the ferry, but they had an address and found a bus. They were dropped off on a dusty gravel road in the late afternoon. Bells around the necks of long-haired sheep rattled in the fields. They began walking, carrying their traincases. Beside them were the twisted trunks of ancient grey-green olive trees. The golden grass smelled of herbs, like sage. Marty felt drained, weary and empty.

"Don't worry," said Kate. "When we get there we don't have to do anything." She had pushed them all the way to this Greek island in the hopes of sitting on a sunny beach on the blue Mediterranean.

All of a sudden as the road twisted, a large tree laden with oranges appeared. It looked like a tree in the garden of Eden with its dark green leaves, as refreshing a sight as Marty could imagine along the dry, stony road. Its shining orange globes hung like Christmas ornaments in the light. They sat down on a rock wall to rest for a moment. The wall turned out to be on the grounds of the hostel.

A man at the desk pointed them to a small room with a washbasin, twin beds and windows which looked down through gnarled grey-green trees onto a rocky beach below. The porcelain in the washbasin was cracked, but everything was clean. A fresh wind blew off the sea through the open windows of the spare, white room.

Kate and Marty tried to find the dining room in order to have something to eat, but none seemed to exist. They sat down at tables in the garden. Trees enclosed the small lawn and shadows lengthened. At last a girl came out of the hotel, but there was no menu and they could not make themselves understood.

When she went away, Kate and Marty looked at each other. Here they were. They planned to stay for several days, but the building was virtually empty.

After a little while the girl came back with plates of tomatoes and black olives drenched in olive oil. The olive oil tasted odd to Marty. She wasn't used to it. She badly wanted a piece of bread with butter, but there seemed to be no way to get it.

In the morning, they went down to the rocky beach, but it too was deserted. The sun was brutal and there were no trees. The rocks ran down to the water. After a day on the beach, Marty looked like a lobster. The skin on her shoulders and face was burning. Even her scalp was red under her thin hair. But the sun had knitted her body together, made it all of a piece. She felt burnished by the wind and sun.

No one was about the country villa the whole weekend Kate and Marty were there. Whenever they sat in the garden, a girl brought plates of tomatoes and olives drenched in olive oil. That was all. The rocky beach was also deserted. They ran into a solitary English-speaking guest who told them that the family who ran the hostel was celebrating the Greek Orthodox Easter, the most important holiday in Greece.

Sunday morning bells rang out, but Marty and Kate could not tell where they came from. There was only the small hotel building hidden in the trees and the beach below. Marty would have loved to go to a Greek Orthodox service, but she and Kate were strange holiday-makers and could not intrude on the family's solemn rites.

It was too far to take the bus back to town, but they were getting hungry. Kate managed to buy a can of Spam, some crackers and dried fruit from the hotel. They took it down to the beach, contrived a fire and roasted slices of Spam over the fire for an Easter celebration. Marty wore a long-sleeved shirt and her white plastic rain hat against the sun. Kate's skin was darker and fared better. The beach was too rocky to lie on.

"It's not exactly what I imagined," said Kate, as they sat watching the sun set across the water before going to bed.

"No," said Marty. There was no luxury at all. "But we're making the best of it." The heat made her speechless, lazy. The sun-drenched, empty days were a solace to her little northern soul. The image of the tree with its brilliant oranges hovered in front of her eyes.

The next day they took the ferry back to Igoumenitsa and a bus along the coast road to Athens. The ancient bus careened along roads built at the edge of frighteningly steep cliffs. Far below was the beach. At night they were still traveling. Looking down, as the bus twisted and turned on the road, Marty watched the white surf curling against the shore in the moonlight. The surf was always there, the tides passing in and out in beauty, whether she saw it or not. When she was in cold, rainy cities, the surf still pounded on these beautiful, empty beaches.

In Athens, things were easier. They met English-speaking tourists, ate at blue and white painted restaurants and drank retsina, a licorice-tasting drink, outdoors at tables in the treeless square in the warm nights. Everyone smoked. There were small round breads with sesame, delectable pastries made with filo dough, meat and rice wrapped in pickled grape leaves, grilled meats and yogurt with honey. Nothing tasted like what Marty was used to, but it tasted good. Greece was simple, sun-burnished.

Marty loved the narrow streets not made for cars. She climbed up many steps, looking longingly into courtyards, into rooms open to the sun and swept clean by the wind. Greece felt empty, elemental. So this is how people live, sleep, eat, she thought.

At the American Express office, a letter from Mother and Dad awaited Marty. They had gotten two postcards from her. "Grandpa passed away on March 10," said Mother. "He didn't have to linger too long in his illness and he was surely ready to go, but as Dad said, 'It's a humbling thing to see one's forebears pass away.'" Dad asked, "How could you go to Rome without seeing the ancient Roman buildings, its coliseum and so on?"

Kate and Marty climbed the Acropolis and looked at the marble remains of the Parthenon, acres of white stones against an intensely blue sky. Next to it was the modern reconstruction of a stoa, garish in its glistening, unweathered stone. Built by Americans to assist in studying and preserving artifacts archaeologists found, it looked out of place beside the ancient stone, gnarled old trees and distant views.

Marty tried to feel what Dad might have felt. He had studied Greek and Latin so as to be able to interpret New Testament writings and the church fathers. But, even with all the literature she had read, classical Greece didn't live for Marty. Greece was a dream, dry, rocky, empty, drenched with sun, next to the sea. I could stay here forever, Marty thought. The empty days had loosened some elemental underpinning, awakened senses she didn't know she had. But they were running out of money, Kate was restless. They were expected back.

Kate and Marty hitchhiked north. On the main road, trucks were the most common vehicle. One stopped and they climbed high up into the cab of a great, iron grey truck. It looked old and somewhat decrepit, but they were glad for the ride. The cab was grimy, the seat covered with a dirty blanket. Marty sat on it gingerly.

The driver, a thin, weathered man in old brown clothes, pulled an unmarked glass bottle from behind the seat and began to drink. He handed it to Kate and Marty. A sip of the hot, fiery liquid was enough. "Schnapps," he called it. "Verboten," he said, smiling and drawing his hand across his neck. They had no language in common, but Kate tried. They did not even know where he was from. They were heading north.

In English, Kate talked quietly to Marty about Sam. She would see him soon. Marty did not want to go back to the village of Dahn, Germany. She would drop off in Karlsruhle and spend a few days by herself. They would meet up in Amsterdam a few days later and take a ferry back to England.

The truck headed north all day. Rocky outcroppings laced the fields, where sheep grazed and olive trees leaned into the wind. By evening, they entered a city where there were no lights. "Beograd," said the driver. Marty found it in Yugoslavia on the worn map of Europe on which she was tracing the trip.

The truck's headlights illumined hundreds of people milling in the darkened streets. They passed what looked like a cinema. Even this building was dimly lit, except by headlights. The faces looked aimless and the people didn't seem to speak to each other. What were they doing? Marty did not know, but their anarchy made her glad she was high in the cab of the truck.

The driver, who was wrinkled and wizened though probably not that old, didn't want to stop. He produced bread and sausage and shared them. Marty couldn't eat much of the greasy sausage, but the bread was delicious.

All night they crawled north on the highway, through terrain with no light in the distance. There was no moon by this time and the truck's headlights and a few oncoming vehicles which met them on the highway provided the only light. The driver showed them his bed behind the seat and Kate crawled back to sleep in it, but Marty bounced, going in and out of sleep in the dirty seat in the cab high over the road. They climbed hills and floated down, the driver nipping Schnapps from his bottle.

As the colors of dawn began to pearl the sky to the east, Marty's head was sluggish and felt like it was full of bees buzzing. The driver stopped to get gas. Kate and Marty used the bathroom and the driver bought them Turkish coffee at a shop. It was thick and sweet, full of sugar or honey.

They climbed back into the cab of the truck, which now felt like home. The driver put a gigantic bar of chocolate wrapped in gold foil on the dash. It was at least three feet long! Marty could not believe her eyes. Coffee and chocolate, for breakfast! What a way to live. Kate unwrapped the foil, broke off some chocolate and ate it. Marty was frightened. Chocolate was her undoing!

It rained as they continued north, the wet spring weather making the high cab of the truck an ark which time had forgotten. They would never find land. Kate, thinking of her Sam, was on one trip. Marty was on another. She sat, wonder-struck, nibbling chocolate from the gold foil, so open she could hardly believe what she saw around her. She was sinking like a stone to her own depths, finding space in herself for everything she had seen, letting it take her, carry her off.

The whole trip had been mind-bending, Marty reflected. First something frightening happened, assaulting their senses and making them wonder what to do, and then an entirely unimaginable resolution would take place. One thing after another. It was what they had come for.

At last the truck driver motioned that he would stop. It was the middle of the day. He was going to sleep. They must get out. Marty and Kate thanked him profusely. He had helped them get very far north.

They put on their red and white plastic hats to ward off the rain and stuck out their thumbs by the side of the road. Another truck stopped for them, this one somewhat sleeker, newer. The driver was younger and looked well-nourished, his face smooth and pink. "Deutsch?" he questioned. When they told him they were Americans, he gave a long, low whistle. "Whooo!"

In the late afternoon, the driver said, "Zagreb," and motioned that he would leave them there. "Hotel," he said. "Zehr Gutt!"

The truck pulled up in front of a modern skyscraper with "Hotel International," inscribed in metal letters across the entrance. "Zehr gutt!" said the driver. The girls thanked him and carried their small baggage into the lobby. It looked expensive, but they knew they must pay for a comfortable night.

Surprisingly, it was less expensive than it looked. Marty rejoiced. Perhaps there would be a bed! A shower! Warm food. They were given a key, took an elevator, and found themselves high up in a large room, with windows which looked out into the rainy evening.

The beds were topped with eiderdowns, thick white coverlets stuffed with goose feathers. Marty slipped under one and lay flat on the bed under its pillowy warmth, very happy. It was all she could do, a few minutes later, to get up and wash.

9

Marty was among the many students filling an ancient room at All Souls' College where Isaiah Berlin spoke from an ornately carved wooden lectern. It looked for all the world like a pulpit. Berlin described how dictators such as Stalin, Mussolini and Hitler used Romantic values to fuel their monomaniacal ideals.

"For the Romantics the universe is in a process of forward self-thrusting. There is only the subject, no objective reality. The Romantic mode does away with the idea that there is a nature of things, that science is submission, which originates with Socrates. For the Romantics, the indomitable will can create its own vision of the universe."

"The true self, say the Romantics, seeks the good," continued Berlin, a forceful thin man with a hint of Slavic accent, gesturing with his hands as he spoke. "But perhaps men don't really know what they want. As a superman, a genius, an artist, I can set myself up as an authority over other men. I can give them what I believe they really want, but can't express. I can force them to be free!"

Marty listened carefully. Berlin spoke rapidly, but the import of his words was clear. Without the scrupulous regard for what is, an artist or genius might come to believe he had absolute liberty. The Romantic ideal played a large part in the formation of the pioneer individualists in the United States as well, to both good and bad effect, thought Marty.

When the students streamed out into the sunshine, Marty found herself almost sleep-walking. She felt inwardly justified. She had never seen herself in the Romantic mode. For her, there was a nature of things, a reality outside oneself which could be understood. The real world was in fact what she wanted to study, what she looked for in literature.

Berlin was a Russian, born just before the Revolution. He had come to England at a young age and had been famous in Oxford for a long time. Perhaps the Russians know something the rest of us don't, Marty thought. She remembered the previous summer when she had so enjoyed having a room to herself and reading Pasternak's book, *Doctor Zhivago*. She made a mental note to read Tolstoy, often mentioned in Berlin's lectures. No one had mentioned Tolstoy at Wittenberg College.

Glyn was not at the lecture, but Marty wished he had been. She had seen him several times since getting back from the continental trip, and he had suggested they meet on Sunday for a picnic. She was already planning the food she would bring, influenced by what she thought Irene Magnusson would have done.

On Sunday it rained. Marty carefully prepared sandwiches, raw vegetables, apples, and a bar of Cadbury's chocolate, and put them up in a cunning brown paper bag with a handle, the kind the produce man filled with potatoes from his truck. She met Glyn at the entrance to the Radcliffe Camera as they planned, but Glyn said they must go to his rooms. It was too wet to sit outdoors in the park. He put his arm around her and they walked off, sheltering under Marty's umbrella.

Glyn lived near St. Peter's Hall, his college. They crossed the bridge over the Mill Stream that flowed into the Thames, where ducks gathered. "I usually give them my toast in the morning," said Glyn. They entered an older house, where, on the second floor, Glyn occupied a large room.

At one end was a thin, student bed. At the other, beneath a wall of casement windows, were a wardrobe, his desk and bookshelves, all overflowing. "It's lovely," said Marty. She wasn't sure if it was lovely because he lived there, or if it just was. Rain drizzled down the windows and drummed on the walk below.

Glyn walked over to the record player. "Remember I was telling you how much greater Coltrane is than Miles Davis?" he said. He thumbed through a stack of records and put one on his small turntable.

There was nowhere to sit, so Marty sat on the edge of Glyn's bed, looking around. The room overflowed with the rich furniture of his mind. Like mine, she thought. Books and notebooks, heaped themselves on the desk surrounding a small typewriter. Cartons of books climbed the walls, laid sideways so you could see their spines. The slow, thickness of a saxophone sound filled the room.

Glyn stood mesmerized in the middle, gesturing to Marty silently, "Do you hear that? I mean, really hear it?"

Marty didn't know what she was hearing. She remembered Line telling her about Ellie's husband playing jazz records. But Marty had never sat and just listened to jazz.

The music broke and in the background were keyboards and a shimmering cymbals. An easy rhythm behind them helped Marty move with the music. The saxophone traveled all over. Minutes passed and Glyn lifted the needle on the player.

"It's like Coltrane is mature," said Glyn. "and Davis is still a child."

"Hmmmm," said Marty. She didn't even know what Miles Davis sounded like.

"I think they're about the same age, but Davis sounds lonely. He is trying to compensate in his music, for inadequacy, isolation. The opposite is true with Coltrane. Coltrane tries to find himself, to find genuine responses to the world, to be honest in his experiencing." Glyn looked so serious, standing in the middle of his room, like the professor Marty expected he would become. But would he lecture about jazz? Not in Oxford!

"Coltrane's music states truth in his own terms, not in stylistic mannerism." Glyn came and sat on the bed beside Marty, putting his head close to hers, speaking passionately. "I wanted to get together," he said, "because I need to tell you I can't have a girlfriend right now. We're getting kind of involved, and I just can't." His eyes looked like they were pleading with her.

Something in Marty sat bolt upright when she heard this. Their growing closeness had had the opposite effect on her. She had been wondering how it would feel to settle down in England. But there was nothing she could say.

"I'm sorry," said Glyn, and he pulled Marty up onto the bed, where they lay in each other's arms.

Marty breathed in the moment deeply as she felt strong arms encircling her. The sun shone through the windows all of a sudden, even as raindrops coursed down the glass. Like here, thought Marty. Her inner weather matched the outer weather.

"It's just that I don't have time for a pregnant wife, kids, all that," said Glyn. "I'm going to try for this Shakespeare prize next year, and I have a great deal of work to do on the syllabus I haven't done yet."

Marty could hardly believe her ears. Of course he was right. What they wanted to do, what their bodies had been telling them, led straight to a family. "Thank you for being honest," she managed to say.

"It's like I'm trying to show you in the music," said Glyn. "I want to reach some kind of stature, find an honesty in myself before I can be with another person. I need to know who I am. Coltrane did. It's easy to be conventional, to do what everyone does. But, in a sense, your relations are parasitic, you suck each other dry unless you have some of your own conviction."

Something in Marty was falling away. Here was a real person, someone clear about himself and what he was doing in life.

"I want to have the emotional simplicity and power to be contributive," said Glyn.

All of a sudden Marty wanted Glyn more than anything. Here they were, lying in his narrow student bed, wrapped around each other, the sun sinking on the western windows, shivering the wet drops into brilliant light as it went in and out of clouds. When would she ever meet such a person again, Marty wondered.

"You're being very brave," said Glyn, sitting up at last. The wind blew the rain against the windows. The music coming from the speakers had been silent for some time.

"Yes," said Marty shakily. The pain of what Glyn was saying felt almost worth it, so wrapped in beauty was the afternoon. Marty clutched the moment to herself. She sat up. "Maybe we should have lunch."

They ate the sandwiches, slowly, but neither of them could stomach anything more. Glyn showed Marty the concrete poetry he was working on, the small publications he liked. At last the twilight lowered and the afternoon was over.

"Come on," said Glyn, protectively. "I'll walk you to the bus."

When she got home, Marty could hear the Magnussons upstairs, putting Thea to bed and watching television. She did not go up, but turned on a lamp in the living room downstairs and sat under it in a big, upholstered chair. She took out her book. Slowly, as she read, she ate the rest of the large Cadbury's bar. She felt numb and did not know what to think.

Irene came down in her housecoat and slippers. "Are you sitting here all by yourself?" she asked. She had watched Marty put together her careful little lunch and sensed how important the afternoon's meeting was to her.

"Yes," said Marty stiffly. "Glyn says he doesn't want to get together any more. He doesn't want a girlfriend."

"Well," said Irene. "That's all right, isn't it? You're going home in a month anyway."

"Yes, but we could have had the month!" blurted Marty.

"Oh, Marty," said Irene. Marty could tell she would have liked to bend down and hug her, except that they weren't really family. "You're going to have many adventures in life. Don't let this spoil things for you."

"No," said Marty. "Thank you, Irene. Don't worry. I'll be fine." But she didn't budge from her chair.

From that point on, the days in Oxford took on a valedictory quality. Marty now felt comfortable and wished she didn't have to leave. But Mother and Dad wrote that they were moving that summer and they needed Marty's help. She should come as soon as possible. Marty called Icelandic Airlines and booked her return flight for the end of May. The Magnussons made plans to do more traveling during the summer, when Trinity term was over.

On Saturday afternoon, Rolfe mowed the grass strips between the rectangular rose beds at the back of the house with a hand-mower. Bambi loped about after Thea on her short little legs, and Irene trimmed roses which had already bloomed and now drooped on their stalks.

Marty helped Irene select and cut flowers from the hundreds of roses that had budded out. The garden at the back of this house was an actual garden, laid out and in need of tending. It had hardly any lawn. There was room to put out chairs and sit admiring the roses on warm days, but not much for playing. When Thea wanted to play, she and Marty went to a nearby schoolyard where there were swings and a duck pond.

Before she came to Oxford, a garden to Marty meant a vegetable garden in an American back yard. Yards she knew were not actual gardens laid out with flower beds ranged in regular rows. How many years had this garden been tilled? These roses set out and cultivated?

"I love roses," said Marty, holding the newspaper full of blooms. "They're really the queen of all flowers."

"I don't know much about particular roses," said Irene. "Each of them has a pedigree. Perhaps I should study them." They carried in the mass of roses and Irene found vases to put them around the house.

In the evening, the spring sun shone magically into the Magnussons' dining room as they sat talking, having Thea's favorite dessert, crème caramel, after dinner. The pale, creamy roses Irene had chosen for the room almost matched the light golden walls. Marty mentally photographed the scene. She had not been able to afford film and developing this whole year in Europe, and she had taken only a couple of small photos.

"The Chertoks are going back to Berkeley in the fall," said Irene. "Lidia thinks you should come to Berkeley. Once you are resident in California, the university there is much less expensive. It only takes a year, she says."

Marty pondered this extraordinary idea. She hadn't really decided what to do next year. "Thank you," said Marty. "I'll have to think about it." She struggled with her napkin, covering her embarrassment when the attention turned to herself. It felt like she was always having to explain herself, and in fact she couldn't! She didn't have a job, and she would need one. Everyone assumed she would become a teacher, and she could now get a job teaching in a high school. But if she went to graduate school, she could teach at higher levels.

"The news from the U.S. is interesting," said Rolfe. "Big demonstrations against the war in the cities."

"I'm so happy we are here," said Irene. The Magnussons were staying another year at least. "I'm beginning to feel quite settled."

"Well, we do pay U.S. taxes," said Rolfe. "We are supporting that war."

"It's amazing how long it takes to feel settled!" said Marty, responding to Irene's statement. What a struggle Oxford had been at the beginning, with everything new! Everything! And now it felt familiar. But she was also thinking about Line in Chicago and her activist boyfriend. Line had not written all year. What Marty heard about her was from Mother. The thought of seeing Line when she got home made her spirits rise. Soon!

Irene smiled at Thea, who dawdled over the custard Irene had made, swimming in its own caramel sauce. "I'm glad Thea is getting an experience of living in Europe when she is a little older." Thea had lived in Germany as toddler, when Rolfe got his doctorate.

"Sounds like de Gaulle thinks Britain is as American as we are! He's still opposing British entry into the Common Market," said Rolfe.

"My dear, you have always been more European than American!" said Irene.

Rolfe smiled at her and reached for her hand. "That's why you married me, is it not?"

The spring evenings continued to be beautiful. Marty took the train to Hothorpe Hall where Kate was a housekeeper. Kate too wanted to stay in Europe as long as she could.

Marty and Kate put fresh sheets on the upstairs beds, getting ready for an upcoming conference. The big windows upstairs were wide open to the spring air. This building too was surrounded by gardens and beyond them stretched fields green with grass, hedgerows between them, rolling hills in the distance. The field Marty could see out the eastern window was white with Queen Anne's lace.

"Sam might come for his leave in the summer," said Kate as she plumped a pillow.

"He'll like it," said Marty. "This is a wonderful place." The sheets fresh from the laundry smelled like sunshine. They must have been hanging outdoors.

"Yeah," said Kate. "It's kind of weird. There are always people coming and going and they don't seem to mind who's here! I can't quite figure it out."

"As long as you're a Lutheran," said Marty. She wasn't paying to stay at the house. She thought it was because Kate worked there.

"Maybe that's it," said Kate. "It was meant for refugees. Maybe we're refugees from America!"

"I wish I could speak to Glyn before I leave," said Marty wistfully. "Maybe at a Warner lecture. But he doesn't want to see me."

"He's right about getting involved," said Kate. "He sounds pretty studious."

"It's incredible," said Marty. "Being a scholarship student, coming from Sheffield, makes him appreciate his education more than most Oxford students. Makes him more serious. Nothing has been handed to him on a silver platter."

"It makes sense," said Kate.

"We didn't have class distinctions at Wittenberg," Marty said. "At least I never felt them."

"I did," said Kate darkly. "People with more money. People with educated parents. They have a leg up over someone just off the farm, like me."

"We're poor as church mice," said Marty. "But I never feel less than other people." The two of the stretched sheets across mattresses and then blankets and puffy comforters full of down. "I just love featherbeds," she said. "I wish we had them in the U.S."

"I felt inferior," said Kate. "That's why I always tried so hard in college."

Marty sighed. "Yes, my problem is I can't make myself understood. I have all kinds of ideas, and I don't feel they are any less important than anyone else's. But they just get all jumbled up in my brain. It might be because I don't understand myself!" It felt good to talk to Kate, who was her equal. "Glyn is much more mature than I am."

"Sounds like it," agreed Kate. "But it's all in front of us. We've got our whole lives to figure things out. Why should we worry so much?!"

"It's kind of painful," said Marty, "being in love. Don't you think so?"

"Yes," said Kate. "But I like it. It gives me hope and things to plan for!"

"Not me," said Marty. But there was no doubt in her mind that she was in love, that she had fallen in love on an afternoon of sun and rain in Oxford, England. She thought about asking Kate what she should do next year. Kate had left her teaching job because she had been too restless at a small Christian academy in South Dakota. But Marty realized she did not want to know what Kate thought.

The evening was long and warm enough to be out. After supper with the Hothorpe staff, Marty wandered out through the gardens towards the fields. The sun was setting beyond the hills and Marty walked into the glow it made around trees and grasses. Small wildflowers threaded the greens with color.

Under a hawthorne tree covered with white flowers in the hedgerow that separated the Hothorpe Hall grounds from the fields, Marty hunkered down in the grass. I'm going to stay here until I know what to do, Marty told herself. The sky spread out beyond, turning opalescent colors, mauve, blush and lavender.

I'm going to do exactly what I want, because that is the only way I can figure out who I am. I don't want to be conventional, Marty insisted to herself. I won't be satisfied with a conventional life. I must find my very own life.

Line never seemed to have this problem, Marty thought. She always knew what she wanted. Mother teased Marty for being so involved in her own self. Mother, like Line, believed in a life of service. But what she had seen in Europe had convinced Marty that there was more than one way to live. I must find my own, she thought. The elemental spareness and simplicity in Greece, as if it had been washed with sun and sea, showed that one could live in beauty. Though of course, it might be selfish.

It grew dark and Marty could hear people talking in the garden. "Where is that girl?" said Kate to a friend.

But Marty didn't budge from her spot. Next year, she thought to herself. Next year I can be myself. California actually sounded like a good idea, far from anyone she knew. Next year she would do exactly as she pleased so as to find out who she really was. Irene's gentle prodding and Glyn's manifesto both sounded in her ears. Who are you? What do you want to do? Not what other people think you should do, but what do you want to do?

It was quite dark when Marty went into the hall and found Kate in the room they shared. "Where were you?" asked Kate.

Marty smiled. "At the bottom of the garden." Within herself she made it into a code word: at the bottom of the garden, at the edge of the setting sun, where I am going to be my own exact self.

Marty did see Glyn before leaving Oxford. She stood near the front of Blackwell's bookshop one afternoon, looking at the poetry books, trying to familiarize herself with the modern ones she didn't know. She heard Glyn's voice and through the window saw him talking to a friend. Spring sunlight played on his golden head. Mortified lest he see her, Marty faded into the darkness at the back of the store.

Again, at the last lecture for the term by Professor Warner, Marty did not trust herself to go and sit beside Glyn. The simple observation of his blonde, beloved head, his worn corduroy jacket across the room was enough for her. She did wonder whether he saw her in the new turquoise coat Irene had chosen for her. It was quilted, cut in a Mod princess style. Marty adored it and felt she looked almost stylish. How many gifts the Magnussons had given her.

Warner spoke about the importance of Virginia Woolf's Modernist prose. "Woolf said that as of about 1910, human character changed, and modern novels must reflect this fact. She gave as an example of this change in human character that, whereas the Victorian cook lived like a leviathan in the lower depths, modern cooks were forever coming out of the kitchen to borrow the *Daily Herald* and ask advice about a hat!" Warner gave a poetic flourish to the phrase.

Marty remembered the summer in which she and April had lain in the grass in Cardinal, April's love of Woolf. How long ago? Almost three years! But Marty had not paid any attention to Virginia Woolf since. She made a mental note to read Woolf, adding the books Warner mentioned to a long mental list.

Marty compared her love for Glyn with that for April. She had loved April, but held her at arm's length because she could not have a family with a girl. But it was easy to imagine a future with Glyn. Work, children, home. All of it fitted. Marty felt hot, and then chilled. She dared not turn her head to look at the tousled blonde head on the other side of the room.

The castle with Glyn Marty had built in the air had no foundation. She must go home, put this promising relationship out of her mind.

Thousands of miles would separate them. Marty dragged her attention back to Mr. Warner's lecture.

"In *To the Lighthouse*, Woolf treats themes of marriage, time, and death. In a further development of her subjective mode, she abandons plot. Unity and coherence are provided instead by imagery, symbolism, and poetic elements." This was the novel she and April had read. Marty tried to remember, but all she could recall was a woman painting a picture. She could not remember if anyone ever went to the lighthouse.

After the lecture, Marty would have liked to go up and thank Francis Warner for all he had given her during the year. She had lived for his lectures. But surely Francis Warner hadn't noticed Marty's avid face among his students.

She was also too shy to tell Glyn goodbye. She slipped out a side door in her turquoise coat, and down the street. She would write Glyn a letter when she got home. It felt safer.

The precious school year in Europe was over, the time in which Marty was free to think. She was back at the beginning, less sure of who she was than when she had come. But she was ready, ready to begin the next chapter.

10

For Line, rotation through the many wards of the Cook County hospital was a constant adventure. She would have liked to settle down and stay in one of them. But the year of school was moving quickly, more than half over.

One day, on a surgical ward, she was surprised to find a young black woman she had befriended when she had a child a few months earlier. Dorothy, inexplicably, had a broken femur. She was in traction, with a cast from the waist down and could only move with the help of straps above her bed.

"What are you doing here, Dorothy?!" exclaimed Line. She stood at the foot of the bed looking at her chart. "Broke your leg did you?"

Dorothy looked up at Line. "Could say that," she said low.

Line looked hard at her. Three months ago Dorothy had given birth to a little girl who was put up for adoption. She was only 17 and no father was listed. Line had tried to talk to her, but found that Dorothy would say little except that she lived with her mother, stepfather and brothers, and that she had dropped out of school.

The baby was adorable. "I can't keep it," Dorothy told her as she stroked the tiny coffee-colored face. "My Momma wouldn't have it in the house." Tears slipped down Dorothy's face and Line's heart went out to her.

Line tried to be warm, but impersonal in her work. Professionalism was stressed again and again in school. But it was very hard when some of the mothers she worked with were younger than she was. She could not help but put herself in their shoes, as Mother had often suggested. She was also not sure what happened to these tiny unwanted babies. Foster care and adoption, she hoped.

Later that day, Line asked an intern how Dorothy had broken her leg. She found that with passionate interest and quiet good sense she could get information she wanted from the doctors.

Barnes pulled out the x-rays. "It wasn't easy. A very sharp blow to the femur," he said low. "That's a hard bone to break, but here you see the fracture. It's in three pieces."

Line looked quizzical.

"She's actually pretty lucky. If it had been just a little higher, we would have to try and repair her hip and that is pretty dicey! Looks to me like she was protecting herself, curled up, and someone hit her with," he shook his head, "maybe a baseball bat?"

Line's eyes opened wide. "She's still a minor. She's only 17! Would social services do any good here?"

"Go ahead," said Barnes. "Give it a try."

Working with Dorothy over the next few weeks, helping her use bedpans and wash, Line could not help but get more involved. Dorothy, though passive and shy, seemed to like being in the hospital.

One morning a dispirited woman sat beside Dorothy's bed, complaining, low. "I can't do it all myself," she was saying.

"This is my Momma," said Dorothy to Line, who arrived with a tray. "She works an evening shift at the factory."

The woman nodded to Line, but she seemed angry at Dorothy. Line was puzzled. She knew that Dorothy's mother relied on her to help at home with her younger brothers and half-brothers. Everyone suspected that Dorothy's stepfather had been the father of the baby girl she bore.

Perhaps the mother wished she herself was in the hospital being looked after.

Line did more listening than anything. She wanted to understand Dorothy's situation before trying to drag in social services, which could be brisk and lack compassion. Line begged her fellow student SueAnn to come and talk to Dorothy, who might tell SueAnn, also black, more than she was willing to tell Line.

Over a chili dog in the hospital cafeteria on a hot, breezeless day, SueAnn told Line what she had learned. "She won't say that her stepfather hit her, but I'm sure that's what happened. He's a good guy, she says. But he drinks and turns nasty." SueAnn looked away. Line knew SueAnn's mother wouldn't let her father in the house if he had been drinking heavily.

"A baseball bat is more than nasty," said Line. Big fans at the windows dulled the clatter of dishes, trays and conversation.

SueAnn continued, "She won't talk about the baby either. I bet she just got fed up and tried to keep him from getting at her."

"She told me she was depressed about giving up the baby," said Line. "So hard."

"I'm glad she's standing up for herself," said SueAnn. Her face looked hard and set. "That's a good sign."

"There must be someone Dorothy can turn to," said Line, sweating in her uniform in the hot room. "Maybe an aunt or a grandmother or her church? How can there be no one who can help her?"

"The hospital buys her time," said SueAnn. "When she gets out, she ought to be able to get away. She's almost 18."

"But SueAnn, will she?!" asked Line. "She's kind of passive. She's going to have another surgery to put some pins in. But she needs to get to school! To find something of her own!" Line echoed the thoughts she would have had, if she were Dorothy.

"I'm glad she's having more surgery," said SueAnn flatly. "But family is family. No one else cares about you as much." She adjusted her long legs and wiped her mouth with a paper napkin. "She's worried about her little brothers."

"But he's assaulting her! This is a terrible injury, and I'm sure it isn't the first," said Line leaning forward and gesturing. "She's trying to resist and this is what she gets?!"

"Blessing in disguise," said SueAnn. "The good Lord works in mysterious ways." She looked crisp and cool, her starched white hat a contrast to her dark skin.

Line sat back. "You are going to make a good nurse," she said to SueAnn.

"And so are you, Line," said SueAnn, smiling. "It takes all kinds, you know."

"Maybe," said Line. "But no one should be fearful in their own home."

"I know, I know," SueAnn shook her head. "You are right, but there it is! We girls got to stick together. I don't think Dorothy's mother is much help. Now if it was my Momma, there wouldn't be any of that goin' on," she said emphatically.

"Yeah," said Line, chagrined. "I still wish we could do something." She turned the problem over in her mind. She couldn't wait to talk to Stephen about it.

Saturday when she went down town, Line could wear what she wanted. She was proud of the jeans she had found at a thrift shop, which she wore with a sleeveless shirt and thongs on her feet. Her thick red-gold hair curled down around her shoulders. She had not seen Stephen for two weeks and was well-aware that he had just come from the SDS summer convention, where Line suspected there were lots of barefoot girls with long, blonde hair.

They met under the monumental statue of the Bowman, Line's favorite of the two lean bronze warrior-on-horseback sculptures at the edge of Grant Park. Stephen looked thin and harassed as usual, but a big smile lit his face when he saw Line. He too wore blue jeans and a denim workshirt, his faded army green book bag slung over his shoulder. He had grown a mustache.

Line dropped the basket she was carrying with the lunch. She tweaked the new sandy-colored mustache and sought his lips underneath it. "Now who do you look like? A professor, or a Beatle?" she asked.

"If you can't beat em', join em'," said Stephen sardonically. "You are a sight for sore eyes," he said, pulling Line toward him and running his hands down her hips in the new jeans.

"You taste like coffee," said Line, contentedly. "Just like you usually do."

The asphalt jungle of buildings, streets and paving was hot and they headed straight for the edge of the lake, where they sat under a shady tree, letting the breeze blow through them.

"Looks like we men are due for some atonement," said Stephen when Line told him about Dorothy.

"Atonement?" asked Line. Light and shade passed over Stephen's skin as the branches moved above him.

"Sorry," said Stephen. "I just mean that our 'male chauvinism' as Jane Adams is calling it, is beginning to be noticed!"

"Chauvinism?" said Line. She didn't really know what it meant.

"At the convention, we approved a report from the women's group which insisted that we deal with our chauvinism, and that women get full participation in SDS."

"Wow," said Line, "that's a first." She resolved to find out more about how it had all gone down from Kay. "But how about you? How was it for you, Stephen?"

Stephen sighed heavily. "I think of myself as a brilliant organizer, but it is becoming impossible. I can't organize these anti-intellectual, anarchic hippies!" He rolled over on the grass and looked up at Line.

When she didn't say anything, he said: "But on the other hand it doesn't matter. SDS is all we've got, except for single-issue groups. It's like a steamroller; it's flattened out the Left and gathered up all these people who want to make a difference. It doesn't really matter whether it's organized or not!"

Line sighed. "I wish there was some way to make a difference for Dorothy. And some others I see in the hospital. I think I want to be in obstetrics," she confided.

"That reminds me," Stephen said. "Your friend Pearl wants you to call her. She doesn't know how to reach you, but she wants to talk to you." He dug into his wallet and produced a slip of paper with a phone number on it.

"Sure," said Line, wondering what that could be about. She lifted her damp hair off her neck and piled it high on her head. "I wish I could go home," she said all of a sudden. It had been a hard year and she had almost no time to do anything but study, work and sleep. She fought hard to keep Saturdays free to see Stephen.

"You need to get out of town!" said Stephen.

"Yes," said Line, sadly. "I do. Mother and Dad are moving this summer, and Marty's home, and I'm sure Paul is too."

"Home from Oxford?" asked Stephen. He always perked up at the mention of Marty, who was a reader and intellectual.

"Yes," said Line. "I feel bad about her. She's sent me postcards from Europe, but I haven't sent anything."

"You know Line, I get to travel a lot. I'm in New York every once in a while. What would it take for you to go home?"

Line sighed again. "I don't want to ask Dad for the bus fare," she said. "It's probably not so bad now, but they're moving to western Iowa, and then it would be more."

"When are they moving?" asked Stephen. He reached up and drew Line down beside him on the grass. "You're so brave," he said, "and you ask so little, Line. I think I'm going to chauvinistically help you get home!"

Line looked at him with big melting eyes. "You would?" Stephen got only a small teaching stipend, but she knew that his parents had plenty of money. They both worked, owned a building in Brooklyn and there were no other kids. "There's a break in our LPN training schedule in August. But they might have moved by then," she said doubtfully.

"It's okay," said Stephen. "A few extra dollars for the bus. It'll be fine."

"Oh Stephen," Line said. "That would be fantastic!" All of a sudden it was all Line wanted in the world. To go home and see everyone. And it seemed possible! "Stephen, you are the best!" She rolled on top of him and attacked him with kisses.

"Hey! Hey!" said Stephen.

Line felt like a puppy, frolicking in the grass. Beneath her was Stephen's old army map bag full of hard-edged books. A book with a hand holding up a gun on its cover and the word 'Revolution' in the title slipped out. She remembered the lunch. "Hungry?" she asked.

"Sure," said Stephen. He sat up, the breeze ruffling his hair.

"I wish I didn't live in such a conservative place," said Line, pulling plump black cherries out of a plastic bag. "I've been hearing about a food co-op, but it's so far away, and I don't really have kitchen privileges where I am anyway. I can't wait until this year is over and I can get a job and move in with some good people."

The cherries glistened in the moving sun and shade of the tree above them. "I mean, of course I live with good people," said Line. "But they're not like us, and they're not young!"

Stephen spit cherry seeds far into the distance. "I know, I know," he said. "I'm hardly ever home. But people are starting to talk about how you live being your politics."

"The personal is the political," quoted Line. "Well I can't live my politics right now. I guess that's what's bugging me."

"You'll get there," said Stephen. "I'm proud of you, Line, for finding something you want to do and are good at. And you are making a difference. I'm sure of it."

"Are you trying to tell me to be patient?" Line teased, accusingly. She threw a cherry at Stephen. "It's all I've heard my whole life! And you're the last one I expect it from!"

Stephen deftly caught the cherry. "Ooooh," he said provocatively. "You're asking for it now, aren't you!"

"No, no!" squealed Line, putting her hands in front of her face. "I'm not! I swear!" She stood up and made ready to run, but Stephen just leaned over and tackled her legs, bringing her down beside him again. "Truce?" she said.

"Truce," said Stephen. He fished out more of the black cherries. "So good. Not my usual fare."

"Stephen!" said Line. "They're only in the grocery stores for a little while in the summer. You must have some!"

"I am, I am." The dark bing cherries disappeared under his mustache, one after the other.

When Line called Pearl on the telephone, Pearl said she wanted to talk in person. Could Line meet her at a coffee shop?

After school one day Line dashed into the coffee shop where Pearl sat, smoking a cigarette and drinking tea she had seasoned with lemon and sugar. Line was in a rush to get back up to the Lutheran home for her evening job, but she tried to appear relaxed. "I don't need coffee, thank you," she said, gesturing to the waitress. Fans in the doorway, sucked the heat out of the room.

"How are you, Line?" asked Pearl, with her sweet, Southern graciousness.

"I'm fine," said Line. "running from place to place in the heat, as usual. But it sounds like I will get to take vacation for a week in August. I can't wait!"

"The heat's bad here in August," said Pearl. "You're lucky." She moved slowly, raising the cigarette to her lips and blowing the smoke out above her. Line noticed the thick eyeliner under her eyes, but she wasn't wearing lipstick.

Line wondered whether Pearl was going to take her time getting to her question. "Did you go to the convention in Ann Arbor?" she asked. "Stephen said there was a women's resolution."

"I did go," said Pearl. "I must say, Line, it's so refreshing to be in women's meetings. I can talk and people listen! All of a sudden we are no longer invisible!"

"What's chauvinism, anyway?" Line asked. She hadn't wanted to ask Stephen. She didn't like sounding stupid.

Pearl giggled. "It's the belief men have that they are superior to women, especially intellectually. It's how we've all been treated by men, so that they don't have to listen to us or deal with us."

Line considered. "I guess so," she said. "I'm not so political as some of you are. So maybe I haven't noticed."

"The system needs to be named and challenged," said Pearl. "Someone came up with the name 'male chauvinism' so we could see it. Believe me, if you had sat in as many meetings as I have, you would have noticed!"

Line sighed. "I fall asleep in those meetings."

"There might be a reason for that!" drawled Pearl. She lit another cigarette and artfully dragged on it.

"Did you want to see me about something?" Line asked. She smiled at Pearl who looked like she might melt into the stiff upholstery of the booth where she sat. "I have to get back up north for work, though I'd much rather sit here all afternoon and talk to you."

"Sorry," said Pearl. But she looked uncomfortable. "It's just that … Some of us thought that, since you're working in a hospital, you might know some doctors we could trust."

"Doctors?" asked Line.

"You know," said Pearl, off-handed. "To help if you get pregnant and don't want to be."

Line looked at Pearl, her eyes narrowing. "But there's Planned Parenthood," she said.

Pearl cocked her head to the side, as if Line should know better. "Well, you know," she said. "Maybe you didn't think ahead!" She leaned forward, conspiratorially. "Or maybe you were raped!"

Line looked as if she was trying to imagine this circumstance.

"But there are also a lot of really poor women, who don't know what to do, how to get birth control," said Pearl.

"I know," said Line. "I've met them. They're in the hospital having babies at this very moment."

Pearl warmed up, seeing that Line was with her. "We were talking in the women's group one day, and a couple of us said people had asked if we knew anything about abortions. And so we thought, I mean it's illegal and all, but we thought we might do some counseling. Be able to give direction. And we're looking for doctors to help. Someone said you worked in a hospital, and I said I'd ask you." Pearl looked at her. "Strictly in confidence and all."

"Of course," said Line. "But I don't think I do. I'm really interested in pregnancy, and obstetrics. Because of the women. Our patients are these amazing women in tough situations. And I've been wondering what can be done for them."

"Yes!" said Pearl. "That's what we want to do! We are giving out a number, and if the person asks for Jane, we will know what they want."

"I hate the idea," said Line quietly.

"So do I," said Pearl. "I'm on the pill myself. But I do think a lot of women need this service. The Clergy Consultation Service we work with told us they get up to 15 calls a day! Mostly from really poor women."

Line shook her head in disbelief. She had gotten pills from Planned Parenthood when she was spending so much time with Stephen at the SDS national office. But she had gone off them since she and Stephen hardly had a chance to spend the night together. She didn't like the pills and thought they made her more emotional.

"Well, anyway, Line," said Pearl. "Keep your ears open. If you hear of someone, you'll let us know?"

"Sure," said Line. "Thank you for calling me, Pearl! It's good to see you! Kay told me about the Westside women's group. I'm hoping to come sometime. But I work so much now!"

Pearl picked up her teacup. "Yeah. We had no idea how much we women needed to get together! It feels so good to talk."

Line took the el north, standing in the heat, holding onto a strap. Bodies surrounded her, though most people looked as neat as possible. The people going north were mostly white at this time of day, women going home with shopping bags hanging over their arms. It wasn't quite rush hour yet. Line felt strong and sure as she moved about in the city.

Line was saddened to hear that abortion was used to prevent unwanted children. Birth control beforehand was much more sensible, she thought. She did not plan to ask any doctors if they could help, but who knew. Maybe she would overhear some information that might help.

Everything made Line think about her values. It's the city, Line said to herself. In the city, anonymous people moved around next to each other as if in a hive of bees. So many possibilities and circumstances to learn from, both failures and successes. In the towns Line grew up in, she was prevented from knowing things by Dad's status as a pastor. People whispered behind their hands or stopped talking when the pastor's daughter showed up. Things happened in those small towns, but Line had to intuit the circumstances. There was history, but she never knew enough.

Dad and Mother knew more things than they told their kids. They talked to each other, but left their kids free to explore on their own, both mentally and physically. Even now, there was a conspiracy in the family to prevent Kristen and Hanna, the "little girls," from hearing the bad language and adult references Line, Marty and Paul used.

Line felt glad she was in Chicago, where so many people had come to find a better life. Many, both black and white, had come up from the South to get off the meager farms where the landlords bled them dry. Line was also learning about the Philippines from girls in her class. The Filipino girls weren't curious, stuck together and didn't volunteer for anything, but they were warm-hearted and hard-working. There must be reasons for all of these things.

I didn't even know what Mother and Dad were like until I got here, Line thought to herself. Stephen's parents sounded very different. He talked to them more frequently than she talked to her family. Both his mother and father got on the phone and harangued him, and he had to stand up for himself, insist that what he was doing was right.

By contrast, the Mikkelsons assumed that no news was good news, that Line was fine until she stated otherwise! She had been so desperate to get out into the world and they had let her. When she didn't go back to college for her senior year, Mother and Dad did not rail at her. Line supposed that they left things in God's hands, trusting things to work out over time. The mills of God, grinding slowly and very fine. They do trust me, thought Line. It was a good feeling.

A newsboy at the station held up a newspaper with a big black headline: "Newark Race Riot," but Line didn't have time to stop and look. The station clock told her she could just get to the Lutheran home in time. She hurried along the shady afternoon streets.

The Lutheran home might not be a very progressive place, but it was comfortable and Line was well-loved.

"How's it goin' Line?" asked Mr. Anderson when she came into the room. He lay on the bed staring at the ceiling after a nap. The smell of pot roast drifted across from the cafeteria.

"Just fine, Mr. Anderson," Line answered. "What are you thinking about?" Mr. Anderson was as mentally sharp as anyone in the place at 96. He had been a cattle dealer and paid attention to politics. Line loved hearing the odd things he sometimes said. She helped Mr. Anderson pull the suspenders up over his plaid shirt.

"Need that oil can today, Line," he said. "Did you bring it? Need to oil up these rusty joints!"

Line giggled appreciatively. She moved his wheelchair over to the bed and helped him gingerly slide into it.

"I was thinking about Teddy Roosevelt," he said. "The radio says there's a riot in Newark. I was thinking about Teddy, and what the ole' Bull Moose would have done about it."

Line wracked her brain, trying to remember what she knew about that particular Roosevelt. "Isn't he the one who liked to speak softly and carry a big stick?"

"Yup," said Mr. Anderson as they wheeled off toward the dining room. "You got it Line! You are a smart girl, and you'll go far."

Line had questions of her own. Race riots were another aspect of cities, people living close to each other. They came from frustration at injustice and lack of equality. A riot against 'the man' was a better thing than hitting your stepdaughter. But how could all of this be remedied? And when had babies begun to be unwanted? These are my questions, Line thought. She did not think Mr. Anderson would have any answers.

11

Paul didn't have much to do the last evening the Mikkelsons spent in Montauk, a warm day in July. The packed moving van was gone, leaving at night so as to arrive in the morning. After the family had supper with one of the neighboring church families, Paul stalked the back yard. He had mowed the whole place two days ago, and the scent of the lush grass was strong in the lingering heat. The sun lay low on the horizon.

The ginkgo biloba in the middle of its square of lawn next to the vegetable garden, was Paul's favorite tree. It was a remnant of a whole phylum of plants which no longer existed, with fan-shaped leaves that turned pale yellow in the fall. It had been small when they arrived ten years ago, but now was at least twice as tall as Paul. He marveled at this tree, which had withstood the deep winters.

The trees Dad planted, loaded now with small green apples, were taller too. Paul visited the lilac, the hated asparagus bed. No one had done anything with their own large garden, as they wouldn't be there to harvest. Next year it would belong to a new pastor and his family.

Paul walked through the hedge where the chipping sparrows nested. It separated the Sherwood's tiny house from the parsonage. The orchard and garden were going wild, beautiful in their way. Long, lush grass grew under the fruit trees. Wizened old John, whom Paul had loved to talk to, had died and his wife moved on to live with her daughter in another town.

Wandering around the side of their own house, Paul looked in on the boarded up entryway, his "office," a weathered little room with peeling paint where he had kept bug collections when he was younger.

"Want to go down to the creek?" Marty asked Paul, appearing in the long rays of sunlight with Kristen and Hanna behind her. "We should go before the sun sets!" she said when Paul nodded.

The four of them walked in a disheveled group out of town, past the Catholic cemetery and down the sandy lane which led to the creek. Paul trailed behind Marty, who held the hands of the little girls. They all wore shorts in the warm weather, Hanna dancing up and down, and Kristen plodding slowly.

"Doe, a deer, a female deer; Ray, a drop of golden sun," sang Hanna.

"Mom says I could maybe get a dog when we move," Kristen told Marty.

"Oh?" asked Marty. "Would you take care of it?"

Paul smiled. Marty couldn't help but play the mother. She loved being with her little sisters.

Birds sang evening songs and the sun lay golden on the right sides of the girls, flattening them a little into silhouettes. Up ahead Paul heard the creek gurgling over the rocks.

The first thing Paul did when Dad said he had accepted a call to Haroldson, was get out a map and look at the rivers. He was fascinated about how water came up from the earth, meandered downhill into rivers, which kept joining other rivers. He had followed this creek's twists and turns into the Turkey River, which led, of course, into the Mississippi. The river near Paul's college was part of the Cedar River watershed. Which, also, eventually ended up in the Mississippi. Paul wondered if he would ever put a canoe in a northern river and follow it down.

Hanna was the first to take off her shoes and wade into the creek, bending down to look into the shallows. Willows hung over the stream in long strands where the titmice and sparrows were settling down for the night. Paul heard a frog beginning its night-time patrol. Trees on the far bank shaded the creek so it was more like glass than a mirror. Paul peered down at the shining pebbles on the sandy bottom. In the deep still pools, water striders skated on the surface.

Paul walked into the water where sand had collected. His bare feet sank in and the water around them rushed away. It felt like the earth moved under him, water streaming downhill. The water was powerful, and in a hurry, that was for sure. Paul didn't want to go anywhere. He wanted to stay there, with his feet planted in the creek.

Marty, as always, knew what time it was. When the sun altogether disappeared and the pale sky became pink and purple, darker in the east, she dragged the little girls home. "You can stay if you want, Paul," she said. "But I have to get up early!" She and Dad were leaving at dawn, trying to beat the moving van. Mother and the girls, and Paul in his little Lark, would start later.

"Bye, creek," said Hanna, waving her little hands as they walked up through the willows. "See you later, alligator!"

Paul reluctantly followed them. He wasn't sentimental about Montauk and he wouldn't really live in Haroldson. But he felt like a transient, a passing stranger, a small ephemeral being washed along in a great sea. Too many moves. The family was always moving. Where was his own life? What should he do with it? How could he make a stand in the great wash of time?

Mother and Dad had "hired" Paul that summer to help move. He was on hand when the family drove to the airport to pick up Marty, who sported a mod-style turquoise quilted coat and a way of speaking that sent the little girls into gales of laughter. She had picked up British expressions and shortened her vowels, unbeknownst even to herself! Kristen and Hanna goaded her into talking, to listen.

But then there had been all the packing. Paul did not know how the Mikkelsons accumulated so much stuff! Mother saved old magazines she intended to read when she had time and took home discards from the school library. Dad collected electronics and radio equipment, archery equipment and now, cameras! Boxes of old negatives! China and cooking utensils, musical instruments, furniture and bedding went into boxes, which were now on their way to Haroldson.

Paul could not imagine himself the head of a family with so many things to pack and then unpack. He wanted to be a lone wolf, ranging across the country with nothing to his name and no one to answer to.

That night Paul stood under the big nondescript elm in the front yard, looking up at the sky. The sky would be the same 250 miles to the west. On the surface of the earth, it was such a small move it would hardly be perceptible. The sky is my home, Paul said to himself. Men kept putting satellites up in it, but they couldn't do much with deep space. It was something you could count on. For billions of years, long before people, the sun and its planets and their moons had been predictable.

Paul found the move arduous, but interesting. For the first time the Mikkelsons moved into an almost new parsonage. It had been built at the same time as the church across the street, with multi-colored bricks placed vertically, and long, vertical windows. The parsonage looked, people said, like a dentist's office. It was plopped down in the middle of an empty square of grass. There was a garage, but no garden. Inside, however, it was spacious and all of the space was useful.

Everyone unpacked and stowed things, including a new washer and dryer, and new furniture. By Mother's birthday in late July, the house was under control. Kristen and Hanna were deputized to make the cake. Paul overheard them as he passed through the kitchen with boxes of books.

"Why is it called 'devilsfood cake'?" asked Hanna, reading the box of cake mix as Kristen dumped its contents into the mixer along with an egg and some water.

"It's the opposite of angelfood," said Kristen. Angelfood cake had a fluffy white texture and was served with fruit and whipped cream.

"But Mother's an angel," said Hanna.

"It's too hard to make angelfood cake," said Kristen. "Besides, Mother likes devilsfood." She turned on the mixer. "Butter and flour the cake pan," she said with three-years-older authority. "I'm going to need it in a minute."

Paul loaded books onto the blonde bookshelves built into the downstairs den. In the family room next to it, at their old dining room table, Marty cut carefully around a thin paper pattern pinned to cotton dress material with a pinking shears. An old television, Dad's ham radio desk and the sewing machine had been stuffed into the room.

"You know," said Marty to Paul as they worked, "I'm so happy Mother and Dad got this house. Mother's never had a chance to furnish things nicely. I wonder if it's because she is teaching now."

"Probably," said Paul. "They don't seem to be hurting these days."

"I can really see her taste, her love of nature," said Marty. "Earth colors, gold, green, brown." Mother had bought a maple dining room table with maple chairs to match.

Paul could see what Marty meant. On the accompanying maple hutch, instead of the delicate china cups she used to display, Mother had arranged handmade ceramic dishes and colorful carved wooden birds attached to driftwood. They were set off by a pair of thick candles Dad had melted down from the beeswax ends of church tapers. The new furniture in the spacious living room floated on a thick gold carpet and real drapes, not homemade, hung at the windows. A sheaf of gladiolas left over from church graced the table.

Just off a spacious foyer, Dad's study was also carpeted and quiet. A wall of shelves held the books he had used at the seminary. His modern desk was flanked by comfy upholstered chairs for people who came in, shut the door and sought his counsel.

With craft materials and games hidden downstairs and out in the garage, a modern kitchen and the spanking new laundry room, the house was as up-to-date as it could be. It looked as though Mother and Dad had become prosperous.

Paul organized books as well as he could, literature in one place, nature books, textbooks which collected after people went to college, library rejects.

"I'm glad it's so cool down here," came Marty's voice. Her oddity and Britishness had receded quite a bit in the month she had been home.

"Yup," said Paul. He went back out for another load of boxes. Neither he nor Marty would be in the house long, so they had flipped for the two extra rooms. Paul was sleeping on a hide-a-bed in the basement den, where he was unpacking books. The smell of chocolate cake baking wafted past Paul's nose as he passed through the kitchen.

Mother sat hemming a dress with her needle and thimble in a lawn chair outdoors on the tiny patio, looking out across the back yard. "So Paul, will you get the coals going for the barbecue?" she asked.

"Sure," said Paul, changing direction. Dad was in the garage, organizing a tool shelf. Paul found the old Weber charcoal grill and coals that had come all the way from Montauk. He set them up in the middle of the flat backyard. He got out a propane torch and began firing the coals, focusing on one at a time.

The sun beat down in the middle of the day. Trees marched down the quiet street at regular intervals, but only a block beyond the church, the fields began, leading to the horizon, as far away as the eye could see. Telephone poles and their sagging wires also marched down the straight streets. No hills prompted curves around them. Paul recalled how straight and flat everything had been in North Dakota when he was little. Western Iowa had gently rolling hills, but not like those near Montauk.

Paul didn't have to get used to Haroldson. After another year at Astoria College, he planned to finish his B.A. at a college on the Red River, on the border between Minnesota and North Dakota. The north, with its woods and lakes, called him. Soon he would be making his own decisions.

Imagining himself in Dad's shoes, Paul wasn't sure he could be a pastor. Dad and Mother were busy getting to know all the people in the new parish. Being a pastor was a gift of service and Dad took spiritual responsibility for a large group of people. Though Dad seemed to love his work, Paul could see the stress on him. Paul thought he wouldn't mind the impermanence as much as being a member of an institution. He would rather have been a scout, an Indian brave who traveled through country he knew well, leaving no track or trace.

As he stood firing the coals, Hanna, in a long skirt of Marty's and a little bib apron came around the corner followed by Marty with a camera. "How do you solve a problem like Maria," sang Hanna as she danced. "How do you catch a cloud and pin it down?" Marty held a boxy camera, looking down into its viewfinder. Partly fueled by Marty's interest, Dad had begun to pick up old cameras at the second-hand stores and outlets he frequented.

Mother was an appreciative audience. Kristen too, stolid and silent, appeared behind her.

"Get Kristen a rake," said Mother, "and take a photo of them as the American Gothic couple."

"Ooooh!" said Marty. "Perfect!" She went to the garage and returned with a rake. Placing Kristen and Hanna next to each other in front of the rhubarb patch (the only plant in the middle of the lawn), she handed the rake to Kristen to hold up. "Now look at Hanna. Hanna, you should look slightly down." Marty clicked the camera, then turned it on its side and wound the film. "Now Kristen you look straight ahead, and Hanna at me. Perfect!" she said.

"Is that Dad's camera?" asked Mother.

"Yes," said Marty. She came toward Paul and took a photo of him moving the coals around the grill with a tongs.

"I feel bad you have so few photographs from your European trip," said Mother.

"Oh it's okay," said Marty. "I couldn't have carried a camera with me, anyway. Just too much to worry about. I did take notes." She approached Mother and the camera clicked again. Paul could hear the film being wound to the next number.

"I think these coals are about ready," said Paul.

Dad set up a card table in the flattest part of the yard and everyone brought out food. Paul grilled the hamburgers, spatula in hand. There were lawn chairs for Dad and Mother. The four kids sat on the ground with their plates.

"I guess it'll be too late to photograph dragonflies emerging this time of year," said Dad. "Some year I want to get that process!" He was talking about the dragonflies at Lake Michigami, which hatched from aquatic larvae known as nymphs early in the year. They were beautiful to watch, green translucent bodies pulled from a stiff, brown thorax. During one long summer day their bodies hardened and turned black as their wings dried and carried them away. They fed on the mosquitoes which were so plentiful in June and lessened as the summer wore on.

"I'm sorry we will have so little time at the lake this year," said Mother, "but I'm worried about the new library. There's a lot of work to do!"

More books, thought Paul. Books were everywhere. It was the family business. He wished the canoe wasn't up at the lake, that he could take it to the nearby Little Rock River and explore. But there wouldn't be much time for that either this summer. The best way to canoe on a river was to have someone put you in upstream and collect you later downstream. Another year, maybe.

"That laundry room would make a great darkroom," said Dad. "It's got water and you could put trays and an enlarger on the washer and dryer." Paul caught him looking at Mother with a speculative look. Poor Mother! Her precious new laundry room, after all those years of ringing wet clothes out of the old Maytag in dank basements and lugging them up the stone stairs to be hung out in all weathers.

But Mother didn't seem unhappy about the idea. She knew who she had married! They were both full of ideas for things to try and things to do.

The girls cleared the dishes into the house and, smiling sheepishly, Kristen brought out her cake. It was a sheet cake, a little lopsided because the oven racks weren't level. Four large candles and eight small ones arranged on the cake were lit with tiny flames in the sun.

Dad began the birthday song in his fine tenor. Hanna boisterously hugged Mother as she finished singing.

"Make a wish!" Hanna said. "Don't tell!"

Mother closed her eyes for a moment, but then blew out all the candles. Paul thought that she must have almost everything she wanted. Usually she just wanted the family to be together. Ellie was in Italy with Bruce and their two children, but Line was coming to the lake. They would pick her up from the train in the Twin Cities.

Mother hugged Hanna to her and confirmed what Paul thought. "Thank you all," she said. "You are my birthday present. I can't think of anything more wonderful than all of you." She looked at Dad, who smiled one of his warmest smiles back at her.

"It's lopsided! Kristen made it lopsided!" crowed Hanna, as Kristen cut the cake in pieces. Kristen hung her head, looking a little crushed.

"Hanna," cautioned Mother. "The cake is lovely! What did I tell you about that?"

Hanna didn't look like Mother's words phased her, but she rejoined saucily, "If you can't say something nice, don't say anything at all." Paul could hear her imitating the voice of Thumper, the rabbit in the Disney movie *Bambi*, the 45 rpm record of which the little girls played often when they were younger.

Mother put her arm around Kristen. "Thank you for making the cake," she said. "You know it's my favorite."

Kristen looked at her gratefully. She took everything, even what her little sister said, seriously. She began picking the candles out of the cake. "The big ones are for ten years," she said, as if Mother didn't know.

"Ice cream?" asked Marty, diverting attention. "Anyone want ice cream with their cake?"

Late that afternoon Paul took the Lark and drove the few miles to the Little Rock River. He went by himself, taking the cracked plastic transistor radio he and Dad had made a few years ago. He felt he had earned the right to a few hours alone. Being with the family was good, but he also liked being by himself.

He parked on the road and walked toward a place where it looked like he could approach the river. It was a real river, gliding past full and thick even in the dry part of the summer. But unlike the rivers of eastern Iowa which cut gorges as they flowed, the Little Rock ambled slowly through flat land. The water was brown, full of silt, the banks held by the roots of willows and a few oaks.

No one was around, just a few cars passing on the road above. In breaks between the willows, Paul saw cows in a pasture on the far side. The lush growth of summer softened the river's edge, making it look tranquil. Probably some fish in there, but it wasn't the first thing Paul thought of. His hands ached for a canoe paddle, not a fishing pole.

The banks had receded somewhat, exposing an edge of rock and shale on the side Paul stood on. He hunkered down on the rocks, idly skipping a piece of shale upriver along the calm, flowing surface into the setting sun. A few riffles sounded loud as the water made its way over rocks in the shallows. Birds were settling down for the night, making sleepy noises.

Paul sat quietly, listening and watching. He didn't see much in the way of animals, besides the cows. Animals didn't want to be seen, but there might be some crepuscular activity in the dusk after the sun set. In fact, there was a nighthawk, with its grating "auk, auk," it's particular song of praise. Paul tried to see it picking the bark for insects, but the leaves of the oaks were too thick.

Paul went back to the car, got the radio and settled down on a grassy bank. He turned it on and twisted the dial to WCCO. Yes! Here was Halsey Hall's cigar-stoked gravelly voice resonantly announcing the Twins game. Another thing Paul could count on, no matter where he lived.

Harmon Killebrew was having a great year. A month ago he had struck the longest home run ever in the Minnesota stadium, landing a ball on the second deck of the bleachers. The Twins were in the pennant race this year, though it was a bit early to see what would happen.

"Holy cow!" sang out Hall, as Killebrew hit a homer, cracking the ball with his powerful swing. No one on base, but a solid hit. The arc of the hit sang through Paul's body as he listened to the cheering crowd. He could not have been happier, listening to Killebrew's hits by the side of the tame little river meandering through the fields.

Baseball is a kind of praise, Paul thought. A way of thanking God for the physical bodies we've been given. A day seldom passed that Paul didn't think of Oddmar, the director who died on Paul's choir tour, and his belief that everything in the world praised the Lord.

Paul could have watched the Twins on television, but he didn't want to insist the family television be tuned to the game. Since Line had left, no one cared about baseball and Paul had gotten so used to Halsey Hall on the radio that his imagination made up the scene. With a radio, the solitary pleasure was all his own.

Absorbed in the game, Paul didn't hear an older man stop on the road and come down into the brush near the river. When he saw him, Paul turned down the volume.

"Evening," said the man, touching an old baseball cap on his head. "I saw a car I didn't recognize up on the road. Just stopped to say hello."

"Evening to you," said Paul, affably. "I'm the son of the new Lutheran pastor over in Haroldson. I've never been here before. Just watching the river and listening to the ball game."

"Good!" said the man. "This is my land along the river, here. The state's trying to buy it up, though. They want it for a recreation area."

"A recreation area?" asked Paul.

"Yep," said the farmer. "Sounds like that's where the money's goin' to be. I just might sell!"

"Recreation. Does that mean hunting and fishing?" asked Paul.

"Yep. Wild turkey, deer, bass in some parts of the river. It's a good river," said the farmer. "But it didn't ever seem that I owned it!"

"Not the river, no," said Paul.

"Well," said the man. He took off his cap and scratched his head, showing a white forehead above his red face. "Recreation. That's where the future's at. Say, what's the ball game?"

"Twins," said Paul. "They're winning."

"Good!" said the man. "My grandfather came out here, bought this land after the Civil War. I never lived in Minnesota, but I'd say it's a pretty good state."

"Good ball team," said Paul.

"Well, greet your Dad for me," said the man, ambling off back to the truck Paul could see up on the highway. But what was the man's name? Paul had no idea. He felt like a stranger. Would he always be the new guy? The stranger?

Recreation, Paul thought. It sounded like management, institutions. Farming was one thing. It was necessary. But God's wild earth didn't really want to be managed. Paul liked park rangers. But, trying to imagine himself in their shoes, his innate dislike of uniforms surfaced. He couldn't imagine himself policing parks, picking up the trash left by people out recreating themselves.

Fingers of unease crept into Paul's solitary evening. He could probably go another year before he made up his mind about being pre-seminary. Everyone expected it, expected him to follow in Dad's footsteps as a Lutheran pastor. But once he was a junior in college, he would have to know. Dad always said that it wasn't easy, that if you didn't feel called, you shouldn't do it. Paul shrugged off the question. Not tonight, he thought, as the nighthawk called from nearby. "Auk, auk," not tonight.

Paul turned up the radio to hear Halsey Hall's gurgling laughter, like sand over rocks. "We better tell our audience what's going on," said the other announcer sitting next to him. Paul was right back in the game.

And the river, oblivious, flowed right on past.

12

Walking home from school the first day with William Chertok, a dark, mop-headed seven-year-old, and Janet, his plump eleven-year-old sister, Marty was frightened. Arriving in Berkeley, California, only two days ago, Marty barely knew her way around, and she must get these two kids to trust her. Though her stomach flopped around vacantly, Marty kept her mouth shut and tried to appear calm. It was hot and she was wearing a sweater she didn't need. After all, it was September, wasn't it?

Everything was familiar to Janet, and Marty relied on her. Janet had been the playmate of little blonde Thea in Oxford. Marty had spent a lot of time with the two girls. After a year in England, the Chertok kids both expressed their delight at being back in America. For Marty, the strangeness of her surroundings was even more intense than when she traveled to Oxford.

"What's the name of this tree?" Marty asked. Facts were safe. The kids found it odd how little Marty knew about their part of the world. In Berkeley the trees were a different color; in general, grey green and sage instead of the lush, wet greens of the Midwest, or England for that matter. Marty hardly wanted to touch the trees, they were so dry, spiky and strange!

"Eucalyptus," said Janet. She stopped and picked up a pale, slender leaf, cracking it and smelling it. "Smell," she said, handing the leaf to Marty.

Marty inhaled the pungent smell. Spicy, but not like pine. William collected the blue-green nuts which lay on the ground around the tree. He handed one to Marty.

"See," he said. "Some of them have four seed-holes and some have five."

"They're lovely," said Marty, turning the rubbery nut over in her hand.

"Dad doesn't like eucalyptus," said Janet. "They're full of sap which burns quickly. He says they're a fire hazard."

"The trees are beautiful," said Marty, looking at the peeling strips of bark which hung down from the smooth trunks of a row of trees along the road at the edge of a park.

"Come on," said Janet. "I want to get my homework done so I can watch television." That was the rule in the Chertok household. "I think Julia's on tonight!"

"Homework on the first day!" said Marty.

"Not me!" sang out William. "I don't have homework."

"Well, come on," said Marty, taking his hand. "I'll play you a game when we get home."

"Battleship?" asked William. He was fascinated by the paper game Marty was teaching him.

"Sure," said Marty. Near the house the smell of redwood chips used as mulch around the plants reached Marty. She couldn't get used to the fragrant warm air. It was wonderfully pleasant, but when would it end? Would it be cold later?

Once home, in the Chertoks' spacious, airy Spanish-style house, William threw down his small school pack and his shoes, walking barefoot on the smooth, hardwood floor. Marty wanted to do the same, but she reminded him gently, "Your mother will be home soon, William. I don't think she wants your stuff spread out all over the house."

William looked at her, but he picked up his things and put them in his own room. Janet sat down, spread out a book on the dining room table and kicked off her shoes. She began writing in pencil, digging into the paper, her dark head to one side. The windows were wide open and the dry, aromatic air breezed into the house. Marty could not believe how warm it was.

A little later, Lidia Chertok, their mother, hurried into the house with a chicken cacciatore she had purchased at a favorite shop nearby. Her dark hair was cropped close to her head and her skin was tan and healthy-looking. "Clear up your homework," she said to Janet. "Dinner will be in half an hour!"

Marty heaved a sigh of relief. Lidia was home! Lidia put the chicken and sauce into a large pan on the stove to warm it. Marty washed lettuce leaves and spun them in the salad spinner to dry them, as Lidia showed her. Janet set the table in the spare, elegant dining room, with plates and napkins in dusty golds and oranges. Mother would have liked it, thought Marty.

The Chertok family felt strange to Marty. Non-practicing Jews, both Lidia and Boris had parents who went from Russia to Los Angeles at the turn of the century. Boris was a brilliant physicist, working at the labs in the hills above Berkeley, and teaching at the university. Lidia was involved in the influential Berkeley City Club. She had encouraged Marty to come and live with them because Marty could pick up the kids after school, allowing Lidia to work part time and spend more time on committees.

For Marty, coming to California meant gaining California residence so that she could go to graduate school, putting off decisions about her future another year. It did not make Dad and Mother happy. They could not understand why she wanted to go so far away and do something which did not further any of the hopes they had for her.

But Marty wanted to be closer to the making of culture. Ever since learning to read from the Dick and Jane books as a little girl and seeing how different their lives were from her own, she had wanted to live closer to places she heard and read about. Oxford was tantalizing, but now Marty had to make a life of her own. She had no idea how to do it. She was blindly feeling her way. The Chertoks' offer was put out lightly, and Marty, without knowing what she was doing, accepted.

Lidia's table was less European than Irene Magnusson's. Vegetables and salads played a big part. Marty, who did not like salad, had never seen anything like it! But she was learning. The salad spinner used centrifugal force to send the water away from the lettuce. She shook up an oil and vinegar dressing in a jar to Lidia's specifications.

Dinner was not served in courses. Everything was put on the table at once, the chicken in its delectable sauce, rice and salad. When Boris, walked into the house, everything was ready. Lidia, like Irene, made sure everyone sat down together and talked about what had happened to them that day.

"How was school?" Boris asked William. Short, dark and full of esoteric thoughts about mathematics and physics Marty could not fathom, Boris was fully present to his children. Lidia told Marty that Boris refused to do work that led to destructive weapons, which limited him, but allowed him to sleep at night. It was mind-boggling to Marty, that she would know anyone doing this work.

"Okay," said William manfully cutting pieces off his chicken. "We're supposed to bring something from home and talk about it tomorrow."

"What are you going to bring?" asked Boris.

"A comb," said William.

"A comb?" said Boris, looking at Lidia, whose eyes were laughing.

"Yes. I'm going to play it like Uncle David showed me."

"With a piece of tissue paper over it?" asked Boris.

"Yup."

"Hmmmmm," said Boris, letting this piece of information stand. "And how about you, Miss Janet. How was your class?"

"Boring," said Janet. "But I knew that," she said smiling. "Just vocabulary and spelling and that stuff." Oddly, it was Janet who took after her father in scientific interests. William's talents ran to art and music. Janet was clearly too bright for normal classes in some areas, lagging behind in others.

"You'll need all that stuff," said Lidia meaningfully, "sooner, rather than later, to become an articulate, well-rounded person."

"I know," said Janet. "But it's boring."

"Open your eyes and look at things differently," said Boris. "Life is only boring to those without eyes to see. Your brother's not even bored by a comb!"

"Julia's on tonight," said Lidia to Janet. Though she was much less apt than Irene Magnusson to sew, Lidia did take a lively interest in cooking. She encouraged Janet to see the physics in cooking, how heat changed ingredients and melded them together.

Janet's face perked up. "Maybe she'll drop the chicken!" said Janet, hopefully.

"We missed her last year when we were in England," said Lidia to Marty. "You never know what's going to happen on her show! We really missed California!"

"How was your day, Marty," asked Boris. "Getting used to the place?"

"Yes, thank you," said Marty, working on her salad. She had prepared for this question, since everything was still so foreign and tension lurked in every corner. "I walked over to campus. So many beautiful trees. And the creek!" Redwoods planted many years ago along a creek which came down out of the hills and flowed through the campus made wonderful, shady spots to sit.

"Just a few years ago," said Boris, "that campus was overrun by the Free Speech Movement. Kind of incredible that it had to happen at all! Surely at a university one would expect to be able to express oneself freely."

"Boris was one of the faculty members involved," said Lidia, her vehemence betraying how deeply the issues cut with them. "Academic freedom is still in question. Faculty members have to sign loyalty oaths!"

"The students' protests did help affirm civil liberties protected in the Constitution," said Boris evenly.

"But look at the backlash!" said Lidia. "Ronald Reagan, of all people!" Reagan had just been elected governor of California based partly on his intention to 'clean up the mess in Berkeley'!

"Academic freedom wasn't an issue in England," mused Boris. "People I met took it for granted. But Oxford and Cambridge weren't state institutions. It seems they had to fight for religious freedom at one point, but that was long ago."

Marty listened, chewing her salad. She knew it was healthy, but it took so long to eat!

"I'm glad these things come up in our country," said Lidia. "It's good to air our views. Promotes diversity. We're having an introductory meeting for a women's discussion group at the club this week. You must come, Marty!"

"I would like to," said Marty. Lidia was a forceful person. Marty worried it would be a struggle to be the self she really was inside, as she had promised herself. On the other hand, Lidia was so different from Marty that Marty didn't know how to please her. She might just have to be herself around Lidia in any case!

After dinner, the girls rushed the dishes into a dishwasher and gathered in front of the television in the family room. Lidia and Janet loved Julia's breezy manner and her insistence that anyone could master the techniques of great cooking.

"Queen of Sheba cake!" crowed Janet as Julia began describing the chocolate almond cake she planned to serve at a champagne and coffee party. Janet leaned over a hassock, her face only a few feet from the black and white screen.

Lidia took notes on a page of looseleaf paper she would put in her recipe notebook. She got excited when Julia melted the chocolate in dark Jamaican rum, placing a small pan in hot water. "See," she said to Janet. "Chocolate reacts to heat in a certain way!" Julia was very specific about smoothing the chocolate and not allowing it to become hard or granular.

Marty was impressed to see that Julia knocked a little cream of tarter into her hand instead of using measuring spoons when she beat the egg whites. Marty could not forget the reprimand she had gotten in 4-H for doing just this! "She's both very precise, and a little imprecise also," said Marty. "She's obviously working from lots of experience!"

"This bit of batter on the edge of the spatula is for the cook!" said Julia, licking it. "That's part of the recipe," she said, deadpan.

"Ooooooh!" said Janet. "Can we make this one? Please?"

"I think so," said Lidia. "It doesn't look too bad."

"It's such a small cake, though," said Janet. "Could we make two?" But before the program finished, Julia explained that French cakes were small, so you didn't have too much on the plate. She decorated the cake with blanched almonds.

"So much trouble for a small cake!" said Lidia. "But I suppose she's right. We'll try it."

Marty recalled the birthday cake her younger sisters had made for Mother's birthday only a few weeks ago. A big lopsided sheet cake, made and frosted with Betty Crocker mixes. It was certainly not a European cake such as those Irene had made in England, or Julia Child now displayed.

"What a lot to learn!" said Marty. She imagined her own kitchen, in which she would one day beat egg whites and make cakes from scratch.

"I'm sure Irene's cakes looked like that," goaded Lidia.

"They were wonderful," admitted Marty. "But we ate so many delicious things!" She could see that Lidia envied Irene in some respects. The good food had left Marty rueful and plump. She could not pass it up! Partly she had felt stress at not knowing how to help the Magnussons. She had slimmed down some over the summer at home, but she still felt bigger than she wanted to be.

"Well," said Lidia, standing up. "Bed time. Let's go see what William is doing." She stroked Janet's glossy black curls. "Good night, Marty!"

I could almost be part of this family, thought Marty, except that my skin is so pale. Her own hair was darker than any of the other Mikkelsons, though not black. She went to bed in the small room Lidia had prepared for her, leaving the window open to the fragrant night breeze.

In the morning, Marty took a shower after Boris and his children had left for school. The walls of the lovely golden bathroom were covered in yellow ceramic tiles. It showed that the house had been built in the 1920's and never remodeled. Indeed, the sink and fixtures were so solid and beautiful, you might never need to replace them. Windows on either side of the sink let in the lambent morning light. A long hose allowed you to take the showerhead down and use it all over your body.

Lidia was having another cup of coffee when Marty appeared. She looked relaxed and lovely in a wraparound skirt with a tee-shirt in warm colors that went well with her skin. "I'm thinking about my day," she told Marty. She was barefoot, but a pair of canvas espadrilles had been kicked under the table. When she was at home, Lidia spent her time reading and writing and prodded her children into doing the same. A Hispanic woman came in to clean the house. Even the garden was tended by other hands.

Marty poured herself coffee and made herself a piece of toast. She gingerly sat down at the table, not sure whether Lidia wanted her presence or not. Marty's mornings were free, but she was hoping to get typing work so as to earn some spending money. Her agreement with the Certoks was for the school year.

"Are you going out exploring again today?" asked Lidia.

"Yes," said Marty.

"So you'll pick up the kids," said Lidia. "I might leave you some instructions on what to do about dinner. I'm thinking of a lasagna. I'll put it together this morning and you can throw it in the oven this afternoon."

"Sure," said Marty. "Whatever you like. I'm anxious to help!"

"Here's a list of Russian authors I made for you," said Lidia. "You should have a look at the *New York Review of Books* too. They have great articles on literature. You are welcome to look through our books, and read them, if you are careful of them. If I were you, I would start with Tolstoy."

"We read Dostoyevsky in college," said Marty. "But I didn't like him nearly so much as Pasternak's book."

Lidia looked hard at Marty. "*Crime and Punishment* I bet," she said. "Sounds pretty Lutheran to me!" Lidia had gotten some understanding of the Lutheran church from Irene and Rolfe Magnusson the previous year.

Marty smiled at her. "Right," she said. "I didn't even read the whole thing, I don't think."

"Like I said, start with Tolstoy," said Lidia. "Read *War and Peace*. Now there's a project for you!"

"Thank you so much, Lidia!" said Marty. Isaiah Berlin had cued her about Tolstoy. She couldn't believe her luck in finding another sophisticated couple to learn about the world from.

It was almost a mile to the university campus, but Marty loved the walk. She didn't expect to wander into lectures, as she had in Oxford, but she hoped to be able to use the libraries. All along the streets were interesting trees and houses, surrounded by unusual plantings. Roses, certainly, but also many other plants. Grasses, cactuses and flowering shrubs. Marty wished Paul had been there to see them.

Marty walked up through the middle of campus, past the campanile and into a meadow under some trees that looked more familiar to her, deep green oaks. Just above was a building with a deck and inviting windows, the woodwork around them painted a bluish green. Marty plopped down in the grass under a tree, writing a little in her notebook, but also keeping an eye on the attractive building.

Students passed up and down on the sidewalks, but the meadow didn't seem to be on any of the main campus paths. At noon, Marty heard the bells of the carillon playing a classical piece from the campanile tower, but still not many students were near. In the building above, which had a wooden shingled second story and a stucco base, a few people emerged onto a deck and sat on the edges of a wall, casually talking.

Using her best skills of fading into the woodwork learned in Oxford, Marty walked up to the building and entered. Dark wood paneling made the large room feel cool and Marty sank down into a huge green leather chair, letting the effect of the room wash over her. The furniture looked crafted to be in the room, including the lamps. Over a large fireplace hung a bust of John Galen Howard looking at an architectural plan. He had supervised much of the campus architecture, according to a card posted near.

The many-paned windows looked out into the sunny meadow surrounded by oaks. Marty did like being in a dark place looking into a lighter one. The carpets and materials were muted, rich colors. Ceilings felt low and dark. Marty walked through the open building, enjoying the deep luxury of carved wood and beautiful light.

What made such a building so special, Marty wondered as she walked through. The way it related to the natural world around it was different from any she had known. It felt like an indoor space which wasn't separate from the outdoor space around it. The Chertoks' house had some of this feeling also. That's it, Marty thought to herself. In California people didn't have to protect themselves from snow and icy winds and weather. The massive stone castle-style buildings she had known in Oxford were bastions against nature, nothing like this beautiful, low-slung building.

Marty kept going, heading down onto Telegraph Avenue through the Sather Gate. Throngs of students came and went. Long hair, drugs, denim and tie-dye had spilled into Berkeley from the 'Summer of Love' in San Francisco, if they weren't indeed born there. Barefoot, disheveled people were everywhere among the students, who dressed as Marty did in buttoned shirts and skirts or trousers. Political groups manned tables full of books and leaflets. On street corners, hippies in exotic imported clothing sold handmade jewelry, leatherwork, incense and Asian textiles and sculptures at small tables.

Marty looked at her watch. She had just an hour before she must go to Janet and William's grade school. Lidia had told her about a famous coffee shop further down the street she wanted to visit. She walked quickly up Telegraph, past all the bookstores she would one day explore. Nothing like Blackwells, of course, but bookstores where she could stand and browse.

Blue and white stripes on an awning announced the Café Mediterranean. It wasn't a clear European blue, but a greyed Pacific blue, Marty noticed. Braving the dirty kids leaning against the wall outside begging her for change, Marty went in.

The Café Mediterranean was famous for the political discussions which took place there and European coffee drinks. Marty stood in front of the massive hand-lettered board describing all the things you could eat and drink posted high above the servers, who stood in a kind of corral, making food and taking money.

Take your time, she told herself. Order exactly what you want. Marty asked for a toasted bagel. She could not afford espresso coffee drinks. The Chertoks would pay her a small allowance, but so far Marty only had the money Dad had given her. She recalled with a pang how difficult the year in Oxford had been when she had so little money she had eaten six-penny chocolate bars for lunch. In chocolate she now tasted humiliation. For the first time in her life, she didn't crave it. When the bagel was ready, Marty asked for butter to put on it.

Marty took her plate to a table on a second level balcony, where she sat looking out at the floor below with its large black and white tiles, and into the street. It was probable that many of the people in the café were not students. Marty wished she had allowed herself more time to sit and dream and write in her notebook.

At the table next to Marty, a young man about her age had stretched his long legs under the table and leaned back. Peering through long hair and glasses he held the *New York Review of Books* up to his face. On the cover was a cartoon of a black man with a huge afro under the title in red: "The New Left: Chicago and After." Line, thought Marty, equating Line with Left-wing Chicago. Certainly Stephen, her boyfriend, was.

Marty had just seen the actual, laughing Line at the lake. Line airily described the hospital where she worked, all of the interesting people she was meeting. She told Marty that women were getting together to talk, since the men didn't have the patience to listen to them. Marty envied Line the purpose she seemed to have in life.

At another table, three young women smoked cigarettes, holding them artfully in one hand as they talked to a big, affable man with a red bandana tied around his forehead. What were they doing, thinking about? The girls wore their hair long, with light gauzy clothes, and were laden with scarves and necklaces. The breeziness of people in California was charming. It was almost like the architecture. With such nice weather, what was there to worry about?!

Marty ate her bagel as slowly as she could. Tobacco smoke blew through the room, but the butter on the sweet hot bagel tasted of home. Everything around her was interesting. What if she had grown up in California, or in a city, she wondered. It seemed that there were so many more possibilities here. She might have become a fashion designer, an architect, a textbook writer or a cook! In the Midwest, the only avenue available to someone like herself was teaching.

Though she sympathized with the students on the Left, Marty did not feel especially political. She would march against the war in Viet Nam if she had the chance, but she was more interested in inner revolution. She wanted to learn. And explore! California was thrilling. And she lived here. She would have time.

But today Marty must go, she must go back north, pick up the kids and spend the breezy afternoon in the Chertoks' lovely house. She wanted to be early, be dependable for Janet and William. That was where her bread was buttered, and Marty didn't forget it. Another day she would come early and have more time to sit in the café.

13

At the food co-op in February in Chicago, Line could not find much in the way of vegetables. She was shopping with Stephen, hoping to make soup. Cabbages, a few carrots, apples, oranges, onions and potatoes. That was it. But Line did not want to give up and buy frozen or canned vegetables. She was feeling especially happy these days, the first days of her real life.

"Dried beans?" asked Stephen, standing in front of a bushel of large white beans. "I think my mother made bean soups in the winter." The food co-op was run out of a garage in Hyde Park. The only heat was from an oil burner in the corner, which kept things from freezing at night. Cold beams of sunshine fell on the bins and bushels of vegetables, dust motes rising in the shafts of light.

Line did not know much about dried beans. "How do they work?" she asked, picking one out of the bushel and holding it up. "Don't you have to cook them forever?"

"Nah," said Stephen, laughing at her. "Didn't Adele Davis teach you anything? You soak them overnight and then they cook up pretty fast."

Line sighed. "I don't think Mother liked beans. The only ones we had were canned kidney beans in the chili or canned baked beans."

"Well, come on, new frontiers and all," said Stephen. "We'll find a ham hock or something to put in. It'll be delicious!"

Line took the onions, carrots, cabbage and soup beans over to an old-fashioned cash register, where Mark stood, bearded and amiable. "Top of the morning to you," he said. He pushed down the cash register keys with mittened fingers, taking Line's money. He put the vegetables into a worn paper bag and gave the bag to Stephen.

"How's it going, man?" asked Stephen, anxiously. Mark was an acquaintance, an SDS friend, and shopping at the food co-op was a revolutionary act. But no one else was there at the moment.

"Good!" boomed Mark. "Can't complain. Keeping our ears open and all. If you know anyone who can help find us more supplies, let us know."

"But how about customers?" asked Stephen.

"Plenty," said Mark staunchly. "They come and go. Don't worry. Come spring, it's going to take off!"

"Right on," said Stephen warmly, holding up two fingers. "Peace, man!"

It was a clear day, but the wind blew off the lake ferociously, and everyone they saw hurrying along the street was wrapped to the eyeballs in scarves and winter coats. Stephen, who had lived in Hyde Park much longer, steered Line toward a butcher, where he gleefully bought a ham bone for 50 cents.

"My mother would never have done this!" he said to Line. "So you're not the only one doing new things." Though his parents were Jewish,

Stephen told Line he didn't turn up his nose at any food. He was skinny as a rail and mostly lived on coffee, peanut butter and brown rice.

Now that Line had her first job in the obstetrics ward at Cook County Hospital, she had rented a small apartment on South Harper in Hyde Park with Lenore, a friend from LPN training. The two girls were enthusiastically buying second-hand pots and dishes and making themselves a home.

Line worked four days a week and every other weekend on the afternoon shift, 3 to 11 p.m. She did not like coming home on the el at 11 p.m., but it couldn't be helped and she did not tell Mother and Dad about some of the things she had seen or some of the questions she was asked on her way home. She was getting tougher, learning not to respond, to move with great purpose through the scary night. Lately it had been too cold for anyone to stop long anyway.

At the apartment at the back of an old brick building, Lenore was in the bathroom with the door shut. Emerging with one towel wrapped around her body and another around her long, reddish hair, she squeaked at seeing Stephen, "Hello!" and dashed into her room.

Line giggled and put the groceries in the tiny kitchen. She pulled out the small paper bag of beans. "This is all fine for tomorrow," she said. "But I guess we'll have to have eggs or cheese sandwiches today." She found a large bowl, poured in the beans and covered them with water.

Stephen took off all his outer clothes, and slouched down on the day bed covered with an Indian bedspread. There was only one bedroom, and Line had agreed to pay a little less and sleep in the living room on this bed. The apartment was dark, the windows at the back looking into a snowy schoolyard lined with bare trees. A small circular table near the window served them for dining. Line came and sat beside him, kissing him in the warmth.

Stephen's hands traveled over Line's body. "You know what I'm hungry for," he said softly.

Sensations of all kinds flowed through Line. She had begun to suspect she was pregnant, but she wasn't sure. Her breasts were tender and she felt a euphoria she couldn't explain. It was just a change in her usual state, a feeling of peace and satisfaction. But it was overlaid by fear. She had stopped using birth control pills during the year of nursing school, and Stephen used a rubber when they slept together.

Lenore's bedroom door opened, however, and she entered ostentatiously. "Are you guys making lunch?" she asked.

"Yup," said Line, pulling away from Stephen. "Do you want a cheese sandwich?" She got up and went into the kitchen. She pulled out the large cast-iron frying pan and put it on the gas stove.

"Gee, I wish we had a television," said Lenore, shaking out her wet hair. "I'd like to watch the Olympics!" It hadn't been easy for Line to find a roommate. Most of her friends lived with their families. But Lenore, like Line, had come to the city by herself in search of work and education. More than anything, she loved sports. She also worked a night shift in a hospital, so odd hours prevailed in the apartment they shared.

Line could see that Stephen looked weary. "Yeah, I try to catch the news on tv, but newspapers also work," he said.

Most of Stephen's efforts were still directed toward ending the Vietnam war and stopping the draft of American soldiers. The recent North Vietnamese offensive during Tet, their new year, had made the likelihood of the United States winning the war look impossible as well as immoral, in the opinion of Stephen's friends. But they knew more about it than most people in the United States. A photograph of a man with his hands tied behind his back, being shot at close range on a busy street in Saigon rose up on newspapers everywhere that month. The unforgettable image flashed through Line's mind when she thought of the war.

Line cut cheese and put it between two slices of bread. She buttered the outsides of the bread and fried it in the cast iron pan until the surface was crisp and buttery and the cheese melted inside.

"I wish I didn't have to go down and watch Peggy Fleming with Mr. Pickett," said Lenore as they ate their sandwiches. Mr. Pickett, their landlord, lived in the basement. He had given up the apartment to the girls when his wife died of cancer. When they moved in, they found hair curlers and hand lotion in the cabinet in the bathroom. "But I'm going to," she said.

Line smiled at her. "Be careful," she said. "Mr. Pickett seems a little overly friendly."

"Who's Peggy Fleming?" asked Stephen.

"Peggy Fleming?!" said Lenore. "She's a figure skater who might win the gold medal for us at the Olympics! Stephen! Where have you been? Her skating is so beautiful it makes me cry."

Line looked off into the austere view of bare trees caked with snow and the white schoolyard beyond the window. "I'm just glad it's warm," said Line. "Mr. Pickett does seem to have a good furnace."

After lunch Lenore left and Line and Stephen lay on the daybed. "I'm starting to wonder if I'm pregnant," Line blurted. "Remember that time we thought the condom leaked?"

"What makes you think so?" asked Stephen. "Maybe you're around mothers and babies so much you're contact pregnant! You know, like contact high." He whispered, playfully stroking Line's stomach and running his hands down her broad hips.

"Maybe," said Line doubtfully. "I feel really good!"

"You better find out," said Stephen. "That's a serious statement. I don't want to talk about it if it isn't true."

"Yes," said Line. "I better find out." It sounded as if Stephen would take it seriously, if it were true.

"You haven't been around SDS people lately," said Stephen. "Things are growing more ominous every day. The new people want to put their bodies on the gears of war, as they say. Hayden's working both ends against the middle, talking to politicians like Robert Kennedy. He and Rennie Davis want to go along with Dr. King's plan for a march on Washington, with a mule train which will then head toward Chicago for the convention in August. But there are other factions who want violence. It isn't a time to be having kids, I don't think."

"And where are you?" Line wanted to know. "What do you think?"

"I'm trying to pull people back to the center, to the purpose of SDS. It's still the strongest, most Left organization we've got," Stephen said. "But it's a strain. There's ideologues in there who want it to be even more radical, more Marxist."

"Marxist?" asked Line.

"Keep throwing the word 'bourgeois' around, like 'bourgeois civil liberties,'" said Stephen. "'Bourgeois marriage'."

Line got it. He's trying to warn me, she thought to herself. She sighed. She loved Stephen, but he kept insisting he couldn't have a normal life until the war in Vietnam was over. "Bourgeois," she answered, trying to see it on page. "I can't even spell it!"

"That's why I love you, Line," said Stephen, holding her tighter. "You don't have an ideological bone in your body!"

"I've been thinking about the SDS cat," said Line. "If you hear of any ideological kittens being born, I would like one now that I have a place of my own."

"I'll keep my ears open," said Stephen.

That week, Line began to make inquiries at the hospital. While making the rounds of her patients as she came on shift, she asked a woman who had just had her third child how she knew she was pregnant.

"Well, what got me this time was I was expecting my period, and instead I just had a little spotting. I remembered that had happened before, and sure enough, this little one arrived!"

"How long after?" asked Line.

"Oh, about nine months, eight months, I don't remember," said the woman, cradling the tiny boy who lay swaddled in cotton against her chest.

Sitting at the nurses' station late that night, recording patient information for the day on their charts, Line took her cap off and let her long hair down. She hated the hat, which bobbled around on her head when she was working. But she wasn't supposed to touch it, as it was never clean enough. Warren, a brilliant young black woman whose whole family was helping her get through medical school, took each chart as Line finished with it.

"How are those twins doing?" asked Warren.

"One of them got to go home," said Line. "But the other one is still in the incubator. Lungs aren't very strong. It's a tough time of year to be born."

"He'll be fine," said Warren, knowingly. "If it's tough at the beginning, his life is bound to get better."

Line found it especially hard, in the incubator room, not to cradle and caress the babies. The incubator babies were treated according to rigid schedules. They might have been in a row of test tubes, thought Line. She avoided the room because of how alien it felt.

"His parents didn't seem too worried," said Line. "They were joking that they might forget to come and get him. That they didn't need two more mouths to feed!"

"Sad," said Warren, absently as she wrote down a number.

"Is there a way to know for sure you're pregnant?" Line asked.

"There are blood or urine tests," said Warren. "But they're more accurate after the first month or so. Missing a period is still a pretty good early indicator."

Line sighed. She didn't pay a lot of attention to her monthly timing, but she would from now on.

"Are you worried about it," asked Warren.

"Yeah, maybe," said Line softly. "Thank you," she said. She befriended the interns who worked long, ridiculous hours at the hospital as part of their training. They came and went so quickly it was hard to get to know them, but they were as interested as Line in the intricacies of childbirth and she could ask them questions. She liked the older doctors too, the ones who had been delivering babies so long it gave them humility and compassion.

There were others, both doctors and nurses, who were rigid about efficiency and method. Time and numbers were important to them and they went about with set faces. Cook County hospital was terribly busy all the time, with people flowing through in all states of duress. Line knew that some of the doctors and nurses were protecting themselves, using scientific procedures to justify it.

Line did not want to become like them. Her gift was for patient care, for having her eyes wide open and hands ready. Watching, she tried to understand a physical situation before someone even used words to describe it. Since birth was normal and sometimes not very complicated, Line had learned a lot about what normal pregnancy was like. The mothers were all a little different however, and she tried to ease their fears and pain.

By the middle of March, Line was almost certain she herself was pregnant. She did notice a little spotting and she had not had a period for many weeks. She mentally dragged her feet, not wanting to discuss it with Stephen. As she had hoped when she found the apartment near his, she was seeing more of him, but now they were a little formal with each other and carefully avoided the topic of pregnancy.

At last, however, Line got the young intern Warren to confirm her pregnancy with a blood test. Even though she had known it, the news hit Line like a ton of bricks. It was way too early for her to start having babies. She was 23, would be 24 in May. Mother had Ellie when she was only 22. She was married and had a husband who loved her, but it had not been easy because Dad was still in school.

Line had taken care of her sister Ellie when she had her first baby at 21. Ellie was lethargic and exhausted, but Line felt fine. She felt more than fine! She was elated. And impressed that this baby had gone to such lengths to be conceived, the sperm slipping through a hole in a condom to meet her egg.

Line could put off talking to Stephen no longer. At the end of March, on her day off when she knew Lenore would not be home, she invited Stephen to come for a meal.

Slushy snow was now interspersed with puddles in the schoolyard at the back of the apartment. Line went out on the porch, a sort of balcony built out over the basement level. She could imagine setting the table back here during the summer under lush trees in the heat. And how big will I be then, she asked herself. Everything now related to her pregnancy.

Stephen arrived at the door with a box. He put the box on the floor and opened it. Inside was a small black kitten with white socks and a white nose. Line was overcome! "Ohhhhh!" she said, picking up the kitten. "Is it old enough to leave its mother?" she asked. She held it close, stroking it.

"About six weeks, we think," said Stephen. He looked proud of himself. "I have news too," he said. "LBJ isn't going to run! Isn't that amazing!"

"Wow," said Line. "I guess he's realized how unpopular he is."

"Yup," said Stephen. "Said so himself at the end of his speech today. Something we're doing must be working!"

"Well, that changes things," said Line, struggling to imagine Stephen's feelings, whereas all of her own were wrapped up in the life growing inside of her. She found an old green sweater and curled it into a nest for the little kitten on the daybed. Its eyes opened sleepily, but it didn't move as she put it down.

Line checked the stew she was making, roast beef, potatoes, carrots and onions. It was bubbling nicely.

"Come outside Stephen," she said. "Smell the air." She pointed to the tree branches hanging over the small porch. "See the buds?" she asked. A cold, grey twilight hovered in the sky.

Stephen stood there quietly. "Change in the air," he said. "Can't be bad!"

Line took his hand and put it on her own stomach. "I'm definitely pregnant," she said.

Stephen looked startled. "How long?" he asked. "Is there still time?"

Line knew what he meant. Some of the women she knew were involved in Jane, a secret group which helped pass on information and contacts for women who wanted to have an abortion. But Line involuntarily put her arms around her stomach, as if it were full and round. She was already protecting this child, who was fighting to make his way into the world.

"Plenty of time," smiled Line. "It'll be born about the same time as the presidential elections."

"No," said Stephen, hesitantly. "I mean …"

"I know what you mean," said Line. "But I'm going to have the baby. If you don't want to share it with me, I'll put it up for adoption. I don't want to have it alone. It needs a father." Line's clarity and ability to say exactly what she meant had come from weeks of already living with the baby.

But Stephen leaned down, putting his head in his hands on the railing of the balcony. "Jesus Christ," he said. "It's just too much!"

Line put her arm around his shoulder. "It's not too much," she said. "We're old enough. You just said change was in the air!"

"But it's so hard!" Stephen looked ashen. "There's still so much to do!"

Line turned and went back into the apartment, shutting the door on the cold March air. "Come on," she said. "Let's have dinner." She lit a candle and put it on the table.

She ladled a plate of stew out for Stephen and one for herself. She was thrilled to be eating for two. She wanted to share her delight, but Stephen wasn't taking it well.

"I got the vegetables at the food co-op," said Line proudly. "It was full of people! I don't think you have to worry about them any more. In fact, Mark says they're moving into a storefront."

Stephen picked at his food. "Where?" he asked weakly.

"Not far, over on 57th Street," said Line. "I can't wait for the warm weather! Right now it's been cold so long I can hardly remember what it was like!"

"Line," said Stephen abruptly. "I have to think about all this. I can't just tell you now how I feel about having a child."

Line was not surprised. She put her hand on his. "It's okay," she whispered. "Take as long as you need to. Everything's going to be fine." But a shiver of fear ran through her. She hadn't thought about telling Mother and Dad she was going to have a child out of wedlock. That would not be easy. A child was a very public thing, belonging to a family no matter what.

The following Thursday, Dr. Martin Luther King was shot and killed. Everyone Line knew was galvanized by it. A pall fell over the hospital where she worked. So many people in Chicago had come up from the South to find work and still had relations there. Whispers started to go around about people leaving to protest, and injured protesters came into the emergency room, though that was far from Line's ward.

Line knew Stephen was working to organize the protests which erupted all over the country. When she finally talked to him on the phone, he said, "It's genocide! It's the end of working with the system. It's time to act!"

Line couldn't do much more than whimper. She had her own moral problem to deal with. "But Stephen," she said. "What about the baby?"

Stephen groaned. "I'm sorry Line. Give me another week."

It was another long, agonizing week for Line. Every day she worried about what Stephen would do. At night she curled up with the kitten Lenore had named Munchkin and spoke to it like a friend. "I know he loves me," she told the little cat. "I know it's hard for him too."

Line imagined Stephen talking to his parents, whom she had never met. He was close to them, though they lived in Brooklyn. They shared his Leftist tendencies, though they wished he would finish school and get a good job in a university. His mother worked in public health and they still paid Stephen's tuition, though he was almost 26. From what Line knew, she was sure Stephen's parents would think she was taking advantage of him.

But it was up to Stephen. There was nothing Line could do about it. If he didn't want to have a child with her, Line would have to say goodbye to him. That scared her even more. It wasn't that she was so worried about being married. She just felt that they were already married in their own eyes. Stephen was her best friend, her refuge. He knew more about her than anyone did, even Marty and Paul. He was the root of the life she had made for herself in Chicago.

Stephen's friends in SDS were also a huge influence, Line knew. The Freemans were good, family people, and so were some of the more sober, older SDS members. But Line did not know the new members, who Stephen said were more radical in every way. From what he said, they did not trust institutions, slept with each other in many shifting configurations and cared for nothing except political effectiveness.

During the previous year while Line had worked to get her nursing license, supporting it by working at the Lutheran home, she had not gone to the SDS office once. It had moved, was actually closer to the hospital. But when they were able to meet, neither Stephen nor Line wanted to share each other, though they filled each other in on everything that was happening.

Besides what Stephen told her, Line heard about SDS in the women's group whose meetings she attended when she could. Most of the Westside Women's group had some connection to SDS through their own political work or because they were involved with its members. Kay Freeman made sure Line was included.

But Line felt most of the women in the group were on a different planet than she was. They were bent on making their way in the larger world and being heard. Line wasn't worried about any of that herself. She wasn't a speaker. She had learned that her gifts were in her hands and in her body. Working in the hospital deeply satisfied her desire to make a difference in the world and she found her friends among other young nurses, none of them very well off or politically ambitious.

Line did not want to go to any of these women with her problems. As she went about her work that week, she weighed everything in her life against the possibility that Stephen would not want to have this child. Perhaps he found it more important to lay his body upon the gears of the war machine the country had become. Perhaps he didn't want to bring children into a country where blacks and poor people were treated so badly.

Line knew she could probably work up until the child was due, then put it up for adoption. Nothing in her external life would have to change. But everything would change.

By the end of the week, Line was a basket case. When she talked to Stephen on the phone she was limp as a dishrag.

"Don't make dinner," he said. "I'll pick you up and we'll go out." His voice was calm and steady.

It sounded promising. But Line was still deeply frightened, bracing herself internally for disappointment.

When Stephen came to the door, however, Line relaxed. He had a power and freshness about him she had hardly seen since she first met him. He was holding up a rickety black umbrella in the rain and invited Line under it.

Line hardly knew where they were as they rushed down the street, but all of a sudden they entered a club off an alley with a thin neon pink light over the door. Stephen handed some cash to the man at the door and they were seated at a small round table in front of a stage. Blue and white checkered cloths covered the tables, with an ashtray and a candle in a glass lantern on each. Around them, a few people were seated, drinking and smoking. Mostly business men in suits with their ties off, but a few women with pouffy hair and sleeveless dresses.

"My Dad told me to find this place," said Stephen, looking around. "Line," he said quickly, placing his hands on hers, "will you marry me?"

Line broke into tears. "Yes," she said. "Yes." Salty liquid streamed down her face. She licked it from the corners of her mouth.

"Good," said Stephen. "That's settled." He lifted a finger like the city boy he was and a waiter came over. He ordered a gin and tonic for each of them and snacks. "Art Hodes is playing tonight," he said, leaning in and whispering in Line's ear. "Came from the Ukraine, but he plays all over New York and stuff."

In a few moments three men came out on stage and a balding, older man settled in at the baby grand piano. A black man took up the bass fiddle and yet another sat behind a drum set. With no introduction they broke into a quiet, energetic piece of blues music. Art's mobile, genial face shook in time to the music he was playing, the bass player smiled and the drummer brushed the tops of his snares and cymbals with metal brushes.

Stephen lit a cigarette and sat back. Line watched him, seeing with wet eyes a Stephen she hardly knew. Tears collected in the corners of her eyes and coursed down her cheeks. She could not stop crying as the trio played. Just as she had tried to tell him, Stephen now seemed to know there was life outside SDS. It would go on, no matter whether the country was at war or not.

14

One night a rap on Paul's dorm room door told him he had a phone call. This was so unusual that he rushed down to the end of the hall to take it. Mother was on the line! Ordinarily, if Mother and Dad wanted to contact Paul, they sent a postcard.

"Please come home next weekend, Paul," said Mother, getting right to the point. "Line's arriving with Stephen and they're going to get married. His parents are coming too. They're all driving out from Chicago."

Paul was thunderstruck. "Line?" he said.

"Yes, Paul," said Mother. "She told us she and Stephen are going to have a baby and she asked if Dad would marry them. Or at least have a service of blessing."

Mother's voice was quiet and calm, even though Paul knew she must be upset. It was terribly sudden. Paul mentally re-arranged the lab books he was supposed to annotate for freshmen biology students and the library research he wanted to do that weekend. School would be out in a month and things were catching up with him. "Sure," he said. "I'll be home Friday night."

"Good," said Mother. "You can be the best man. Marty doesn't have enough money for plane fare, but we'll just do the best we can. Stephen's parents are coming out from New York!"

"Ah," said Paul. That was probably the most upsetting thing for Mother. Paul knew they were Jewish. "And Dad can marry them?" He was puzzled.

"Well, he's investigating," said Mother. "In any case, it will be an ecumenical affair!"

"Well," Paul said, "It will be good to be home. I might bring some work with me. I'm supposed to be writing a paper on Thoreau. But I can't wait to see you all!"

"Me either," said Mother. "Thank you, Paul, for arranging time to be with us. Is everything going well with you?"

"Sure," said Paul. "Smooth sailing here! But I'm busy." He didn't want to take expensive minutes on a long-distance phone call when he would see the family soon.

"Well, good night," said Mother's voice. "We'll see you Friday night."

Paul hung up the phone, shocked. Mother was clearly in a tizzy, but why wouldn't she be? Paul admired Line for coming right out with it. No pussyfooting around for Line! But he could just hear Dad's bitter comments. Television and magazines were full of discussions of parents not understanding their children: the "generation gap" it was called. Dad didn't like the younger generation's idea of "free love" one bit.

At the Mikkelsons' house on Saturday an atmosphere of nervous anticipation reigned. Aunt Rose had also come to see her niece's family, adding formality to the proceedings. Frodo, Kristen's black lab, which Paul was surprised to discover was allowed in the house, danced around, his nails scratching the tile floor.

The Cohens drove up in a rented car. Line stepped out of the car first, but Paul could see nothing different about her. She looked relaxed and happy to see everyone in the early May sunshine, not like a prodigal daughter. Stephen too looked spiffy, in a pullover sweater and jeans.

Paul realized that Line had never been to Haroldson before. Last summer she had come directly to the lake to see her family. He could not imagine what she, or the Cohens were seeing when they drove in to the small town.

The Cohens were about the same age as Mother and Dad. To Paul they looked like middle class Americans. Mr. Cohen wore a suit and a bow tie. Mrs. Cohen also wore a suit and carried a handbag. They were city people and indeed, when they entered the foyer of the modern parsonage, they exclaimed at the amount of empty space!

"Our townhouse in Brooklyn is crowded to the gills!" said Mrs. Cohen.

"Well, you've lived there forever," said Stephen. "My grandparents bought it in the 1920's," he explained.

"Yes, Jacob runs his law practice out of it," admitted Mrs. Cohen.

"This is my sister, Rose," said Mother. "She has just retired from being a grade school superintendent."

"I did get to go to New York once with a girlfriend," said Aunt Rose, inclining her head as she shook hands. "But I didn't get to Brooklyn."

"Best little town on the planet," said Mr. Cohen. "We're very partial to our Senator, Bobbie Kennedy. He's been a real force in our community these last few years. Understands our problems."

"Would you like some coffee," asked Mother. Everyone was on their best behavior, speaking warily to each other.

"Sure, sure," said Mr. Cohen. "Thank you so much for having us on short notice. Never know what these kids are going to do next!" Paul caught his broad wink and hoped that Dad would warm to Mr. Cohen.

Paul wanted to listen to the Cohens talk, so he could hear their unusual accents. But Dad ushered Stephen, Line and the Cohens into his study, where chairs had been arranged. Mother took in coffee and a plate of cookies and closed the door.

Nothing in Dad's experience had prepared him for a wedding like this, he had told Paul. And in fact, it would not be a wedding. Line and Stephen had taken blood tests, gotten their license and had a civil ceremony in Chicago, at Dad's suggestion. The meeting with the Cohens was to go over the words of the blessing of the union Dad had put together.

Much of the Christian wedding ceremony came straight out of the New Testament. For Lutherans, the words spoken at a marriage, like all words, were actions. But marriage was not a sacrament. It was the union of two people in the sight of God. The way in which they lived and raised their children was up to Line and Stephen. There was nothing Mother and Dad could do about that, and there wasn't time for the usual counseling Dad offered new couples. But at least they could meet Stephen's parents and see into whose hands they were commending their daughter.

Aunt Rose, Paul, Kristen and Hanna, left out of the meeting, each had things to do. Paul and Hanna drove to a neighboring town to get hothouse tulips and camellias, which Aunt Rose made into corsages. They also practiced the duet they would sing at the service. Kristen made Mother's usual Sunday dinner, laying chicken breasts on top of Minute Rice, topping them with canned soups, and putting them in the oven to bake.

When everyone emerged from Dad's study, Paul felt a genial mood pervade the house. Dad was at his warmest, Mother her most gracious. By now they knew something about the Cohens and the Cohens knew something about them.

"We do have one thing in common," said Mr. Cohen, touching Dad's back with his hand as they walked out together. "People with the surname Cohen, which means priest, are descendants of the priests that served in the Temple in Jerusalem 2,000 years ago. It's one of the most common Jewish names in the United States."

That night the dining room table was crowded with seven places, Aunt Rose in the place of honor as the oldest person. Paul set up a card table for himself and the two younger girls. He could overhear the grownups talking, but mostly he felt a little left out. There just wasn't room for all of them at one table.

Mr. Cohen described his immigration practice, which involved many Russians and people from Eastern Europe. The Cohens, Jacob and Sima, had met in Brooklyn in high school. Jacob arrived in America as a little kid. Sima's parents also had left Russia.

"After the war, we had a young couple from Estonia staying with us," said Mother, "until they moved further west. I think they ended up in Seattle."

"We could have moved west," said Mrs. Cohen, "But my parents didn't want to leave their friends. My father was a furrier, and he'd heard you didn't need furs in California! So they stayed. And we did too. I couldn't leave them. They went through so much to get here. But Stephen now, he takes it into his head the neighborhood's too small for him. Decides to go to the University of Chicago!"

"And gets himself in a mess of trouble!" said Mr. Cohen. "But we're proud of him. Stephen's become a real mensch." Mr. Cohen attacked his chicken breast with his knife and fork. "The government needs waking up. And these young people! Think they can take on the Pentagon, no less! Drummed LBJ out of office!"

"What's a mensch?" asked Aunt Rose.

"A mensch is a fine human being," said Mr. Cohen. "Surprises me to say so!" He looked wryly at this wife and then over at Stephen. "Sorry, son," he said. "I do think well of you and what you are doing."

Paul listened in awed silence. The Cohens' Brooklyn accents and talk about the great world made Paul feel that the life he saw on television had stepped off the screen and into their home. Having these worldly guests in their home was a test of the whole Mikkelson family.

"Your candles are like Shabbat candles," said Mrs. Cohen, referring to the two beeswax candles on the table. "Shabbat is our day of rest," she said. "We don't observe Shabbat very strictly, but it is nice to remind ourselves."

"The seventh day," said Dad.

"Yes," said Mr. Cohen. "It starts on Friday evening. We're not even supposed to drive on Shabbat. But then, in New York we hardly ever drive anyway." Paul could hardly imagine being in a place where you didn't need to drive.

Mother asked Hanna and Kristen to serve ice cream after the meal. Kristen didn't need prodding to be respectful and quiet. She sturdily cleared plates and brought them out to the dishwasher. Hanna had managed to keep her small, irrepressible self quiet and contained so far, but asking each person whether they wanted chocolate or vanilla, and whether they wanted a cookie, she turned up her winsome blonde face as if romancing them.

"How can I refuse a little girl like you?" asked Mr. Cohen, his Adam's apple bobbing. "I'll have vanilla, and a cookie."

"She almost looks like a little boy," said Mrs. Cohen in hushed tones while the little girls were dishing ice cream in the kitchen.

Paul smiled. He had thought the same himself, but no one in their family ever said so. He noticed that Stephen didn't say much during dinner, and neither did Line.

Finally, the Cohens left for their motel, leaving Line and Stephen to sleep in the downstairs den. Aunt Rose, Mother and Dad were exhausted and went to bed, but Line said she was too excited to sleep. Paul could not resist staying up with her and Stephen.

Sitting in the dark in the living room, the only light coming from the kitchen, Line's face shone beside Stephen's pale one. But Paul had no idea what to say to them. Line's experience was by this time so far from his own he could hardly imagine it.

"The house is so beautiful," said Line. "I had no idea."

"First new parsonage they've had," said Paul. "But not much of a yard."

"Nothing like Montauk," agreed Line. "Mother said you will sing tomorrow. Thank you! And for coming home on such short notice."

"Sure," said Paul.

"It's your last year at Astoria, isn't it? God, the time goes so fast. I can hardly keep track!" said Line. "What are you doing next year?"

"I'm going up to Trinity College next year, on the Red River," said Paul.

"Wow," said Line. "Maybe you'll get back to Bryson." She turned to Stephen. "I'd love to take you there someday. It's so tiny! We grew up and went to grade school in the wilds of North Dakota." Bryson had been one of Dad's first parishes.

"This town is pretty small, it seems to me," said Stephen.

"Yup," said Paul. "I do intend to go to Bryson. No one's ever been back. Not even Dad." All of a sudden he remembered playing gypsies around the big tree at the back of the schoolyard with Line and Marty, and the day he had finally been able to climb it. "I wonder if the big tree is still there," he mused.

Line sighed. "So long ago," she murmured. "It was a tree in the schoolyard we all loved," she said to Stephen. And to Paul, "It's so weird coming here and not knowing a soul. Do Mother and Dad like this town?"

"I think so," said Paul. "I don't hear them talk about it much. The farming's different than Montauk, more field crops and less livestock. And they are making friends. They've been here almost a year now."

"A year!" said Line. "I have no idea where the time goes."

"You're busy," said Paul. "And your life is completely different. You probably hardly even think of us out here."

Line looked a little stung. "It isn't that I don't think of you," said Line. "I am our family," she emphasized. "I carry you in my heart, in all of my organs. Everything I do has you in it."

"Yeah," said Paul evenly. "I'm sure the same thing will happen to me."

"I was so happy to meet your parents," said Line to Stephen. "It's like they care about family as much as we do! It's such a relief!"

"You can imagine how strange it is for them here," said Stephen. "I don't really think they've been west of New Jersey before! And their neighborhood is a little bit like the south side of Chicago. It was thoroughly middle class and Jewish, but a lot of blacks moved in to work in the big shipyards. Kennedy, as my Dad said, studied poverty in our area and his programs are now being used elsewhere."

Paul listened, fascinated. He hardly knew any black people. He tried to imagine what having a furrier for a grandfather would be like. No one he knew wore furs, which were very expensive.

But to Paul's chagrin, Line turned the attention back toward him, asking him straight out, "Are you going to be a pastor, Paul? At the lake last summer you said something that made me wonder."

"What did I say?" Paul asked, looking down at his hands. He felt like Line was invading. He didn't even ask himself this question. But that was Line. So direct. So willing to get right down to the nitty gritty. And she was right. He was going to have to know soon.

"You said you thought the Lutheran church wasn't 'big enough'," said Line. "I can't remember what it wasn't big enough for."

"I don't know either," said Paul. "I'm trying to be open to the call, but so far it isn't very clear to me."

"Don't do anything until you are sure," said Line. "That's the one thing I've learned. Find what you are most interested in. I love nursing, and no one ever even suggested it to me. I had to find it myself." She stretched and yawned. "Maybe for you it's music," she said suddenly.

"Nah," said Paul. He echoed Line's yawn. "The natural world comes way before that. I'd like to work outdoors more than anything. That's why I want to go up to Trinity. It's almost North country." All around them the silent house breathed and Paul felt himself expanding into the quiet that he loved.

"The North country," said Line. "Wow, Paul. Maybe you've got something there. It's big enough, that's for sure!" She stretched and leaned toward Stephen. "Bed time, my love?" she asked.

On Sunday morning the Cohens walked across the street to the Lutheran church with Aunt Rose and the rest of the Mikkelsons, except for Dad who was already there. Standing up in his white surplice, during the announcements he acknowledged the presence of their honored guests. Afterwards the Cohens took the Mikkelsons to Sunday dinner in a neighboring town. "Just think," Paul heard Mrs. Cohen say to her husband. "A town without a motel or a restaurant. It's amazing."

The service of blessing went off without a hitch as far as Paul could see. He stood up on one side of Stephen and the little girls in their Sunday dresses stood next to Line. Line wore a short cotton dress printed with peach and rose-colored flowers and carried tulips. Dad wore his surplice and gown, with a green silk stole.

Paul noticed that Dad did not invoke the name of Christ or the Trinity of God the Father, Christ the Son and the Holy Spirit as he usually might have. He noted that the solemn union of two people in marriage in the presence of God is meant for their comfort, whether they prospered or not, and that all who witnessed this wedding were bound to love and bless the new family they were undertaking together.

Hanna sang "He's Got the Whole World in his Hands" by herself while Paul played guitar. She and Paul sang "Tell Me Why" together at Mother's suggestion, to remind Line of the times the family sang while traveling in the car. "And I will tell you, just why I love you." Paul took the higher part, blending with Hanna's sturdy little alto. Finally they did "Let Us Break Bread Together on Our Knees." Paul chose the old Negro spirituals because Line and Stephen had met in Alabama. The songs were also large in the national consciousness after Martin Luther King's death.

Stepping back up beside Stephen at the altar, Paul handed Stephen the two gold rings he had been asked to keep in his pocket, and Line and Stephen vowed to love each other until death parted them. They slipped the rings on each other's fingers and Dad said, "Let your love for each other be a seal upon your hearts. Let us pray."

After blessings and prayers, Paul placed the wine glass tied up in a white cloth which Mr. Cohen had given him near Stephen's foot. Stephen smiled at Line and Paul heard the muted crunch of broken glass.

"Mazel Tov!" said Mr. Cohen from his pew. He had explained that there was always some bitterness in life, and that breaking the glass was meant to remind people of this.

"It's bitter, make it sweet!" called Mrs. Cohen. Only she and her husband and Aunt Rose sat in the church pews. Mother was at the organ, ready to play the processional. Stephen kissed Line and they all processed down the aisle to the front of the church.

Mr. Cohen and Dad collaborated on taking photographs. Dad had two cameras which he put on a tripod, one after the other. Mr. Cohen took shots of the wedding party, Paul took some and Dad took others. The photographs would probably look as though it were a normal wedding, guessed Paul, though the bride was not wearing a white dress. No one would know how small it was.

The party was very short because the Cohens wanted to get back to Chicago that night. Mother had found a woman who specialized in wedding cakes. She served the cake with punch at the parsonage. Everyone sat around the living room, watching Stephen and Line open their few wedding presents. But then the Cohens, including Mrs. Line Mikkelson Cohen, got into their rented car and left.

Their leaving left a big hole in the atmosphere at the Mikkelson house. Dad permitted himself one wry comment. "Guess they don't need a honeymoon," he said. "I think they've already had it!"

Mother just looked at him. "I'm glad that went so well," she said gently.

"He looks like a fine young man," said Aunt Rose, "and it's impressive that his parents came all the way from New York."

"I agree," said Mother. "But I am glad it's over! Do you want another cup of coffee, Rose?" The two of them sat down to kibitz about the event.

Paul carried the heavy punch bowl into the kitchen. It was still half full. Kristen was loading plates and cups into the dishwasher with the black Frodo at her feet. Hanna had disappeared.

"Hey, Paul," said Dad, following him. "I want to get up to the lake and plant a few trees yet this spring. Do you want to come with me and open up the place?"

"Sure!" said Paul. He was feeling let down after all the excitement, but Dad was full of energy. Paul knew he must settle down to his books. In clear weather it took about two and a half hours to drive back to school. He would leave after supper and drive in the lengthening spring light.

"Let's see," said Dad. "We could leave on Thursday night, and come back on a Saturday." Everything Dad did had to work around his pastoral schedule. "Confirmation is next week, but the week after would work. How about it?"

"Sure," said Paul. "You know I wouldn't miss a trip up north! That'll give me enough time to arrange my school work." He would say goodbye to Astoria in a few weeks. He felt ready. He had gotten all he could from the school.

When Dad picked Paul up Thursday afternoon at college, he was driving the old Ford Country Sedan station wagon. He was gunning it on the dry highways because he wanted to reach the Badoura tree nursery before it closed that afternoon. It was hours away. Dad had planted trees and shrubs the year before, but he was even more excited this year.

"In about 15 years, your mother and I will retire up to the cabin," Dad said as they drove north. "I've already been thinking about it! Course we'll have to winterize it, but your Mother and I have all kinds of ideas! I want to build a little boathouse near the lake soon, maybe a bird blind out in the woods. We could put a darkroom in the basement, off your room probably," he said. Dad turned off the large highway onto a smaller back road. He knew the route like the back of his hand.

"I found a photographic enlarger at a sale," he said. "There wasn't time to show you when you were home for Line's service, but I've been trying it out."

"We can develop our own photographs?" Paul tried to imagine the possibilities.

"I brought a few along," Dad said. "I'll show you when we get there. We got some great photos of Line and Stephen and the family."

The Badoura nursery was at the edge of a big state forest just south of Lake Michigami. It had been started in the 1930's to promote the planting of native trees and shrubs. Dad needed no encouragement. He wanted to control erosion on the hillside which dropped down to the lake below the cabin. He also planted along the boundaries of their land, making privacy between the cabins. Trees provided cover and food for the wildlife he wanted to attract as well.

At the nursery, the minimum order of bare root seedlings was 500. "Looks like we've got our work cut out for us," Dad said as they loaded the boxes into the back of the station wagon. He had ordered white pines, spruces and birch, all of which did well in their wet, sandy soil. For the hillside, there were fast-growing caragana shrubs, which had a pod-like seed and yellow peaflowers in the spring.

As they went further north, the trees rose majestically on every side. The great winter hush of snow was gone, and the lush, wet land that it left was warming up, thick mats of green undergrowth beginning. Moving up through the trees was like a processional in a cathedral. Dad and Paul became increasingly quiet.

At last they reached the gravel road which led off the main highway around the lake. The tires squished over the wet sand and Paul opened his window to let in the intoxicating smell of pines and the thick humus under the trees, undisturbed all winter. Dad drove slowly and the two of them looked hard out the windows to see what they could see.

"Not many people up here this time of year," said Dad. A few wooden signs pointed down driveways to people's cabins deep in the woods, but the big silver Mikkelson/Bakken mailbox had been taken down. Dad drove down the two ruts that were the driveway to the cabin and parked. The air was cold and damp as Paul got out. It was twilight and tiny leaves quivered on the birches and poplars. As always, the first thing they did was take the path which switchbacked down the hill to the lake.

The lake was high, brushing up against the trees at its edge. Paul put his hand in to feel how cold it was, knowing the ice had disappeared only recently. "I sure would like to be here to watch the ice break up sometime," he said.

"Yup, me too," said Dad. "Like I said, when we get all snug and retired, we'll get to see the whole year round up here. Can't wait."

Fifteen years, thought Paul. That's a long time to wait. But he didn't say so out loud. The sky stretched far across the lake, azure and lavender toward the west. The south side of a large, freshwater lake was surely one of the best places Paul could imagine from which to observe the world.

Dad began climbing back up to the cabin and Paul followed. Dad turned the key in the lock and they entered the spacious wooden building. Cold and damp lay like a pall over the furniture which had looked so gay last summer. The cabin wasn't insulated at all. When it was built, no one expected to live there all year.

The electricity and gas were on, but the water was not. A valve kept water from entering the cabin during the winter so it wouldn't freeze in the pipes and burst them. Dad connected the electric pump while Paul carried dry wood up and tried to get a fire started in the black iron Ben Franklin stove which now sat squarely in the middle of the big room.

When Dad came up from the basement, he went to the sink and turned on the faucet. Reddish water spit and snorted as it came out of the tap. He let it run, water coming up from the deep well below. "Have a glass," said Dad, pouring one for Paul.

The icy water tasted like iron and other minerals as Lake Michigami was near the Minnesota Iron Range. It was a taste Paul loved. Home. The little thought sneaked into his consciousness. You could have Iowa with its fertile fields and mild people. He much preferred northern Minnesota.

That night, Paul and Dad piled all the blankets they could find on top of their beds. By morning the Ben Franklin was cold and any warm air had leaked out the wooden walls, leaving the cabin as cold as the out of doors. When Dad got up, he put on a warm woolen jacket, turned on the gas and heated water to make coffee and oatmeal. "Have to get to work," he told Paul. "It's the only way to keep warm around here!"

The sun came out and fell hot on Paul's jacket toward the middle of the day. But carting seedlings around in a wheelbarrow and carefully planting them also kept them warm. Paul breathed in deeply as he drilled small holes in the ground with a trowel and carefully inserted the bare roots, tamping new soil around them. The soil was soft, sandy and wet but the sun wasn't strong enough to make it steam.

"Perfect planting time!" sang out Dad. "Couldn't have timed it better!" He walked around, inspecting the springy green fingers of pine and spruce he had planted the year before.

Paul took off his jacket and let the dirt run through his hands. Home, he thought as he smelled it. This is where I want to be.

15

Marty, at the Café Mediterranean in Berkeley, carefully arranged her coffee and bagel at a small marble table near the window. The May sunshine was intense, but a breeze wafted in through the door. Across the street the awning of Marty's favorite used bookstore proclaimed the name: Moe's. Street people hung out in front of it and students passed back and forth. It was hard to tell which was which any more.

Marty wore a dark cotton shift dress she had made the previous summer, fitted around the bust, a dress Irene Magnusson might have worn.

She was feeling pretty in spite of her glasses, her arms bare, dark hair swinging around her shoulders. She felt thinner too. California, the simple, fresh food at the Chertoks, had been good for her.

Deliberately Marty slowed down her movements as she sat down. She stirred sugar and half and half into her coffee slowly with a spoon. Doing this she took herself out of ordinary life for a moment, making a small ritual of her freedom and selfhood. She contemplatively raised the cup to her lips with both hands.

Every day that spring was warm and breezy, but a little ominous. The school year in Berkeley was coming to a close and Marty had not solved the riddle of what she should do next. She would stay in the Chertoks' beautiful, spacious house during the month they were in Europe that summer. But after that, she must move on. The Chertoks wanted Janet, who would be 13 that summer, to grow up and take more responsibility.

Marty thought of Line, now married and pregnant. She wished she could see her, ask her how it felt. Line was certainly getting on with her life. Marty had the vague idea of finding a room in one of the many student apartments in Berkeley. But she must find a job in order to pay for it. By September, she would be a resident of California for a year and eligible for lower tuition at the university. But what should she study?

Marty looked over to find someone was watching her. Had she seen that blonde head before? Perhaps here at the Med? She finished the sweet, buttery bagel, wiped her fingers and pulled from her bag Pasternak's letters to his Georgian friends, a translation Lidia had just gotten.

The Chertoks' Russian backgrounds and interests had influenced Marty greatly. In the previous year, Stalin's daughter, Svetlana Alliluyeva had defected and published her memoirs. The Chertoks also followed the show trial and conviction of Andrei Sinyavsky and Yuli Daniel. They saw it as an end to the thaw in relations with the West Khrushchev had promoted. Was it too late to study Russian?

All of Pasternak's autobiographical writing was now available in translation. Marty chanted his name under her breath together with that of his friends: Pasternak, Akhmatova, Mandelstam and Tsvetaeva. She herself wanted to write, but not now. She was too young, had not lived enough. And she was no poet. Nor scholar, she thought sadly. What could be made of her own odd mix of interests?

Marty felt the eyes of the blonde guy upon her again. He stood up, came toward her and asked, "May I interrupt you?" His mop of hair was longish, curly at the ends, but he was clean-shaven and wore a white button-down shirt with a pair of jeans.

"Of course," said Marty, immediately self-conscious. She had been feeling pretty, but this golden creature made her feel she was pasty white, not tan like a California girl should be.

"It's like you've arranged the space around you," said the young man, pulling a chair backwards to the small marble table and sitting astride it. "It's interesting." Around his shoulder on a strap was a black cardboard, cylindrical case. He took it off and put it beside him on the floor.

Marty looked nonplussed. She took off her glasses, putting them on the table on top of her book. "Interesting?" she managed. The young man looked like some of the well-off students at Oxford, sporty but also languid. Such men didn't usually talk to Marty.

"Sorry," said the young man. "I'm Erik," he held out his hand. "I've seen you here before."

Marty shook Erik's warm, dry hand. The skin on his powerful arm was a warm golden brown against the white of his rolled-up sleeves. "I'm Marty. I do love this place." She looked around.

"Yeah," said Erik, following her glance. "It's great. But I'm not sure exactly why. One of my teachers, I'm an architecture student," he said, "is always asking us to think about how much life there is in a space. Why some spaces have more life than others."

Marty looked around. "It's my bit of freedom, having coffee here in the mornings."

"Freedom from what?" asked Erik, looking at her with slightly mocking eyes.

"From my job," said Marty. "I'm sort of an au pair girl. I live with a family. In a few minutes I have to go pick up the kids from school."

Erik waggled his head, considering, but he didn't look away. "Books about Russians," he said. "Notebooks. Looks like you study too."

Marty looked a little desperate. "I just don't know," she said. "I just don't know what I'm studying." Something about Erik's questions, the intensity that lay just under his indolent pose, made her want to answer him with absolute truth.

"Hmmmm," said Erik. "You'll figure it out. Maybe it's just life."

"Life for certain," said Marty, agreeing. She felt panicked. Was it okay to be talking to this attractive stranger? Shouldn't she be leaving for the school? She put on her glasses and looked at her watch. It was a little early, but she began packing her books into her bag.

"You're a busy girl," commented Erik. "What are you doing Friday night? Want to meet here?"

"Okay," said Marty, mentally scanning her immediate future. "I can do that. I'd like to." She beamed at him, as she stood up, trying to be relaxed and sure of herself. "What time?" she asked.

"Oh, around seven," said Erik. He hadn't moved, was watching Marty.

Something about his gaze relaxed Marty. She breathed deeply and gathered up her things, offering her hand to Erik. "Nice to meet you," she said. "I'll see you Friday night." Or not, she thought to herself. It didn't really matter.

Marty walked out of the Café Mediterranean and down the street, not turning back to see if Erik's eyes followed her, though she felt them. She had met a few men that year, but no one she liked had asked her out. The Chertoks' friends were mostly professors. There were graduate students around, but they were more fascinated by Boris than by Marty. She had also done some anti-war work with Lidia, but she met few single people. She was studious and lonely, but quite happy.

I must find a job, Marty thought as she walked through the beautiful, tree-filled university campus. I can't float around on campuses any longer. There must be a place where people need me, thought Marty.

On Friday, somewhat to her surprise, Erik was waiting for her at the Café Mediterranean. He didn't want to stay there and talk, however. He hustled Marty down the street to his car. "Electric Flag," he said mysteriously. "Come on!" He was wearing jeans and another white shirt with a sweater around his shoulders. He put his hand on Marty's waist as they walked.

Marty had never been to San Francisco by herself. The Chertoks visited the natural history museum and aquarium in Golden Gate park, taking Janet, William and Marty. Another day, they went to the Legion of Honor perched on a cliff above the ocean, a grand building with many white columns and Rodin statues. Marty had the impression there wasn't a lot of art in San Francisco. Nothing like there was in London. She had so little money she didn't dare go to San Francisco and explore, though she thought it could be done on a bus.

Erik's car was a big roomy Plymouth Fury, turquoise blue and a little banged up. "Had it for years," said Erik offhandedly. "I can sleep in the back seat if I want to."

The evening sun glistened on the Bay as the big car lumbered up the freeway and onto the bridge between Oakland and the city. Erik pulled Marty over to him across the big seat. "What you doin' over there?" he asked. He put his arm around Marty's waist and left it there, driving with one powerful brown hand. The high steel girders of the bridge were a triumphal arch leading to glory as they went through a tunnel and the white buildings of the city came into view.

Marty tried to decode Erik's attractive combination of insouciance and arrogance. The crisp East Coast look came from a prep school in Massachusetts, where he had followed his father and brother. But he was from Los Angeles, where his father worked in television. At Berkeley, he was in a five-year architecture program, with one more year to go. "And then what?" asked Marty.

"San Francisco here I come!" said Erik. "I'm sure I can find work. Ain't goin' back to LA, no way!" He had an odd way of slipping into a patois Marty didn't recognize, though he looked like a person who spoke the King's English.

When they got to San Francisco, Marty tried to pay attention, but the streets confused her. Erik tried to turn on to Market, but it was full of construction. "Oops, forgot about BART," he said. Wooden bridges crossing tracks, zebra caution tape and orange and yellow signs littered the street.

"BART?" asked Marty.

"Bay Area Rapid Transit system," said Erik, expertly crossing the street and getting caught in a maze of diagonal streets. "They're building a tunnel deep underground. It'll go under the Bay. They found lots of wooden ships rotting down there."

At last Erik parked at an angle near what looked like a white capitol building. "Lock your door," he said. "Lots of street people around here." He rolled up the windows, grabbed a paper bag from the back seat and drew Marty along the street.

As they crossed Market Street, Erik pointed out how it ran diagonally through downtown, a white wedding-cake sort of building with a clock tower dimly visible in the distance. Lines of people stood along the sidewalk against the building on the other side. A big marquee proclaimed Electric Flag and the Don Ellis Orchestra were playing at the place, the Carousel Ballroom. Erik pulled the two of them into line and Marty had time to notice that most of the people were hippies.

Marty didn't feel too out of place. She was wearing jeans and a white teeshirt under the fawn-colored hooded sweatshirt she had found when Janet was reading *Harriet, the Spy* that spring. Janet had one too and so did William! All of them wanted to look like Harriet.

Harriet even had glasses, which helped Marty. But she was conflicted about them. She wanted to see everything, but Erik was being proprietary as they stood in line. He put his arms around Marty and, pushing her against the white wall of the building with his whole body, gave her a kiss. Marty surrendered, reaching up a hand to take off her glasses. His hard body against hers felt better than anything she could remember. She kissed Erik back and put her glasses in her pocket.

"Need a joint?" asked a surreptitious voice at Erik's elbow.

"Nope," said Erik, turning toward a dark figure. "Got one!"

Suddenly the line began to surge forward, carrying Erik and Marty with it. Near the door, while Erik paid for the tickets, Marty could just see a big purple and green poster with goo dripping down onto the figures of ghouls. The letters "Electric Flag" were made like weird limbs and reminded Marty of a picture in a Dr. Seuss book. Marty felt so out of her depth, she resolved to just be quiet and see what happened.

Erik went very close to the stage and settled them on the floor. The room was filled with acrid smoke which obscured the colored lights on stage. Erik opened the paper bag and took out a bottle of wine. He took a swig and handed the bottle to Marty. Out of a thin, silver cigarette case, he took a rolled cigarette, lit it with a butane lighter and took a deep pull, blowing the smoke up toward the ceiling.

Marty lifted the bottle to her lips. It tasted like the sweet sherry she had drunk in Oxford, under much different circumstances.

"Want a taste?" asked Erik, handing Marty the cigarette.

"I've never smoked," she said.

"It's weed," said Erik. "Just try a taste."

Marty took a small puff on the cigarette and handed it back to Erik. It was hot and nasty in her throat. Who could like such a thing?

"I've got brownies too," he said loudly into Marty's ear. "Just in case we get the munchies." He looked at her significantly.

"I do like brownies," Marty said. "Anything chocolate is fine with me!" She spoke loudly, but the people milling about and music on the amplifiers drowned her out.

A black man and three long-haired white guitar players came out on stage. Everyone stood up and yelled as the black man, in an Afro and dark glasses, began singing blues. "Charlie Allen," said Erik in Marty's ear. How did he know?

The crowd moved toward the stage. Colored lights played over the band, glinting off the guitars, which were tethered to a big bank of amplifiers. People around Erik and Marty were dancing, surging with the music.

Marty loved the dark rhythmic singing. She closed her eyes and let her body follow the music, exploring it. "Wade in the water," sang the vocalist with a dark, rough power. "Who's that young girl dressed in red? Wade in the water. Must be the children that Moses led." In between songs Erik handed her the bottle of wine and she took another drink.

Don Ellis turned out to be a guy playing jazz trumpet, electrified! It was amazing. Feeling a little drunk blurred the outlines of sounds, just as watching without her glasses made things hazy and indistinct for Marty. The trumpet player was trying things out. The crowd stamped and yelled. "They don't get it," said Erik. "This isn't the right place for that kind of music. These people want rock and roll!"

But Marty was beginning to worry that it was awfully late and the third act still hadn't come on. She was feeling nauseous with everyone pressing in on her. When the orchestra left the stage, Marty asked Erik, "Shouldn't we be getting home?"

"Home?" Erik looked at Marty, incredulous. He put his arms over her shoulders. "It's just getting started! Wait 'til you hear Bloomfield!"

Marty looked up at him, realization of what she was doing dawning on her. She had had no idea what he meant when he suggested they go out Friday night. Mentally, she began backtracking. She had told the Chertoks she would be out that night, but they would expect her home late.

"I think the Chertoks might wonder," said Marty. "It's getting pretty late, isn't it?"

"Hey," said Erik, persuasively pulling her toward him. "Didn't you say you were free, white and 21, and all?"

"Yes," said Marty slowly.

"I thought we'd go over to my friend Jamie's house, in the Haight. Big old Victorian. We could go over there, have breakfast, go home and take a shower! Pretty as pie," said Erik, pressing her to him.

"Breakfast?" squeaked Marty.

"Do you want to call your family? Let them know?" asked Erik. "They don't need you for anything do they?"

"Okay," said Marty weakly. "What time is it?"

Erik looked at his watch. "About midnight."

"Midnight!" said Marty. "It's too late to call them!" Pictures of the Chertoks' closed bedroom door, the porch light they would have left on for her flashed in front of Marty's eyes.

"Well, I'm sure they're not waiting up for you," said Erik callously. "They'll get over it if you don't show up." He pulled out his little silver case and took out another joint. Lighting it, he passed it to Marty. "Here, have another toke."

Marty pursed up her lips and drew a little smoke in, coughing. "I'm really feeling sick," she said. "Could we move back?"

They pressed back through the crowd and found places to sit against the back wall near the door, where there was less smoke and more air. Mentally, Marty reviewed her situation. She was fine. The Chertoks didn't really need her. She was certainly old enough to do as she pleased. She didn't want to let them down, but she also really liked Erik. And she was certain she wouldn't be able to find her way home by herself. She was feeling woozy, but the cold night air helped.

"Want a brownie?" asked Erik, pulling a saran-wrapped package out of another pocket. "My roommate made them. There's a little hash in them, but not much."

"Oh my God!" said Marty. "I don't think so." She'd heard about hash. It was even stronger than weed. But she was ashamed of being so resistant to everything. "I'm sorry, Erik," she said anxiously. "This is all new to me." All of a sudden she was afraid she would never see him again.

"It's okay," nodded Erik sweetly. He looked the essence of cool, leaning back against the wall as he smoked, his blonde hair tousled around his face. "I like getting little girls into trouble."

When Electric Flag came on, Erik paid attention, but Marty was feeling overwhelmed. Mad, jigging, dancing people stood between them and the stage. The music, the wild guitar and the heavy duty drumming, seemed to go on forever, with people clapping, whistling and shouting after every song.

"This one's for you," said Erik in Marty's ear as the band started a new song.

On stage, someone was singing. Marty picked out the words. "Groovin' is easy, if you know how, baby, ... it doesn't have to be, so hard on you!"

Erik danced, pointing both hands at her and bobbing his head, "It's easy to see, baby, you're nobody's fool. But you won't be nothing, baby, by staying cool."

How could they have written this song, Marty wondered. It was about her!

At last the band disappeared and people started walking out into the darkness. Erik seemed to be wide awake, but Marty felt like she was in a dream. They found his car and Marty let herself be taken to an apartment somewhere, she didn't know where. Erik's friends let them in and they climbed ornate wooden stairs to a big living room, where people lay around on couches, not talking, just listening to soft music. Green, acrid smoke rose in the air.

"Brownies?" asked Erik, putting the remaining brownies out on a coffee table. Marty was happy to see that some of the people were girls. Long haired girls with long legs stretched out, relaxing. Erik and Marty sat down in the corner of a couch, wrapped around each other and snoozed.

Toward morning Marty woke up. Light fell dustily in between the slits around a dark curtain on the window on one side of the room. She untangled herself from Erik and went looking for a bathroom. She was feeling much better.

The bathroom was off a long hall which led back to a light-filled room. In the mirror, Marty was surprised to see that she looked fine! Tousled hair, but clear, fresh skin, she thought. She still had her bag and her glasses. Whatever had happened last night, she could see that she was okay. And surely she could get home by herself now, if she had to.

Drawn by voices, Marty went back to a big, kitchen where three girls were sitting around a table, drinking coffee. Marty felt ashamed. She didn't know any of them. "I'm Marty," she said hopefully. "I came with Erik."

"Oh, Erik!" said a woman who wore a robe made out of a hand-printed sepia Indian bedspread. "He's one of my oldest friends. I'm Jamie." Jamie waved her hand in the direction of a big gas range. "There's coffee, if you want some."

Marty went over to an open shelf and took down a mug. She poured in a little coffee, trying to be as inconspicuous as possible as she sat down. But she pricked up her ears when she heard the conversation.

"I'm working temp for this office," said one of the girls. Thick eyeliner leaked down onto her pink cheek. She stretched and yawned. She was wearing a short purple velvet dress with black tights and boots. "An insurance company. Boring as hell, but it pays the rent. I really ought to find something better."

"Good tips at my bar," said the third girl, who probably lived in the house, as she too wore a colorful robe over silky underthings. "I like it better than Macy's, that's for sure!"

It dawned on Marty that single young people lived in San Francisco! Jamie said, "I need an aspirin." She left the kitchen and returned with a big, plastic bottle, shaking it. "Anyone want one?" She looked provocatively at Marty.

But Marty shook her head. "No, thanks," she said. "Can anyone work temp?" she asked the girl with the runny eyeliner.

"Sure. All you have to do," she replied, "is go down to the agency, take a typing test and they'll find temporary work for you. I swear, it's easy."

"Do you have to wear a suit and all that?" asked Marty.

"No, no. Just a nice blouse and skirt."

"A short skirt," said the girl who tended bar. "The guys like it. I don't know if it helps at the agency, though."

"What agency," asked Marty. "In the City?" She was already understanding that there was only one City. San Francisco!

"There's a bunch of them," said Jamie. "Look in the yellow pages. Under Employment Agencies."

Wow, thought Marty to herself. If only it were true.

"Those are great boots," said Jamie to the girl with the eyeliner. "Did you get those at Macy's?"

"Emporium," said the girl.

"Good morning sunshine," said Jamie as Erik shambled in from down the hall. She shook the bottle of aspirin at him. "Want one?" He looked sleepy, but very sexy. The tousled look sat well on him, Marty thought. She noticed the girls, except for Jamie who acted like a sister, instantly became self-conscious. She didn't dare show that she was his girl. Was she?

"No thanks," said Erik. He pulled his silver cigarette box out of his pocket and opened it. "Things go better with toke." He lit up a joint and took a drag, passing it to Jamie, who got up to pour a mug of coffee for Erik.

When it reached Marty, she took a small breath off the joint, but its acrid taste hadn't improved. She lifted her coffee mug to her lips and drank, wishing she dared find some milk and sugar. The coffee was hard-edged and bitter.

"Do you have a phone I could use?" asked Marty quietly. She did not like being in anyone's debt, but the Chertoks might be up now and ready to answer. Forces were colliding in her and it didn't feel one bit peaceful. "I need to call Berkeley."

"Sure," said Jamie. "Over there," she waved her hand.

"I'll just be a minute," said Marty. She got on the line and when Lidia picked up the phone she apologized for worrying them, and said she would be home soon.

"One of the tenets I live by," teased Erik. "It's easier to ask forgiveness than to get permission." He speared half a donut from a plate in front of one of the girls and ate it. As the girls giggled, he said, "Oh, was that yours? Sorry!"

"Think you can get by on charm, don't you," said Jamie. "Well, you probably can!"

"Doesn't work in school, though," said Erik, showing some chagrin. "They want you to work! Speaking of which, I've got some drawing to do. Guess we better get going."

Jamie put her arms around him as they left. "Don't be a stranger, Erik," she said. Had she been his girlfriend, Marty wondered. Probably.

As they drove out of town, Erik asked, "Got time to check on a building I'd like to show you?"

Marty felt sardonic. In for a penny, in for a pound, she thought. It couldn't be much worse. "Sure," she said. She couldn't fathom the rough maze of streets they traveled, crossing Market and into what seemed to be the thick of the downtown. I'll have to get a map, Marty thought. She loved maps.

"It's just been built," said Erik, "by Skidmore, Owings and Merrill." He parked on an empty street and took Marty up steps to get to a wide plaza a floor above the street. Across the cement plaza was a tall dark building with trusses making x's across its sepia-colored glass face. "That's the seismic structural bracing. For earthquakes," said Erik.

The building was huge, but looked cool and simple. They walked toward it, past a fountain of splayed out pipes. Water poured from each of them making it look like a big dandelion head, ready to blow. Marty drew her hand through the water.

An open passageway allowed them to walk right beneath the building, still above the street level. Acres of grey stones set in cement formed the walkways. Beneath the building were smoothly carved marble and alabaster animals. Monumental, but intimate.

"Benny Bufano," said Erik. "Come on." They came to a green square of grass, surrounded by stone steps. In the middle was a bronze horse with its neck straight and stiff. In fact it wasn't really a head, just a suggestion. A balcony walkway over the street below led to housing. They paused on the bridge over the street, looking up the straight street climbing a hill, shiny in the sun with little parked cars glinting on both sides.

On the far side, walkways went between brilliant white townhouses set off by garden squares planted with grasses and weeds, and pools of water lined with stones. "It looks Asian," said Marty. "It's beautiful." The buildings made her feel hushed and expectant, looking all around her.

"Sort of Mediterranean too," said Erik. "I'd love to live here. Definitely a Pacific influence, but we live in this Mediterranean climate. Couldn't be better."

Marty looked at him, standing there in the sun. There was no hint of the stoned, hip persona now. What a set of contradictions he was.

When they got to the Chertoks' house in Berkeley, Erik went to the front door with her and introduced himself to Lidia. He turned on the charm and took the blame for keeping Marty out overnight. "I thought she knew what going to San Francisco might mean," he said. "But I guess she didn't."

"I know what San Francisco is like," said Lidia knowingly. She looked approvingly at Marty's catch. "We're just finishing a late brunch. Want to join us? I think there are bagels and lox left."

Erik looked at Marty beaming. "Sure," he said. "Sounds great!"

16

A thick canopy of leaves hanging from trees in the backyard made Line's Chicago flat very pleasant in the summer. She and Kay Freeman drank iced tea on the balcony porch, which looked out on the lawns and softball fields of a schoolyard. Kay was older than Line by at least six years, and she had just had a baby son, much to Line's delight.

"You guys really need to get out more," said Kay sympathetically in the low, guttural voice that Line loved.

Line was working evening shifts on an obstetrics ward at the Cook County hospital, which allowed her to have Kay over on a Thursday morning. She sighed. "I know," she said. "I want to, but Stephen isn't Bernie. Stephen is swayed by these younger movement guys who are getting so impatient."

"I know them," said Kay. "They're desperate to have some influence on the convention." The Democratic convention would be held in their very own city, only a few days away. Line had hardly seen Stephen for weeks. He was manning phones for the hundreds of people who were pouring into the city, training marshals for the protest marches they expected and working on printed materials as he always did.

"They will," said Line. "Of course they will. I just hope Stephen gets home in one piece!" Protests had become increasingly violent since the death of Martin Luther King in April and Bobby Kennedy in June. Everyone was losing patience. Line did not have to indicate her big belly to Kay.

"You see," said Kay. "All the more reason to get out to movies or restaurants. Round out your life. Tough things will happen to all of us, but worrying about them is not going to help."

"Of course you're right," said Line. But what both women knew and neither of them said, was that Line, married only five months, had much less ability to influence her husband than Kay, who had already been married ten years. Line and Stephen were being tested in the fires of their new marriage, great civil unrest and the immanent birth of their first child. The uncertainty hung in the air, almost palpable.

Kay tried to cut through it with the air of an elder sister. "Don't worry, my girl," she said. "How are you feeling physically?"

Line relaxed. It was good to have Kay to talk to. "Wonderful! I've been surprised at how peaceful and good I feel. So contented. I was born for this, I know."

"I'm so glad," said Kay. "Little Abe is utterly worth the pain. But I'm not sure I'm made for it. I'd rather be in a lab or a classroom!" Kay was working on a degree in biology. "But having children is part of having a balanced family, and I was nominated!"

"I have to wear Supp-hose at work now," said Line, "to keep my varicose veins from acting up." She reached down and smoothed her bare legs with her hands. "They do help," she said.

"Yeah, I heard," said Kay. "On your feet all evening. I admire you."

Line saw Munchkin, her black and white cat, off in the distance, stalking something. She laughed. "It's so funny," she said. "All of us in our little white uniforms, pretending to be so professional, when really we're just rats in a maze, trying to help out the other rats. But I like being an animal. Don't you?"

"A mammal," said Kay, "definition: usually a warm-blooded, hairy vertebrate which suckles its young. But not always. Whales are mammals too."

"I've seen so many births now," said Line. "They're all different, but all the same."

"What's strange," said Kay, standing up, "is that I felt like I gave my body up to others. Poked and prodded by everyone. And it's still true. Now I feel like I belong to Abe." She went back into the apartment, where Abe slept in a little bassinette.

Line stood up too. "Want some more tea?" she asked. She had filled a pitcher with ice cubes, sugar and slices of lemon as her Southern friends had shown her.

"Sure!" said Kay, letting her sleeping baby lie. She settled back down in a lawn chair, looking out over the green playing fields and trees. Far away, someone was cutting the grass with a mower. "I'll get Stephen to take you to *2001*," she said. "It's a great movie. In Cinerama! It's weird, but thought-provoking."

"Not this week, I don't think," sighed Line, returning with the pitcher. "I'm going to the rally at the coliseum, but I'm afraid to go on any marches."

"When are you due?" asked Kay.

"First week of November, right about election time," Line said. "Fine time for a new baby, isn't it." There was an edge of bitterness in her voice.

"Believe me," said Kay. "We talked about this a lot before we had Abe. But we're not getting any younger and we believe. All of this ferment is shaking up those old boys in Washington. Things are better for me than they were for my parents, and I'm sure they'll be even better for Abe." Kay smiled ruefully. "How's that for a pep talk!"

"Good!" said Line. "I don't really need convincing. I'm really pretty happy!"

"The good thing is, we can choose when to have kids now," said Kay. "Although, I know your little girl or guy is something of a surprise!" Bernie and Kay were Stephen's main mentors and confidants. They had surely been in on helping him decide to marry Line.

"I think he or she just wanted to be born," said Line. "Put up quite a fight!"

"After the convention," said Kay. "I'll make sure Bernie leans on Stephen. There'll be time for you guys to go out then."

Line didn't say what she was thinking. Lack of money also made the beginning of her marriage difficult. In the summer, Stephen depended on the small sum his parents sent him as an allowance. SDS tried to pay him $10 a week, but couldn't always. Line's income from the hospital was the major portion of their money, and she was saving as much as she could against the time she would not be able to work. At least by that time Stephen would be back on the university payroll, working as a teaching assistant.

They didn't need much. Line felt rich in culture and the Mikkelson family had never been well off financially. But she hated to admit to friends that she had no money to do anything but pay rent, take the bus to work and eat. She was using the food co-ops and all of her ingenuity to eat healthily for herself and the baby.

"Thank you," said Line, shyly. "I look forward to it." Line didn't like feeling humble. She wanted to feel equal to her friends. "Are you going to march next week?"

"Oh yes," said Kay, "get little Abe started off on the right foot! He's still small enough to carry." She looked back into the room where Abe slept. "He's been such a good baby." Kay stood up. "I should be getting home," she said, collecting her things. "I must admit I'll be glad when the convention leaves town and we can get back to normal life!"

"Normal life!" said Line, laughing. "What's that?! I'd really like to see some of it!" She brought the pitcher and the glasses into the tiny kitchen. Following Kay to the door, she put her arms around her. "Thank you Kay for all your influences," she said, her heart full.

"I'm happy for you, Line," said Kay in a low, resonant voice. "Take good care of yourself."

Line could hear hidden messages in this. Kay knew much more about Stephen and what was going on in the movement than she did.

When Line arrived home at 11:30 p.m. after her hospital shift, Munchkin curled his body around her tired legs as she unlocked the front door. He could get out the back and jump down from the balcony into the gardens and school yards below, but he couldn't get back in. Line picked up the cat and buried her nose in his fur. At least he was home to welcome her, though Stephen wasn't.

Line felt she hadn't talked much to Stephen in weeks. Who knew where he was. She had given up asking, seeing the warning look on Stephen's face. "Don't push me," it said. "I've done what you wanted, now let me do my thing." She was sure he wasn't telling her everything, protecting her.

The tiny apartment was on a floor above a basement and didn't get a lot of light. It was protected from the great heat of the day, but when Line was gone, stuffiness built up. She opened the door to the hall so the night air could blow through from the open door to the balcony at the back. She checked Munchkin's food and water and watched him settle on the daybed, wrapping his lithe body into a curled ball.

Line turned off the lights and sat in the old wooden rocker she had found at a second hand store. It was hard to calm down after a shift at work and coming home on the noisy el train. Late at night the train was full of black faces coming to their homes on the South side. Hyde Park was surrounded by the black ghetto. Line was used to it, but there was always some edge of tension. She was a woman and she was white. Would some guy, black or white, prey on her? Line was quick and purposeful when she walked.

Line put her hands around the little body growing inside her and rocked. The open doors allowed her to hear the low drone of television coming up from Mr. Pickett's place. Mr. Pickett owned the building and lived in the basement.

A lullaby crept into Line's head and she sang softly to herself, "Go tell Aunt Rhody, go tell Aunt Rhody. Go tell Aunt Rhody, the old grey goose is dead." Line wondered to herself how this sad song had become a lullaby. Maybe because of its simple, quiet melody. She thought she heard Mother singing it to her, or maybe Aunt Rose. "The one she's been saving, the one she's been saving, the one she's been saving to make a featherbed." It was comforting to have the thought of Mother with her.

Line did not even want to know what was going on with the movement. When she had last seen the leaflets and books piling up on tables around someone in a park, one sign among many said, "Smash monogamy!" Stephen may have wanted to do that, Line thought. She imagined him with a girl, maybe the sweet blonde Allison, a privileged young girl who knew Spanish and wanted to go to Cuba. Allison was free, unencumbered. Green-eyed monsters grew in Line's insides, eating away at her peace.

Other things too had been bothering Line. Extra jars of Vaseline, a stack of red bandanas and a pair of goggles appeared. What was Stephen planning? She stood up. She would never get to sleep this way.

Line shut and locked the front door. She drank a glass of water from the kitchen tap and lay down on the bed she and Stephen shared. Sleepy and heavy, her body lulled itself. Line remembered the hot nights she and Stephen had gone out and sat on the point at the edge of the lake all night with their neighbors. She hoped Stephen wasn't out there tonight.

Later, deep in sleep, Line heard a key turn in the lock. After some water running sounds, Stephen slipped into bed beside her. Holding Line tightly, he stroked the bulge at her middle. "How's my baby?" he asked.

"Your baby?" asked Line.

"You, my Line," Stephen said. "You're my baby. How are you?"

"I'm fine," said Line sleepily. And she was.

Convention week was hot and wild, the streets full of people as Line tried to get to work. She conserved her strength, as the hot weather was hard on her and she didn't want to trouble the baby growing inside her. At night she took Munchkin into her lap, and turned on the small black and white television Stephen used to find out what was happening in the outside world. It looked as though Mayor Daly's riot squads were everywhere and protesters challenged them against the backdrop of the convention meetings.

Stephen had told Line SDS wanted to get the attention of the "children's crusade" which backed Eugene McCarthy. "There is a system — call it imperialism — that must itself be challenged," they wrote on the big newspapers posted everywhere called the *Street Wall Journal*. Stephen was in the thick of it, marshalling attention, posting news, setting up meetings and rallies, moving quickly about the city he knew so well.

When Stephen came home for a shower and fresh clothes early Monday morning he told Line that all day long Grant and Lincoln parks were full of workshops, tables full of books and pamphlets, and speakers on all kinds of topics. "You'd love the brown bread people are baking in coffee cans. Looks like a mushroom when it comes out, so delicious," Stephen told Line, knowing her weakness for good bread. He slathered peanut butter on their own bread and stuck the sandwiches in his backpack.

Line, sitting in the rocker, watched. "Bring some apples with you," she told him. "You can't live on peanut butter!"

"Your friends from the Medical Committee on Human Rights are here," Stephen said, meaningfully. Line had worked with the MCHR in Selma, where the two of them met, only a few years ago.

"I'd love to see them," said Line plaintively. "But I have to work!"

"I'm glad you have to work," said Stephen evenly. "I'm glad you're not out on the street these days."

"Or nights," said Line pointedly. She knew as well as Stephen that the city, between Mayor Daly, intent on cracking down while the Democrats were in town, and movement people, intent on action, was a tinderbox.

"We can't get permits to march and curfews are set," said Stephen. "It doesn't look good. Streets near the amphitheater where the Democrats are meeting are sealed off." He swung his backpack over his shoulder and came over to Line. "But don't worry," he said, kissing Line's forehead. "The crowd is so huge, it isn't likely to be me who gets busted up."

Line lumbered out of the rocker and reached her arms around him. "Lenore and I are coming to the rally on Tuesday," she said. SDS and the Mobe, a national committee to end the war in Vietnam, had contracted the coliseum to have an Unbirthday Party for LBJ. Line's former roommate Lenore had moved out when Line and Stephen married, finding herself another place to live in Hyde Park.

"Good plan," said Stephen. "But it'll be a huge crowd. I might not see you. Promise you'll hang to the back and not get in trouble."

"We will," said Line as they walked to the door. Line wondered what else he had in his little backpack. Protection against teargas probably, and who knew what else.

At the rally, Lenore and Line laughed at the antics of Abby Hoffman and the yippies, nominating Pigasus, a young, pink pig, for president and bringing him out on stage. "We demand that Pigasus be given Secret Service protection and be brought to the White House for his foreign policy briefing," said Jerry Rubin, his arm in a cast from street fighting the night before.

Line was thrilled to see Dick Gregory, a black comedian, who was running for president as a write-in candidate. He had been an activist for years, turning stereotypes to comedic advantage. In June he had gone on a hunger strike in jail in Washington State and had been sent to a hospital when he got down to 135 pounds, too weak to move. But there he was, tiny on the stage in front of the huge audience in the vast coliseum.

People are small, Line thought. She was near the back of the auditorium, but microphones allowed her to hear everything. On television, and sometimes in movies, you saw huge heads hanging like expressive clouds in front of you, their eyes wide, looking directly at you. But very few people got this kind of close-up.

When Phil Ochs took the microphone, Lenore stood up, her red hair hanging down her back. Ochs' sweet singing, all lonesome up on stage with his guitar, was very romantic. Lenore leaned down to speak in Line's ear: "That's the revolutionary I'd like to take home," she said. He looked clean cut in a white shirt and sportcoat, his longish hair swept to the side.

"Sit down!" said someone in back of them, but Lenore wouldn't. Line wished she could see Phil Ochs better. "Call it 'Peace' or call it 'Treason,' Call it 'Love' or call it 'Reason,' But I ain't marchin' any more, No I ain't marchin' any more," he sang. All across the big, barn-like structure, people stood up, holding up their right hands with two fingers extended in a victory sign. Tears came to Line's eyes as she stood up too, raising her hands for peace.

Stephen was somewhere up front. Line saw him at the side of the stage now and then. After the rally, she and Lenore took the train home.

"I ain't marchin' any more either," said Line to Lenore. "I need to take care of this baby."

"Right on," said Lenore, as they came down the steps of the el into the brightly-lit train station. "I'm going to see if Mr. Pickett is still up."

When Line woke up in the morning, no one was beside her. She was wringing wet from sweat and worry. She drank coffee out on the balcony under the peaceful shade of the trees and vowed not to turn on the television. At 2 p.m., she put on her hospital whites and took the el train to the stop where she usually got off for work. She threaded her way through the afternoon crowds, and took a bus to the hospital.

At the nurses' station, when Line appeared in her stiff white hat, her hair pinned high on her head, a distraught father complained that his wife almost had her baby in their car. They had been held up at every turn by crowds. "Two bridges sealed off! What do I care who they elect!" he said intensely. "Where are the police who can help me? Protect me? They're all lined up in riot gear at Grant Park!"

It was hard to know what the man wanted, what his complaint was. "Your wife is all right now, isn't she?" Line asked, trying to calm him. "She's here in the delivery room?"

"She's here," the father said belligerently. Sweat stains were visible under the arms of his sport shirt and he seemed to take up the whole room. "I hope she's okay."

"I'll go check," said Line, looking at the charts in front of her. "Mr. Tobiasz?"

Hot, stuffy air filled the hospital. Up and down the corridors, heat hung like a fog. Sweat dripped down Line's back.

In the delivery room, a noisy fan tried to dispel the heat. But there, in a pool of sweat, lay Mrs. Tobiasz, dark sweaty hair swirled on her pillow, with a tiny baby on her chest. Dr. Anderson was cutting the baby's umbilical chord.

"What a lot of dark hair that little guy has," said Line admiringly.

"It's a little girl," said Dr. Anderson.

"Can I tell her father?" asked Line. "He's out at the nurses' station, upset." Mrs. Tobiasz seemed rather out of it, her eyes glazed over.

"Sure," said the nurse in charge. "She'll be in her room in half an hour, after we've had a chance to clean her up."

At the nurses' station, Line explained. "You've got a little daughter, Mr. Tobiasz. With lots of dark hair!"

Mr. Tobiasz threw his hands up in the air and then knelt on the floor, "Ah, thanks be to God and to the Virgin. Ah, my little Paulina. Thank you, thank you," he said.

"Paulina?" asked Line.

"Her name's Paulina," said Mr. Tobiasz. He clasped his hands and stood up, his presence becoming smaller. He went over to the chairs in the waiting room and proceeded to pray, his body rocking back and forth.

Toward evening Line took a break. She walked out into the street to get some air and stood silently watching as cars drove up to the emergency entrance, divulging people with bloodied heads and broken bones. Bloodied policemen also got out of squad cars.

Interns with stretchers rushed out to meet the cars, but many people hobbled in by themselves, their friends holding them up. Line thought she saw Kay Freeman driving one of the cars. "Oh my God," Line thought to herself. As soon as a car was emptied it rushed off into the twilight. "Is this a war zone?" Line wondered, stricken. Policeman standing by arrested one bandaged man as he limped out of the hospital.

In the lobby of the hospital, a television was on, tuned to a quiz show. As Line watched, the news broke into the show. Near the Hilton Hotel, students waved their hands in the air, chanting "the whole world is watching, the whole world is watching," as club-swinging, Mace-spraying policemen dove into the crowd. Line saw a man with a Red Cross armband clubbed and kicked down.

On television, it looked like a window of the hotel broke and photographers, policemen, and protesters raced through the shards of glass into a bar off the Hilton lobby, scattering drinkers, breaking more glass. Jumpy cameras registered the chaos.

But Line couldn't watch any more. Tense and exhausted, she took the elevator back up to the obstetrics ward. In her mind, she was with Stephen, wondering where he was and if he was getting hurt. But she must go back to work.

At the end of that long shift, Line couldn't wait to get home. She rushed off the train and over to South Harper. The flat was empty. She went down the stairs to Mr. Pickett's, where she was not surprised to find Lenore sitting on the couch, dipping her hand into a bowl of potato chips.

"They've finally done it," said Mr. Pickett in a stagy whisper. The sound on the television was playing very low.

Hubert Humphrey, his jowly face animated and huge on the screen, was accepting the nomination of his party, banners waving and balloons rising around him.

"Well, that's that," said Lenore, flatly. Like Line, she was an LPN. Politics didn't mean that much to her. "Life goes on, I guess," she said, looking up at Line.

"Have either of you heard anything about Stephen?" asked Line hopefully.

"Not a thing," said Mr. Pickett, dancing around the apartment. "Sure was a night, though. Riots on television! Dan Rather got punched in the stomach!"

"Oh God," said Line. If that had happened to Dan Rather, what on earth had happened to Stephen! She didn't hear herself swearing any more, though Dad had pointed out in a recent telephone call that she was. Taking God's name in vain. It seemed justified, under the circumstances.

"Well, you were at the hospital," said Mr. Pickett. "Did you check to see if he was admitted?" He seemed exhilarated by the fighting.

"No," said Line. "I didn't think to. I'm more worried he's in jail."

"Well, don't worry," said Mr. Pickett. "I'm sure he'll turn up soon."

Line went upstairs and fell into a fitful sleep. She was exhausted.

Stephen had indeed been arrested. He had a black eye and was covered with bruises when he arrived home at 5 a.m., waking Line. He seemed pleased, however, hardened, wearing his wounds with pride. He was charged with endangering public safety, disorderly conduct, mob action, and resisting arrest, but had been bailed out by other SDS members with funds set aside.

"It's not the first time," Stephen told Line, peeling off his shirt to reveal taped ribs and blue and red patches of blood veins rising on his skin. "But, it's the best."

"Did they get your kidneys?" asked Line, her face ashen.

"Some," Stephen said. "I don't remember. They don't stop after they've got you. They keep going!" He flopped limply on the bed.

"Bastards," said Line softly. She took ice out of the ice cube trays and put it in plastic bags, bringing them to Stephen. He held one up to his eye.

"When did it happen?"

"In the afternoon," said Stephen. "After we lost the peace plank and this kid climbed up the flagpole. We lost Rennie. I don't know where he is. After we got bailed out, I went over to the office where they were making the daily wall poster. It's a good one! People are fed up."

Stephen fished in his jeans pocket and pulled out a wad of notes with his other hand. "Lost my backpack," he said. "But I got this!" He read triumphantly from the notes with his good eye: "Those of us who have been in the streets for the past five days don't care whether McCarthy wins or loses. Now that's he's lost, we still don't. Only the youth of America and the Vietnamese will stop the war in Vietnam; and only the youth and the black people of America will create the new life. This, not a liberal Senator's political career, is our struggle."

Stephen put down the grubby piece of notepaper, his face shining. "It's just the beginning, Line," he said.

Line could not help it. She turned away.

17

"Could you hand me that level, Paul?" yelled Dad. "I just dropped it."

Paul saw the steel level with its two bright yellow-green inset liquids in the dry leaves at the base of the concrete foundation. Above, Dad was framing out a small, almost square room he called the "beach house," built near the shore of Lake Michigami well below the family cabin. Paul retrieved the level and handed it up to Dad.

It was a blowy day and tree branches shimmered and belled out like sails around them. Whitecaps rose on the crests of the waves below on the lake and the sounds of wind and water were loud. Leaves shook against each other in the birches and in the taller pines the boughs heaved and soughed under a low cloud cover.

Paul felt exhilarated by the wind as he stood on the woodsy bank, handing up two-by-fours to Dad. He couldn't think of anywhere he would rather be. The smell of the new wood wasn't as strong today. It took heat and sun to bring it out.

They had laid the floor of the little house on a cement block foundation, and now Dad was establishing the frame which would hold up the walls. Inset into the hillside, the building would have a place to store boats and tackle beneath it, while making a room above for sleeping or observing birds and wildlife. Dad had helped his father do construction work during the summers between college and seminary study. There was little about building that Dad didn't know.

The noise of the wind kept Paul and Dad from talking as they worked. Paul loved Dad's observations, but he was beginning to find differences in the ways they related to the world. When Dad came up to the lake he was so full of ideas he couldn't rest, and neither could Paul! Paul preferred contemplation, observation. He wanted to just be in nature, but Dad was always moving, planning, working. He took Mother on canoe trips in the evenings, or went for a swim in the lake, which was calmer and warmer in the evenings than it was all day. But during the day there was "no rest for the wicked," as Dad often said!

"Did you have to be so wicked then?" Paul said wryly. He didn't usually try to tease Dad, whom he regarded with the greatest respect.

Dad gave back an ironic, complicit smile, but he didn't say anything.

Paul, again this summer, had been co-opted by Mother to stay at the lake while Dad was away and help with the beach house when Dad came up. Paul was perfectly happy with the arrangement. There were no great summer jobs for him. In the fall he would leave for Trinity College, which was a hundred miles west of the lake

Paul held studs in place as Dad carefully toenailed them into the base with long nails. "Start them straight," he told Paul. "Get the point in. Then you can find the angle." He showed Paul how he started the stud about a quarter inch out from where he wanted it, allowing for the hammer hits, and braced his toe against the stud. The sound of the hammer rang out against the rushing wind.

"Ok," said Dad. "I'm ready for another one." Paul brought over one of the two-by-fours they had carefully measured and sawed off, placing it at the pencil marks they had made on the base.

At last they heard the cowbell calling them to lunch. It brought Kristen up from the lake, where she had been throwing sticks into the choppy waves for the black Labrador retriever Frodo. Paul had found that, even when exhausted, Frodo would still leap into the frothy lake after a stick, thrashing and shaking water everywhere as she climbed out onto the dock.

Inside the cabin, Hanna sat cross-legged in front of a shoebox she and Aunt Rose had made into a theater with tiny figures for King Arthur, Guinevere and Lancelot. "I wonder what the king is doing tonight," she sang gravely to herself. Mother had indulged her by purchasing the *Camelot* LP that came out that year and Hanna knew every song by heart. "How goes the final hour as he sees his bridal bower being regally and legally prepared?" she sang in the exact nuances and rhythms of Richard Harris.

Paul smiled at her as he washed his hands. Did she know that the love between Lancelot and Guinevere was illicit? Paul doubted it.

"Well, Humphrey was nominated at last," Aunt Rose greeted Dad and Paul. She had brought a television up that year, to watch the news. The signal wasn't strong in the under-populated North Woods and "snow" covered the screen, obscuring the picture. No one could watch it long.

"I guess no one is surprised," said Dad.

"No," said Aunt Rose. "McCarthy conceded late last night. Lots of demonstrations still."

"You didn't see Line on television, did you?" asked Dad.

"No," said Aunt Rose. "I'm sure she's taking care of herself. That baby must be getting big!" She looked across at Mother, as if they had been talking.

The baby was due in November, Paul knew. If he were watching television, he thought, he'd be looking out for Stephen.

Aunt Rose and Mother laid out the lunch food, smoked whitefish from Morey's Fish House in Motley, cold cuts, sliced tomatoes, lettuce and pickles for sandwiches. Morey's was far from the lake, but Dad had brought a delicious freshwater fish, Northern pike, smoked to perfection so they could eat it cold. Regal in its brown paper, the delicately-flavored fish rarely lasted more than a day or two.

"I was wondering," said Aunt Rose, "whether you could rig the antenna of the television a little better, Carl. I'd really like to watch the Twins' games!" She looked conspiratorially over at Paul, knowing he listened to the Twins on the radio. The Twins weren't having a good season, but you never knew. Paul's favorite, Harmon Killebrew had ruptured a hamstring in the All-Star game and was out for the season.

"Sure," said Dad. "I'll try." Everyone had ideas about what Dad could fix or build when he came up.

Paul basked in the relaxed homey-ness of the cabin. Six people sat down to lunch, the most they would have at one time that summer. Paper rustled, milk was poured. Paul made himself a sandwich.

At the screen door stood the tall shape of Uncle David, who had walked over from his beautiful log cabin next door. Built by a company with special machines to strip and mill logs to exact matches, the cabin had a sleeping loft and a large stone fireplace. Paul thought it the epitome of cabin perfection.

"Hello!" Uncle David called. "Thought I'd catch you all together. Share a barbecue tonight?" he suggested. "It's just the three of us." His three older daughters were off living their lives, but his son Matthew, halfway between Paul and Kristen in age, was with them.

"Sure," said Aunt Rose to her younger brother, who taught at the Lutheran seminary in St. Paul. She looked toward Dad. "Shall we start the fire about 5 p.m.?"

Mother beamed impishly at Uncle David, who most embodied the wry Norwegian looks and character of their mother. "We got peaches yesterday," she said, "which means we are making your favorite pies!" The early loss of their father bound Mother, Rose and David tightly. Mother had been only seven when he died.

"If you're making pie, I'll be over earlier!" Uncle David left without coming into the cabin.

Paul's memory called up the taste of Mother's pie, peaches steeped in brown sugar and butter. There hadn't been ripe peaches for a year.

"Can we have S'mores tonight?" Hanna asked, turning up her small winning face. "Even if we have pie?"

"Not tonight Hanna," said Mother gently. "Peach pie will be sweets enough."

As Paul finished lunch he thought longingly of the book Mother had said he would like. It was down in the basement, lying on his bed. How nice it would be to curl up with a book for a while.

But Dad was raring to go! "Come on Paul," he said. "Let's see if we can finish that framing today." It was true that Dad only had a week of vacation. They must finish the beach house before they left the lake, as it would sit under deep snow all winter.

By evening, the wind had died down considerably. The light of August evenings left more quickly than it had in June. Paul already felt the hint of the dark and cold to come. After the barbecue, he went down to the dock, feeling how short the time at the lake was, how many sunsets he had already missed.

Above him, smoke from the wood coals wafted on the breeze as Matthew and Kristen heated green stick wands in the fire and trailed them about. Their parents had retreated to the screened porch off Uncle David's log cabin to have a cup of coffee.

Paul wondered how long it would take Hanna to figure out that he had brought the guitar down to the dock! He played a few, tentative chords. Music, voices, everything carried over the still lake. Paul was shy, but he couldn't help strumming as he watched the sun go down. He was experimenting to see whether he could actually do both at the same time.

The sun blazed a trail directly toward Paul on the water, setting more to the south on the horizon than it had in early summer. Paul played a piece of Ecclesiastes turned into a folk song, now famous. "To every thing, turn, turn, turn, there is a season … and a time to every purpose under heaven." The chords were easy, C, F, G with a few minor chords thrown in. Hanna appeared just as the sun went down in a pink haze.

Hanna knew the words to this song too, of course. Her memory for songs was amazing. Her appearance made their duet public. Paul suspected Dad, Mother, Uncle David and Aunt Eileen listened from the screen porch above. "A time to get, and a time to lose; a time to keep, and a time to cast away." Hanna just liked to sing, standing on the dock as if on stage, her face warmed by the reflected evening light, her legs brown and sturdy.

When they finished, Paul said, "A time to watch the sunset," stopping. He acknowledged to himself he couldn't really sing, play and watch at the same time. He strummed a few chords as Hanna sat down beside him.

The afterglow of gold and peach on the underside of the clouds left trails of, there was no other word for it, glory. Reflected in the expanse of the glassy lake, the color made Paul ache for the fact that he would soon be stuffed into buildings again, following routines of classes and meals that did not let go. The call of a loon echoed over the water, sadly now, Paul thought. Was he being sentimental, anthropomorphizing the world to match his feelings? The picture of stern old Mr. Johnson in his greenhouse back at college came to him. Mr. Johnson insisted Paul observe precisely, see everything he could, find words to write down what he saw. Like Darwin did on the Beagle.

"That purple cloud looks like a magician," said Hanna.

"Yeah," said Paul. "I see it."

"That's his hat, like Gandalf," said Hanna, stretching out her hand.

"Yup," said Paul. "Getting kind of flattened." Another loon skimmed the lake on its belly and stopped, a dark silhouette settling beside the other. The color on the lake was fading.

From up above in the trees came Mother's voice. "Come on, Hanna. Bedtime."

Hanna stood up. "I have to go," she said formally to Paul. "Good night."

"Okay, sleep tight. Don't let the bed bugs bite," said Paul. He was excited. Now, at last, he could be alone in the woods. What should he do? A night canoe ride along the shore? Go to bed with his book? Slip along the road to the swamp? The delicious possibilities loomed in front of him as he carried the guitar up to the cabin.

The big dragonflies had eaten up a lot of the insects from early summer. Horse and deer flies were still around, but they were mostly a problem when you were sweaty in the hot sun. Not at night. Paul considered the moon, a waxing crescent, going down in the west already at 9 p.m. It was a clear night and the stars would be bright. A few shooting Perseids would be left, though they peaked a week ago.

Paul slipped the canoe off its mooring on some old rubber tires and into the water. His eyes were used to the available light of the sky. He moved slowly in the shallows along the shore, taking deep drags with the paddle and trying to be as quiet as possible. Chipmunks and squirrels scrabbled along the shore. Up on the hill, lights and people moved, bits of conversation floated down and screen doors swung shut. The lake was at its most populated in August.

Paul breathed in the cool night air, listening. He wondered whether he enjoyed the solitude more because he lived in a family. Probably. He found it easier to think about Hanna and Kristen, Mother, Aunt Rose and Dad, to really see them, when he wasn't with them. Did that go for Line and Marty, he wondered. He would have loved to have one of them in the canoe with him, talking softly. But they were far away. It would never happen again.

Paul headed east, away from the silver crescent. The half light of the hidden part of the moon was almost visible. The Milky Way was thrown out across the sky, all of its pinpoints of light making a dense ribbon. He picked out his favorite summer stars, Arcturus in the Herdsman Bootes, and Vega in the Lyre. They were friends. Nothing could change them. Their movement across the sky was absolutely dependable.

The air grew chill on the water. Paul imagined the hundreds of lakes across the state all still under the sky. No one needed to observe them. They just were, at all seasons of the year. How much effect did the moon have on these lakes, he wondered. There were no tides, as on the great oceans. But gravity must be acting upon them in some way. I need a base, thought Paul, a place from which to watch and measure things.

Though the lake seemed a stable influence, one Paul could count on, it was a summer place and it belonged to Aunt Rose. Dad was slowly building up equity in the property. One day he would insulate it and make it an all-year-round place to retire, as he and Mother wanted.

Mother kept lists of all the birds she saw, and some nature journals, but Paul did nothing. He could not get enough of feeling the air on his skin, the damp smells of humus and pine, the tastes of the iron-laden water, the chitterings of small animals, calls of birds and the wind, the colors and changes on the earth. He felt terribly lucky to be in good health, to be free. And when he was able to be outdoors he didn't want anything to come between himself and the elements.

Paul dipped his paddle into the water, turning the canoe back towards home. In June, when he first arrived, the lake had been close to freezing and few people had been about. Everything happened quickly in the northern summer, the sun, the heat, the birds nesting and procreating, the lush plant life. The lake was busy with comings and goings, but the sun had peaked. Life was getting ready to go dormant again.

Creeping noiselessly along the path, Paul went up to his room in the base of the cabin. A de-humidifier ran most of the day to try to rid the place of damp, but Paul turned it off when he got into bed. He turned on the light and pulled out the book Mother had given him, *The Immense Journey*, by Loren Eiseley.

Great spaces opened in Paul as he read about the earth before men, before angiosperms, when great redwood trees had been the only plants and reptiles roamed the world. Eiseley had been a bone hunter, a paleographer. Only when flowers and grasses got going was the earth ready for large mammals, and people. Paul could not put the book, offering Eiseley's speculations about evolution, down. Only when he saw the sky brightening at his window did he realize he wouldn't be able to stand up that day if he didn't get some sleep. He guiltily put down the book and fell asleep, the vast spaces of the earth before people filling fitful morning dreams.

That morning, when the frame on the beach house was up, both Paul and Dad put the plywood walls in place. The woods rang with the sound of their hammers. The breeze was not as strong today. The new wood smelled delicious and light and shadow shook about them as leaves moved delicately high in the sky. Paul pretended to himself that he was wide awake and soon, rhythmically swinging a hammer, he forgot that he had hardly slept the night before.

A wall of holes for windows looked out between the trees to the lake. Dad had set smaller window spaces on either side. Looking through them gave Paul a different view of the world. The water, the woods were seen from new angles from inside the building. Making new views was one of the things restless, evolutionary men did.

The next day Dad and Paul set the windows Dad had purchased in place. "We need to go into town and look at roofing materials," Dad said. A flat ceiling, which was also flooring, had been laid on top of the frame, but Dad was still pondering the roof. He wanted it to be flat, so people could take chairs out and sit on it, but a flat roof in snow country was never a good idea. He paced around, looking at things and thinking.

Paul hunkered down on the new roof, looking out at the water, waiting. It was late afternoon and Kristen and Hanna were swimming with their cousin Matthew, splashing around in rubber inner-tubes a little way out from the dock. Uncle David, on the platform above the dock, poked through his fishing tackle. Unlike Dad, he loved fishing and was planning an expedition for that evening. He wanted to go to a nearby lake which was said to have Northern Pike in it.

"Guess we better just go," said Dad finally. "Maybe they'll have some ideas at the hardware store."

Dad and Paul hiked up the path and looked in at the cabin to say where they were going. Dad had a cup of coffee and they each had one of the cornflake bars Aunt Rose had made, peanuts and cornflakes melded together by a thick caramel syrup.

"I don't think we need groceries," said Mother. "But please bring home some milk."

Paul was relieved. He hated long forays in to the grocery store, time better spent elsewhere. If he were in the wild, he thought, he would just have a big sack of potatoes, a sack of peanuts and eat them until they ran out! But Mother always had ideas. This year she didn't ask Paul to run out and look for milkweed pods and wild food. She was fascinated by a Navajo rug weaving kit Kristen had started. It was just a square frame, with yarns strung across nails to make a warp and woof. Mother wanted to do some weaving herself.

Dad drove the Ford station wagon, now weather and people-worn, in to Walker, a resort town on the huge Leech Lake. Once they got off the gravel road which circled the lake, the highway was smooth asphalt, wide and edged by forests. "Up here," Dad said, "everything always becomes more clear to me, everything that seems fuzzy down where we live."

"Me too," said Paul. "That's why I like the North country."

"All this conflict," said Dad. "This student unrest. The most important thing to me is relationship. Relationship to God, to family and each other. If you get your relationships right, you will not have much else to worry about."

Paul didn't like conflict one bit. In the natural world, there was certainly conflict, but it didn't have all of the social and cultural strains he felt in people. People always seemed to want different things.

"In Haroldson we've got all sides of the political spectrum," Dad continued. "The Eliasson's daughter was thrilled with Bobby Kennedy. She met him somewhere along the line and went to Washington this year to work on his campaign. She was devastated when he was killed. That family is very liberal. But we've also got the Republican contingent, who are angry at the lack of patriotism they see in young people. Not supporting our troops."

Paul was all ears as Dad rarely spoke out.

"I do see that there wasn't any other way to get past segregation than for the government to step in, in some of those deep South states. But if people had their relationship to Christ foremost in mind, they could get past their prejudices. Martin Luther King showed that."

"He was against the war too," said Paul, remembering what Line had told him.

"It's a terrible war," said Dad. "So much suffering on all sides. The United States doesn't want to wimp out, but it sure isn't going anywhere. Totally different than our involvement in World War II."

Paul heard Dad's perspective clearly. Dad never talked about his younger brother Marshall who had been killed in France shortly before World War II ended. Dad had been spared because he was studying at the seminary, but that had been a righteous war in his eyes.

"As a pastor, I focus on Christ's loving kindness to all, redemption and its power. Then I am in right relation to the Lord, and to all of his people."

"Yeah," said Paul, understanding all of a sudden. "It puts you above the conflict."

"Not a popular place to be," said Dad. "But I never worried much about being popular, as you know." He looked over at Paul and smiled.

"Yeah," said Paul, musing. He thought of the stories he had heard about Dad in college, sleeping on the roof of the dorm, refusing to smoke or drink, making his way out of an immigrant family towards being a spiritual leader. Paul knew that Line had never gotten along with Dad particularly well, but Paul found Dad and his idealism easy to love and respect.

At the same time, Paul wanted to tell Dad: I'm not you. Let me be myself. He wasn't ready to say it out loud yet.

"I really don't understand what Marty's going for," said Dad. "Do you? Wants to live in the big city, maybe? But wouldn't Minneapolis do? I think I understand what Line's doing better than I do Marty!"

Marty's letters were full of the interesting Jewish family she had lived with and of her fascination with the West Coast. She had moved into the city of San Francisco and was living with a bunch of friends. She worked in an office doing secretarial work and was taking photography classes at a free university. She sent a few photos she developed herself, of flamboyantly dressed people lazing on the grass in a park. They looked like hippies with their long hair and peasant clothes.

"Got me," said Paul. Marty had sent him a letter at school, but because he wasn't much of a correspondent, there had only been one. "Maybe she just has to move away to find herself?"

"Find herself!" said Dad. "What's there to find?!" Dad made a turn onto another smooth highway, and spacious automobile lots began to appear. "I've given Marty the name of one of the guys I went to Seminary with. He serves a church in San Francisco she could join."

Paul looked noncommittal. He certainly couldn't answer for Marty.

"Like I said, relationship is what's important," Dad said as they arrived at the outskirts of the town. "Get your relationships right, and it will all fall into place. We love and trust you kids," said Dad. "I'm sure you know that?"

"Yes," said Paul. "I do. And I bet Marty does." The old gang was in disarray. He wished he knew more about Marty and Line. Their freedom to make their ways in the world was enticing, however. It would be a little while longer before Paul could. He was following the path expected of him, attending another Lutheran college in the fall to get his B.A., but he did not know how best to use his gifts. Or even what they were.

Walker had one main street which roughly skirted a huge lake. It was reputed to be very quiet in the winter, when only locals lived there. But in August it was bustling, the hub of many surrounding resorts. Vehicles lined up at the stop light, and people thronged the sidewalk. Dad drove up to the flourishing hardware store and parked.

The front of the hardware store was stocked with fishing tackle, big rubber waders, camouflage suits for hunting, tents and guns. Though people hunted deer, geese and pheasants in Iowa, Paul never saw open displays of rifles like these. It showed him what Northern preoccupations were!

Paul let Dad go on ahead into the construction section. He was mesmerized by a display of beautiful brown leather Chippewa lace-up boots. A thick pair of socks, and how deep into the forest one could go in them! His feet would feel like heaven!

Next to the boots were tents. And sleeping bags. All of a sudden Paul's sleepiness caught up with him. He wished he could take one of the warm bags and wrap up into a warm ball on the forest floor somewhere.

Except for the time he and Dad had borrowed a tent and canoed up the chain of Gulch lakes, Paul had never camped. He imagined that a tent would allow him to stay out in the woods forever, mosquito free! A tent could be carried and placed anywhere, a little house on your back. And a warm sleeping bag would also help him to stay out later in the year.

Paul sighed. Desire for things rarely came over him. He usually tried to see how much he could get by without. But the woods were fascinating in the fall. When he went back to school, Paul always felt the melancholy of knowing that things were happening in the woods without him.

Tents, good boots, sleeping bags drew Paul toward adulthood. Dad was helping him pay for his education, but Paul would have to buy these things himself. He wanted his own money and his own life. Two more years at least before any of that happened, but it was coming. He could smell it! Marty and Line could have their old cities. It was not in a city that Paul wanted to find himself.

18

Marty could not get over how simple it was to live in San Francisco. She had a room in a communal flat on Cole Street. She slept on a mattress and kept her few possessions in wooden Chinese packing cases which could be found on Grant Street. She made food in the kitchen at the back of the shared Victorian-era house. For the cost of a dime and a nickel, she took an electric trolley bus downtown to a job at which she did typing for a legal publisher. And she opened her first bank account. It was all she needed.

Of course there were problems. Sometimes the guy who lived in the large basement room played music much later than Marty wanted to overhear it. Sometimes the kitchen was crowded and people didn't do their dishes very quickly. Friends of her housemates came and went at all hours, including her own friend Erik. Marty didn't have much to call her own. A window that looked into a light well and a door that closed. It was usually enough.

What she did have was the city, a vast public space she could borrow freely. And she was making friends. It had been a while since Marty knew many people of her own age. The city was full of them, fascinating people with all kinds of stories. It was said that "all the loose nuts and bolts rolled out to the West coast," as in a drawer which wasn't flat. Marty didn't mind being one of them.

On Friday night, Marty, Joyce from Indiana who was half Korean, and Lana from New York walked over to Andy's, a Russian bakery on Haight Street, a block from their house. A bit of grey, pillowy fog rolled up over the hills, as it had every night for the last month.

"Where's the summer?" whimpered Marty, as she pulled her sweater tighter around her. "I want it to be warm!"

"It will get warm," said Lana. "Too warm. I love our built-in air conditioner!" Lana had been in the city for a year already, an authority Marty trusted. She was a colorful, full-figured person with thick curly red hair which she pulled back off her freckled face.

"When?" asked Marty plaintively. "It was warm in September last year in Berkeley."

"Any minute now," said Lana. "Don't worry."

Marty had spent the foggy month curled up under a cotton-covered feather comforter Kate, who had married her Army boyfriend in Germany, had sent from Europe. The house was cold and damp around the edges, though it could be enchanting when light filtered into the rooms.

At Andy's the smells of spiced meats and steam from soups cooking on big iron ranges at the back of the large room warmed the chilly night. The dining tables were not separate from the kitchen, as if they had been an after-thought. From a deep fryer, an older woman in a big white apron lifted fragrant piroshki, yeast dough wrapped around ground meats, onion and herbs.

"Just like home," said Joyce, sinking onto a padded kitchen chair at a formica table. Andy's was a favorite because it was cheap and had a warm atmosphere.

"Like home?" Marty asked. It wasn't like her home. "Did you have big vats of soup and meat in the kitchen?" It was hard to imagine the farm Joyce lived on with her silent Korean mother.

"Yes indeed," said Joyce. "Lots of people to feed on that farm. My mom was always cooking." Black hair streamed down her back. She looked like a little girl, but Marty knew her to be tough-minded and practical.

"Not like my home, either," said Lana. "Even though my mother had all those boys after me. She managed the household, but she didn't cook much or clean."

A thin woman tucking bits of graying hair under her kerchief came to take their order, writing it down in Russian on a pad of green-lined paper. She had a thick accent Marty yearned after. She'd been reading Russians in translation and wanted to hear the actual language which must be as full of rich life as English.

When she left, Marty asked Lana, "Did you ever wonder whether you would have gotten along better with your mother if she had been a different sign?" She was fascinated by the astrology that spun around their heads as if it were real.

"Maybe," said Lana. "She didn't really want a self-centered little Leo like me around, I don't think."

Marty, a Capricorn, got along fine with Lana, but she had never been her own Mother's favorite, who was born on the same day as Lana. Mother was indelibly attached to Line, no matter what Line did.

"So what's Erik?" asked Joyce.

"Scorpio," said Marty.

"Oooooh," said Joyce. "Watch out! Every Scorpio I know is too intense for me!"

"I know," said Marty, ruefully. She had found her room through Erik's old friend Jamie, and she saw Erik himself almost every week when he came to San Francisco. But he was unpredictable. Marty did not know whether she was his girlfriend or not.

Marty's pelmeni, pockets of ground meat and herbs wrapped in thin dough, arrived in a broth topped by a big dollop of sour cream. She breathed in the unctuous steam rising from it.

"Why are fatty things so good?" wailed Lana, crunching into her piroshki.

"It's because fat carries flavors and aromas," said Joyce. "Can I taste that?" she asked, fork poised above Marty's dish.

"Sure," said Marty.

"Korean food is full of chili peppers," Joyce said. "But mother tried to cook what my dad wanted. He said he couldn't taste the food when it was full of chilis. I think, in Korea, they were trying to preserve the food, or mask the tastes if the meat was old."

"Is Korea tropical?" asked Marty.

"Not really," said Joyce. "I went with my mother when I was in high school. It was beautiful. Her family has a farm outside Seoul. They've never gotten over her marrying an American soldier."

"That's amazing," said Marty. "Are you glad she came to America?"

"Yes!" said Joyce. "Women have a chance here. I don't even speak Korean! And I like being bi-racial. You get the best genes from both sides."

"Good way to look at it," said Lana.

Marty could have sat there all night, talking to her two friends. No one knew or cared where she was. It was heaven. She didn't have to do a thing until Monday when she next went to work. She looked around, wondering whether the way her friends were dressed depended upon their sign. Marty knew astrology was superficial, but she found this sort of classification fascinating.

"I wonder if I like black so much because I'm a Capricorn," said Marty. She had changed out of her work dress as soon as she got home and was wearing a black cotton turtleneck under a sweater, with a pair of jeans.

"I'd never wear black," said Lana. "I like red! And green and gold. And all of their off-shoots. Autumn colors, even purple if there is enough red in it." She wore the cotton dress she had worn for work, short, red with a gold paisley print in it. She turned to Joyce, who wore a plain blue, little girl dress. "What about you? You're a Cancer, right?"

"Yeah," said Joyce. "I'd never wear black either. I like light colors, maybe a pearly gray. But my colors change with the season too."

"You're taking this whole astrology thing much too seriously," said Lana to Marty. "I think our clothes have more to do with our personalities."

"You have to admit, though," said Marty, "that Allie looks like a perfect Pisces in those floaty clothes she always wears." Allie hung out with the guy downstairs who played music a little too loud. Long blonde hair flowed down her back and she wore thin wispy clothing, layers of it with beads. Or long velvet dresses, which were in style now, except that no one wore long dresses to work.

"It's her personality!" insisted Lana. "It's just who she is!"

Marty was grateful to her friends. Nothing was off limits, though people didn't often talk about books. Marty was shy, but she loved Lana's forthright, intelligent talk. In small groups she felt free to talk as well.

"What are you up to tomorrow?" asked Joyce. Since their families were far away and not a force drawing them, weekends were spent exploring and having adventures.

"I'm going to the Cannery," said Lana. "I need to send my mother something for her birthday." The Cannery was a renovated brick building on the northern edge of the city full of interesting shops. Once that part of town had been a produce market with canning factories. It was also home to a fleet of fishing boats. Now it invited tourists. Below it was a park and a public beach. "Want to come?"

"I'll come," said Joyce. "I love it over there. I love Design Research." A store which sold colorful modern furniture, dishes and textiles, it was the only outlet for a stunning brand of Finnish fabrics and clothing, Marimekko. Some of its goods, beautifully displayed against the brick walls of the old building, were even affordable.

"Yeah," said Lana. "That's the place to shop for my mother." She looked at Marty questioningly.

But Marty was thinking about photographs. She was taking a course in a free university. "I need to do some developing," she said. "The dark room isn't open on Sunday." For a small membership fee, Marty had learned to expose photographic paper using her negatives and an enlarger. She could hardly believe she had the means do this and had taken to photographing friends. Not seriously. She had no intention of becoming a photographer. It just helped her to see. To look at things.

"Okay," said Lana. "I get it. Art before friends." She smiled mischievously at Marty.

Marty ignored her. Lana never got seriously upset.

On Saturday, time disappeared entirely as Marty worked in the low reddish light of a large, airy communal dark room in a city park building. She had brought glossy 8½ x 11 paper to print on and the large negatives made by the Brownie camera Aunt Mabel had given her. The room smelled of chemicals she couldn't entirely identify, partly the acetic smell of the stop bath, perhaps.

Marty followed directions closely. She focused and spotted the image first as light poured down through the negative and onto the white plate at the base of the enlarger. When she was happy with it, she turned off the light and carefully placed a thick piece of glowing paper. Using the second hand on her watch, she turned on the light, exposing it briefly, and then placed the paper in the developer.

Marty diddled the paper with a tongs as she watched the image come up. She was short so when she photographed the lanky figure of Jack up close, he towered over her. He held something in his hands, examining it, while behind him in the light stood the handsome Nathan. It was a gorgeous photograph. No one else could have taken it. It was Marty's point of view, her very own eyes.

Why did a photograph seem more real than actual life? You could stare at it, looking at every part as long as you wanted, while you couldn't do that in real life. In life, everything was always moving, changing. Framing too, placing a border around a scene, gave it weight, created something from the shimmering ever-changing face of life.

Marty put the photograph in the stop bath, then the fixer. The wet prints were put in big rollers to squeegee out the chemicals, then dried. The people working at the studio would put them in a cubby for her when they were dry. The backs of her prints were marked with her name.

What Marty liked best was photographs of people. Photos of the natural world did not do it any justice, particularly not in black and white. But developing photos of people often caught something. They were so complex, even in two dimensions. Both complex and simple in their beauty. Endless exposures of a person turning, moving, even blinking, each showed something different about them, as film demonstrated.

It wasn't hard for Marty to get her friends to pose! She generally photographed outdoors because there was enough light. A few of the photographs were taken in her friends' flats, against the paisley backgrounds of Indian bedspreads bought at Cost Plus and hung on the wall. In flamboyant clothing against this rich background, smiling faces with perfect skin stood out, showing the bone structure, the emotional tone of the moment.

Marty framed by instinct, placing people's eyes high in the frame, giving them space to look into if they were looking to the side. Marty had no art education whatsoever, no idea about what she was doing. Occasionally she cropped out extraneous things in the edges of her original photograph. But mostly she just went with the naturalistic image she was able to get, picking and choosing among exposures to keep only the best ones. It all cost money and Marty had little to spare.

Marty's friends liked the results. But when Nathan's lover Jack asked Marty to take a few shots of Nathan to help him get modeling jobs, Jack deemed the printed results "unprofessional." Marty was a little hurt, but Jack was from New York and knew what he was talking about.

Marty had tried to do what Jack wanted, but the focus on the lens of the Brownie camera was soft and, she had to admit, dust showed up on some of the prints. She did not intend to become professional. She was just having fun, learning to see, capturing moments in time.

Marty finally collected her things. It must be afternoon and she was hungry. The sky was brilliant when she emerged from the reddish semi-darkness, but wisps of fog were moving in again. She could have taken a bus to get home, but it was only about a mile. Marty set off walking, buying a jelly doughnut at a corner shop nearby.

Marty preferred trees to shops. Avoiding Haight Street she took a route through the Panhandle, a thin strip of park that started at the end of the long Golden Gate Park, and continued into the residential districts. From one side, Marty could see the houses on the other, but it was full of trees, eucalyptus, Monterey pines, cypresses and acacia.

These were the trees that made the landscape of San Francisco so different from any in the Midwest. They were different colors! Grey-green, sage green, the acacias a grayish yellow green Marty had never seen before. None of them were really deciduous, though they changed throughout the year, the acacias flowering yellow in February. Drought tolerant, Marty knew these trees helped tame the sand dunes and wild winds that had made the western part of the city a wilderness only 100 years ago.

Marty nibbled the sugary crust of the doughnut. Doughnuts tasted like freedom. They were cheap and here she was, walking along, eating one without caring who saw her. Despite her longing for warmer weather, Marty felt a fierce loyalty toward San Francisco. Never had she met so many people who felt so congenial. Never had she found so much she wanted to do and think about. Nowhere had she felt so stimulated and so free.

Moving to San Francisco had been a way to make money and become independent. It didn't mean Marty would never go back to school, she told herself. It just put off all those decisions while she explored this diverse, unexpected place.

Marty walked slowly through the Panhandle. Often in the mornings, people did martial arts here, but it was too late in the day for that. Now, in the feathery afternoon light, children played on the playground equipment, a basketball game took over the court and people sat under trees, eating and drinking. Marty looked long at a black man wearing a long coat, elegantly reading a large book as he stood in the chiaroscuro light under a tree. Marty took a mental image of him, knowing she wouldn't dare disturb him with a photograph even if she had a camera. It would be taking advantage.

A wave of homesickness washed over Marty, making her heart feel hollow and lonely. She missed the empty plains under the light-filled sky, the green colors of the Midwest. San Francisco skies were obscured by buildings, except at the edges of the city. But freedom to think as she pleased was worth the loneliness.

Maybe she was homesick for Lake Michigami? Marty had spent summers there, canoeing in the soft warm evenings on the lake. But not this year. The family had probably just left, everyone going back to school. Marty wondered how Line, who was about to have her baby, was doing. Stephen was slightly injured in the demonstrations at the Democratic convention, she had heard. Line might still be working at the hospital. Marty hoped they were happy. She could not even imagine where Line lived.

Marty turned the key in the lock of the red Victorian building. She picked up the envelopes which scattered the floor of the hall under the letter drop. One was from Kate in Europe! The house felt quiet. Marty sank into a big velvet chair in the living room, opening the packet pasted with foreign stamps. Kate was doing collages of cutouts from magazines, with poems she was writing. Bitter ones. She seemed to hate being a housewife, made only for cooking, cleaning and sex. She begged Marty for news.

Marty could not understand. What could Kate possibly want? Marty wanted to be a housewife, imagined creating beauty around herself. Kate must surely live in beauty in the folksy cottages in southern Germany. Why wasn't she happy? Marty would write her a letter soon, but not tonight. Tonight she planned to go to a movie with Franci, a friend who loved films as much as she did.

Marty hunted for pieces of last week's Sunday *Chronicle* stuffed under magazines on the table. She found the pink Arts section and searched through the liner notes about the films currently playing. In front of each one a cartoon of a little man either jumped off his seat, sat clapping, sat bolt upright or slumped over. If reviewers hated a film, he wasn't even in his seat.

Marty picked up the telephone and called Franci. "The movie at the Cento Cedar is called *Accatone*," Marty said. "I've never heard of it. The director is Pasolini."

"Are you looking at the paper?" asked Franci. "What's the little man doing?"

"He's sitting up, clapping his hands," said Marty.

"Hmmmm," said Franci. "It's Italian. How bad could it be?"

"Okay," said Marty. "Do you want to see it?"

"Sure," said Franci. "I'll meet you at the coffeehouse at 7 p.m."

The Cento Cedar was in an alleyway at the edge of the Tenderloin. For Marty, almost any foreign film taught her something, took her somewhere. Growing up in small towns without a movie theater, Marty had seen few American films. It was only when she went to Wittenberg College, which served up Bergman, Bresson, Italian films and French new wave films, that she had begun to see movies.

Marty was early, ordering herself a cup of French roast while she waited for Franci. Maybe I frame photographs based on the movies I've seen, she thought.

The previous Saturday night, Marty and Franci had talked to an amazing guy who seemed particularly interested in Marty. He was hip, smart and intellectual, as well as good looking, perhaps a few years older. Marty hoped he might again come to the cinema that night. Their conversation had been magical across a candle-lit table, ranging rapidly through literature and movies.

What attracted people to Marty, she wondered. What did people see in her? Her intensity, her groundedness, her intellect, her star-shine? She didn't think she was pretty. Jack hit it on the head when he said she was "pretty enough." He meant, thought Marty, that no one who asked her out would be ashamed of her. It was important. Guys wanted a good-looking woman on their arm.

Marty was not beautiful. But she was smart and that went a long way in life. It made her an excellent companion for herself. But she also wanted a boyfriend. She wanted to be Iris Magnusson or Lidia Chertok. She wanted to be in the middle of a rich family life, with a husband who loved her, a household which flowed from her fingers. She didn't expect it to happen over night, but she did long for it.

Perhaps Marty should have found a guy in Cardinal, Iowa, at college, as Mother and Dad expected. But she hadn't. The guy she liked best, Glen, found another girl.

Erik, who was studying to be an architect at Berkeley, took Marty to concerts and to visit his friends. But Marty was afraid to ask him how he felt about her. She did not want to presume. She felt he was glamorous, rich, in a world she wasn't sure she belonged. Marty thought him exciting, but not a person she could take for granted. She had no idea whether he wanted a family.

Franci arrived in a bustle of energy. "Is he here?" she whispered, as she leaned in to greet Marty, remembering the handsome guy from the week before.

"I don't think so," said Marty. "Maybe he'll come."

Franci stood at the counter, ordering a cappuccino while Marty watched. Franci wore a pair of beautiful tall boots Marty longed for. When I have enough money, Marty thought. Franci's peasant dress in a dark print with small flowers on it nipped in at the waist with a wide belt. Franci sewed her own clothes. She was educated, the same age as Marty. She wasn't as beautiful as April had been, didn't like to read as Lana did, but Marty liked being with her. Franci was smart and active, well-rounded.

"So, what's happening?" asked Franci, sitting beside Marty with a steaming cup.

Marty smiled at the familiar greeting. "Not so much. I spent the afternoon in the darkroom. How is it that when you cut things down to two dimensions, you actually see more?"

"I don't know," said Franci. "Art sort of elevates things. But it's more about the perception of the creator. The point of view of the artist."

"Oh, I don't know about that," said Marty. "The viewer completes the picture. We're all artists. I love that dress. I bet you made it!"

"Yes," said Franci. "It feels thrilling that I can make whatever life I want. Pick my lifestyle. Not like our parents, for whom everything is so rigid."

"Yours?" asked Marty. "Mine aren't really rigid. But they have to fit into the small towns they live in. They like them! I'll never forget Mother laughing at me because I identified with Carol in *Main Street* trying to get some culture into her small town. Mother thought the joke was on Carol! That Carol didn't understand or appreciate her surroundings."

"My parents are really competitive," said Franci with a hint of malice. "Things always have to be just so. They have to give the best dinners, have the best house. Dad has to make the most money. Ugggggh!" Franci moved her head and shoulders vigorously as if shaking something off. "I'm so glad I got away! Lucky I wasn't a guy, too. My brother considered becoming a Jesuit before he came to his senses."

Marty did not understand the East Coast where Franci's father worked as a chemical engineer. Franci and her brother had gone to famous East Coast schools, but Franci had dropped out when she got mononucleosis. Marty met her at work where they both used Dictaphones to type manuscript prepared by lawyers for a legal publishing company.

"It's hard for me to relate," said Marty. "I felt homesick today. But I also love San Francisco. I feel so free here!"

"Me too," breathed Franci in agreement, her body arranging itself decisively in her chair.

Pasolini's film turned out to be about a guy who lived on the wages his girlfriend made as a prostitute. He was practically a street person, a handsome one. In the end, after dreaming about his own funeral, he was killed on a motorcycle.

"I don't get it," said Franci angrily afterwards. "Despicable guys. Living off women. Who ever heard of such a thing?"

"Sorry," said Marty tentatively, apologizing for the choice of movie. Her eyes felt large, her neck tense from straining to understand. "I don't get it either. Disturbing. It was beautiful, though. In places. The music …" A weighty Bach oratorio lent the story its tragedy.

"I like French films more," said Franci. "Truffaut. I can usually see myself in a Truffaut film."

"I've seen some great Italian films," said Marty. "Antonioni. Fellini." She didn't really want to talk about it. The best thing to do with a film, any film, was let it settle to the bottom of your life. See what happened.

"More coffee?" Marty asked, looking in the door of the candle-lit coffeehouse with disappointment. She still did not see the inviting stranger from last week. She had taken for granted she would see him again, but he had not taken her phone number. He too must have been depending on the supernatural power of the city to help them find each other.

"No thanks," said Franci. "It's late. I want to go home."

The two girls headed toward Market Street where most of the buses congregated before fanning out across the city. Marty was pensive and Franci sleepy. Everything can't be magical all the time, Marty thought. Freedom didn't guarantee it.

The images from the film passed in front of Marty's eyes. Two dimensions once again, with an added auditory sense. And time. Pasolini saw beauty in everything. Even degradation. It was there, if you framed it right.

19

"What I do at the hospital is hard work," said Line to Mother, at the other end of the phone line. "I'm on my feet all day. But I think I can keep going another week or so."

"Please be careful, Line," said Mother's soft, gracious voice. "I'm sure you'll do just fine with all that background you've had now."

"I keep remembering taking care of Ellie," Line said. "Bruce wasn't home and I had to get her to the hospital. At least Stephen's here, though he has a lot going on." She sat in the wooden rocking chair, the black, curling phone cord pulled tight across her big belly. Outside the October rain came down, making puddles on the porch and the empty schoolyard beyond.

"You've had a lot of experience, Line," said Mother, reassuringly. "Is your apartment warm?"

"Oh yeah," said Line. "And a friend is giving me some baby clothes. I'm sure you don't have any left!"

"No," said Mother. "Ellie might, but she's so far away!" Ellie's youngest was already four and growing up in Italy. "You're all so far away!"

The heavy thud of the downstairs door announced Stephen's immanent presence. "Actually I hear Stephen, back from class," said Line. "Everything's fine there, Mother?"

"Oh, yes," said Mother. "School's underway, the usual. We've heard from Paul, who is a little overwhelmed on that big campus, but he's fine too!"

"Marty?" Line was bad at communicating with people, but Mother was the hub of the family wheel. Everyone talked or wrote to Mother.

"We do get letters," said Mother. "She got a permanent job with a publishing company, says the fall weather is lovely. I'm afraid we've lost her to that beautiful city!"

"Oh, don't worry," said Line. "She'll be back." A whoosh of cool air and Stephen stood behind Line, kissing the top of her head.

"For visits," said Mother. "She writes about her appreciation of our family, now that she is seeing so many different people with less advantages than you girls had."

"Here's Stephen to say hello," said Line, handing him the phone. A grey twilight was settling in, the windows growing dark. The room filled with the sweetish smell of baked vegetables.

"Hello, Lois," said Stephen with careful formality. He hadn't seen enough of Mother to know her. "How are you and yours?"

"We are very well, thank you, Stephen," said Mother. "We're looking forward to your news, in a few weeks."

"Yes!" beamed Stephen across the phone. "You'll be hearing from us!"

"And greet your parents," said Mother. "Carl and I enjoyed meeting them."

"I will!" said Stephen. "Here's Line." He handed Line the phone and turned on the lamp. A low light flooded the room. Silently, he brandished a large glossy *Life* magazine at Line, but Line didn't know why.

"It's so good to talk to you, Mother," said Line, taking the phone. "We're thinking of all of you!"

"God bless you, Line," said Mother. "We're thinking of you too."

Line leaned over and placed the phone handset back on its base. She reached up, drawing down Stephen's face to give him a kiss.

"Big article on SDS in this *Life*!" said Stephen. "They even quoted me, but they didn't use my name."

"Is that good?" asked Line.

"It's a surprisingly sympathetic article," said Stephen. "It says SDS is the most vocal representative of the movement, and that most campus activism starts with us."

"Let's see," said Line. She flipped through the magazine and found, in the midst of ads for Coca-cola, electric heat and Toshiba televisions, a long article filled with black and white protest photographs.

Stephen leaned over her. "Toward the end, they quote various people without naming them, calling us 'tacticians.' 'The Establishment has lost its conscience,' that's me," said Stephen. "They came to a meeting at headquarters. You know how it is. Probably we were all talking at once! They did spend time with a few guys, Ogelsby and James."

Line was lost in reading. "Are you pleased?" she asked.

"Damn right," said Stephen. "Students are joining up in droves, also. About time. There ain't no place to be today but in the movement."

Line looked up at Stephen. "I'm proud of you," she said, choosing her words. "This confirms everything you work for. But I'm glad you are teaching again, and working on your degree. There's more to life than politics!"

"No!" said Stephen. "It's all politics!" Stephen's strong, wiry body flopped down on the day bed.

"Okay, okay," said Line. "I know what you mean. But ever since I've been pregnant, I feel that this kid, this life in me is more important than anything. I've been trying to protect it."

"Me too," said Stephen. "I don't want our kid to grow up in a military industrial complex! But it's gotten so corrupt, it's bound to implode. I don't see any future in it." He was in a rare optimistic humor.

"Good," said Line, curtly. "Then I'm not going to worry about it!" She stood up, pulling down the big tee-shirt she wore as a maternity smock. "Supper?" she asked. "I've got some potatoes baking and a squash." She looked anxiously at Stephen. If he wanted meat, he must bring it home himself. She would have liked some too, but she was pinching pennies against the days she wouldn't be able to work after the baby was born. Luckily Stephen now got a stipend for the teaching he was doing.

"Sounds good," said Stephen. He didn't move. Even though it was Saturday, he had been out early, training with his affinity group. They did exercises and judo, practicing for the next street fight. Then he went to the SDS office, sometimes the university library. Line did not always know where he was. Stephen didn't tell her everything.

Moving about the kitchen and setting the table, Line tried to rein in her sharp tongue. She contented herself with asking, "How was your day?"

"Pretty good," said Stephen. He stood up and went into the tiny kitchen, looking in the refrigerator. "Do we have any of that cheese?" He asked.

"A little," said Line. "It's there, in the door."

Stephen sliced himself some cheese, eating it right off the knife as an appetizer. "Kind of wet this morning out in the park. But we warmed up exercising, and then at the office. As I told you, memberships are pouring in and campuses are erupting everywhere. There's so much to do!"

"I know," said Line gently. "I hope other people are helping you."

"Well, Rennie's still in the office, but Tom Hayden and Todd are out in California. Don't blame them, really," said Stephen. "Things are erupting there too."

Because she didn't see much of him, Line was jealous. She hoped Stephen wasn't getting involved with the movement women he worked with so closely. Some of the conflicting radical ideologies were hostile to 'bourgeois' institutions. Line was worried that Stephen felt hijacked by their pregnancy and marriage.

Normally Line was not afraid to bring her fears out into the open, but now, just before the baby came, she didn't want to fight. Stephen always assured her that he was faithful. He was more grown up than others. But she knew he also felt the intense pull of the people around him. Most of them were now younger than he was at 26.

"How about you, my love?" asked Stephen. "What did you do today?"

Line dreaded the question. On her days off she was lethargic, loved staying around the apartment. She was surprised to find she could brood for long hours, sitting in the rocking chair, playing with her long hair, petting Munchkin the cat, and listening to music on the radio.

"I went to the co-op," Line said. "And Lenore tried to teach me how to knit. I'd love to learn, but I'm all thumbs," she said ruefully. "You don't really have a handy wife, I'm afraid." She pulled a ball of yarn stuck with needles from under a pillow on the daybed where she had stuffed it. A loopy square of green knitted cloth hung from one of the needles. "See?!"

"My wife is wonderful," said Stephen, coming toward her and trying to encircle her big body with his thin arms. "I don't want her any other way. I happen to know that her hands soothe new mothers almost every day, and that she herself is going to be a wonderful mother."

Line whimpered. She longed for Stephen's arms when he was gone so much. But she was also glad he wasn't hanging around the house, watching her as she galumphed around. She was getting bigger and bigger. It wouldn't be long now.

Two days after Line did her final scheduled shift at the hospital, she woke up in a tangle of wet sheets. It was early morning, the windows dark. She got up and went into the other room as quietly as possible, letting Stephen sleep. Turning on a lamp, she paced back and forth in the tiny apartment, trying to get the feel of the contractions that had started dragging at her lower back.

Line knew that early labor was to help her cervix open slowly. Even though it was her first baby, she was determined to try to get by without much pain medication. One of the women on the obstetrics ward told her labor didn't feel like pain as much as a terrific, earthy force, working to push the baby out into the world. Line tried to imagine the contractions as a natural force, like weather or a storm kicked up in her body.

Not knowing whether the baby was a boy or a girl, Line had taken to calling him or her little Bobbie. Walking through the house in the early morning she began crooning to the baby. "Now don't you take forever, little Bobbie," she said. "I don't want to fill us full of drugs just because you're taking forever." If the baby took days, she knew a mother could become too exhausted to push it out.

Hours went by and the grey light beyond the windows began to reveal the bare tree branches at the back of the apartment. Line poked her nose out the door. The air was wintry and brittle, cold as ice. She put a kettle of water on the stove and made herself a cup of weak tea. When the contractions grabbed her back, she sat for a moment, trying to stretch and breathe into them.

After a while Stephen stumbled out into the light. It was Friday and he had an early class. Seeing Line up surprised him. She was sitting in the rocker, but as a spasm grabbed her, she closed her eyes and held onto the rocker arms. Stephen stood watching. "I think it's going to be today," said Line, as she opened her eyes.

"Today?!" said Stephen. "Shall we go to the hospital? Are you ready?"

"No," said Line. "I don't want to go just yet. As soon as I go, I'll lose control of the whole thing. Let's wait as long as we can."

"But, we have to get a cab!" said Stephen. "There'll be traffic!"

Line could almost see the adrenalin surging through him. She sighed. "Yeah," she said. "I guess you're right. But, please, make some oatmeal. I think we can wait a little longer." She stood up and walked around, moving the muscles that had tightened up with pain.

"I'll cancel my class," said Stephen. He reached for the phone.

With Stephen on the phone, another contraction began. Line had no idea how close they were to each other. She rolled her eyes back in her head and went with it, stretching, feeling, letting it happen, a force that was going to let her finally meet this little Bobby who had made his home inside her.

"Hold me," she begged Stephen when he put down the phone, wide-eyed, paying attention to her face. "Just hold me." She slumped on the daybed.

"I'm glad little Bobbie isn't waiting until election day," said Stephen, a trifle grimly, as he lay down beside Line and stroked her.

It was the beginning of a long day. Late in the morning, Stephen and Line went to the hospital. Line was tired and anxious, but she tried to be patient with the hospital protocols and procedures. She waved goodbye to Stephen. He must stay out in the waiting room.

Hospital personnel took over Line's body, monitoring her and treating her impersonally, just another baby factory. But she had expected it. She felt lucky that at least she knew the staff. Dr. Anderson, grey-haired and warm, was on duty when she arrived. She hoped her labor wouldn't take long and he would be the one to deliver little Bobbie.

Line did not want to stay in bed. She kept moving about, circling the small delivery room, sinking to her knees when the contractions came. She was trying desperately to relax and not let it get to her. The nurses were tolerant, at least at first. They knew Line and admired her stubbornness and strong will. They weren't anxious to tangle with her.

Between contractions, Line saw that the sun had come through the clouds and was sinking behind the buildings. Orange streaks lighted the white room. Line wanted to open a window and look out, but she was too tired. She sank into a little puddle under the window, waiting for the next earthquake to take her. She wished she could be outdoors, having her baby at the edge of a rice paddy, as Vivian, who had been to Vietnam, said women there did. But it was darn cold in Chicago in November.

At last Line began to feel something change. "I have to push, I have to push," she said urgently to Jamison, the attending nurse who had been there forever. "Please get the doctor," she begged.

As she had seen some mothers do, Line got on her knees on the bed and pushed. When Dr. Anderson arrived, he was as appreciative as he had been with all the other births she had seen him attend. "Good girl, Line!" he said. "Keep it coming, keep it up! Almost there!"

Line pushed, rested and pushed again. She gave up on her body. It didn't belong to her. The baby had taken over.

"Hey!" said Jamison. "Got those boy's names ready?! Looks like you are delivering a little boy, Line."

Line felt the wet slithering of the baby between her legs. She rested her face in her arms and sighed deeply. A raucous wail came out of the tiny mouth that Line couldn't see. "Another push," she heard. "Just one more. Come on Line!"

Line pushed and then sank onto the bed. Dr. Anderson was cutting the cord, freeing her from her son, who was now an independent being. Line was exhausted. She tried to turn over but she couldn't, crying from exhaustion and relief. She just wanted to see the baby.

Jamison was swabbing Line's lower parts with a wet towel. "Did good, Line," she said. "You did great!"

"A healthy boy," said Dr. Anderson's voice. "No visible problems!"

At last Line managed to crawl up on the bed and turn over. The baby was floating over near the darkened window in the doctor's arms. He put the baby in a scale and a nurse measured the dark red, howling little body. How cold and cruel the world must feel, thought Line. "Please," she reached out her arms. "Please may I have him?"

Finally they wrapped the little boy in a blanket and put him in Line's arms. Line closed her eyes, feeling his tiny heartbeat next to her chest. "Baby, baby," she said softly, tears rolling down her wet face. "You've just done the hardest thing you'll ever have to do! It'll all be easy from now on," she whispered. "I promise."

Line was transferred to a clean bed with wheels and she and the baby went rolling down the hall to a recovery room. Line clutched her son. She did not know what to call him. Probably Christopher, she thought. That was the name she and Stephen favored for a boy. She wondered whether they had told Stephen, and whether he would come. Recovery room protocol was left up to the staff. Line herself usually encouraged the father to enter.

Line was left alone for a few minutes, bending down to snuggle the tiny red baby. She felt great, as if all her fears and anxieties had been lifted. Her body had cooperated and here she was with a tiny, healthy boy.

All of a sudden, Stephen appeared! "We're getting special treatment," he said. "They love you here. I'm so proud of you! Let's see the little guy!"

Line felt wonderful. She gave Stephen her widest smile. Stephen, smelling like coffee and tobacco, leaned down and kissed her. She directed Stephen's attention to the sandy-haired little wrinkled head at her breast. "He looks like you, I think," she said. "Look how red his skin is. He's a toughy. How would you like to come out in the cold like this after all this time?"

Stephen looked wryly at the baby. "I wouldn't want to come out either," he said. "It's a rum go out here, little guy. But we'll take care of you." He stroked the little face with a finger. "And how are you, my love, my Line," he asked.

"I feel wonderful," said Line. "Tired. He came pretty fast, really. I was lucky." She leaned into Stephen's thin body. She was shaking and wet with perspiration again.

"You've got to rest, my girl," said Stephen softly. "You're amazing."

Line felt Stephen was insulated from her, though, drinking coffee, reading probably. He was coming from some other mental place.

"Christopher?" asked Line.

"Sure, Christopher," said Stephen. "Christopher Carl Cohen. I'll tell them at the desk."

"I wish I knew more about breastfeeding," Line said. She knew the nurses would soon come to take Christopher and feed him a bottle right away. She had seen mothers breastfeed their new-born babies, but she had neglected to find out how to do it. Christopher slept but his little mouth did appear to be sucking. And Line's breasts were heavy and even felt wet. The gown she wore was open at the back, not the front. "Help me Stephen," she asked as she struggled to get out of it.

Naked, Line sat holding Chris to her breast, feeling rebellious and pleased with herself. But Christopher wasn't getting the idea. "Oh, please," said Line, hoping he would take her breast before anyone came to take him away.

But Christopher didn't. Jamison came, took Christopher and told Line curtly to cover up and get some sleep. Jamison made a face at Stephen, as if he were the problem.

Line sighed. "I know we could do it," she said, dropping her empty arms. "If we just had some time. I've been almost naked all day! Who cares!"

"You can do anything," said Stephen. "I'm sure of it." He looked concerned, but out of his depth. He'd never spent any time in hospitals.

Line was glad he had seen her frustration, had seen that giving birth wasn't simple. "I'll figure it out," Line said confidently. "It won't hurt him to have formula and breast milk too. Your milk dries up if you don't breast feed," she said to Stephen. "I'll keep trying." Mother had not breastfed any of her six children. At the time doctors insisted formula was better, but Line wanted to do things 'naturally,' with as little help as possible.

The next few weeks went quickly. Line drank in the baby, watching him grow. She was easy with babies, had helped take care of her little sisters. And she did manage to breast feed Christopher, though it hurt at first. He was hungry! Especially at night. Line eventually loved having his little mouth at her nipples as if she were a mother goat or a sow.

Snow fell, Nixon was elected President, and Thanksgiving came. Line and Stephen were invited to Bernie and Kay Freeman's house for dinner.

It was a clear, bright, cold day. Most of the leaves on the trees had fallen, opening up the avenues to the sky which was as crystal blue as the inside of a bowl. Stephen carried the pumpkin pie Line had made from a large can of pumpkin and a Betty Crocker crust. It wasn't as pretty as the ones Marty made, Line thought, but no one knew that, and it would taste good. She felt strong, and so happy as their little group trundled down the sidewalk towards Hyde Park.

"It's my favorite holiday!" said Bernie, greeting them at the door. "It's so American. We all celebrate in the same way!" He led them into a large room, the sun intense behind the gauzy curtains.

Kay's little boy Abraham, now seven months old, sat gurgling and drooling in a little high chair near the dining table, his fingers trying to grasp the crackers Kay had put out for him. He tried to cram what he picked up into his mouth! Beside him was thin, dark Nancy, artfully folding napkins. She too was a long way from home, had been gathered up by the Freemans for the holiday.

Line held up her little son, wrapped like a package in several blankets, and Nancy reached for him. "Ohhhh," she said. "He's darling!" Christopher's skin had now taken on a pale cast and he had large, dark eyes. She carried the little boy into the kitchen to show Kay.

Line was entranced by little Abe and tried to point Stephen in his direction. It wouldn't be long before Christopher would be sitting up and drooling as Abe did. But Stephen was excited to have his mentor, Bernie Freeman, all to himself. The two of their heads pressed together as Bernie prepared drinks, talking heatedly.

Nancy handed the bundled Christopher back to Line. "Rather traditional roles we are all playing here," she said sardonically. She and Kay, and occasionally Line, were all in a women's group, collected from those in and around SDS.

"Oh it's all right!" said Kay, rushing in with a steaming bowl of green beans. "Bernie helps me clean up. He helps with everything, actually!"

The only other guests were two students from India. One was from Goa and the other from the north, from New Delhi. "We found each other at the university, but we have to speak English to each other," the taller, dark Bengali said. "Our languages are totally different!"

"Yes," said the shorter man, in carefully accented English. "I was raised a Catholic, speaking Portuguese. My father has ambitions for me. But recently Goa joined India as a state. I am happy to be studying mathematics in English!"

The two men, drinking gin and tonics from small glasses, fascinated Line. She cradled the sleeping Christopher as she sat talking to them on the daybed under the wide windows which looked down into the sere and empty park. "And what are you studying?" she asked the Bengali, who was wearing a suit and tie. She was ashamed that she hadn't gotten his name straight.

"I'm studying physics," he said. "But also music, literature, history. It's quite an interesting time in the United States. I have learned much from Bernard and Kay," he said. His English sounded more British than American.

A large turkey, stuffed with celery, rice and onions, mashed potatoes with turkey gravy, green beans, cranberries, a sweet potato casserole and salad were arrayed on the ample table set up in the middle of the room. "Bon appetit," said Kay, invoking Julia Child as she invited her guests to sit down.

Line put the sleeping Christopher on a blanket on the wide daybed, tucking cushions around him. He was too little to roll around and fall off.

When Kay asked Bernie to give thanks, Line listened hard. The Freemans were also Jewish. Though Stephen hardly mentioned it, Line had begun to wonder whether his background might become important now that they shared a son. Bernie said, "Let us join hands and give thanks."

Line bowed her head and linked hands with Stephen, and Nancy on her other side. "For the abundance of food on this table, for those who have helped prepare this sumptuous feast," said Bernie in a sonorous voice, "for the roof over our heads, the clothes on our backs, our health and wealth of blessings including these two tiny sons; for the opportunity to celebrate with family and friends and for the freedom to pray without fear in this great country, we thank you Lord, for these, among your many, many gifts."

The Goan student crossed himself, like a good Catholic.

"Were you ever a cantor?" asked Stephen.

"My father was," said Bernie. "I might have been, if I was still active in the synagogue."

"Just imagine," said Kay, "we're going to have Nixon in the White House. For four years!" she said. "And we are still thanking the Lord." She giggled, passing the mashed potatoes.

Line laughed. She couldn't help it. Did it really matter so much who was in the White House?

"He has campaigned on a promise of peace," said Bernie.

"Humphf!" said Kay. "As if we should pay attention to a campaign promise!"

"He wants 'Peace with honor'," quoted the Bengali ominously.

"No longer possible," said Nancy contemptuously.

Line sighed and looked over at her sleeping child. Kay was cooling a bit of mashed potatoes to put on little Abe's tray. "If only," Line said, "our children could grow up in a world without war."

"We have a wealth of blessings in this country," said Bernie. "It would be a sin not to admit it." He raised his glass with a ringing, "L'chaim!"

A chorus of voices answered him. "To life!" "L'chaim!" "God grant it!" Silvery wine poured down Line's throat. To life, she thought. To what comes.

20

Marty was terribly excited as she came down the jetway in Minneapolis just before Christmas. She had not been home in a year and a half. Longing to see her family, but equally desperate to preserve the self she felt she had attained, her whole body was filled with anticipation.

There, among the strangers in heavy winter coats, scarves and boots collected in the ugly airport light at the gate, she picked out the beloved faces of Dad and her two young sisters, Kristen and Hanna.

Dad's warm face was split by a grin which stretched from ear to ear. There was a little bit of grey in his crew cut, around the temples. Marty embraced him. "Oh Dad, it's so good to see you!"

"And you," said Dad. "You're lookin' mighty chipper."

"You too," said Marty shyly. She bent down over Kristen and Hanna, but not very far! "Kristen!" she wailed. "You're almost as tall as I am!"

Kristen, stolid and earth-bound, smiled self-consciously. "I am, aren't I!" She stood next to Marty, moving her hand from the top of her head to measure where it hit on Mary's body. There were only a couple of inches to go!

"She's going to be taller than you, Marty," said Dad, looking on indulgently.

"And Hanna!" said Marty. "You've been growing too!"

"I'm eight now, Marty," said Hanna gravely. "What did you expect?!" Hanna's solemnity against the striking lightness of her hair and face, was always a surprise.

Marty looked at Dad, as if she were Mother and these were their two young children. Indeed, as a baby, with fifteen years between them, Marty had carried Hanna everywhere.

Dad drew them off in the direction of the baggage claim. "We're not the only ones who are looking forward to seeing you," he said. "Paul went to get Line in Chicago, and Mother must be home by this time too!"

"Line?!" asked Marty.

"Yep. Mother's idea. Paul had the time and he just drove off in the station wagon. Took a sleeping bag. I'm not sure yet if Stephen's coming, but certainly Line and Christopher. They should be home tomorrow!"

"How exciting!" said Marty. "A real Christmas with all of us. I can't wait to see Christopher!"

"Almost eight weeks old now," said Dad. "None of us have seen him yet."

It snowed as Dad drove home in Mother's Plymouth. Slow, steady flakes came at the windshield like a fantasia of light, lit by the headlights which bored into the dark in front of them. Dad drove slowly, confidently.

Marty felt blessed. "I'm sorry it's so far," she said to Dad. He must have taken the whole day to come and get her. It was a four-hour trip on a good day, slower in the evening storm.

"Oh, you're welcome," said Dad. "You take the trouble to get out here, and believe me, we'll help! I can tell from your letters that city is seductive, but we'll put up a fight!"

"Thank you," said Marty. "Don't worry, Dad. I've been so homesick, sometimes. But I also really love it."

"Well, save your tales," said Dad. "Mother will want to hear them too."

When Line arrived with Paul the next evening, Marty was so excited that she felt the roof of the modern house in Haroldsburg might blow off! Everyone talked at once and Christopher was passed around, carefully. Most of the family had eaten supper already, but Line and Paul hadn't, so some of the lasagna was heated up for them.

"I've never had a baby of my own," said Hanna, solemnly, looking up from where she sat on the sofa with the wrapped bundle in her arms.

"He's just starting to smile," said Line. "He's amazingly responsive now. See, he's watching you. Imitating." Christopher's face was a healthy pink, his big eyes followed movement and people, and his little hands reached for things. Marty thought that Line's face looked thin, despite her recent pregnancy. No less shining. In fact, perhaps it shone more than ever. But Marty could see tension, even suffering.

"Take your time," Mother told Hanna. "Let him get used to you. Don't rush him." Mother's arms looked hungry, waiting her turn.

Marty was patient too. She had enjoyed lots of babies. And she knew that she and Line would have plenty of time to talk, as only they could. She looked around the room, trying to decide why the atmosphere was so easy among all of them.

The scene was that of a crèche, with the focus on the swaddled baby in the center. Mother sat protectively next to Hanna, who held the baby. Line, on the other side, ate from a plate of lasagna. Kristen stood behind Mother, watching closely. Paul too was eating from a plate, as he stood in the doorway. Dad hovered in the background, listening, taking time out from his many pursuits for a change. Frodo, the black Labrador, lay at Mother's feet. Low lamplight warmed the faces and made pools around the room.

"Paul was amazing," said Line. "There were cars in the ditch all along the icy roads today, but Paul just kept going! Nothing stopped him!"

"Snowed all the way?" asked Mother. She hated to drive in snow and ice.

"Not all day," said Paul. "You know how highways get. Cars warm them up and then they freeze again. Slippery. No. The weather was pretty stable, cold, grey skies with some snow flurries. There was more snow the day before, when I drove up." Paul looked like he always did. Steady, intense, quiet. He had just turned 21, Marty realized.

"We got that snow coming down from Minneapolis," said Dad. "Pretty socked in all over."

Marty imagined Paul and Line, driving across two states in the big Ford station wagon on the icy highways. Paul's good leg was his right, which could probably handle riding the gas all day. Marty had driven that car when she took driver's training. At least it had an automatic transmission.

In San Francisco, the atmosphere could be mellowed with music, or grass, but people were so different that Marty liked being with one person at a time best. Here in the Mikkelson household, where there were now five adults and three kids, harmony reigned. It was probably Mother, Marty thought. Everyone deferred to her, and she always directed the attention to the littlest person in the room, or sometimes the eldest. It was a structure you could trust. Mother and Dad tried to be fair to everyone. Marty knew she too would get her turn.

"Could we make lefse?" asked Line. "I've been dreaming about it!" Grandpa Mikkelson had died and Grandma was in an old folks home. Grandma could not send lefse as she did most Christmases. They must learn to make it themselves.

Marty caught Dad looking at Mother mischievously. Hmmmm. What did that mean? "We could try," answered Mother. "We could get the recipe from Aunt Hilda, and use the pancake griddle."

"Not potato lefse!" said Line. "I hate it!"

"Okay, okay!" said Dad. "We hear you! We get a few old Norwegian delicacies as gifts, but it does seem they are dying out."

"Sandbakkels," said Mother. "Sometimes rosettes or fattigman." Sandbakkels were sugar cookies; rosettes were made from a light dough, deep-fried around patterned steel irons and dusted with sugar. Fattigman, or poor man's cookies, were also a sugary pastry deep-fried in knots.

"Flatbread?" asked Marty. She remembered piles of thin sheets of crackling wheat bread given to them by older women in Montauk. Spread with butter, they were delectable.

"Probably not," said Mother. "I don't think anyone makes it."

"And klub?" asked Paul. "Anyone make that?"

"I don't think so!" said Mother, shuddering with distaste. Klub was a blood pudding Grandma Mikkelson made with flour and suet and stuffed into intestines.

"All poor man's food," said Line, "according to Mrs. Jacobson. I was surprised to hear that!"

"My mother was a hired girl for a while," said Dad. "Her family came from Norway because they were poor. She learned how to make all those things as a girl."

"Amazing how stratified it all was," said Mother.

Mother wouldn't touch klub, but Marty thought it was delicious, fried up and spread with butter. Dad and Mother were certainly from different sides of the Norwegian culture. It's perfect, thought Marty. I'm the daughter of an educated peasant and an aristocrat!

"Well, anyway," said Line. "I want to learn how to make lefse. And not with potatoes!"

"I made ginger crinkles," said Hanna. "Almost by myself! Could they have one?" she asked, looking up at Mother.

"Sure," said Mother. "Kristen, why don't you bring out those cookie tins."

Kristen returned from the kitchen with several painted tins, opening them on the coffee table to display their contents. "The little wafers are mine," she said modestly. One tin held white chocolate studded with toasted almonds.

"Oh my goodness," said Marty, reaching for a piece of the almond bark. It was very sweet and tasted like vanilla. "It's heaven!"

"Mother made that," said Hanna, from her perch on the sofa. It was clear she was restless, and Mother took the tiny wrapped Christopher from her. Hanna jumped up and carried tins around. "You have to try my ginger crinkles!"

Marty wished she hadn't been so hasty. She took a ginger crinkle from Hanna, but the little wafer cookies, frosted with pink and green frosting also looked attractive.

"Take it easy, Hanna," said Mother. "We don't have to eat everything at once!"

Line looked as though she were going to cry. "Oh," she said, reaching to hug Mother. "It's so wonderful to be here, surrounded by your warmth and abundance!"

"Yes," said Mother, smiling at her with characteristic dignity. "We don't have to stint at Christmas!"

Christmas was a busy time in a Lutheran parish. Having collected their children all in one place (except for Ellie, who was still in Italy with her family), Mother and Dad went to bed. Kristen and Hanna were sent to bed too, but Marty, Line and Paul were much too excited. In fact, thought Marty, this is what I need. She could not think how long it had been since Sparky and the gang had been together. It was a miracle. She held Christopher, smelling his milky, sweet skin.

"I'm going to make some coffee," said Line, quietly. "It would taste so good with cookies, wouldn't it?"

Coffee sounded decadent to Marty, who had begun to notice that her stomach wasn't happy if she drank too much. But Mother and Dad's coffee was not very strong. "I'll have some," she whispered.

"Paul?" asked Line.

"Absolutely!" Paul was rummaging in the cookie tins.

"You look sort of thin," said Marty to Line. "Are you okay?"

"No," said Line, sighing. "I'm not okay. But it isn't anything anyone can do anything about. And I'm not going to think about it for a week! I'm just going to enjoy myself and eat everything in sight!"

"Me too!" said Marty. She did not feel deprived. In fact she was plump from all the delicious food she was able to find in San Francisco. But no one made sweets as fine as the Mikkelsons'. She was not going to worry about overeating during the holidays.

"Well what is it? What is bothering you?" asked Marty, when they were all in the living room, drinking coffee from pottery mugs. "You can tell us," she wheedled. "We won't spill the beans to anyone else."

"It's Stephen," said Line. "He can't let go of the revolution. In fact everyone I know is getting more militant all the time! Nixon says he wants peace, but they're dropping tons of bombs on the Ho Chi Min trail in Cambodia and all these guys had to go back to Vietnam who didn't want to."

Line paused to sip her coffee, but the words poured out of her. "Then the campuses are erupting and we're very aware of the Black Panthers around us, who are being hounded terribly by the Chicago police. Stephen is teaching, but he spends long hours at the SDS office. He's also training in a guerilla cadre, for street fighting. I know he doesn't tell me everything he's up to. He has very little time for us. It really wasn't the best time to have a baby," she finished finally.

"Oh Line," said Marty. "It can't be true! It's never a bad time to have a baby!"

Line looked at them both miserably. "I'm sorry," she said. "But I really haven't been able to unload much on anyone." She giggled helplessly. "You guys get it!"

"It's okay," said Marty. "You're kind of in the thick of it. The rest of us lead lives of quiet desperation, while you are on the front lines!"

"Huh!" said Line. "Both of you look as happy as clams." Christopher whimpered a little, and Line picked him up and, expertly lifting her sweater, gave him her breast. Marty was stunned. Here was Line, going before as she always had. But no one said a word.

"Not many clams as happy as I am," said Paul, reaching for another cookie. "I didn't get into choir this year. I kept going back for tryouts, but they said they had too many good tenors. I just quit going back. But school is really interesting. A friend of mine took me skiing! It opens up a whole new way to look at the woods! Following rabbit and deer trails through the snow. I can't believe it. It's like when I first started canoeing!"

"And you don't have any problem with it?" asked Marty. She tried to imagine Paul hunkered down on a pair of skiis.

"Well, it's cross-country," he said. "I use one leg more than the other, but I can do it. And really cover a lot of ground!"

"Wow," said Line. "I'm so proud of you!"

"Yeah!" said Paul. "I just have to save up, get some handed-down skis or something. You wear these shoes that fit into the skis. They're not that different than regular shoes. And you wax the skis depending on the kind of snow you're in."

"I'd like to go," said Marty. "It sounds fun."

"How about you, Marty?" asked Line. "What's San Francisco like?"

"Amazing!" said Marty. "I feel so free there! It's sort of unpretentious and everyone's in the same boat, arrived from somewhere east, no family, no connections. We make our own! I'm living in a house with four other people, most of whom I like. There's always something going on!" Marty wished she could say something about Erik. She didn't want to admit even to herself that she was in love with him. But he was too unpredictable to call a boyfriend.

"And, how about your job?" asked Line.

"I got a job in a publishing house, typing of course. They publish legal books. I type up what the lawyers dictate about cases. It's not so bad. And there are a lot of interesting people there too. Hardly anyone reads as much as I do, but they like movies and music. Everyone loves music! Have you heard the *White Album*, by the Beatles?"

"Nope," said Line. "Our life is all politics, it seems. One good thing. The women are getting together more. We have a women's group. I would go crazy without them! Some of them have kids, and we're talking about co-operative child care. This little guy isn't ready for that, but maybe this summer," Line stroked Christopher's face with a little finger. She deftly lifted him and held him against her shoulder.

"Can I hold him?" asked Paul. He hadn't had a turn.

"Sure," said Line. She wrapped the little blanket around Christopher and put him in Paul's arms.

Marty mentally photographed the scene as she sipped coffee and ate more almond bark. What wealth was spread in front of her. Here was her family, almost snowbound in a cozy house, as in *War and Peace*, but the most current news of the day came to meet her in these vivid presences.

"So what about school?" asked Line, as Paul settled back into a chair. "Have you figured out your major?"

Paul all of a sudden looked anguished, shaking his head. "I don't know, I don't know," he said. "I have to start taking pre-seminary classes. But I'd really rather be in biology, or botany." He looked down at Christopher, who was smiling. "Yes," Paul said, smiling broadly at the small face. "I think I'm really more of a scientist! What do you think?" Christopher's tiny hand reached toward Paul's glasses. "No," said Paul. "Those are mine."

"You've got to face it," said Line, provocatively. "You are a person who can't do what he can't do. I've always know that about you."

"Did you guys see the article about Robin Graham traveling around the world in the *National Geographic*?" asked Paul. "It's here somewhere. He's a few months younger than me! I got out the globe and followed him with my finger. I was so right there with him!"

Marty listened, astounded at her quiet brother. "You're not thinking about that, now, are you?"

"Well, imagine," said Paul. "Being in Samoa and waiting out the hurricane season. You'd learn a lot! I don't know much about sailboats, though."

"Wow," said Line. "I think you had better put off the sem!"

Paul sank back into the chair with his bundle in his arms. From the look on his face Marty could tell he had never thought of that.

"Put it off?" he asked.

"Yeah, just put it off," said Line, waving a careless arm. "Don't do anything until you are sure about it. As they say, there are lots of ways to skin a cat."

This resonated strongly with Marty. "You are so right," she said. "If we'd grown up in a city, we would have had so many more ideas about the future. Maybe I would have been an architect! Or a photographer. There are so many possibilities!"

"I couldn't put off that little guy," said Line, "and I don't regret it one bit. But I'm afraid for us. So much violence all around."

"Not here," said Paul. "Or in Moorhead, Minnesota. Some guys are getting drafted, but they are finding ways out of it. And some of them want to go."

"I must say I notice a lot less violence in San Francisco than I did last year in Berkeley," said Marty. "The riots at the Oakland induction center were some of the worst yet. And Oakland is the birthplace of the Panthers. Oakland's really scary. But in San Francisco, there are concerts in the park almost every weekend. It's like a big party. Everyone dresses up, and they're so stoned they don't seem worried about anything!"

"Hippies and yippies," said Line, with some distaste. "Actually, I like the yippies. Abbie Hoffman is so funny! I saw him at a big gathering during the convention. And SDS does need to lighten up!"

"I love the feeling of freedom I get in San Francisco," said Marty. "I never knew I wanted it so much! It can be lonely, sometimes, but it's worth it to find out what I want to do, what I think. I need it. There's almost no one like me there!"

"Really?" asked Paul. "I always think we're sort of normal."

"We are," said Marty. "But a person from a big family, who grew up Norwegian Lutheran, lived in Europe and likes serious books and foreign films. Not very common." Marty got up. She wanted more coffee. But she was also worried she wouldn't sleep. "You know we could go on all night," she said, standing in the doorway to the kitchen. "Do you think we should go to bed?"

"No!" said Line. "We're just getting started!"

"We should really go to bed," said Paul. "We've got a week to talk."

"Yeah," said Marty. "It isn't fair to everyone else if we're washouts in the morning."

Line conceded. "Thank you, guys," she said. "You have no idea how happy I am to be here." She took Christopher from Paul, throwing him up on her shoulder.

Abundance appeared to be everywhere. Marty was astonished at the wealth of things that appeared under the Christmas tree. A kit to build a fiberglass canoe for Dad, a table loom for Mother, cross-country skis for Paul, and an amazing red robe quilted with gold thread for Marty. There were all kinds of smaller presents for Line, Christopher and the younger girls. Mother loved holidays and she had money to spend!

Marty tried to love the robe. She didn't like polyester and didn't want to wear it. But Mother had tried to please her, not something she usually did! The robe was also long and warm, and Marty did like its Chinese red color.

When every other present had been opened, Dad pulled out a flat one for the whole family. "You open it, Kristen," Dad said. Inside was an electric griddle, especially made for lefse! That was why Mother and Dad had shared a look, realized Marty.

On Christmas day, after church and a big turkey dinner, Line and Marty organized themselves into a lefse making team. Line mixed up the dough and let it sit before rolling the pieces out.

Kristen was desperate to help. "You can fold and flatten them," said Marty. "Get some clean dishtowels and maybe a bowl to put over them, so they don't lose their steam after they are cooked." Christmas music played on the phonograph. In the next room, Mother laid out her loom and studied the instructions, Hanna dancing in the background.

Line cut the dough into lumps and rolled each one out on the kitchen table, using lots of flour and a special, grooved rolling pin to roll it extremely thin. When it was thin enough, the floury pancake couldn't be handled. Marty slipped a carved wooden stick under it and carried it over to the hot griddle, smoothing it out. Dad had sanded the edge of the stick down very thin. The lefse browned quickly. Using the flat stick Marty flipped it, so it could cook on the other side.

There was no yeast in the dough, but it was a soft, rather than a crisp flatbread. When Marty felt it was done, she used the stick to pass it to Kristen, who folded it once and then again, and stacked it in the towels, using the steam to keep it soft and pliable.

Kristen looked up at Marty joyfully. "It's always more fun when you come home," she said. "I wish it were like the old days."

Marty looked at Line. Kristen and Hanna were so different from each other. They played some games together, but Kristen liked to spend time with Frodo outdoors and Hanna was totally absorbed by books and music.

"The old days?" asked Marty questioningly.

"You know. You guys tell stories about the big tree, and ice skating and playing 'my hopes.' And we don't do any of that," scoffed Kristen.

"I guess it was because we were so close in age," Marty replied. "But you are luckier in some ways. Mom and Dad were poor when we were growing up. And Paul was sick, and often not here ..."

Kristen looked stubborn. "I still wish it was like the old days. There's not even *Amahl and the Night Visitors* on television!"

"I wonder why," said Marty. She missed it too.

Line laughed at them, energetically rolling another very thin piece of lefse. "Appreciate what you have, Kristen," she said. "You never know what's coming."

Marty picked up the dough on her stick and laid it carefully on the hot grill. No grease was used. She handed the finished piece to Kristen and wiped the excess flour, which smelled burnt, off with a rag. "Do you think we could have a piece?" asked Marty.

"No need to wait!" sang out Line.

"Come on, Kristen," said Marty. "Let's share one of those slices."

Kristen uncovered one of the pieces, which had grown more brittle and cracked on the folds as it cooled. Marty spread butter on her half. She couldn't bear to add sugar and cinnamon, as some people did. The sweet taste of wheat with butter was enough.

Paul came and stood in the door, watching them. "Smells good in here! I'd like a piece," he said. Kristen opened up the folded dishtowels and handed him one.

"Remember," Marty said, "when Mother thought maybe we should switch to margarine and Dad put a stop to it? He said life was too short to eat margarine! I know lots of people in San Francisco who think margarine is more healthy, but I still feel like Dad was right!"

"Nothing like butter," said Paul, slathering it on his lefse. "At least to people from the North countries, like us Scandinavians."

"What a Christmas," said Line. "I almost don't believe it!"

Marty agreed. The year before she hadn't had enough money to get home. She had loved learning about Jewish holidays in the Certoks' home, but nothing beat being with her family at Christmas.

21

Registering for classes the second semester at Trinity College, Paul knew he was up against a wall. He must take one direction or another if he wanted to graduate with any sort of useful degree. He was miserable, but he could not goof around any longer.

Mr. Berg, Paul's advisor, wasn't much help. Paul had been in his geology class last semester. "I often think you transfer students don't know what you want," he said irritably when Paul met with him in his office. "What do you want from your college education?" he demanded.

"I'm kind of a generalist," said Paul. "I want a liberal education. But I also need a job. I've thought of myself as pre-sem all this time, but all of a sudden I'm not sure!" He had probably chosen Mr. Berg as an advisor because he would rather be in science.

Mr. Berg sighed and put a hand over his face. "I was impressed with your thoughts on rivers and deltas last semester, but I'm not sure they amount to a career," he said. "Have you talked to your folks about this?"

"I'm the only son in a family of six," said Paul. Only men could become pastors. "I'm close to my Dad and it's always been assumed that I would be a pastor. I can't really talk to them about it."

"Well, I wish I knew you better," said Mr. Berg. "Teaching is a good backup," said Mr. Berg. "But you'll have to take education courses. I guess you got one psych class at Astoria that might transfer," he said, pondering Paul's records in front of him. "Worst case you'd have to take summer classes."

Yeah, thought Paul. That would be tough. "Okay," said Paul slowly. "I guess I better move forward on the theory I'll become a teacher."

"High school science?" asked Mr. Berg. "You can get started, but you'll probably need more education as you go along."

"I love to study!" said Paul. "That's not a problem! I just need to be able to pay for it. Especially if I'm going against the family grain."

Back at his desk in the dormitory that evening, Paul fingered the small ivory Eskimo seated in a kayak Aunt Mabel had given him years ago. Without a dog to talk to, he often used this small carving as a talisman. "What would you do?" he asked silently. The Eskimo's arm was raised, as if about to spear a seal or a fish, though it held no weapon. The ivory was soft and smooth to his touch. Education would have meant something entirely different in the Eskimo's world: life sustaining skills not found in books.

It wasn't as if Paul wasn't religious. He was rooted in his relationship to Christ and the church. It was really a matter of his personality, Paul thought. Even though it appeared from the outside as if Dad took a lot of time for his hobbies and his life, Paul knew that he gave everything, that he was always absorbed by the problems of his parish, by the stresses of preparing sermons every week and the constant question of whether there wasn't more he should be doing. Paul just didn't feel he was prepared for this.

"Full moon tonight, Mikkelson," said Paul's roommate, Wayne Stenson, as he entered. Wayne didn't have Paul's problems. He had his own! Thin and dark, he had studied mathematics his whole life and was something of a whiz, but he didn't want to be drafted and he was worried about it.

Paul knew what a full moon on a clear night meant. When Paul showed up after Christmas with skis, Wayne wanted to go skiing at night. Wayne didn't express himself well, but he was an active guy and had taken Paul out on skis the first time.

"Sure!" said Paul. "Leave after supper?" The new semester had hardly begun. It was the best time to skimp on sleep and homework.

"Yup." Wayne sat down to the fat book on astronomy he was poring over, turning on the desk lamp in the gathering darkness of the late afternoon.

After supper the two of them met back at the dorm. They laced up their cross-country ski shoes, punched them into their skis and headed out into the dark. Paul could wear normal shoes, even on his polio leg, so shoes weren't a problem. It was just harder to find and maintain his center of balance, since one of his legs was so much stronger than the other. He did what he had to, however. Nothing kept him from being outdoors.

The two skiers didn't have to get far from the college before the wide expanse of the sky opened. The moon rose behind them in the east, large and fat on the horizon, a glowing silver white, throwing their blue shadows long across the deep and settled, untouched snow. Paul let Wayne make a trail and he followed, his skis fitting into the grooves in the snow ahead of him. He didn't want to get too tired.

The Red River, the dividing line between Minnesota and North Dakota, was only a few blocks from campus. The river was actually the bed of a glacial lake of fairly recent origin. Paul had not been in Moorhead during the spring yet, so he had never experienced the flooding, which could be major depending on the timing of the snow melt. The river was also unusual because it flowed north, into Lake Winnipeg in Canada.

Wayne powered ahead with long smooth strides, a demon skier. He put up with Paul's steady, slow pace because Paul put up with his speech difficulties. Both of them were glad of someone to ski with. Paul had learned the hard way that he shouldn't travel alone when he had sprained his good ankle badly in the snow and Foxy and Dad had rescued him.

At the river, Wayne turned north. Ice lay on it, but not enough to trust. In the north, winter was actually the best time to get around. It was cold, but snow and ice made smooth plains and reduced the vegetation, so you could see more and move fast. Paul had only been at Lake Michigami once when it was frozen over, but he and Dad had walked out on the ice and chopped a hole in it to see how thick it was.

Paul moved steadily through the thrilling landscape along the icy river. On the right, pine and fir trees laden with snow stood like silent witnesses. Winter was short, but dramatic. Paul thought he saw faint shimmers of green ahead along the horizon. When Wayne stopped for a minute, he pointed them out. "Aurora?" he asked.

"Surely," said Wayne, handing Paul a thermos he had stuffed in a pocket, in which there was lukewarm coffee.

Paul looked up. His old friend Orion now lay on his back along the horizon, his belt pointing down to Sirius, the Dog star. The swift moon had moved higher in the sky, allowing them to see the stars along the edge of the great bowl. Wolf moon, thought Paul. A full wolf moon.

"Wonder if you could follow the river into Canada," said Wayne.

Paul got it. So that's what Wayne thought about. "On skis?" asked Paul.

"Yeah," said Wayne.

"It's only a couple of hours by car," said Paul. "You could take a bus to Winnipeg!"

"Maybe," said Wayne.

Paul could see he was taken with the romance of it. "That's crazy," said Paul. "Breaking trail all the way. Carrying gear. You couldn't get far."

"Yeah," sighed Wayne.

But the idea captivated Paul too. He often imagined the French and Indian trappers roaming the Northlands in the past, using the stars and the rivers to know where they were.

"We better turn 'round," said Wayne, looking up.

"Can you tell how long we've been gone by the moon?" questioned Paul.

"It moves about 15 degrees an hour, I think," said Wayne. "So, I'd say 30."

"Wow," said Paul. The moon had indeed come about 45 degrees over the horizon. They had been skiing for two hours.

Paul let Wayne go ahead, retracing their path and skiing in the grooves of their own outward trail. Without much wind, the temperatures didn't feel worse late at night, Paul noted. In fact, he felt quite comfortable. He was glad for his mittens, which trapped the warmth of his fingers together.

The snow was crisp and dry under their feet. They stayed in the clear areas, but once when they came close to trees, Paul saw a rabbit track, two deep parallel prints in the blue snow, followed by the rear ones in a line. The moon shadows of leafless trees lay like lace across the gleaming drifts.

Close to the river, Paul called for Wayne to stop. Standing absolutely still and listening, they could hear the gurgling and swishing of water under the thin ice. It sounded like life to Paul, like the great artery or vein of a body, pumping liquids north towards its great heart.

They pushed back south, the rhythmic swoosh of their skis too loud to hear any other sound.

When they got to the dorm they stuck their skis and poles upright in the snow by the door. "Great night," said Paul to Wayne, pulling off his mittens and blowing on his cold fingers. His legs ached almost equally, but otherwise, he felt great. "Thanks for the run!"

Paul's bed was welcome, but his heart was full as he lay down. And every night the moon shone like this, whether he went out to look at it or not! A lifetime of moons waxing and waning stretched in front of him.

As the winter progressed, Paul came to like the idea of being a teacher. It wasn't so different from being a pastor and it felt like there was more room for uncertainty. He took an astronomy class and one in beginning calculus, trying to broaden his math and science background. Wayne helped. Though he didn't speak much, Wayne was good at describing math. Paul did not tell Mother and Dad his plans.

One Sunday evening Paul piled into a car with Michael, Doug and Naomi, headed to a small church to play for a Luther League benefit. Paul had been asked to join this outreach group because he could play the guitar. They were a little late, but Michael, tall and assured, with golden brown hair, had his foot heavy on the gas. The car was warm and comfortable, though it was dark and freezing outside.

Doug sat in the passenger seat, the map in front of him, navigating through the thick mists. The irrepressible Naomi, whom Paul had sung with at Astoria College, began singing, "Michael, row the boat ashore, Alleluia." She began with the right words to the folk song, but soon she began making up the verses as she went along, giggling as she thought of the next one and poking Paul with a mittened hand to help her.

"This Red River is chilly and cold, Alleluia.

"Chills the body, but not the soul, Alleluia."

Michael joined in contributing verses. "Douglas, help to navigate, Alleluia; through the mists so we won't be late, Alleluia."

Naomi giggled when she heard new words, but was able to sing as they repeated the phrases.

"Paul will take out his guitar, Alleluia; making love instead of war, Alleluia."

Paul listened to see what they would say about Naomi. "Michael's boat is a music boat, Alleluia; Michael's boat is the music boat, Alleluia." No one had come up with one for her. The music kept rolling, the loudest person driving the next phrase.

Finally Paul had it. "Sister Naomi trim the sermon, Alleluia; sister Naomi trims the text, Alleluia." Naomi collapsed into laughter, her face red and her eyes dancing.

"We should get the kids singing this," said Michael. "Get them to make up their own words!"

"You could do it, Michael," said Doug. Michael was a natural leader, a good speaker and yes, headed for the ministry.

The car was so full of warmth and merriment they almost missed a turnoff. But Doug was using the odometer to check where they were, and they pulled into the lighted church parking lot only a few minutes past the time they were supposed to be there, 7:30 p.m. Paul hastily pulled out his guitar, trying to warm and tune it.

Michael led the brief meeting, which accompanied a bake sale. It looked like the whole church was there, men, women and children of all ages. Michael opened with a devotional passage and Naomi, tall and blonde, spoke too. She was in love with Michael, Paul could tell. They quickly moved on to the singing. Paul loved being part of it.

In the back of the room, Paul spotted a young woman sitting on a chair with her leg in a cast propped up on another chair. After the meeting, Paul got a cup of coffee and a piece of cake and went over to her. Someone had already given her a piece of cake. It was unusual for Paul to approach someone he didn't know, but she looked friendly, perhaps a little older than he was.

"I can't help noticing someone with their leg in a cast," he said. "I had polio myself. What happened?"

"I fell out of a plane," said the girl, who said her name was Marcia.

"You fell out of a plane?" asked Paul.

"Well, not exactly. It wasn't in the air," conceded Marcia, smiling. "That just sounds like a good story. I was getting out of one of the little bush planes in Alaska, and the ground wasn't quite like I thought it would be. And I was carrying a bunch of books. It all went wrong in an instant! And got worse from there!"

"Wow," said Paul. "That sounds tough!"

"It had to be re-broken, surgery, the whole bit," said Marcia. Her face looked a little worn, talking about it. "It was kind of rough. I had to come home. They couldn't take care of me there as well as my folks could."

"Sorry to hear that. What were you doing in Alaska?" asked Paul.

"I'm a teacher," said Marcia. "There are so many people up there, kids back in the bush. They can't get to school, so the school districts send teachers out with books to help the parents teach their kids."

"Wow," said Paul. "By plane?"

"A lot of the time," said Marcia. "Sometimes by train, dog sled. Whatever works. Sometimes the kids go to boarding schools."

Lights were going on in Paul's brain. "And you're from here?"

"Yes," said Marcia. "Born and raised right here. I went to St. Olaf. Alaska sent out recruiters. I guess they knew Minnesotans would be less apt to mind the weather! Forty to fifty below sometimes out there."

"I know," said Paul. "I had an aunt who was a missionary to some of the towns, Shishmaref, Teller. She ended up in Sitka. She's retired now."

"Oh yeah," Marcia warmed to the name. "I know Mt. Edgecumbe in Sitka. It's a high school, a boarding school. Alaska has special problems. Everything is so spread out there! But they discovered oil last year at Prudhoe Bay. All these people want to come in and build a pipeline. Everyone says things are going to change."

"So you're going back?" asked Paul.

"As soon as my leg heals," said Marcia. "Probably not until this fall, though. It's getting close to summer now."

"This is all so interesting!" said Paul. "I'm over in Moorhead, not far away. Can I write to you, or call you? I'm really interested in teaching in Alaska. I've got one more year to go. I'll graduate next year."

"Sure," said Marcia. "I was an English major, and I love to read, so I'm not bored at home. I'm reading up on all kinds of things. But it does get kind of slow some times." She looked up at Paul ruefully. "Everyone's busy."

Paul looked around, "Arrrgh," he said. "I ought to carry a notebook or something." He tore off a piece of the paper tablecloth and handed it to Marcia with a pen and a hymnbook to write on. Paul was impressed with himself. He rarely went up to anyone he didn't know and talked to them.

"Thank you so much!" said Paul, folding the scrap of paper Marcia had written on and stuffing it in his billfold. "So do you work out of one town? Do you have a base school?"

"Oh yes," said Marcia. "I'm in the Denali school district, which is headquartered in Healy. It's not too far from Fairbanks."

"Do you think I could get a job there?" asked Paul.

"Are you kidding! They're begging for good teachers. I get the Fairbanks newspaper to keep up. It's fascinating."

Paul closed his eyes for a moment. A dream was being born. It didn't even seem too far from reality. "Fairbanks newspaper?" he asked.

"*The Fairbanks Daily News-Miner*," said Marcia. "They mail me the Sunday paper, kind of late, but that's okay."

"Could you keep them for me?" asked Paul. "I'd love to see the old ones."

"Yeah, they're starting to pile up," said Marcia.

Naomi came over at this point. "Paul," she said, nudging him. "We've got to go. It's getting late."

"Sure," said Paul. "Naomi, this is Marcia. She's a bush teacher in Alaska but she broke her leg."

"Tibia and fibula," said Marcia, reaching for her crutches. "I've seen enough x-rays to last my whole life!" It seemed that everyone was pulling on coats and scarves, getting ready to leave.

The car was quiet on the drive back to campus. Everyone seemed to be sleepy or thinking their own thoughts. Ideas like firecrackers were exploding in Paul's head, though he kept them to himself. Why had he never thought of this before, he wondered. Aunt Mabel's long career, all of the slideshows and talks on her mission work, the ivory carvings, the hand-stitched Eskimo doll in beautiful furs she gave Mother. The song of Alaska ran through his family and he hadn't paid attention.

But Alaska was the North Country and no mistake. No wonder they looked for teachers in Minnesota! Paul couldn't wait to get his hands on those Fairbanks newspapers. He began writing a letter to Marcia in his head.

Life intervened on Paul's dreams, however, bringing him back, front and center, to the present. By the middle of March, everyone at the college and across the river in Fargo, North Dakota, was aware that the snowmelt was not happening as fast as it should. The cold continued and by the end of the month there was still 8" of snow on the ground. Daylight lengthened and everyone began to watch the river.

Paul walked along the banks. The ice had begun to break up and floated in chunks on the water which moved powerfully north into Canada. If melting occurred in the south but not the north, ice dammed the flow and water had nowhere to go. The ancient lakebed flooded.

"Every 100 years," people said, "we have a really major flood. This might be the one." In 1897 the river crested at 39.1 feet, way beyond flood stage. The towns were much more built up now. Wayne pointed out that the sun in April had the same force as that in mid-August. A sudden thaw might mean disaster.

In the first week of April, temperatures soared to 60 degrees and 2" of rain didn't help. Thousands of sandbags were collected and the call went out for volunteers to build them into levees. Student volunteers, alumni and anyone who could help poured in, from as far away as the universities in Mankato and Minneapolis. As the water rose, major downtown roadways and bridges were closed off, underwater.

Trinity College was on high ground and not in much danger, but the southern part of Moorhead was. The college closed classes down and prepared tons of food and housing for volunteers. Paul went to the gym with other students and found Mr. Berg's team. The athletic teams stuck together. Paul saw chorus members in a group, getting ready to sing work songs.

The first day Paul's group was bussed around by country bridges to provide the brawn for sandbagging in Fargo. Engineers directed operations, telling people where to go and what to do. The sense of rising urgency made everyone work fast. Older men stood on trucks shoveling sand off into the bags. Younger men humped them to where they needed to go.

A line formed, passing the bags hand over hand to an experienced-looking man who placed them on the levee. Shoulder to shoulder, Paul passed the heavy bags along. It rained intermittently and Paul was covered in muck after hours of being on the line. He was hungry, but after a while, when no one left, his stomach shut up and he just kept going.

Spirits were high and wry jokes passed from person to person. It was amazing how people's usual pettiness evaporated under this kind of pressure. Nature was pointing out to men that she was mighty, thought Paul. But men were also Nature. Weather made people band together against it. The sandbaggers were like a swarm of ants, struggling to maintain their small holdings against Nature's great sway.

In the spring evening darkness, Mr. Berg called the group off. Paul got a soggy sandwich and a bag of chips. It tasted better than anything he could remember. "Hot coffee!" shouted one of the girls from the back of a truck. Paul walked over and filled a paper cup from a big silver urn.

The next day, Paul's group sandbagged a coulee which was about to flood into a South Moorhead neighborhood. The water was heavy, churning and roiling along. It could knock a man down if you got in its way. Why does this work, Paul wondered as he passed bags down the line. When they took a break, he asked Mr. Berg.

"Clay and silt fill in the gaps in the sand, actually making the bags a better barrier as the waters rise," said Mr. Berg, standing next to the levee. "See. As it gets muddier, less water seeps through. The bags also are getting heavier, so the floodwaters can't wash them away."

"I guess it's been so long since this happened, no one's figured out a better way," said Paul.

"They need a drainage ditch," said Mr. Berg, "far out around the city, to take the pressure off the river. But that's a big project. Probably a federal project. Things have to get a lot worse before they decide to do that. And sandbags aren't bad. They're cheap and portable."

When they had done as much as they could, Paul went back to the neighborhood to help drag furniture up out of people's basements. Some of the girls had been doing this, but they needed help. Wading through a few inches of water, Paul found someone's guitar in a case, forgotten in a corner. He felt terrible. Would it still play?

One family had a huge freezer full of food down the basement. It couldn't be dragged upstairs full, so they were emptying it, cooking some of the meat and passing it out to people. Paul ate three hamburgers! It felt like a party.

At night Paul slept deeply, but the sense of urgency, of rising water was with him when he woke. The next morning they were told that the river had crested at 37.34 feet, a record. The stagnant water began to recede. But that wasn't the end of it.

It turned out that cleanup was worse than sandbagging. It took weeks. Silt and muck from the river stunk and felt like sewage. Water and plumbing systems were contaminated and everyone had to conserve. Garbage piled up in the street, pieces of old carpeting, furniture and water-damaged dry wall. The sun dried things out, but lines of muck were etched onto buildings at the high water levels for weeks afterwards. Paul felt lucky. His guitar was safe.

School returned to its usual fervor, but no one forgot the flood. "You never know," said Paul's German teacher, who lived in Fargo and crossed the state line every day to teach. "The best laid plans of mice and men, often go awry!"

It reminded Paul of his own plans. He wrote to Marcia and arranged to visit her.

A postcard arrived from Dad. "Call us collect," it said. "We want to hear about the flooding. Love, Dad."

Paul called and told them the part he had played.

"On television it looked like everything was under water," said Dad. Mother was listening in on the other line. "We couldn't tell whether you were flooded out or not!"

"Nope," said Paul. "Quite an experience, though. Rivers are amazing. Especially this one."

"Yeah," said Dad. "By the time it got up to Bryan, where we lived, it wasn't very powerful. I think they built Fargo on a floodplain."

"Yeah," said Paul. "An ancient glacial lakebed." He hesitated, but then blurted, "I wanted to tell you I'm thinking about getting a job teaching in Alaska when I graduate. I talked to someone who is teaching there. They need all the people they can get!"

There was silence at the other end of the line. Finally Mother managed, "Alaska?"

"Yeah, they discovered oil up there and people are going to flock there to work. Schools will be stretched and they will need teachers!"

"You are needed," said Dad, slowly. "Are you sure that's where?" No one said what they were all thinking. What about the seminary, Paul?

"Well, I'm thinking about it," said Paul. He felt elated. He had brought it out in the open. It was all down hill from here.

"We'll pray for you, Paul," said Mother. "As we always do. You will surely find the right path."

22

When Stephen arrived home haggard with worries and fears, Line sat him down in the rocking chair and placed the smiling, pink-faced Christopher in his arms. "Talk to him," begged Line. "He loves to hear your voice." A warm rain was falling and Line had the doors to the back porch open. Munchkin was curled on the daybed, his white paws over his face.

Stephen was a little awkward with his son, but he did relax. Line stepped back into the kitchen where she was grating cheese for tacos, which Ann, a friend from Texas, had taught her how to make with black beans. Stephen sang, a little off tune, "Oh, I ain't gonna work on Maggie's farm no more..." Line laughed because his voice sounded thin and nasal, like Dylan!

"Is that SDS?" she asked. "You ain't gonna work for SDS no more?"

"Ought to be," said Stephen darkly.

Stephen's euphoria over the national prominence of SDS had been short-lived. He was suffering many different kinds of strain. He took his teaching seriously. His small salary was the only money they had. But as a respected long-time member of SDS and a natural negotiator, he was trying to hold the fragmenting ideologies of the SDS leadership together.

SDS was very active, reaching out to members of the black movement, resistance groups, Third World revolutionaries, high schools and labor unions trying to forge a revolutionary youth movement. The national office leadership was trying to shore up its alliances against the encroaching Progressive Labor, a Marxist ideological group which SDS, insisting on open membership, had not been able to shut out. Every meeting, as Stephen reported them to Line, was contentious and unpleasant.

At the same time, the group was suffering the pressures the Nixon administration had unleashed trying to curb the New Left. Many of the people Stephen had worked closely with were no longer in Chicago or had formed other affinity groups, all part of the widening movement. The newer members of SDS were considerably less afraid of violence, and in fact were learning guerrilla fighting tactics from Third World revolutionaries.

Line hated to see Stephen so worn and wasted. She saw little point to endless infighting. She herself would have fallen back on an apolitical stance, thinking only of her own family and baby, except that the women's group she participated in stoutly insisted that "the personal is the political." Women's groups were also fragmenting the movement, though widening it considerably.

Christopher took Stephen's singing in good stride, but he wouldn't fall asleep until Line let him suckle her breast. As soon he was asleep, she put him down so she and Stephen could have dinner.

"So what's going on?" Line asked. They hadn't had time to sit and talk for almost a week.

"Well," said Stephen. "I got ten more colleges rejecting our request to have the June convention on their campus. Guess they're onto us! There's one out east, but Bernardine doesn't want it out in PL territory." He laughed, half-heartedly.

Line smoothed back the long, red-gold hair that curled around her face. Months of not working had made it thick and healthy. She folded her taco over and took a bite. "Not too surprising," she said.

"Everyone's hardening," said Stephen. "Both inside and outside. The revolution has begun, it seems. And you can't make a revolution with a loosely organized group. It has to have discipline. SDS is changing."

"Are you hardening, my darling?" asked Line.

"Yes," said Stephen, quietly. "Yes, I am. Doing nothing, in a time of imperialist violence by one's country, is also violence." Inner fire burned beneath his exhaustion. "I don't mean you, Line," he said. "You're keeping the home fires burning. But for me, it would be wrong."

Line sighed. "You've worked so hard," she said. "Can't you take a break. Let other people take up the cause?"

"People like me are the most important right now," Stephen said. "Voices of reason are few. I feel obligated, with my mediating skills, to hang in there."

Line knew he was right. "I know," said Line. "I've just had enough of the sacrifices we're making." She did not tell Stephen that the event of her day had been being short-changed a dollar. She hadn't realized that the cashier at the co-op got confused as she talked to him. Afterwards, it was too late. And she was too ashamed to insist that the co-op, a righteous organization if ever there was one, pay her back.

Instead, Line stood under the black umbrella with the broken spokes and cried, Christopher in a sling across her chest. A dollar would buy a pound of meat, a couple of dozen eggs, or twenty Hershey bars. She could have used that dollar.

Stephen stood up. "I'm sorry, Line," he said. He kissed her on the forehead and stepped out on the damp balcony, where the evening sun was shining through the clouds. Big drops hung from the overhanging roof, shining with color. He took half a cigarette from a mashed, woebegone pack and lit it with a match.

Line cleared the dishes. She knew Stephen was hiding a lot from her, also. She didn't try to buttonhole him. She was a natural nester, happily staying home for days at a time in bad weather. She concentrated on stretching her food allowance and keeping the atmosphere at home light and cozy.

But her sense of responsibility for Christopher loomed very large. Especially since Stephen didn't seem to worry about Line or plan for his family. Line wondered if she wasn't too independent. Perhaps if she begged or pleaded with him, Stephen would notice. But Line wasn't good at that. She was better at accepting the burdens thrust on her.

"Come here, Line," said Stephen. Line went outdoors. Stephen put his arms around her and they stood looking out toward the budding trees and the low hanging sun. "I'm not sure what the end of all of this is. I know Nixon is getting tired of the war. And more and more people are seeing Amerika for what it is, an imperialist swindle. I do know I love you."

Inwardly Line giggled. It was like a movie moment. But she lapped it up. She needed it. "Thank you, Stephen," she said. "I love you too. I'm sorry for whining. I'll try to buck up."

Stephen's hands traced the small of Line's back and traveled down to her big hips. That night Line went to sleep happy.

But it didn't last long. Line's real worry was about the summer. One evening she sat in the rocker after Christopher was asleep, the cat in her lap. Brooding, she plucked at the fraying ends of her long hair. She really needed to cut them.

Finally, in despair, she fumbled around on Stephen's desk to find the phone card he used when he made long-distance calls from home. She called the phone number she had for Marty, and, amazed, listened as someone said, "Just a minute, I think she's around here somewhere." Line listened to the echoing sounds of people moving around as the phone lay on some table in San Francisco.

"Marty! I can't believe I got you," Line said.

"It's me all right," said Marty. "Are you okay?" Phone calls in the Mikkelson family were serious.

"I guess so," said Line. "I just had to talk. I can't tell Stephen how worried I am. I do have friends, but I don't like dumping all my problems on them."

"I know," said Marty. "I'm so glad you called. What is it? You can certainly tell me."

"It's just that I'm going to have to work this summer," said Line. "And I'm scared to leave Christopher. Stephen is good with him, but he's so involved. He might take him somewhere and not pay attention! The SDS office is awful. It's no place for a baby!"

"Couldn't Stephen get a job?" asked Marty.

"He usually works at SDS in the summers, which doesn't pay much. He seems more committed than ever. If we are going to pay the rent this summer, I'm going to have to work."

"Have you talked about it?"

"I'm scared to," said Line. "The women in my group are forming child care groups. I'll probably have to do that, give him to one of them. But, with the bus and everything I'm gone ten hours a day! And I'll get a weird shift I'm sure. I just don't feel I can count on Stephen. God, Marty. I'm scared to death!"

"You could go home for the summer," said Marty. "Go up to the lake."

"Oh my God, Marty," said Line. "Don't tempt me. But it's like admitting defeat. I can't do that. Stephen and I have to solve our own problems."

"Well, I guess you're going to have to talk about them then," said Marty flatly.

"How are things with you?" asked Line, putting off the thought.

"Good!" said Marty. "I'm still working for the publishing company. Part of the time I'm dialing up a computer in Rochester, New York, and typing index notations into it. The computer sorts them and makes up a comprehensive index for the back of the book. Isn't that wild?"

"Yeah?" said Line tentatively. She found it hard to be interested. "So you like your job?"

"I do," said Marty. "I'm in a pool of people, and they're all so interesting. San Francisco is wonderful. We're always exploring on weekends. Line," she broke off. "Is this okay? Are we running up your phone bill?"

"It's some phone card Stephen has. I think it's okay," said Line. Whether SDS was paying for it or not, she simply did not care. "And are you still seeing the elusive Erik?"

"Yeah," said Marty, softly. "He's around a lot. I'm not sure why he likes me. He's so suave and well-educated. But he does disappear. I just sort of take it as it comes."

It didn't sound like Marty. She couldn't do things by halves. "Maybe we're missing something here," Line said. "Of course I don't know the guy."

"He's gorgeous," said Marty. "And why would he be interested in someone like me?"

"Marty," said Line. "You have no idea how happy I am to talk to you. You're down to earth and level-headed. And you're so far away from the simmering pot I'm in. It sounds positively peaceful there!"

"Actually, there's a lot going on, a strike at SF State. But that doesn't affect me very much. Line," said Marty suddenly. "Why don't you come out here this summer. I could put you up. We'd have a wonderful time."

"Oh, Marty," said Line. "How could I possibly? I don't have any money and I'd be just running away. Maybe I better hang up before I say yes!"

"Sorry, I don't mean to derail you," said Marty. "But if you get in trouble …"

Line decided she had better leave it at that. She said her goodbyes. The call had lightened her, but she still had much to brood about. She had trouble sleeping until Stephen came in very late.

The next day Stephen called Line in the middle of the day. "Bernie Freeman was attacked in his office," he said, his voice low. "He's in Cook County hospital. I think you should come. You might be able to help Kay."

"What happened?" said Line, the blood draining from her face.

"He was found on the floor bleeding. His hand is badly injured and there are craters in his skull. He's in surgery right now."

"Is he okay?"

"No one knows. They're trying to repair his fractured skull, and his hand, but Kay is hysterical."

"I'll be there as soon as I can," said Line. She was shocked and frightened.

It was a bright day in early May. Line dressed and prepared Christopher for an outing. Where, she wondered was Abe, Kay's little boy who was now walking? What a nightmare! She could not get to the hospital fast enough, carrying Christopher in the little sling she had made by tying an old scarf over one shoulder. He was getting heavy, but so far it worked when she wanted her hands free.

When Line got to the emergency room, the waiting room was filled with people. The word had traveled out to the Freemans' friends, which were legion. Almost the whole Westside Women's group was there, though there was nothing anyone could do but mill around and talk in low voices.

Line went up to Kay and knelt beside her. "He could be a vegetable," Kay said, her eyes hollow and gaunt. Abe gamboled about on the floor, playing with blocks and enjoying the unfamiliar party.

"You must trust, Kay," said Line. "The human body is remarkable. It has amazing powers of rejuvenation."

"Thank you, Line," said Kay. "I'll try." She hiccoughed as she gulped in air, trying to relax.

Vivian began scheduling how they could help Kay's hospital vigil with meals and taking care of Abe. Several of the women in the group lived in Hyde Park, as Line did.

Line overheard Stephen talking to someone who must be a colleague. "Someone found him in a pool of blood. It was a good thing they got him here quickly. He might have died," he said low. "Kay says he went to his office to meet a newspaper reporter. Guy hit him on the head with a crowbar and slashed his hand."

Line felt sick and shocked. It was so close to home. In the next weeks, she tried to be there for Kay, but Bernie's parents came from New York, and Kay's life was very full. Line and Stephen could only wait.

A week later there was a melee at the SDS office when Stephen was there. Police arrived, demanding to inspect the premises as a shooting had been reported. A few minutes later, a bunch of firemen also arrived. Mike Klonsky, the national secretary, said nothing was happening in the offices, and suggested that the fire chief alone inspect the place. When he entered, the firemen barged in after him and the police followed. Both sides pushed and shoved and five SDS staff members were arrested and held on charges of "interfering with a fireman" and " battery against an officer."

Stephen spent the entire night trying to raise bail. He was successful and the five were out the next morning, but all of them were now certain that SDS was the target of serious repression. New Left Notes stated: "It is clear that until the power to control the institutions of this society is in the hands of the people, the people will never have justice or freedom. Power to the people! Death to the pig!"

Though spring was insistent, among people, chaos reigned. Campus strikes, arrests, police repression and shooting. That same week they heard that in Berkeley, where hundreds of people had turned a derelict lot into a park, the university sent in police, who cleared the area and put up a chain link fence. A spontaneous riot broke out and hundreds of people were shot and maimed. California's Governor Reagan sent the National Guard to Berkeley to patrol the streets.

Line despaired, worried every day that Stephen would not come home. It seemed that nothing deterred him. At the end of May, Line went to the Cook County hospital to see Bernie. She stopped by the employment office, checking to see whether they needed people and what shifts might be open.

"We can give you a night shift," said the crisp administrator. "We don't have any openings on the obstetrics ward right now," she said. "The night shifts are in osteo and in the intensive care unit, but I'm not sure you have enough training for the ICU."

"Thank you," said Line. "I'll think about it." She was carrying Christopher on her hip, as she and Marty used to carry their little sisters.

Line found Bernie Freeman's room in another building. He sat on the side of the bed, his thin weak legs hanging down, one arm in a cast slung from his shoulder, his head bandaged. Kay stood beside him.

"Hey," said Line, falsely cheerful as everyone was in the hospital. "You are lookin' good, Bernie Freeman!" She went over to Kay and gave her a hug, then kissed Bernie lightly. His skin was looking much better, comparatively. "What did I tell you, Kay. I think you'll be fine, Bernie."

"Fine," said Kay flatly in her rich, dark voice. "I don't know what fine is, but I'll take this over last week! Or even yesterday."

Line settled herself in the visitor's chair. There was nowhere to put Christopher down. She splayed him out on her lap. It was a warm day and the white room felt airless. Abe was nowhere to be seen.

"Not where I was planning to spend my summer," said Bernie in a low, weak voice. Line leaned over to hear him.

"No," said Line. "How's the food?" She felt proprietary about the hospital.

Kay grimaced, but Bernie shook his head. "Doesn't matter," he said. "I'm just happy to be here."

Kay petted Bernie's good shoulder. "Had enough?" she asked. "He hasn't been out of bed yet, but they think he's ready," she said to Line. Her powerful, resonant voice and her stance lent Bernie considerable strength.

Line nodded, relaxing. "It's up to him," she said, but stopped herself. She hated it when people talked over the head of a sick person, as if they weren't there. "You'll know, Bernie, when you're ready. Don't let anyone stop you." Christopher started fussing and she opened her shirt and held him to her breast.

"It's so good to see you, Line," said Kay. "Some people seem scared of us. As if our troubles might be contagious."

"I'm very at home in hospitals," said Line. "When I was 14, I stayed with my brother for weeks while he recovered from a reconstructive polio surgery. He was only ten and in a lot of pain. A hard lesson for a kid to learn," said Line. "But I learned a lot from it too. It's amazing how we get through this stuff."

"Your brother came through?" asked Kay.

"Really well," said Line. "He hasn't had a surgery since, though one of his legs is weaker. He was telling me at Christmas he can ski! He acts like he never had polio."

"Glad to hear it," said Kay. She helped Bernie settle back into bed.

"How's the hand?" asked Line.

"They say it's getting better," said Kay. "We don't know yet."

"And little Abraham?" asked Line.

"He seems okay," said Kay. "But I don't know about that either. Bernie's mother spends most of her time with him, so at least there's some coherence. We need Bernie to come home. I don't like to bring Abe here." She looked anguished, torn between the two people who needed her.

Line remembered Thanksgiving dinner at the Freemans' house, with Christopher only a month old. She picked up a glass of water, "I can't help but remember, Bernie," she said, "your Thanksgiving toast. L'Chaim!"

"L'Chaim!" said Kay thickly. "Don't underestimate it; but don't expect anything either."

"L'Chaim!" echoed Bernie weakly.

At home, Line reported on her visit to Stephen. He had come in late, but in the morning, Line made coffee for him before he left for school.

"Why should Bernie get it?" said Stephen. "He wasn't even a revolutionary! He was well known and he did speak out, but he was entirely non-violent! What sort of country is this, anyhow?!"

"Things happen," said Line softly. The day felt sleepy, the air warm.

"I wish I could talk to him about the convention coming up," said Stephen.

Line just looked at him. "He's really very weak."

"Everyone's writing manifestos," said Stephen irritably. He grimaced as he gulped the too hot coffee, and stood up, putting on his coat.

Line tried to focus. She saw SDS' problems in personal terms. Listening to Stephen, she had gathered that Mike Klonsky's Progressive Labor group was trying to get SDS to align with workers and not get tied up in nationalism, a "bourgeois" idea which prevented workers from winning their freedom from the capitalist class. They saw the black "nationalist" demands for black studies departments and black professors as a danger. They were sure they were on the right side of history.

On the other side was the very active Bernardine Dohrn and the national office staffers, who countered with methods they thought would develop a revolutionary youth movement, mobilize the left into a fighting force and take the revolution to victory.

Stephen sighed. "I guess we've come this far," he said. "We can't stop now. We're telling kids the revolution is here. All they have to do is join. Otherwise it's gonna run right over 'em."

"But what are we going to eat?" asked Line plaintively, following him to the door. "We can't eat revolution!"

"I thought maybe you'd get a job again this summer?" he said tentatively. "Or we can borrow money from my folks. Or I'll get a night job. Don't worry. It'll work out."

"There's the rent too," said Line.

"Yeah," said Stephen, looking sheepish. "I didn't pay the rent last month ... I spent it on bail ..." He had one foot out the door. "I'll see you tonight," he said, giving Line a perfunctory kiss.

Line froze. She didn't say a word. But when Stephen left, she called Marty. "Could you send me a bus or train ticket?" she asked. "I'll pay you back sometime. I just can't stay here," she said.

Quietly, Line began preparing. When the ticket came, she took Munchkin down to Mr. Pickett and asked him to take care of the cat. She was evasive about where she was going or for how long. She called Mother and Dad and told them, but asked them not to tell Stephen where she and Christopher were. "Just say that we are safe," Line said.

Line took some carrots and a bag of peanut butter sandwiches. I can live on them for a few days, she told herself. She packed a few clothes for Christopher and slipped out the door. She left her apartment key on the table, but she did not leave a note. "He probably won't even notice," said Line bitterly to tiny Christopher.

23

On the train, after a surreal afternoon and a night trying to sleep in her coach seat, Line woke up in Denver. Along the horizon was a line of snow-capped mountains. Wow, thought Line. She had never seen mountains, never been west of South Dakota.

An older lady in a cotton shirtwaist who had gotten on the train the night before, offered Line an orange, which she took gratefully. Christopher had been a good traveler, sleeping on Line's shoulder. He was like a piece of clothing. She didn't dare let go of him. While the train sat in the Denver station, Line tried to move around a little, changing Christopher's diapers in an empty seat. She had bought some of the new disposable Pampers that were advertised everywhere, though they were frighteningly expensive.

As the train got going again, Line flipped out the little table arm beside her and peeled the orange, letting Christopher grab pieces and stuff them in his mouth. Two teeth had appeared under his bottom lip and he was beginning to chew on everything. Before long they were both sticky and messy. But who cared. Outside the window beside them, the mountains grew larger, fields reached toward them, the sky was incredibly blue.

"Those are the Rockies," said the lady opposite. "We get the best scenery today. The Rockies and the Colorado River." She wore a corsage of paper roses and leaves.

"Are you from Colorado?" asked Line.

"Yes," said the lady. "I take this trip from Omaha to Grand Junction pretty often. My son lives in Grand Junction."

Christopher seemed pleased to look out the window, watching the landscape change and feeling the pulsing engines moving them smoothly forward. He chewed on the edge of his blanket contentedly. Soon the train began climbing, pines and spruces beside them. When a train passed them going the other direction, giving a long whistle which broke as they passed, Christopher crowed and waved his arms.

"That's a smart little boy you've got there," said the lady across from Line.

Line felt alert too. Stirring a cup of coffee she had bought, the world looked peaceful and full of beauty. Line could not see a shred of violence or revolution in any direction. She realized that she wasn't just punishing Stephen by running away. She was giving him the freedom to choose.

Stephen had been railroaded into getting married by their accidental pregnancy. He wasn't ready for it, clearly more interested in his political work. And that work was so radical as not to leave much room for family. In fact, the majority of the people Stephen knew were against family. Line recognized he had been having trouble straddling his marriage and his hot-blooded friends.

With this in mind, Line felt that leaving was the right thing to do. Nothing was forever. She could go out, visit Marty and see what happened. Leaving had been very tough, but now that it was done, and it had begun to feel right, Line figured she might as well enjoy herself.

Before long, the train entered a long tunnel. "Up above us is the Continental Divide," said Line's tour guide. When they came out of the tunnel, they were traveling along a river which widened as they traveled beside it. Line looked at the lady across from her.

"That's the Colorado," said the lady. "My son is an engineer. He works for a big oil company, trying to get at the oil that's around here."

Time felt funny to Line. It felt like it had stopped, though the train lapped up the countryside and the shadow on her shoulder showed that the sun was moving higher. That afternoon, the mother of the engineer got off the train, handing Line another orange. "Good luck," she said. "Have a good time visiting your sister!"

Line felt like an escaping revolutionary, being aided by the good, common people of the country who didn't know she was an enemy. She was deeply grateful for the oranges.

Another night of fitful sleep followed. In the early light Line heard someone say they were crossing Donner Pass in the Sierra mountains. She felt quite bedraggled, but she took Christopher to the washroom and tried to clean him up. She put on a clean tee-shirt. She didn't have much in the way of resources. Putting on a brave face, she bought a cup of coffee from the porter and settled in.

As the afternoon lengthened, the train dropped down into the California basin, its terminus. Everyone prepared to leave. "Remember Marty?" Line asked Christopher. "She said she'd come for us." But Line had the jitters. She had no idea where they were and very little money.

Stepping down off the long train, Line stood on the platform holding Christopher with her two light bags. Slowly the crowds thinned, and there, as promised, was Marty! Line couldn't help it, a few tears escaped as they hugged.

"Hey, Christopher," Marty said. "You've gotten bigger!"

"I think he likes new things," said Line. "He acts like he loves the train. And he's been so good!" The air was warm, and felt fresh to her. Not like the cloying, humid heat she was used to in Chicago.

"That's good," said Marty. "I hope he holds up a little longer. We'll have to take a couple of buses to get home." She picked up Line's bags and headed them off. "You don't have much stuff, Line," she said. "Do you have a sweater?"

"Yeah," said Line. "I think so. It doesn't matter. I was hoping I could wear some of your clothes."

"Don't worry," said Marty. "There are free boxes on Haight Street. And Good Will has cheap things. But it's cold here in the summer. You won't believe it! It's because of the fog. It comes in at night, sometimes stays all day!"

With Marty negotiating, the girls managed Christopher and the bags on buses over the long Bay Bridge, onto Market Street in San

Francisco. It was a construction zone, laid with huge wooden timbers and marked off with yellow tape and temporary railings where it was torn up for the construction of a rapid transit system. They took another bus up Haight Street to the red house where Marty lived. Everything swirled around Line. She felt a little ill.

Marty let them in to a long hallway with light at the end. Large dark rooms opened off it, full of rugs and couches laid with colorful bedspreads and pillows. In the second room was an upright loom, laced with colorful yarns. Sounds could be heard coming from a kitchen at the end of the hall.

"I've been looking for an apartment," Marty said quietly as she showed Line her bare room. "Something just for us. I can afford it now, and it would be better for Christopher."

"Yeah?" said Line. She felt terribly confused, but perhaps she was just tired.

"Just go chill out in the big room," said Marty. "I'm going to fix us a little dinner. You'll feel better after a good night's sleep! But we should call Dad and Mother and let them know you arrived safely."

"Could we have a shower?" asked Line. She felt grubbier than any time she could remember.

"Sure," said Marty and showed Line how to pull the plastic curtains around the water, which fell into a big old bathtub. The toilet was next door, an odd aspect of Victorian living.

"Thank you, Marty," said Line. "We're so happy to be here! Aren't we Christopher." She snuggled the little boy close to her. His big eyes looked in every direction.

The clean warm water washing over them felt wonderful, though Christopher peed on her toward the end and Line had to start all over. Luckily she hadn't gotten out of the tub yet and dirtied the big fluffy towels. Line put on the cleanest clothes she could find and tied her thick hair in a curling knot on her head. Nursing the momentarily clean little boy, he fell asleep.

The other commune members were washing up when Line and Marty finally sat down to dinner, but Line met them: Joyce who had an Asian cast to her face and long dark hair, Lana with red hair and freckles. Lana gave them half a pan of tomatoy lasagna, which Line and Marty ate along with a salad.

"There's another guy who lives downstairs and uses the kitchen," said Marty. "James. He's a musician and a waiter. He's not around much. You might hear him playing music at night."

"This lasagna is the best thing I ever ate!" said Line. Smells of hot herbs and tomatoes washed up around her. It felt so good to be still, to have good things to eat. Christopher slept on the mattress in Marty's room. Line was glad he was so easy to care for and needed so little.

That night Line slept like the dead. Even Christopher didn't wake up, except to nuzzle her early in the morning. It was Friday. Marty got up and went to work.

By the time Line got up and wandered through the large flat, the house was empty. The air was cool, the sky a feathery grey. Line found coffee in a kitchen cupboard labeled 'Marty' and brewed herself a cup. She liked the idea of living with other people, but it seemed complicated. She made toast and gave Christopher some to chew on.

Clean and rested, Line felt much better. Marty had given her a map and a house key and pointed out that if she walked up the street, she would arrive almost immediately in Golden Gate Park, a famous three-mile long spread of trees, flowers and ponds.

"Be a little careful," Marty had told her. "There are people living under trees everywhere. It isn't that they're dangerous, but there might be some speed-freaks or addicts who want money for drugs. And none of them are very clean."

"We have got to get you a stroller," said Line as she carried Christopher on her hip up the street. He really was getting heavy and he was too big for her makeshift sling. She thought of the photographs she had seen of women in foreign countries with babies tied onto their backs. She imagined making some kind of sling for her back in which he could ride safely.

The park opened out into a wide space very quickly. The sun was beginning to blaze through the patches of wispy grey fog and fell hot on Line's body. It was very pleasant, a combination of heat and chilled air she didn't recognize. A few cars went up the drive, people walked around, park employees cut the grass.

A white, wedding-cake building appeared at the edge of the space. The building was in three parts, like a castle with a sugary dome over the middle. All of it looked fragile, as if made of white painted glass. Formal gardens were arrayed in front of it. Line settled herself in the shade on the grass looking down on the magical building.

So this was San Francisco, Line thought. She had forgotten the noisy, dusty construction-filled streets, the congested traffic and preoccupied people of the day before. Line took in the stillness and the gardens. Christopher beside her clutched at the grass with his little hands. "This is grass," she told him. Sadly, Christopher hadn't seen much grass in his young life. Tiny white flowers could be seen, but no clover, as in the grass of Line's childhood.

Before long a black man in an afro with a red bandana around his head like Jimi Hendrix' came up to her and sat down. Line was wary, but he seemed gentle and wanted to talk.

"Nice baby you have. How old is he?"

"About eight months," said Line.

"I haven't seen you around here before," said the man, pulling out a hand-rolled cigarette. "You new?"

"Sort of," said Line, trying to be noncommittal.

"Used to be a great place." The man handed Line his joint, but she waved it away. "There used to be free food everywhere. Free music. Free stores. The Diggers thought everything should be free."

"The Diggers?" asked Line.

"Hell, you are new," the man concluded. "They were anarchists. But they're gone now. Moved up to the country, I expect."

Line picked up Christopher. "I think he's getting sleepy," she said. "I think we have to go." She shouldered the little boy.

"There's still a free clinic, though, if you need it. Down on Haight Street."

"Thanks," said Line, politely. "It was nice to meet you."

"Sure thing," said the man. "Have a nice day." He stood up also.

Line walked away, heading toward the white building and watching her shadow to make sure she wasn't being followed. In Chicago Line knew lots of black people. Hospital workers usually, most of them nice. But street smarts had taught her to be wary of people who came up to you. They usually wanted something.

On the other hand, Line thought, this guy didn't have the hard-edged anxiety of city people in Chicago. This too was San Francisco. Line inspected the formal flower beds laid out in front of the white building. It was beautiful close up too, but she was sure it cost something to enter. She was perfectly happy outside.

That night Marty insisted on taking Line and Christopher to her favorite Russian kitchen on Haight Street. "We won't be able to eat out often," she said, "but we are celebrating your arrival!" The Russian lady who waited on them brought a little wooden high chair for Christopher.

Line's confidence was returning. She hated being dependent on anyone. "I've been thinking," she said. "I could get some babysitting work this summer. I know you said you could put us up, but I will try to do what I can."

Marty waved it off. "Line," she said. "You're family. You can't imagine how happy I am to have you. And to get to know Christopher."

Line relaxed in the warm, homey atmosphere where huge stainless steel pots could be seen at the back of the room, steaming on an ancient gas stove. The smells of spiced meat hung in the air. "I already like it here," Line said. "But it's so different! Like night and day." She told Marty about her encounter in the park.

"San Francisco is very different from Berkeley," said Marty. "But I've been in the city almost a year now and it feels like home."

"Home?" questioned Line. Christopher slapped the table in front of him with his dimpled hands and Line handed him a bit of cooled piroshke.

"It's serious here," said Marty. "But in a different way than Oxford or Berkeley. Nobody reads here, or almost no one. It's all physical, people doing things, learning things. Trying things and becoming who they want to be!"

"That sounds like what you wanted," said Line, "isn't it?"

"It's the freedom that I wanted," said Marty stodgily.

Line looked at her closely. She did look better than she ever had, Line thought. She was thinner, her dark hair thick, wavy and long. And her pale skin looked better, like she had gotten some sun on it. "You look good," said Line. "You look like you feel at home." Line didn't like to admit it, but she had been so worried that she really hadn't thought of anyone beyond herself and her little family for a long time.

Marty beamed. "It's Erik," she said. "I'm always falling love with someone, Line. I can't help it. Right now, it's Erik."

"I can't wait to meet him," said Line. There was something fishy about this Erik thing. She couldn't tell what it was, but she was sure she would know when she met him. But then, who was she to talk. She hadn't known Stephen as well when she married him as she did now.

The next day Marty showed Line how to take a cross-town bus and arrive near the marina at the northern end of the city. They walked out onto a green expanse at the edge of the harbor where yachts were tethered, their halyards clinking in the breeze. Some people had set up a volleyball net and an Asian man was flying an elaborate kite with his two small boys. Off to the left loomed the famous Golden Gate bridge, red in the sun. On the shore beyond the water were empty hills, little towns and in the foreground the island prison, Alcatraz.

Line was again struck by how different, how benign the Bay felt compared to Lake Michigan. She had loved the Lake, especially in the summer when the city felt like a hot box, asphalt everywhere. But the winds off the Lake were strong, especially in the winter when they made the city bone-chillingly cold. You could sense the industry, the steel mills to the south, the big ships coming in, the raw power the Lake generated.

Here the sun was strong on the green water, there was a light breeze, and the small buildings made everything look tame and civilized. Marty pointed out the bridge they had crossed the first day when they got off the train, the Bay Bridge.

"That's Coit tower on top of Telegraph Hill," said Marty. "And there's downtown. They've started working on the Transamerica Pyramid which everyone hates. It's going to be the tallest building in town. Most people I know want to keep the city low rise and human scale, but the battle over this one has been lost."

Line just looked. "It's a beautiful city," she said. "A white city." The part of Hyde Park where she had lived in Chicago had been largely brick, the streets dark and shady with trees.

"From here you can walk over to Fisherman's Wharf. It's this great place with all sorts of shops in reconstructed factories," said Marty.

Line and Marty walked down to the water, alternately carrying Christopher. They sat on the rocks and ate crackers and cheese. "It all feels so easy," said Line. "Chicago was hard. There are beautiful places there, but it's either too hot or cold most of the time. And it's crowded and scary."

"Don't even think about it," said Marty. "Just take the summer off! You don't have to do anything. In the fall you can decide what to do."

"Oh God, Marty," said Line. "You are helping us so much!"

On the way home, Marty bought a thick newspaper called the *San Francisco Chronicle*. "The Sunday paper, with the want ads in it comes out on Saturday afternoon," she said. "I want to see about rentals."

Christopher napped as Line sank into the sofa in the big common room of the flat when they got home. The room felt put together, a rich wash of color, made up of all kinds of bright textiles which worked together, though nothing particularly matched. The light, which shone into the room in the morning, was entirely gone. "This is really a nice place," said Line.

"It's all Lana," said Marty as she separated the sections of the newspaper and spread it out in front of herself. "She has the knack of furnishing a place." Marty turned on a lamp in order to read the fine print of the want ads.

"Will she mind if you move?" asked Line.

"No, she already has a friend who wants to move in." Marty's head was buried in the newspaper. She wrote phone numbers and addresses in her notebook. "1402 Larkin. I wonder what the cross street is," she said. She consulted a map of San Francisco.

An older paper left out on the chest that served as a coffee table caught Line's eye. President Nixon had met with the president of South Vietnam and announced that 25,000 troops would be withdrawn by September. Did anyone believed him? Line poked through the Want Ads. She wasn't sure what to look under. Domestic help? She couldn't work as a nurse without a California license.

Marty made calls and appointments to see apartments. The next day they set off together, taking buses, carrying Christopher. In the northern part of the city, after meeting with a Hispanic woman named Consuela, the manager, they agreed that the Larkin Street apartment would work for them. Marty wrote a check sealing the deal. "It's a safer area, I think," said Marty. "Just below Nob Hill. I can't wait to explore!"

Line let herself rest in Marty's certainty and enthusiasm. It was a reversal of their usual mode. She was tired. She did not know where she was. So much change.

As she followed Marty down a hill, Christopher on her hip, Line thought of Stephen, who had probably moved into one of the unkempt SDS communes. When she talked to Mother and Dad, they said Stephen had called them, but had not asked where she was. He was glad Line and Christopher were safe, and had passed on the message that Bernie and Kay

Freeman were moving to Santa Barbara, California. Line was not surprised. Bernie was recovering, thankfully.

"You've got to see the ocean," said Marty as they turned on to Polk Street. "Let's just go on the way home. It's easy. We'll take the Geary bus out and watch the sun set. If the fog will let us," she backtracked.

"It's almost the solstice," said Line. They were threading along between people who went in and out of the little shops. "When does it set?"

"Maybe 8:30 or so," said Marty. "Let's go find out! Are you tired, Line? Do you want to go? It's mostly riding the bus."

"Sure," said Line. She had noticed that there was always more walking than she expected in Marty's calculations. But she was game. "Diapers," she said. On the trip she had used disposable diapers, though she was ashamed that she let Christopher sit in wet diapers longer than he should due to her abject poverty. Whenever she could she let him go without diapers, kicking his little naked legs in the air. "The only limit on how long we stay out is clean diapers!"

"We'll stop and buy some," said Marty.

When the bus dropped them near the ocean, Line and Marty walked out on the expansive beach which ran the entire length of western San Francisco. The sound of the breakers rolling in toward the beach was loud and got louder as they walked toward them, long combers edged in white. Clouds lay on the horizon obscuring the sun, but a thin slice of sky showed it might make an appearance as it sank. The rhythmic sound welled up in Line. It was nothing like a lake. It was the ocean, the biggest one in the world.

Line nuzzled Christopher's soft neck and together they looked toward the light. The pulse of the world, thought Line. The pulse of our bodies, salty as we are. She followed Marty who walked along the wet sand at the edge of the surf.

"The tide's in, I think," said Marty loudly, her voice blown back to Line. "There's usually more beach."

The surf moved toward them and Marty skipped away. There were others on the beach, walking dogs and playing Frisbee. "Let's take our shoes off," Marty said. "One of us can stay with Christopher and the other can walk out." She sat on the dry sand above the surf line, took off the leather sandals she wore and rolled up her pants.

Line settled beside her, making a circle of her legs for Christopher to sit in. She smiled widely, watching Marty scamper down toward the water. The sun dipped under the clouds, sending a shining golden ray across the water directly to Line and pinking the clouds above it. Marty was a small dark figure near the water.

Line took off her tennis shoes and felt the large, dark granules of sand, handing some to Christopher. It wasn't a white sand beach. When Marty came back, Line walked toward the water, her feet sinking as the sand ground against itself around them. The wet sand held her better. She stood in the surf, letting a wave roll around her feet and wash back, tugging the sand around her feet as it went. The rhythmic roar of the surf ground along the beach as it came in.

The sun sank, a golden ball on the horizon. The undersides of the clouds turned pink and gold. The sky was reflected in the watery sand, opalescent, an extraordinary display of color and light. The aura of newness hung over everything, filling Line with awe. She walked slowly back up the beach to where Marty sat with Christopher, the noise of the surf receding. She felt like an egg, like a cork bobbing at the world's edge. She was limp and tired but buoyed by the power of the earth.

"It's just amazing," Line said, sinking down. "In Chicago, we get a nice sunrise on Lake Michigan, but I must admit, I hardly ever saw it. Sometimes on my way to work in the winter."

"I don't get down here often either," said Marty. "There's nothing like it though. Someday we'll come down here and I'll bring my camera."

"Christopher," said Line holding her son up and looking out toward the expanse of ocean. "Have you ever seen such a wide sky?"

A week later they moved. As soon as they got the keys, they gathered their possessions into a taxi and left. The shiny rooms had been newly painted. There were a few pieces of furniture, a couch, a chest, a couple of day beds, lamps, a formica table and chairs in the small kitchen. Lana had given them some dishes and Marty bought a black, cast-iron skillet to cook in.

"Do you want the back room or the front room?" asked Marty. It was clear that the front room, with a bay window on the street, had been the living room with the bedroom in back. The back window looked out on a light well and they could hear people talking Chinese in a nearby apartment, washing up pots and pans.

"I don't care," said Line. "But maybe we should take the back. It's a little more private for baby napping. And darker."

"Sure," said Marty. "We can get more furniture at BusVan, but I think this is a good start!"

"It's great," agreed Line.

Marty left to go exploring. She could travel faster and farther alone.

Line lay down for a nap with Christopher. It was comforting to have found a safe place for herself and her son. She could rest up and not worry about money or make any decisions for a little while.

Marty came back full of excitement and a bag of groceries. "There's a 24-hour grocery store only two blocks away," she said. "The cable car goes up California, and on the other side is the Cala!"

"California's easy," said Line. She was starting to feel better.

24

On Friday, when Marty left the office, Erik was waiting in his Plymouth. She knew he was coming, but she still got a rush of feeling when she saw him, looking like both a disreputable bohemian and a shiny-faced architect as he leaned out the window.

Marty crossed the street and kissed him in front of several friends who streamed out the door at Cardigan Shores. She ran around to the passenger side and ducked in, feeling that the whole world was watching. From the radio came a distinctive singing voice Marty had never heard. "I'm gonna get up, make my life shine," it sang in a ringing chorus.

"You do know how to get everyone's attention," Marty said demurely, stowing the train-case she had carried all over Europe beneath her.

Erik pulled smoothly into traffic, looking out the window behind him. "Who cares!" he said, reasonably. "Nobody!"

Marty knew he was right. No one should be jealous, as each person could live his own, shining life. "Who's the singer?" she asked. She loved the relaxed music, horns in the background, sweet, swinging rhythm.

"Boz Scaggs," said Erik. Just then, a bit of saxophone showed up, playing against the drums and background singers. "Smokin'," said Erik. He turned up the sound on the tape deck as they rolled slowly onto the 101 freeway. Traffic was at a standstill as people tried to get out of town on

Friday night. Wisps of fog rolled across the sun. "I've made up my mind," he sang along, "gonna get up, make my life shine."

It was great music. Erik always had the latest thing. How did he know, wondered Marty. Another song started, not so nice. "If you treated me right, I'd be comin' home to you," sang Scaggs. Marty just listened.

"Come here," said Erik. "What you doin' over there." He pulled Marty into the crook of his arm.

It was a long way to Santa Cruz, especially on a Friday night. Marty had no idea where they were going, had never been south of the city. "We're goin' to the redwoods," was all Erik would tell her. He seemed to have friends everywhere. In town, Erik stopped at a grocery store. "They're always hungry out there," he said. He bought bottles of cheap wine, pasta, tomato sauce, onions and hamburger.

Leaving Santa Cruz the road wound through tall straight trunks on both sides. The sky above was thick with fog. "Those are the redwoods," said Erik. "Finest trees in the world. You've seen 'em used on houses everywhere. Shingles. Remember? You don't have to paint them or finish 'em or anything. They look natural, blend in."

A picture slowly dawned on Marty. "Like all those beautiful, dark shingled homes in Berkeley?" she asked. Marty remembered walking through whole streets of houses in Berkeley meant to blend into the trees and gardens around them.

"Yeah," said Erik. "Maybeck. Julia Morgan. The shingles are red when you put them on, but they darken. Last forever. If they're from old-growth redwoods. New ones aren't as good."

"Wow," said Marty.

"I heard of this one house all made from one Mendocino redwood," said Erik. "The Tibbetts house. The guy saved one tree, built a whole house for his daughter when she got married. On the East Coast, shingles are usually cedar." The Plymouth felt big on the narrow curving roads as they wound through the trees.

"Here's the cabin," said Erik. They turned into a thin two-rutted drive. Erik parked at the edge of the path and got out of the car. When Marty pulled out her train case, Erik shook his head. "You don't need that," he said. He handed Marty a paper sack full of groceries.

There may have been light once between the trees, but now grey clouds surrounded them coming down thick and low, water in the air itself. Marty took in the pungent smell of dense piney humus and the wet green ferns below. Standing still for a moment, they heard nothing but distant laughter and water dripping off the trees.

"Look up," commanded Erik.

The trunks reached forever, close to each other. High above were the branches, green clouds touching each other. Marty touched the spongy bark of a tree, a dark red-brown. Walking between the tall columns in the wet, vibrant air felt a little like being in church.

In the center of a clearing was a small wooden cabin with a porch spread with old leather boots and shoes, a bicycle with very thin wheels. Smoke rose from the stone chimney which almost covered one side of the house.

The green-gold smell of sweet smoking weed hit them as they walked up on the porch. Erik went in through the open door, carrying groceries. "Hey," he said to an assembled crowd of twenty people who sat around on couches, stools and the floor in front of the fire. Marty was intimidated by so many people, but no one said much.

Roger stood up to greet Erik, throwing his arms around him. He was slightly older, warm and friendly. "Hey yourself," he said. "Looks like you got just what we need! How'd you know we were hungry?"

"You're predictable," said Erik. "Everyone's always got the munchies out here." He put the bags in the small kitchen on a counter. "This is my girlfriend, Marty. Smells like you've got what I need too!"

"Yep," said Roger. "You came at a good time. Willie just got back with some great stuff. Oaxaca, honest to God. Just the flowers. You've got to try it."

Marty tried to make herself small. It looked as if people were just sitting, relaxed, waiting to see what would happen. They nodded but didn't bother to introduce themselves.

One man, who must be Willie, dressed in dusty brown leather including a leather cowboy hat, stood up and handed Erik the fattest joint Marty had ever seen. He touched it with a lighter and Erik took a long drag, holding the smoke in. Marty could almost see it curling up around his brains. Finally he let some out through his nostrils.

Behind him, Roger handed Erik a small glass. "Here," he said. "Cool that down a little. Want some Marty?"

"Sure," said Marty. She had learned that if you didn't imbibe what everyone else was, they became paranoid you were a cop. The whiskey was hot and fiery going down her throat, but it tasted good after the long drive.

Erik handed her the joint and she took a tiny toke, holding it in but not letting it go down.

"God," said Erik. "That is some kind of weed!"

"Can we make spaghetti?" asked Roger from the kitchen. "Before you guys completely lose it."

Marty went into the kitchen. "I can make the sauce," she said. Before long she was standing in front of an ancient gas stove, browning a big mound of onions, garlic and hamburger in the black cast-iron skillet Roger produced. "Just like home," she said, smiling at him. She felt well-oiled, as if someone had smoothed off the social edges with solvent and inserted her into place. Groovin' is easy, she thought, if you know how.

Roger got a big kettle of water boiling and opened the wine bottles. "Twenty people," he grumbled, under his breath. "And nobody brought nothin' but wine." He smiled at Marty.

No one was going anywhere, though. Somehow the food stretched though Marty only took a few bites off Erik's plate. Sourdough loaves appeared from somewhere, and the last people just got a piece of bread to dip in the sauce.

After eating, people made room for Erik on the couch in front of the fire. Marty slid in beside him, enjoying the heat of his body pressed against her. It was a quiet evening. No one got up and took the stage. Conversation was desultory, between neighbors.

Marty listened and watched, trying to sort out the relationships. Roger kept getting up to throw logs on the flames, which leapt, hissed and crackled. He had a worn, hip look to him, longish hair but no beard. He seemed to be the owner. Willie looked like a Mexican bandito. He had the mustache, leather vest, red bandana around his neck and never took off his hat.

Joints got passed around and everyone had a glass of wine or whiskey. No one played music or sang. The fire was the entertainment. Late that night, Roger leaned over and handed Erik a flashlight. "You guys take the couch in the woods tonight."

"Sure thing," said Erik. He looked at Marty. "Come on," he said, putting a proprietary hand on Marty's waist. It seemed everyone watched them.

Marty was desperate to stretch out somewhere. Erik led them outdoors and back to the car where he took two big cotton sleeping bags out of the trunk.

Just off the clearing, in a slight open space in the redwoods, an old hide-a-bed was stretched out. It looked pretty damp, but sandwiched between the two flat, warm sleeping bags, Marty felt fine. Little noises and rustlings could be heard all around them. Snakes liked warm places, Marty had heard. But they were up off the ground. Hopefully a snake couldn't get into their bed.

Marty stretched her body its full length. At her side, Erik was insistent. She had felt it while they sat by the fire. His hands reached for the skin around her middle and up. She too was flushed and full of the ache which could only be satisfied by Erik deep inside her. His weight on top of her pressed her down. An owl called its soft, unearthly hoot three times from a tree near them, and then again from closer. The two of them fell asleep holding each other.

In the morning, Marty was wakened by flute music drifting through the fog. Above her the tall redwoods stretched up to the sky, their green boughs high above the ground. The damp, dripping air made the evergreen smell of the piney earth strong. An unearthly light, sun trying to break through the fog, surrounded the woodsy bed.

"That's Richard," said Erik, listening to the flute. His warm body stretched alongside Marty, his nose in her neck. "Goes to Stanford. He rides his bike over here on the weekends."

"Over the mountain?" asked Marty, incredulous. She had taken note of the route through the Santa Cruz mountains, the slow chug of trucks up the steep road, the Summit café and the long haul down. It felt like they were going too fast the whole way.

"Guess so," said Erik.

"Was he that tall, French-looking guy?"

"Yep," said Erik. "That's him."

They lay warm in the deep cotton bags, listening to the rustlings, the water dripping off the trees, birdsong. The flute music was slow, something Marty recognized. Peace and time were for once at rest in her.

"Pachelbel," said Erik. "Needs more than one flute, though. It's a canon."

"Where is he?" asked Marty.

"Up in the woods," said Erik. "There's a treehouse back there where Willie sleeps, I think. He's a mule skinner. Roger rents the cabin and Willie's his brother. He comes and goes. He's been all over, up and down the Grand Canyon. There're lots of places you can't get to without mules."

Marty shook her head, incredulous. She could not have even imagined people or places like this. "How did you find them?"

But here Erik had no information. "Don't know," he said. "Just following some friends around, I guess."

"It looks like it might be late," said Marty. "Like the sun is trying to come through. I just want to stay in this bed forever." She rolled over and, leaning on her elbows kissed Erik's eyes. His face was fresh and alive in the vivid, green light.

"You look beautiful," said Erik, brushing some hair out of her face.

Marty wrapped the words around her poor little hungry heart. She had almost never heard them before. "Does the sun ever come down into the trees?" she asked, looking at the cathedral spires around them.

"In the middle of the day, I guess," said Erik. "We should get to the beach though. It's a beach day for sure."

At the cabin, people sat at the edge of the porch, drinking coffee. It looked to Marty as though there was no more food available than there had been last night. When Erik announced they were going into town, two of the younger girls, dressed in jeans, long hair and provocative crocheted tops, begged to go along. Most of the people looked older, wearing worn leathers and patched and quilted cottons. One of the women was knotting something in twine as she sat, a piece of macramé.

The two young women were students, going to the University of California in Santa Cruz. Erik dropped them off at the edge of town and they had their thumbs out almost before they got out of the car. "I'm not too worried about them," he said, looking after them appreciatively.

Erik and Marty went to Denny's and had eggs and bacon for breakfast. Marty felt a little worn, as if she had been deeply used. As she should be, she thought, like a woman. Her head was empty and her limbs felt a pleasurable ache. She was glad for the birth control pills in a plastic circle, Ortho Novum, marked out one for each day for 21 days. After waiting a week, she started the next month's packet. She had gotten them at Planned Parenthood.

Marty spooned cream and sugar into her coffee. She wished she had a bathing suit. A bikini, like California girls. All she had were her jean cutoffs and a white peasant blouse. She wished she was tan and sleek like the students.

Erik sat across from her, quiet, his tousled blonde hair falling into his face. He was achingly handsome, silent. Marty could now understand that with one of his personas, he wanted to be a competent mountain man, like Willie. He had gotten a job drafting at the sleek architecture firm he favored, Skidmore, Owings and Merrill. "You have to genuflect when one of the partners passes down through the desks," he told Marty sarcastically. The main office was in New York with San Francisco a satellite. Marty noted that he was good at getting whatever he wanted, though he stayed as stoned as possible when he wasn't at work.

Line didn't like Erik. She put up with having him around, but she told Marty she thought he was using her. "For what?" asked Marty. What did she have that he wanted?

"Sex," Line told her. "He's not going to stay with you."

Marty didn't care. If he was using her, she was surely using him. She loved the fact that he was educated, from a powerful, well-off family. It fed her own dark ambitions. She wanted, somehow, to play a part in the great world.

But Erik was also too cool for Marty, she felt. He didn't call her for days, even weeks, and then turned up as though nothing had happened. Marty was desperate when she didn't hear from him, but it was always worth it when they did get together. Their bodies matched, whether their heads and cultures did or not.

Denny's was the most American place Marty could imagine. There sat Erik, dipping bacon into his sunny-side-up eggs. Marty sipped her coffee, sighing deeply.

Erik smiled at her. "Happy?" he asked.

"Yes," said Marty. "I loved waking up under the redwoods."

"Yep," said Erik. "Me too." He reached in his pocket, found some wadded up dollar bills and put them on the table. "Ready?" he asked.

At the beach they stretched out on a blanket in the sand, letting the noise of the big surf roll in over them, their bodies somnolent and full of juice. The breeze deliciously played over Marty's body, cooling off the sun's heat which lay on her like a hot human hand. When the fog began to roll in again, Erik stood up. "Guess we better get back," he said.

Marty wasn't sure what he needed to get back to. It was Saturday night and there was a whole day before either of them needed to go to work. Perhaps it was just impatience. Erik never stayed in one place long. She stood up, brushing off the sand and helping shake out the blanket. Driving back, Erik played the Boz Scaggs tape again and another one Marty hadn't heard by The Band.

As they got closer to her apartment, Marty felt the impending rift. She wanted to bring it up, ask Erik when she would see him next. But she also felt it was part of their pact. If she didn't pressure him, he would come back. If she did, he wouldn't.

Erik pulled up in front of her apartment on Larkin Street. "See you," he said. "Give us a kiss."

Marty leaned over and kissed him. His face was flushed with sun. Tendrils of desire rose up in her. She made herself get out of the car, but part of her drove off with Erik, an almost palpable net of connection. It was painful to cut, so abrupt. Marty put her key in the door and slowly went up the stairs.

The apartment was full of people, Line, Jack and Nathan with Christopher on his knee. "Get yourself a glass, girl," said Jack, a genial mood playing over his graying hair and lean physique. He held out a bottle of wine and poured some for Marty.

Nathan, much younger with dark hair curling around his gorgeous head, nodded. He sat on Marty's daybed in the evening light of the bay window. Christopher was getting stronger. He sat up pretty straight and his little hands reached out in every direction.

Line looked happy, smiling. "I'm so glad you're here!" she said, greeting Marty. "I wasn't sure you were coming back tonight. We went to the flea market in Alameda, and guess what Jack found!" She stood up and went into her room. Returning with a cloth and aluminum contraption, she lifted Christopher into it. The little tubular frame stood on the floor without falling over. Putting it on the couch, Line sat down in front of it, strapped it around her chest. "See!" she said. "Isn't that amazing!"

"Turn around," said Marty. It had a high back. "I don't think he can fall out of that."

"No," said Line. "And my hands are free!"

"Wow," said Marty. "We've been needing that!"

"He likes it too. He likes being high up, I think," said Line. She stood up and walked around the room. Nathan stood up too, to show how Christopher could now relate to his face. Christopher chewed on the canvas which was sewn tightly over the tubular frame.

"Teether and backpack in one!" laughed Marty. She sat on the couch and sipped the glass of white wine. The silvery liquid eased down into her heart. She tried to forget how bereft she felt about leaving Erik.

Line took off the backpack and set it on the hardwood floor. "These guys ran out of food stamps and I offered them dinner."

"Sure," said Marty. "Sounds like fun." She was thinking of Roger, feeding a multitude with a kettle of spaghetti. But this was only four grownups.

"I know how to cook two dishes," said Jack with his unique combination of New York hustle and laid-back Los Angeles sophistication. "Eggplant parmigiana and beef stew. I could teach you one of them."

"Eggplant parmigiana!" said Marty. "That sounds exotic."

"It's delicious," said Jack. "But it takes a while to make."

They'd been eating cheese and crackers, but Marty sensed that they were hungry. She stood up. "Should we all go over to the Cala and buy what we need?"

Neither Marty nor Line had ever eaten eggplant. They looked beautiful, dark purple globes, but Marty had no idea what to do with them. Jack showed them how to slice and salt them down to take the bitter juices out, then bread and fry them in olive oil. The slices were layered into the black iron dutch oven with mozzarella cheese, mushrooms, onions, tomatoes, oregano and lots of tomato paste. Over the top Jack shredded Parmesan cheese. An hour later, when everything had melded together, they ate the thick stew.

"Ambrosia," said Line.

Marty hardly knew what was eggplant and what wasn't. Everything tasted so good together. "It's wonderful," she said.

Jack and Nathan ate more than one helping. Marty suspected they had known hunger. Jack, an out-of-work actor, was sick of the rat race. "There's nothing out there," he was fond of saying. He had found Nathan as a kid, hustling on the streets of Los Angeles. The two of them had a strong sense of style and, adding their own value to old misused things, were trying to make a living by re-selling them at the flea market. Marty had met them at the free university, and they liked the household she and Line made up. "Not much nonsense in you Minnesotans," said Jack.

Late that night, when Christopher was asleep and Jack and Nathan had gone home, Line and Marty sat up talking. The dirty dishes stood all around them, but Marty waved her hand. "I'll do them tomorrow," she said.

"Mother forwarded a letter from Stephen," said Line, rather impersonally as if she didn't care. "He says SDS fell apart at the June convention. Can you imagine?" she asked. "Everything he's worked for. The national office is now run by Bernardine and her Weathermen. And the Progressive Labor types have split off. Stephen sounds like he doesn't know what to do. But the trial of the Chicago Eight is about to start. And the Mobe's organizing this big peace demonstration for October."

"What do you want him to do, Line?" asked Marty. She had been pleased to see how comfortable Line was in California, but she did wonder about Line's plans.

"I want him to do something that shows he cares about us," said Line. "That's all I want. I'm not going back until he does."

"To Chicago?" asked Marty.

"The apartment's gone," said Line, "the home we had there. He's living in some disgusting commune where ideology rules. There's no place for me. I think I'm going to have to settle down here." She threw an anguished look at Marty. "What do you think?"

"I think you should stay," said Marty. "Get your California LVN license. I'll help you. Together we can take care of Christopher."

"Do you think so?" Line asked.

"I like living with people," said Marty, "but family feels best." She could see herself and Line under the lamp, reflected in the glass of the uncurtained windows. They were drinking the last of the wine.

"Friends become family," said Line. "But it takes a long time."

"Just settle down here," said Marty. "Leave it open-ended. Who knows what will happen." She'd been doing it for so long now herself, she felt like an authority.

"Jack keeps talking about 'life-style'," said Line. "It's so different here. In Chicago people talked about 'sharpening the political line.'" She giggled. "No one cares about politics here."

"I hear that word 'life-style' a lot," said Marty. "I think it means listening to your own mind and heart rather than copying others. It isn't that no one cares about politics. It's just that here, they really do believe the personal is the political!"

"I like it," said Line. "In Chicago I met so many people whose families had moved up from the South to take work in steel mills and factories. They wanted to take part in the American dream. But their kids aren't so sure about it. The city is brutal and bitter and cold. Here everyone feels more equal to me."

"In Berkeley, at the Chertoks' I knew all kinds of people who read books," said Marty. "But here in San Francisco, I don't meet intellectuals. It's more like, listen to your heart. Live authentically."

"You always were a bookworm, Marty," said Line. "That's never going to change."

Marty thought about the afternoons she stood in the big reading room at the San Francisco public library, pawing through the Russian literature shelf to see if there was anything she hadn't read. Pasternak, Tsvetaeva, Akhmatova, Mandelstam, she named to herself the four poets who epitomized 20th century Russian literature. The reading room was beautiful, shaped a little like the Carnegie-style library she had worked in at Wittenberg. The ceiling beams were painted in subdued colored patterns, "No, that'll never change," she said. "I learn from books."

"And I learn from people," said Line. She sighed. "I hate for Christopher not to see Stephen. But I don't know what to do. He just has to do something to show that he loves us. He hasn't even asked where we are!"

"He's probably trying to get his act together," said Marty. "I think you're both doing the right thing."

"And how about your prince," asked Line, a little sarcastically. "Did you have a great weekend?"

"Really great," said Marty. She rubbed the hollow place in her stomach. Her eyes felt big and soft when she thought about Erik. "A cabin in the redwoods. We slept out under the trees. Owls hooted. We woke up to someone playing flute music."

"Now there's a lifestyle for you," said Line appreciatively.

"The people looked broke and hungry, though," said Marty. "Nobody seems to work. There was nothing to eat until we brought spaghetti."

"Wow," said Line.

"Do you think having lots of dope around would be worth going hungry?" asked Marty. "The people at the cabin looked tamed, or something. Sat there and didn't introduce themselves. Hardly talked."

"You know I don't give a fig for grass," said Line. "Or acid, or any of the rest of it. The body is a temple, after all."

Marty tended to agree. She was thrilled to be independent, to be free to live and think as she wanted. Good food and shelter were the most important. She liked interesting talk, as there was in the university families she had lived with. But Erik was her reality. She could not get around it. He had something she needed, something she didn't understand. The key to her body.

25

It was October and Paul was actively anticipating snow. He couldn't wait to go skiing again. He was practice teaching in the town of Hawley, twenty miles east of campus. Every day, as he drove the little Lark to school, he looked at the trees and the fields, but nighttime temperatures hadn't even gotten down to freezing yet.

Paul pulled into the parking lot of the long, low building, grabbed his new briefcase and went into the teachers' lounge. Mr. Hudson, the middle school science teacher under whom Paul worked, stood beside the coffee machine, drinking black coffee.

"Morning Paul," he said. "Kinda mild out there, isn't it."

"Yeah," said Paul. "Where are all those blizzards and storms we had last year?"

"Keep your shirt on, Paul," said Mr. Hudson. "It'll happen. I can wait! In fact, you should come golfing with me this Saturday. Our golf course is something special. Can you come?" Mr. Hudson's dark hair was carefully slicked down into obedience, but an intensity in his eyes showed that he was someone to be reckoned with.

"Sure," said Paul. "Sounds like fun." It was not a time in his life when he was going to say 'no' to things! He took off his winter parka and knotted the tie which was slung around his neck in a careful four-in-hand. In the teachers' lounge, he was still himself, but as soon as they stepped out into the corridor thronged with students, he and Mr. Hudson would become Teachers.

Paul filled a Styrofoam cup with hot water into which he squeezed a slice of lemon. He had never gotten used to coffee, but the hot water helped his throat. He had been terribly excited about teaching. He saw it as a chance to express all of his fascination with science. But it hadn't turned out exactly that way.

Teaching middle school kids was difficult. Six batches of kids a day entered the science classroom, wired for action. Mr. Hudson, through a combination of age, voice volume, and school customs and rules, managed to command their attention, but Paul was finding it difficult.

The first period was a home room. Mr. Hudson didn't exert much authority during it. Not much had to get done. Students finished up homework, whispered the day's gossip to each other and killed time until their first class. Paul used the time to review the lesson plans for the day, which, to his chagrin, followed the textbooks closely.

When he first thought about teaching, Paul imagined that giving everything he had, his polio experience, bug collecting, guitar playing, love of astronomy, experiments with ham radio and photography, interest in baseball, close observation of plants and small mammals, all of which were part of science, in a sort of free-form educational experience would mesmerize every kid he came in contact with. Working with middle school kids quickly disabused Paul of these romantic notions.

When the bell rang and students left their desks, the smooth surfaces of which were printed with grids as though they were graph paper, another group filed in. After determining who was present and who was missing, Mr. Hudson turned the eighth grade class over to Paul.

It was Paul's favorite class because of a blonde, extremely intelligent kid named Debra. Usually she sat in the middle of the room, stony-faced and frowning, but she warmed to Paul.

Paul began by introducing the chemical compounds hydrogen and oxygen, showing how they made up water, and writing the chemical notation H_2O on the board.

"Water is necessary to life. The human body is 50-75% water. Water has many attractive properties. And we use them every day. For instance, its solubility. Come on up," he suggested. The students grouped themselves around the lab desk at the front of the room, where Paul had assembled dishes of sugar, salt, vinegar and hydrogen peroxide.

"Common sense is going to indicate what the salty water and sugary water taste like," Paul said, preparing solutions. "Taste them," he said, letting the students put their fingers in the bowl.

He demonstrated the surface tension of water collected in a spoon, adhering to itself and filling a tablespoon with more than an actual tablespoon.

"See what happens when you float some pine needles on it," Paul said, handing some pine needles to Debra. She looked up at him as the needles floated on the bubble of water. Of all the students, jostling and rubbing at each other, she was the most present.

"You all know what ice is like," said Paul, taking ice cubes from the little refrigerator below the lab desk. "It is one of the few things that in a solid state is lighter than it is as a liquid."

Over a Bunsen burner, Paul boiled a measured amount of water, showing how the molecules became more and more active as they came to a rolling boil. "You see we've lost some water here," he said, pouring it back into the measure he began with. "Where did it go?"

"Steam!" said Debra. "I saw it!"

"Yes!" said Paul, beaming at her. "Now," he said, drawing the symbol for hydrogen peroxide (H_2O_2) on the board. "Let's add one more molecule of oxygen. How many of you have ever washed out a wound with hydrogen peroxide?"

Many of the students had. "Two oxygen molecules, bonded to each other, with hydrogen molecules on each side becomes hydrogen peroxide, a famous cleaning and whitening compound." He showed the students how a solution of water and hydrogen peroxide could cleanse a stain off a counter.

"My mother uses it to lighten people's hair," said Addie. "I saw the bottle."

"Exactly," said Paul. "Try floating the pine needles and the ice on it, Addie," he suggested. By itself, the hydrogen peroxide was slightly more viscous than water.

A ripple of pleasure ran up Paul's spine as he looked around at the kids crowded around the lab desk. Perhaps he was getting through to them! "Most of us have only seen hydrogen peroxide in a dilute solution," he said. "It can be dangerous, as are lots of chemicals. The point is, everything in our world is composed of chemicals with interesting and different properties. Water is the most ordinary thing in the world. But how interesting it is."

"Okay, students," Paul finished, "Please take your seats and we'll talk about what you need to do for next week's class."

As the students filed out, Mr. Hudson congratulated Paul. "Good work," he said. "Any time you can get them to listen. Especially all of them!"

Paul ducked his head in pleasure. Teaching was hard, but he did love the upturned faces.

"So tomorrow," said Mr. Hudson. "Be sure to wear warm clothes. It might seem strange to you, but there are many of us who just can't get enough golf!"

Paul started up the Lark in the chilly air and drove back to the college in the golden evening light. The angle of the sun had moved into its winter part of the sky, far to the south, he noted. He was pleased with himself.

When practice teaching began, Paul felt he was painfully back in Montauk, the new kid who was ignored because he couldn't run. Most of these students too were more excited about games at recess and whatever made them part of the group than learning. We are herd animals, Paul thought, visualizing a herd of impala bounding across the savannah as depicted in *National Geographic*.

Public school, if Paul had forgotten, was not designed to excite students. It was designed to make sure each of them shared the knowledge currently known to man. As a teacher, Paul had to be aware of everyone in the class, spooning information into their brains so that they could walk away enlightened on basic, commonly-held points.

Once he accepted this, Paul became as interested in this problem as he was in any other. At least he was well aware of who his students were. Most of them came from farms and the towns which served the little community with its great grain elevator. Wheat, corn and soybeans grown in the area were shipped by rail into the cities for processing into bread, oils, animal feed.

Debra intrigued Paul the most. He could only guess that the subtleties of the way he spoke about things might have captured her notice. She got a sullen look on her face when Mr. Hudson used the implied threat of his intensity to keep the class in order. Addie's mother probably ran a hair salon in town.

The outsider students, isolated either by their intellect like Debra, or their differences, excited Paul. Mr. Hudson spent most of his time insisting on the attention of the whole class, and getting it. Paul had tried Dad's method of talking very quietly, but it just didn't work. Perhaps, under the terms Mr. Hudson had set up, the kids expected something else. There was little time to devote to individual kids, but they did make teaching worthwhile.

In Moorhead, Paul pulled into the house near campus where he lived in a basement apartment with three other guys. Wayne, his cross-country skiing friend, had indeed disappeared when he got drafted that summer and was rumored to be in Toronto. No one was really sure.

An envelope with the return address of Healy, Alaska, in Marcia's handwriting lay on Paul's desk. One of his roommates had put the ivory figure of the Eskimo in his kayak on top of it. Paul decided to save it until he had had something to eat. He was ravenous!

The kitchen was empty, Friday night, and so was the refrigerator. The bucket of chili Paul had made last weekend was gone. He opened a can of baked beans and put the beans in a saucepan to heat. Luckily there was a package of wieners in the fridge, and he cut up a few and threw them in to make the beans taste better. He imagined he was cooking himself a meal in Fairbanks. It would probably be a lot the same!

Paul ate a few crackers as he heated up milk and stirred in cocoa powder. In his room he stretched out on his bed with the hot cocoa and the letter nearby. He didn't want to go to the football game as his roommates probably had, especially as he had agreed to meet Mr. Hudson the next morning.

Marcia wrote that she was happy to be back in Alaska, teaching at a small village school. There were only three teachers handling eight grades of school, but the classes were small. She wrote how painful it was for the village to watch the high school students take off in airplanes, headed for boarding schools in Fairbanks, Sitka and Oregon. The whole village missed them. Marcia had some of their brothers and sisters in her classes.

"Kids leaving home at 13 and 14. It's terrible," wrote Marcia. "But, it's been going on for a long time. Many students don't go to high school. Only the brightest ones." Marcia judged everything by Minnesota standards, Paul realized.

Paul had been thinking hard about what to apply for in the Alaska school system. He had decided that he would try to stay in Fairbanks. He wanted to live in one town and get to know it, use it as a base. From living in small towns, he felt he knew quite a lot about village life. He also expected that high school students would be more knowledgeable about their surroundings and he could learn from them.

From what Marcia said, some native Alaskan students from villages boarded with families in Fairbanks and went to high school there. Paul got the sense that a deep divide existed between the native Alaskans and later settlers to the region, who came mostly from the "lower 48" to harvest Alaskan resources, create recreational facilities or to homestead. Paul tried to read between the lines in the Fairbanks newspaper about high school basketball games, for instance, and see how it was going. But newspapers only skimmed the surface. He needed to be there!

The Fairbanks paper crackled with excitement about the pipeline which oil companies wanted to build between Prudoe Bay in the north and Valdez in the Gulf of Alaska. Other ideas, such as shipping the oil, had been suggested, but all were fraught with possible environmental disaster. Alaskan native claims had to be settled before a pipeline could be built. Negotiations between the federal government and the newly-formed Alaska Federation of Natives were underway.

Paul ingested all of it, as if he were already there. He was determined to live in Alaska as he wanted, to explore and try things and learn firsthand all he could. It was a frontier, in a way, and he thought he had found a way to go to it. He was trying to draw Mother and Dad into the adventure as well, bringing home stacks of Fairbanks newspapers. Though they were disappointed Paul wasn't going to the seminary, they probably held some hope that he might later.

For his own part, Paul wanted to keep everything open, to be a blank page on which life would write his story. He wanted to live in a diverse group of people and see life without blinders. He felt strongly about his relationship to Christ, but he wanted to step away from churches, from the certainties they held dear.

Paul was pretty sure he could get a job in the Alaskan school system as they were chronically short of teachers. He would graduate in June and wanted to get to Fairbanks early in the summer, when there was still enough light to get adjusted to the place. The land of the midnight sun. As soon as the new year rolled around, Paul planned to start writing to the Fairbanks school board.

Musing thus, Paul picked up his guitar and strummed. The song in his head was "Michael, Row the Boat Ashore," the one his group had been singing when he had first met Marcia, sitting with her broken leg at a Luther League meeting. The room was warm, and he fell asleep in the lamplight.

Paul waked up when his roommates came back with a six-pack of beer, to celebrate the victory of the Trinity Cobbers. In the early days of the college, a rival academy had ridiculed Trinity as a bunch of Norwegian "corncobs." "Lutefisk and lefse, yah, yah, yah," they yelled. Over the years, Trinity had taken the slur and turned it into fun, using its maroon and gold school colors for a corncob logo, and a mascot called "the Kernel."

But Paul was too sleepy to stay awake. He was hardly invested in college any more. In eight months he would be gone. His friends could celebrate and drink all around him and he didn't even hear it. He went to bed dreaming of the coming winter in Alaska.

In the morning, he left before any of the revelers was awake, getting into his car and taking the highway to the town of Hawley. The golf course was south of town. Paul parked by the club shack and waited for Mr. Hudson. There was still no frost, though the Lark was too cold to sit in.

Paul got out and walked around in the thin, early sunshine, stamping his feet, looking across at the wide expanse of lawns and trees.

Mr. Hudson stepped out of his car too, slapping his chest with his chilled hands. He wore a thick woolen lumberjack shirt over some sweaters and looked very different than he did at school. "Brisk!" he said. "Don't worry, we'll warm up soon." He dragged a bag of golf clubs from his trunk. "Now Paul," he said, intensely. "I just want you to have fun."

The golf course was deserted. The lawns were probably not getting the attention they did in the summer, but they were stunning to Paul. A landscape manicured within an inch of its life. It was like a game board, as of course it was. A physical game board with human counters moving through the links, trying to better their scores.

"It's one of the best courses in the area," said Mr. Hudson. "Makes Hawley one of the best little towns around, too."

Paul tried to keep down his iconoclasm, tried to take it all in. It didn't matter that Neil Armstrong had set foot on the moon in July that year, or that thousands of people had just demonstrated all across the country against the war in Vietnam, the biggest peace demonstration ever. In Hawley, Minnesota, boosters such as Mr. Hudson were intent on proving their small island was the best on earth. A golf course proved it!

Perhaps it was. Paul had no rejoinder. He could not say that he liked wild places better, that imposing such order on a place, making it into a playground for men horrified him. He could not currently conceive of ending up in Hawley, Minnesota. But, as people said, if you named the well you wouldn't drink from, that might be the one you must.

Mr. Hudson showed Paul how to flex his knees and stand, how to bend at the waist as he swung. He demonstrated why he chose certain clubs, how par was set and what constituted a swing. It was all very absorbing. Paul tried.

"Being short is a good thing in golf," said Mr. Hudson. "You're more grounded. Widen your stance a little."

Mr. Hudson was a few inches taller than Paul, who wasn't short, really. Paul rarely thought about his height, as his legs seemed much the greater challenge. He was actually a good athlete, broad-shouldered and strong. But he couldn't run.

"Golf is a math game," said Mr. Hudson. "Distances, weight, club length, muscle mass used to drive. I find it all fascinating."

Ahhhh, said Paul to himself, getting it. He remembered how Dad used to go hunting with Archie LeBlanc in order to get to know him and see whether he could get Archie to go to church. As a result, Archie converted Dad to bow and arrow hunting! And Archie did come to church once or twice, which was chalked up to Dad's power as a pastor. Here was Mr. Hudson, trying to convert Paul to golf! Paul felt glad he had no need to convert Mr. Hudson to anything.

The sun came through finally and the day turned warmer. "Call me John, for Chris' sake!" said Mr. Hudson, as he took off his coat at the fourth hole. "Where the hell shall I put this?" he wondered, hanging it over the bag of clubs on its little wheels.

Paul was happy to take off his coat too. It made it easier to swing. He knew he would never think of John Hudson as anything but Mr. Hudson, however. He would try.

By the 16th hole, Paul's legs were feeling tired. He was pleased to note that the holes were laid out to end up back at the club shack where they had started out. Paul wasn't doing too badly. Mr. Hudson's strokes were only a couple over par, and Paul was five or six. Still, it wasn't bad, he thought. He especially liked it when he got onto the putting green and tried to tap the ball into the hole.

"Beginner's luck," said Mr. Hudson when Paul's ball rolled into the hole.

Paul laughed. "Ender's luck too," he said. "I don't think I'll be much of a golfer."

"Why not?" asked Mr. Hudson.

"Heading to Alaska next year," said Paul.

"Alaska!" said Mr. Hudson. "Now there's an adventure for you!"

"Yeah," said Paul. "My game is chess, which I expect will come in handy during those long winters!"

"Guess you're right," said Mr. Hudson. "Look's like they opened up for us," he said as they went into the small building that served as a clubhouse. A few tables were arrayed around the room, which sold golf supplies at one end. "Let me buy you a cup of coffee," he said. "Or do you want a beer?"

Paul wavered. He didn't like either one. But he was a grownup now. And he was sure he was going to have to get used to beer. "I'll have a beer," he said manfully.

They sat down at a table and Mr. Hudson leaned back expansively, his hands behind his head. "If I was a young man like yourself," he said, "Alaska might be the place I'd go too! Heard they discovered oil up north there."

Paul explained everything he had learned about the negotiations that were going on in Alaska over the pipeline. "They're short of teachers," said Paul. "But the real reason I want to go is to get out in the wilderness. There're almost no roads! Bear and moose. And I really want to experience the extreme seasons, the northern lights and midnight sun."

"Yeah," said Mr. Hudson. "I read Jack London once. You know, the Klondike stuff. It's a rough place, though, Paul." He looked at Paul intensely, and Paul knew he was thinking about Paul's polio. Would Paul be able to handle an outdoor life?

"I'm trying to be realistic," said Paul. "I'm not expecting to homestead. I hope to live in Fairbanks and teach in the high schools. That'll give me time in the summers to get a little further out into the wilderness. Maybe work in construction or something. I know my limits," he said.

"Hope so," said Mr. Hudson. "I wouldn't want to hear that you'd frozen to death somewhere off where nobody could find you."

"Plane crashes," said Paul. "That's the number one problem. They use small bush planes to get around. As if they were cars. And I'm not sure pilots know what they're doing all the time, from the sounds of it. But I had an aunt who was a missionary there. She was just below the Arctic circle in Nome and Shishmaref. She spent 30 years there!"

"Ahhhh," said Mr. Hudson. "So you're following in her footsteps."

"Not exactly," Paul admitted. "I'm afraid I'm not serving the people the way she did. I'm doing this more for my own interests at this point."

"It's not a bad reason," said Mr. Hudson. "Education is a service, believe me! Alaska became a state when?" He scratched his head.

"In 1959," said Paul. "I remember having a little flag with 50 stars on it above my bed." He did not mention that the bed had been in a hospital and he had been undergoing painful reconstruction surgery on his legs.

"Wow," said Mr. Hudson. "It's only been a state for ten years! And here they discover oil. Those kids are going to need you! Civic education, the bedrock of our democracy. We all take it for granted. But I've been places where they don't understand it. Korea, for instance," he said. "Democracy has a long way to go in the world."

"Yeah?" asked Paul. He knew Mr. Hudson had been a fighter pilot at one time.

"Well, I didn't see much of Korea," admitted Mr. Hudson. "I was in a bomber squadron at the end of the war, a kid really. I flew planes above North Korea, spent a few weekends in Seoul. But it's nothing like here. It gives you perspective."

"How?" asked Paul. He could see history passing across Mr. Hudson's darkening face as he went back over the years.

"Women, mostly," said Mr. Hudson. "Asian women are nothing like American women. They're almost a different species."

Paul tried to imagine what Mr. Hudson was talking about. He felt grateful to be discussing the world with Mr. Hudson, who was surely trying to initiate Paul in some way. Paul was glad he had gotten to work with a male teacher. He had grown up mostly with sisters and was still trying to figure out the features of what he found to be the male preserve.

"I guess I don't really know what you mean," said Paul. All of a sudden Paul longed for Line and Marty, for the world they had known together. There had never seemed to be much difference between girls and boys when he was growing up. Everyone was equal. Everyone worked, though women's work was different.

"Don't worry," said Mr. Hudson. He waved his hand dismissively. "There's plenty of time for a guy like you. You're going to do fine, Paul. A good teacher. Mostly because you're interested in what you're doing."

Paul nodded and Mr. Hudson continued, standing up and stretching. "This might be it for this season. Every round I play I think, well maybe that's the last one."

"Yeah," said Paul. "Bound to snow sooner or later." He expressed his appreciation, thanking Mr. Hudson kindly.

Driving back to the college Paul thought about his sisters. They were meeting people from subtly different cultures too. Line had married one. Stephen and his family from New York had been a surprise for the Mikkelsons.

Feeling less bound by his Lutheran background, Paul was also meeting people very different from himself. He was grateful for the integrated and seamless Norwegian Lutheran culture he grew up in, but it was only in getting to know diverse people that he could really see his own culture. Another stab of longing to see Line and Marty and compare notes hit him.

High wisps of cirrus cloud gathered in the west, driven by some type of weather front, perhaps. I want to live in one place long enough to know it, thought Paul. I want to be an old guy who knows what the weather is going to do just by looking at the sky. Maybe that place would be Alaska.

26

Line picked up the telephone in February and, incredibly, heard Stephen's voice at the other end of the line. She had not talked to him since she left Chicago nine months before. She was so surprised she could hardly speak. But there was his voice, sounding sad, anguished and also, strangely exalted.

"The Chicago seven have been acquitted of conspiracy," Stephen said. "We are so glad. Some of them have lesser charges, but the acquittal has us all reeling!" He sounded as if Line would be greatly interested by this fact.

Line was interested. She'd been following the television news. But she was much more interested in what Stephen could possibly be thinking about his son, his wife. She had not stopped thinking about him, but she had resolved to do absolutely nothing about her husband. She read his letters but did not answer them. She was happy with the life she was making for herself and Christopher. She did not think she could go back to Chicago. "Yes," she said softly. "I'm glad too."

"Line, my baby," Stephen's voice sounded anguished. "I think about you all the time. And I'm faithful to you in my fashion."

"Yeah?" Line waited to hear more. She didn't want to hear how faithful Stephen was at this point. She wanted to know his plans. Actions spoke louder than words, as her Mother had always said.

"Your Dad gave me your phone number. How is Christopher?"

"He's fine," said Line. Christopher himself had left his wooden train and come up to her at the sound of voices, putting his hands on her lap as she sat on the sofa. He batted little hands at the black object which had taken his mother's attention. Tears welled in Line's eyes.

"And you?"

"I'm fine, Stephen," said Line.

"Line!" wailed Stephen. "I'm so glad to hear your voice! Please talk to me!"

"I don't have anything to say," said Line. She had thought about Stephen every day over the past months, silently arguing with him, cajoling him, but her dignity protected her. She was sure she was in the right and that it was up to him to close the gap between them.

"Oh, Line, my Line," said Stephen. "I want you here with me."

Line was silent. What could she say? Christopher's curls frothed around his head in the sunshine, as Stephen's must have when he was little.

"I know you think I've given myself over to revolution. But it's starting to feel like history," said Stephen. "Fred getting killed made me terribly angry, but I can't go the route Bernardine and the Weathermen are going. Fred himself said that their violence is hurting the community."

Line listened. She knew, from reading his letters, that he was talking about the killing of Fred Hampton, the promising young head of the Black Panthers in Chicago, just before Christmas.

"Things are changing," said Stephen. "People are calling Altamont the end of the Sixties. You weren't there were you?"

"No," said Line. Altamont was far out in the California countryside. No one she knew had been at the Rolling Stones concert at which the Hells Angels had tried to impose order and several people had been killed. Dad must have told Stephen she was in California too.

"Line," said Stephen. "This is amazing. I'm so glad to be talking to you! Line," Stephen paused. "Please wait for me. I'm trying to finish up my Master's and then maybe get another degree in history, so I can teach. Will you come if I get settled somewhere?"

"I'm not 'coming' anywhere, Stephen," said Line.

"Well, will you think about it?" asked Stephen. "I want to see you. And Christopher. I bet he's walking by this time."

Complicated algorithms rose in Line's head. She did not want Stephen dropping into Christopher's life unless there would be some continuity to it. "I told you once that I didn't want to have a baby by myself," said Line carefully. "It's been tough on Christopher. You can't just drop in on us and then leave again."

"No, no," said Stephen. "Of course, you're right. But Line, will you think about it?"

"Yes," said Line quietly. "I will. But I have to go now." She was anxious to get off the line before her self-respect wore too thin.

"Oh, Line, I love you," said Stephen. "I'll write to you. Please write back to me," he begged.

"Goodbye, Stephen," said Line, tears welling in her eyes. She put the phone back in its cradle and gathered her son into her arms. Tears spilled onto his soft sweet skin and the little plaid shirt she had bought at Goodwill. How hard it was to be alone.

Wiping her eyes, Line smiled at Christopher. "You," she said. "You are so sweet. What shall we do today?" she asked. She did not even want to introduce the concept of father to the little boy whose Dad was so distant.

The winter sun coming in the southern windows lay in big flat lozenges on the floor by Christopher's toys. It never ceased to amaze Line that the middle of the day could be so warm in February. "Let's go out to the abandoned garden," she said to the little boy. He reached up his hands and played with her red-gold hair.

Line put on Christopher's jacket and carried him down the steps and out to the sidewalk. She set him down and let him walk on the little legs that were growing more sturdy the more he used them. Line slowly followed him up the sidewalk. Every part of the street was sun-washed. The light-colored buildings reflected the light and there were few trees.

At the smooth stone steps leading to a church, Line let Christopher climb. Though she was having trouble getting used to such a different environment, San Francisco represented safety. She blessed every day that she and Christopher could go outdoors.

Line was working now, four evenings a week at Children's Hospital. At the neighborhood playground, she had found a friend, Samantha, who could take Christopher for a few hours in the afternoon. Marty came home from work, picked him up and spent the evening with him. If Marty wanted to go out, Samantha kept Christopher until Line came home at 11 p.m.

Line was glad to be working and have money. Though she was on an oncology ward, she was hoping to get back into obstetrics when the opportunity came up. And it was good for Christopher to play with Samantha's little girl.

Having made a life for herself independent of Stephen, Line could think of him freely. She still didn't want to raise Christopher by herself and, if Stephen bridged the gap between them she would be glad. Living with

Marty was fine, except that Marty did not seem to be able to say no to her insidious boyfriend Erik.

Line did not regard Erik as a good person. She felt there was something sinister behind his charm. He drove Marty crazy with his absences, and once in a while, like last weekend, the two of them were insufferable. They had taken tabs of acid in the front room and been loud and giggling all night while Line tried to sleep. They didn't keep Christopher awake, but when Line found them in the kitchen in the morning, hazy-faced and grinning from ear to ear, she could hardly be civil.

No one drove Line from her home, however. She hunkered down, shared the coffee and the box of sugary doughnuts they were eating and gave one to Christopher. Line trusted Marty completely, but less so when Erik was around.

"Come on, Christopher," said Line, standing up and taking his hand. Feathery acacia trees bloomed yellow and a few ornamental cherries put out pink flowers on branches with no leaves as yet. It was stunning. Line was sure that in Chicago a stiff wind still blew off the lake making the air bitter with cold. Spring was slow to come in Chicago, but in San Francisco the only thing that made it winter were occasional weeks of cold rain.

Today the sky was a brilliant blue. Christopher's small steps eventually brought them to the top of Russian Hill. Pausing at the corner of Greenwich, Line looked out at the Golden Gate Bridge to the north. The green water was dotted with the white sails of boats. But the wind coming over the crest of the hill off the water was cold.

When they got to Lombard Street, the austere buildings on Alcatraz looked very close. Once an island prison, it had recently been occupied by Native Americans. Line wished them well. She took Christopher's hand, leading him down Chestnut toward an empty lot.

Opening a decrepit wooden gate, Line lifted Christopher up the cracked stone steps into the garden of a large old home. All that remained were the foundations and the garden walls. It was Line's favorite place. She loved wandering around, looking at the overgrown vegetation. The top of the hill where the house had been was clear and sandy. Further back a few trees provided shelter and grass, tall from the winter rains, followed the slope down.

Line sat down in the hot sun out of the wind, letting Christopher wander. She identified sourgrass with its yellow flowers and miner's lettuce. Neither of them were familiar to her. The twisted grey-green twigs of a rosemary shrub were awash in blue flowers. Clumps of lavender and mint gave off their smells in the heat of the sun. Marty wasn't much help identifying these plants, but Line had found a friend who was.

A few weeks ago, Line had stumbled on a group walking through Golden Gate Park on a Thursday morning. With a shock of white hair, big tufted eyebrows and a goatee that stuck out, Joe Miller and his wife Guin led the walk. Joe was a kind of mystic, who, Line learned, refused to be any kind of guru or spiritual teacher. Joe told people, "This isn't something you can go to India and get, or the moon, or South America! It's inside you. Just be still and find it."

To keep up, Line carried Christopher in the backpack Jack had found for her, though he was getting too big for it and was very heavy. When she couldn't get close to Joe, Line walked near Julia, who knew a lot about plants. Julia pointed out the succulents, the madrones and manzanita, the pampas grass and herbs. She had lived in the dry desert of California all her life. Julia asked Line to go Sufi dancing on a Saturday night. "You can bring your son," she said. "He'll probably sleep right through it."

The plants that survived in California were able to conserve water, or get along with little. Generally the only rain that fell all year was in the winter. The fruits and vegetables were different too. Avocados and artichokes, pomegranates and kiwi fruits, things Line had never seen before. Grapevines and olives flourished on hard, stony, dry ground.

Line felt like a tough desert plant. The stored-up love and affection she had gotten from her family she doled out lavishly to her son. For slightly different reasons, she loved California as much as Marty did. She could not imagine what Stephen could do to entice her back east. The women's group in Chicago had made the place bearable, and Line had loved the feisty people she met at the hospital, but it didn't compare to the ease of living with family in the warmth of this sun-drenched coastal city.

Line brought herself up short. She must not think about Stephen. She was with her son in an abandoned garden at the top of Russian Hill in San Francisco, surrounded by plants. "Be, just be," she heard Joe Miller's voice shouting. "There are three things you need for the spiritual path, common sense, a sense of humor, and more common sense." Joe's message was something Line could get behind. The future must take care of itself.

The hot sun was a warm embrace. Christopher handed Line a wild California poppy, a brilliant orange. He sat down on the remains of an old sidewalk and picked up snails with pudgy fingers. No one needed to tell Christopher to "be"! He was like a little Buddha, lifting his arms up to Line.

Line could barely remember the young self she had left behind in Chicago, the angry self who had wanted to fight for justice. Christopher had brought her fight home. His immediate welfare was more important than any political use Line could be. She was glad to hear that Stephen was turning away from the violence which still erupted everywhere. Bomb threats were constant across America. The Bank of America downtown looked like a bunker. What earthly good was all this?

Line picked up Christopher and set him on her hip, walking quickly down the hill home. She would feed them lunch and go to her shift at the hospital. She hoped that Christopher would sleep a little before they had to leave.

On Saturday evening, Line took the bus to the base of Oak Street, carrying Christopher. She joined a group of people in long, flowing clothes streaming into an old building with a large foyer and a ballroom beyond. The skirts on the women's colorful dresses were floor length and the men wore caftans or long shirts from India and Tibet. Some of them carried drums, guitars and other, less recognizable, stringed instruments.

The ballroom was empty except for the people. High lamps flared light out on the ornate woodwork and fluted columns, but the ceiling was very high and there wasn't enough light to keep the room from being mysterious. Piles of coats and shoes were pushed against the walls. Line looked for Julia among the people standing around talking on the shiny wooden floor.

Julia found Line first. "Line! You came!" she said. Julia's long hair was loose, trailing down a long pink dress embroidered with big, bright flowers.

Line felt Julia's arms around her and Christopher. "Yeah," she said. "I traded my shift at the hospital with a friend. The dancing sounded like so much fun when you told me about it. I love your dress," she said.

"It's a Mexican dress," said Julia modestly.

Line's own long peasant dress was gathered at the scoop neck, the arms and under her breasts. Marty had sewn it out of lengths of woven purple and white cotton.

Julia inclined her head toward an old man in a loose caftan with a beard and thick-rimmed glasses on his nose. Long white hair flowed around his head. "That's Sufi Sam. He's studied psychic and mystical spirituality all his life. His wealthy family rejected him. Once when he was in the hospital he was told by a divine presence that he would become 'the spiritual leader of the hippies.'" Julia giggled. "And here we are, the hippies!"

Line was not a hippy, but their approach to life intrigued her. If you left out the drugs, they were a little like what Line thought the early

Christians must have been like. They didn't worry about money and status all the time, were free to smell the flowers.

Christopher wasn't the only little kid in the room. As the dance began, Line stood over to one side with another woman who held a small child. Swaying to the music, she waited until Christopher seemed to be falling asleep. Then she put him down in a nest of coats and shawls and joined the dancing.

Sufi dancing used verses and songs from many spiritual traditions. "May all beings be well, may all beings be happy, peace, peace, peace," sang Sam. It was easy to join the circles, following the person in front of you, moving as they did. "Head in the clouds, feet on the ground," shouted Sufi Sam. Line followed. At first she was nervous and kept returning to Christopher, to see whether he was all right. But he slept soundly.

In one dance, everyone reached out their arms to their neighbors, touching them on shoulders and waists. Line felt hands, one on her shoulder, one on her waist from the short person to her right. She didn't know any of these people, but it felt good to be locked in the circle. Then the group held hands as they sang "Allah, allah, allah." The words were simple, opening the breath and the heart.

Line leaned into the rhythms, letting her body sway and move. Harmonies high and low reached her from people who knew the songs, singing with the guitars in the middle of the circle. At last things began to wind down. "Thank you for the gifts, of this day and every day," they sang. Then just stood quietly, until Sam released them. "Go with God!" he sang out.

Yes, Line thought to herself. I can do that. She found Christopher and thanked Julia for inviting her. "It's not like there's anything I am forced to believe," she said.

"Oh no," said Julia. "The idea is that there is truth in every tradition. The Sufis gather them all up. I test blood work at the University of California," she said. "I need this. It's a complete reversal of that structured, rigid world. I love it."

"Hope I see you next Thursday in the park," said Line. She held the sleeping Christopher against her shoulder. "I work nights so that's easier for me to get to. I love hearing you talk about plants."

"I love plants," said Julia. "I want to learn more about them, and about how to use herbs for more natural healing. I think the Native Americans know a lot more than we do. The Chinese too."

"My sister found me a book about gypsies in New York. There's a lot of herbal information in it," said Line. "Juliette de Bairacli Levy wrote it," she said stumbling over the odd name. "She walks the streets with her kids and her dog and writes about trees and herbs. It is such a different perspective on cities."

"I've heard of her!" Julia looked excited. "She's a veterinarian. She has written about curing horses and dogs," said Julia. "I'd like to read that when you're done." The two of them flowed down the marble steps out of the building and stood on the sidewalk in the dark with all the other people, loathe to leave.

"Sure," said Line. "I'll bring it on Thursday." She realized it was the kind of exchange she had been looking for all of her life. Line loved learning, but she wanted to know things not taught in schools. Julia shared her interests.

That week, on the small black and white television Line rented to keep in touch with the world, she heard that students had set fire to a Bank of America near Santa Barbara. Line knew the Freemans had moved to Santa Barbara. She thought Bernie had taken a job at the university there. Line had not been in touch with them. She felt sad she was such a bad correspondent, wondering whether Bernie was well enough to teach. She would love to talk to Kay but it felt beyond her powers at the moment.

The next afternoon, Jack and Nathan came to the house. They brought a bottle of wine, crackers, cheese and a salami. Line took plates and knives into the living room with its bay window looking out on the street. Marty was at work. She could always be counted on to leave the front room neat.

Christopher stood in the circle of Line's arms as the four of them sat companionably on the daybed and the sofa, picnicking on the food.

"My dad was a stockbroker," Jack said. "Walked around New York with a handkerchief full of gemstones. He'd take them out and look at them in the sun to remind him of beauty." Jack had grown up in New York, but also worked as an actor in Los Angeles.

"Wow," said Line. It was a world she could not imagine. She was thinking of Juliette in New York, who reveled in plants and trees instead of gemstones.

"I was the bartender in *North to Alaska*," said Jack. "And I worked in an underground movie, *Chafed Elbows*. You'll probably never see it. Very funny. It satirized everything!"

"If they ever play them on television, will you let me know?" asked Line. "I'd like to see you in a movie."

"Sure," said Jack. "Loved the guy who made *Chafed Elbows*, Robert Downey. But they won't let it out. It's too dark, too right on."

Line handed Christopher another cracker. He seemed to like the strong tasting cheese.

"Nathan was an extra in a film just before we moved here. Shot up in Washington State. There's a fire in a village and he's passing buckets along a line of people. Look for it. I don't think it's out yet. It's Robert Altman, with Warren Beatty and Julie Christie in it."

Nathan never said much. He looked like a dark gypsy himself, curly hair surrounded by a halo of sunlight. He smiled and nodded as Jack told Line about the movie, as if he was remembering the scene. "Pretty damp up in Washington," he said.

"Totally insane profession," said Jack, darkly. "We're much better off here."

Nathan had grown up in Los Angeles. He was younger than Line, had never been to much school. Jack, urbane, handsome, sure of the stupidity of American culture, was Nathan's teacher. And Line and Marty's also.

"So Line," Jack said. "I did have an ulterior motive in coming over here. According to the paper they're broadcasting reruns of *The Avengers* with Diana Rigg today. And you have a television! Could we see if it's on?" Jack and Nathan lived in a peaceful apartment in an old Victorian. They had covered the walls with Indian bedspreads from Cost Plus and filled sunny corners with the marijuana plants Nathan was trying to grow. A haze of pot smoke often filled the place.

"Sure!" said Line. "It's in the back room." She knew it was a mess, the bed not made, Christopher's clothes strewn about. But maybe Jack and Nathan didn't care. She stood up and led them back to her room, Christopher toddling after.

The light was never bright in Line's room. From the window open on the light-well you could hear the neighbor Chinese people speaking to each other as they chopped vegetables in their kitchen. But in the subdued light, Christopher could nap almost any time of day.

Line turned on the tiny television which sat on a Chinese wooden box. Jack and Nathan stretched their long bodies out on Line's mattress, and Jack fiddled with the channel buttons.

"You've got to see the beginning," said Jack, as the series began.

Line marveled at Jack's prowess, turning on the television at just the right time. In front of her on the tiny black and white screen, a man fell on a chessboard, a knife protruding from his back. Another nattily dressed man in a bowler picked up the bottle the man dropped and poured two wineglasses, handing one to a thin, dark-haired woman in a leather suit who was putting a gun in her boot. They clinked glasses and walked off.

"Ahhhhhh!" said Jack. "Great style!"

Line watched closely. "It's her eyes," she said. "They're full of mischief!"

"Mischief!" said Jack. "Insouciance!"

"What does that mean, Jack?" asked Line. She reached out a hand to quiet Christopher, who lolled about with his head in her lap, entranced by the many people in his room.

"She doesn't care. She's beautiful. She's witty and amazing and can turn anyone on. On top of it, she's indifferent! It's the ultimate sexiness!"

Line, flanked by Nathan and Jack, watched the program avidly. On television Steed was the staid Englishman to Mrs. Peel's modern presence, the perfect foil. Steed was entranced by the delicious Mrs. Peel but possessed of his own certainty.

In a little while, the door opened and Marty appeared. "Come and watch," said Line. "It's almost over."

"I wondered what was going on," Marty said, but was quieted by the fact that no one looked up from the television screen. She knelt behind them, watching.

When the plot had thickened and come to an end, Steed got into an ancient road car and Mrs. Peel climbed into a sporty convertible.

Jack stood up. "You see what I mean?" he said.

"Yes," said Line. "I do. She's beautiful."

"Hello, Marty," said Jack. "How was work?"

Marty wore black tights, a grey woolen skirt and a black sweater. With long dark hair and thick glasses, she looked like an intellectual. Line laughed to herself. She remembered what Jack had once told her, "You girls have a certain bovine beauty," he said. Against the slim Mrs. Peel, she and Marty did look like a couple of cows in a field. But Line didn't repeat this out loud. Poor Marty was sensitive.

"It was okay," said Marty. "It looks cozy in here. My feet are all wet from trudging around in the rain."

"A glass of wine?" asked Line. "Jack and Nathan brought it. I think there's some left."

"Yeah," said Marty. "That would do it."

Line stood up and everyone followed her into the front room where empty wine glasses, plates of cheese and cracker crumbs littered the floor. Line looked at Marty, but Marty appreciated Jack's take on life as much as Line did. Marty would not complain. Line handed her one of the mismatched wineglasses they had bought at Goodwill. "Cheers!" she said. "Not quite Mrs. Peel, but it will have to do!"

"You girls do very well indeed," said Jack evenly. "We always enjoy coming to your place."

Line wondered what Jack saw when he looked at them, coming from the sophisticated places he did. She wondered what Stephen would think of them all, should he all of a sudden be dropped into their apolitical midst. I guess it's good I'm thinking about him, Line thought to herself, hearing his voice in her head. She didn't want Stephen to be history.

27

That spring Paul spent endless hours contemplating the routes west across country. He wanted to leave early in the summer, but he could not resist a stop in San Francisco, even though it would have been much shorter to go directly through Canada. Mother and Dad encouraged him.

"Take your time, Paul," said Dad. "You'll probably be driving a lot if you insist on living in Alaska. But you may not always have the time you have now."

Paul appreciated it. He did not have money of his own yet, and Dad gave him some to get started. Dad also gave him the Ford Country Sedan, which he thought would probably make it to Fairbanks, but then must be laid to rest!

Paul planned to camp in the station wagon, using his fabulous new sleeping bag, his most precious possession! It was a feather-filled US Army mountain bag that Dad found at a surplus store. They didn't buy a tent as Paul didn't think it would be much use in Alaska. Dad helped him lay carpet squares on the bottom of the station wagon as a cushion.

As to the routes, Paul knew he must make time across the big states, but he had never been west and every place was seductive. It was difficult to choose! The end of the route had to be from Salt Lake City through Nevada, on Route 80, as the most direct. But there were several ways to get to Salt Lake.

Paul packed the station wagon with his few possessions, trying to stay light on the books but including his warmest clothes and his guitar. Early one morning, Dad, Mother, Kristen and Hanna got up to say goodbye. It was eerie. Paul had always stayed close to home, but now he didn't know when he would next see his family.

The first day Paul made it mostly through South Dakota on the long flat highway. He paused to pay tribute to the Missouri River as he crossed it, and drove north around the Black Hills. The town of Spearfish, South Dakota, sounded like an auspicious place to stop. He found a campground along Spearfish Creek. It was a clear, mild night and the sun went down behind some willows. Paul made a wood fire and cooked up potatoes and onions in a small black iron skillet. The Dakotas felt familiar to him, as if he had hardly left home.

Almost no one else was using the campground, but a person about Paul's age emerged from a Volkswagen camper van, came over and offered him a can of beer.

"Looks like you're by your lonesome here," the man said, one hand straying over his beard and mustache.

"Yep," said Paul. "Just cooking myself some dinner. Want some?" He indicated the pan he was stirring with a spatula.

"Sounds great," said the man, who said his name was Jimbo. "Nothing like the smell of onions to draw a person!"

Paul took the beer and the two of them sat at a picnic table, eating out of the skillet. Jimbo was also crossing the country, but in the opposite direction. He was going home to Wisconsin after a year at school in Denver. "It's a great place," Jimbo told Paul. "In sight of the mountains. Kerouac spent some time there. Neal Cassady's home town."

Paul knew who Kerouac was, but that was about all. "Kerouac?" he said.

"Yeah, *On the Road*, like we are," laughed Jimbo. "He was always crossing back and forth. But *Visions of Cody* is about Denver. Great book." Jimbo took a drag on a handmade cigarette and Paul smelled marijuana. "Want some weed?" he asked.

"No thanks," said Paul. He wasn't planning on getting anywhere near Denver. It was too far south. "I've never been west," he said, "but I'm not going to have much time for sightseeing. I've got to get to Fairbanks while there's still some light! I want to be there on June 21. And before that, I want to spend a week in San Francisco with my sisters."

"Yeah, yeah," said Jimbo slowly. "Sounds like you've got a lot goin' on." He went back to his Volkswagen and brought back a couple more beers. Paul refused the second one.

"You've got to stop at a hot spring though," said Jimbo. "They're all over the place. Nothing like it. Hot water coming right up out of the ground! Indian Springs near Denver has thermal springs in caves! It's my favorite thing about the West."

"Sounds wonderful," said Paul.

"Yeah, I'm lookin' forward to some good Wisconsin brews," said Jimbo. "But I'm already missing the girls and the hot springs." He laughed largely, slapping his thigh.

At night, Paul left the back of the station wagon open. The creek was too fast-moving to spawn a lot of mosquitoes. The sound of the rushing water in the canyon below the campground lulled Paul to sleep.

The next morning, cold air surrounded him. Paul moved only his eyes in the luscious warmth of the sleeping bag, watching the sky lighten. His body was stiff, partly from having to stay in one position while he drove the long miles. But he got up, ate a banana and set off again.

Wyoming felt like the west. It wasn't a straight shot, as the highway through South Dakota had been. Paul drove down to Casper. As he stopped for lunch, he thought of the Friendly Ghost, but the town was loaded with its own history. It had been named for a young lieutenant killed by an Indian warrior near the fort his father commanded. Paul longed to stick around and learn more, but after downing a hamburger, he kept going.

The Rocky Mountains began to be visible as Paul left Casper. He went south and traveled beside the railroad for the rest of the day, coming to Green River by evening. The Green had recently been dammed, which made a wide, placid river through a "flaming gorge."

Paul found a campsite and again coaxed a small wood fire into cooking his onions and potatoes. In the dimming light at sundown, he poured over his road atlas. Water from the Green flowed south into the mighty Colorado, through the Gulf of California which divided Mexico, and finally into the Pacific. Essentially, Paul had reached the Continental

Divide. He would have loved to put a canoe in, right where he was and let the river carry him south, taking his chances.

But Paul was driven by his goals for the summer. He had a job teaching at Lathrop high school in Fairbanks. He hoped that if he got to Fairbanks early, he could get some work, maybe construction work, for the summer and get oriented before school started. He figured his first year of teaching would be so strenuous he wouldn't be able to explore much.

Pounding through the salt flats of Utah and the Nevada desert at a steady pace over the next couple of days, Paul grew tired. He hated having to rush through places. Loren Eiseley had been a bone-hunter in this country. Many towns were named for springs, but he had no time to investigate.

At last, Paul crossed the Sierras and floated gently down into the fertile central valley of California. A beautiful bridge carried him across the San Francisco Bay into a city of tall white buildings.

Paul didn't like city driving any better than Dad did, and this city was especially confusing. Line said their apartment was in the north, so Paul tried to stay north, stopping to ask directions several times. Clouds obscured the late afternoon sun. At last, after bumbling around, Paul found Larkin Street, but there was nowhere to park!

Paul pulled into a driveway and rang Line and Marty's bell. Both of them came clamoring down to greet him and Marty got in the car to help look for a parking space on the narrow streets. The houses and apartments crowded right down to the sidewalk. It looked like some of them had garages, but you couldn't park in front of the driveways.

"In the evening everyone's come home from work and it's harder to find parking," Marty said. "It isn't a city to drive in. We get along just fine without a car here."

"I can see that!" said Paul. "I need a car to explore in Alaska. And this old tank isn't going to make it much further anyway, Dad says."

Marty turned her head to look at the packages and bags strewn throughout the back of the station wagon. "Oh," she said. "All those big family journeys. It's unbelievable that you came all that way in the old Country Sedan!"

With Marty directing, they finally found a spot and left the dusty old car. It was chilly and Paul's skin was prickly from being hot and sweaty as he drove. "Cold," he said, as he pulled on a flannel shirt. "I've been hot, driving through the desert. None too clean, either." He smiled at Marty as he rolled up his sleeping bag and put it in a stuff sack.

"Don't worry," said Marty, pulling her sweater around her. "We are just so glad to see you!"

The yellow disk of the sun showed through the drifts of cottony clouds. A flight of seagulls caught Paul's eye, flying in a cloud, turning and twisting. High up were patches of blue sky.

"It's the fog coming in," said Marty. "We're so close to the ocean that it really affects us. San Francisco Bay is just over that hill. Hot air in the valley sets up a current, drawing in the fog through the Golden Gate. It's the one thing I don't like. We hardly ever have a really hot night. Of course, it's nice air-conditioning, but I miss the Midwestern heat in the summers."

"Wow," said Paul. "Every night?"

"Pretty much," said Marty.

Paul was disoriented, but Marty pointed the way. "We're on the base of Nob Hill." She pointed. "See, the Bay lies to the north. You came in over the Bay Bridge, over there."

Buildings surrounded them on all sides, their metal gates and doors right on the street. To his left Paul could see buildings climbing the hills.

"The main part of the city is over there," said Marty. "I used to walk over Nob Hill to my job in the morning, but now my job is South of Market, too far to walk."

"There're hardly any trees," said Paul.

"Sometimes there's a little yard behind an apartment building," said Marty. "But this part of town is old and dense. It all burned during the earthquake and fire in 1906, and then it got rebuilt."

At the apartment, they went up the steps to the first floor where Line stood in the doorway with Christopher, a small vivid person on his own two feet, blonde hair curling around his face. He smiled up at Paul and chortled when Paul picked him up and nuzzled his neck. Line led them into a large room with a sofa and a daybed snugged into a bay window without a shred of curtains. Paul sat on the daybed with Christopher reaching up to his scruffy beard and longish hair.

"I hope he's not thinking you're his 'D-a-d,'" spelled Line, quietly. "I haven't spoken to him about his D-a-d in a long time."

"Stephen?" asked Paul cautiously.

"We're talking," said Line. "But I don't want Christopher to think about him unless I know Stephen will be there for him." Line filled wineglasses to toast Paul's arrival. "L'Chaim!" she said lifting her glass. "To life!"

"Cheers," said Marty.

It was very odd, after moving west for days, to be sitting quietly among his sisters! Paul drank down the wine, which tasted rather nice, if somewhat tingly. Line and Marty looked different than what Paul was used to. Line wore a long dress with a scarf wrapped around her shoulders. Marty wore jeans, belted with a big buckle and a black turtleneck top. Both of them had long hair hanging around their shoulders.

"So have you become Californian?" Paul asked.

Marty and Line looked at each other.

"It's the freedom," said Marty. "I miss things about home, but I wouldn't give up the intellectual freedom for anything!"

"Safety," said Line, quietly. "I feel much safer here than in Chicago. I hate to say it, but it's true." She looked darkly from Paul to Marty, then took Christopher from Paul and hugged him. "Kent State, the Weathermen, bombs everywhere. I'm so glad we're here."

"You know," said Paul. "I'm impressed with how Dad and Mother have helped me, even though they wanted me to stay closer to home and go to the seminary. Dad told me that they had a call to Washington State when they were younger, and they really wanted to go. But they both felt they must stay in the Midwest, close to their families."

"Dad was the only son after his brother died in the war," said Line. "And Mother was the youngest, the closest to her mother."

"Maybe you are living out one of Dad's fantasy lives," said Marty. "They helped me go to Oxford, when it was an economic burden on them. And then I kept going! I'm sure they want me to settle down nearer home too."

"Dad even bought new tires for the station wagon!" said Paul. "Along with everything else. It was like he was going himself!"

"It takes courage to do what you're doing, Paul," said Marty. "I don't think I'd have the guts to go live in Alaska."

"I'll send you guys some of the newspapers from Fairbanks," said Paul. "They're just people living there, like everyone else. Aunt Mabel was a pioneer. She lived out in the wilds of Shishmaref and Nome. But Fairbanks is a boom town, it sounds like. I want to use it as a base."

"A boom town!" said Marty. "I've been headed towards more civilization, not less!"

"It's the relation to wilderness that I'm interested in," said Paul. "Alaska is vast, most of it unpaved and unspoiled. I want to see what happens there."

"Hungry?" asked Line. "We've been expecting you all day. It's so wonderful you're here!" She put Christopher down and headed toward the kitchen.

Paul stood up and stretched. "I'll eat whatever you've got," he admitted. Christopher stood below him looking up. Looking out the window Paul noticed that in the lighted apartments on the opposite side of the street, people were moving about. How strange a city was! Paul picked up Christopher and they all converged on the tiny kitchen.

"We all used to think Line was the rebel," said Marty, "but I think I'm just as much of a rebel as she is these days!" She laid out plates on a formica table.

"Having a kid makes it different," said Line. "Your kid's more important than you are. But I'm still counter-culture, don't you worry!"

Paul laughed at his sisters. They had been living together for almost a year in this apartment. It was such a delight to be together again!

Dinner was a plate of brown rice topped with cut up carrots and broccoli. "It's the quintessential hippie meal," said Marty. "But we'll have hot fudge sundaes for dessert. Whenever Line or I have had a bad day, we take each other out to Blum's down on Polk Street for a hot fudge sundae. It's a historic San Francisco candy company, with a drug store counter and booths, except that everything in it is pink! Pink walls, pink leather seats. It's just amazing."

"Oh," said Line, "but we have to take him to Ghirardelli Square. I like their chocolate much better. Blum's is too sweet for me."

Both of them chimed in with all the places Paul must go while he was in San Francisco for a week. He listened to the unfamiliar names Line and Marty mentioned, but then he broke in. "There's only one thing I really need to do," he said. "I need to get my feet in the Pacific. I'm not going to live by the ocean. This is my only chance."

"No problem!" said Line. And she and Marty began a heated discussion of their work schedules. It was Monday night, and it turned out that from Wednesday to Friday, they had opposite day and evening schedules, so as to take care of Christopher. The next day, when Marty was at work, Line, Christopher and Paul could go to the beach on the streetcar.

That evening, Paul stretched out in his sleeping bag on the floor in Marty's room behind the sofa. He could have slept on the sofa, but it was old and the springs were unreliable. He didn't mind the floor.

The week of running around the city with Marty or Line or both went quickly. Paul found that the city did have trees along some streets and especially in the parks. No amount of walking inhibited them. Christopher either tagged after them happily, rode on Paul's shoulders or was carried on someone's hip. They left the station wagon where it was parked, moving it only on street cleaning day.

They visited the red Victorian house where Marty had lived before Line came, and Marty proudly introduced her brother to Joyce and Lana. They stopped at Jack and Nathan's 'pad' at the back of a mansion, where the walls were hung with Indian bedspreads and the smell of patchouli tried to overcome the thick odor of weed.

Paul went to the dark room with Marty where she developed photographs she had taken. In one of them, all three Mikkelsons sat on a hillside with Christopher in front. "We've got to send that one home," said Marty. "I'll make you a copy too, Paul."

Paul walked with Line through Golden Gate Park, trailing after the wild-looking Joe Miller as they talked to Line's friend Julia, who identified herself as a "herbalist."

On the days Line went to work, Paul stayed with Christopher until Marty showed up in the late afternoon. He loved it when the little boy waked from his nap, sleepy and cuddly. They put on sweaters and Paul followed Christopher, his blonde curls wafting about his head. Christopher's little legs plodded the sidewalks up the hills, stopping to investigate everything from steps to stones to bird droppings and flowers. What a different childhood he had from Paul's.

"It's going too fast!" wailed Line on Sunday morning as they sat about, drinking coffee and eating toasted bagels. "We want you to stay forever!" Christopher tromped happily on the colored cartoon pages of the Sunday paper stewn about on the floor and the sofa.

Paul pulled out the road atlas and poured over the highways. "Remember those commercials for tires or trucks they were testing on the Alcan Highway?" he said. "I think they got into my blood."

He didn't have a definite schedule, but he figured it would take at least a week to drive north, and he wanted to be in Fairbanks by midsummer. "I knew it would go quickly," Paul said. It was the middle of June. He would have to leave in a day or so.

"Let's go to the tea garden," said Marty. "Paul hasn't seen it. And then we could go out to the beach one more time," she wheedled.

"Good idea," said Line.

It didn't take long for the three of them to get ready. Christopher was always ready! They waited on a corner for the electric-powered trolley bus. "Get a transfer," hissed Marty as they boarded, paying two dimes each to ride. The bus wasn't very full on a Sunday morning so they all got seats.

Lurching up the street, the bus made no noise except for the whine of the wheels. "Remember when we used to play 'my hopes' on the prairie in North Dakota?" asked Line. "When I come back from the hospital late at night, I have to wait for this bus. I stand there looking for its headlights saying to myself, 'My hopes! My hopes!'" She laughed.

When they got off on Sixth Avenue, Marty dragged them a block down to Clement Street. "There's a great second-hand bookstore there," she said. "Green Apple. The bus turns around here. We'll have time to look." The store had hand-made wooden bins in front of it full of paperback books. But Christopher didn't allow them time to browse. He kept pointing at the buses, trucks and cars as they went past.

Another big municipal bus took them into the park and they got off on a large concourse. "That's the DeYoung Museum," pointed Marty, "and over there is the aquarium." Between the buildings was a large space with a band shell at one end. It was full of odd trees with thick trunks sprouting wands of new green leaves and fountains.

"The park was once nothing but sand dunes," Line said. "The ground's been prepared over many years for its current vegetation."

Paul followed Line and Marty to an ornate wooden gate, its multiple roofs carved and painted.

"The tea garden is very old," Marty whispered as they stood outside the gate. "It started in the last century. That tree is full of cherry blossoms in March or April." She pointed to a tree at the edge of the gate. A wall enclosed the garden.

"Can you tell it's her favorite place?" asked Line.

A weathered wooden moon bridge was humped over a stream just inside the garden. Christopher's legs were almost long enough to reach the wide steps, as he climbed with Paul's help. Line and Marty watched. They were surrounded by small trees in perfectly-trained shapes, flowering azaleas, meandering streams, bamboo and, on a little rise, a teahouse open to the air.

They wandered around, looking at the statues of Buddha, the manicured lawns, the large goldfish in the ponds, the iris. Every vista was foreign, miniature and beautiful. Line led them to the teahouse. Shaded by a wooden roof, they sat along tables looking out toward the garden. A blackbird came right up to the table, tame as could be. Line waved it away.

"Three?" asked a girl in a patterned silk kimono, who arrived to serve them. She returned with a black iron teapot, three small china cups without handles and a plate of cookies. Christopher fisted a cookie and began chewing on it. Marty poured the tea.

"I'm sure you can understand why I like it," said Marty. "Even though it's crowded with people in the summer, and feels foreign, every bit of it has been touched by people's thought. It makes me more conscious. I slow down my movements, especially if I come alone, and I see everything really clearly."

"We can go away and leave you to your heightened awareness," teased Line, sipping from one of the tiny cups.

"I love it when you're all here too," protested Marty. "I'm just trying to explain something to Paul." She took Christopher on her knee.

"Never mind," said Line. "I'm just trying to get your goat."

Marty's goat was still easy for Line to get, Paul noticed. He was thinking about the golf course he had been on in October with his master teacher, Mr. Hudson. "Someone took me golfing last year," he said. "And I'm struck by how much more pleasing I find this man-made landscape than I did that one. I was horrified by the golf course, I don't mind telling you. Man over nature, subduing it into a sterile playground for himself. Like a game board."

"I think the Japanese work more with nature," said Marty.

Paul eyed the carved stone fountains, the low fences made of bamboo. Nothing he could see was made of metal or plastic. "I'm sure it is just as much work to take care of this garden as a golf course," he said, taking a bite of a sweet cookie topped with an almond. "But it doesn't turn me off."

"It's beautiful," said Line. "You're looking for unspoiled wilderness, but this is surely a reminder of the good men can do, making gardens. I'd love to have one myself," she said wistfully.

"Ever since I've left home, I've been grateful to Mother and Dad for the love of nature they gave us," said Marty, jigging Christopher up and down on her knee. "Partly it's that when I see the problems other people have with their families, I'm amazed at how wonderful ours is."

"Everyone is so different!" said Line. "And you find it most when you listen to people talk about their families, their intimate lives. Jack and Nathan, for instance. They can't imagine how we grew up, and I can't imagine how they did!"

Paul looked closely at his sisters, at the water dripping through a bamboo pipe and into a stone boat, at the perfectly trimmed pine trees, at the steaming teapot. "Well," he said. "We're a long ways from the plains of North Dakota here!"

Line mockingly had the last word, as usual. "Listen to us," she said. "Being sentimental old codgers. Just because we're together for once and Paul's leaving for the wilds of Alaska. We'll get together again. You can bet on it."

"Yes," said Paul. "Family's the best." The picture of Mother and Dad waving goodbye with Kristen and Hanna beside them as he pulled out early in the morning arose before him like a stab in the heart. He felt almost stupid, knowing how lonely he would be when he woke up in Fairbanks far from anyone he knew. But there was no going back. He had been planning this trip and he wanted it and now he was going to have to do it.

"I try to tell Mother and Dad how much I appreciate them," said Marty. "In letters. But of course I'm not going home."

"They know," said Paul softly. "I think they know."

Connie Kronlokken

ACKNOWLEDGEMENTS

The author would like to thank her siblings, cousins and friends who have shared in the experiences of which this is a fictionalized account. She would particularly like to thank Susan Korn who took the cover photo, and Marshall Tate, who allowed the use of his image! She also thanks Don Starnes for his cover design and for his support throughout the project.

ABOUT THE AUTHOR

Connie Kronlokken grew up in a large Norwegian/Danish Lutheran family. She spent her childhood in small towns across Minnesota, North Dakota and Iowa. In 1969 she moved to the San Francisco Bay Area and now lives in Los Angeles with her husband Don Starnes. Connie studied filmmaking in Denmark and has been a student of yang style tai chi for more than 25 years. She loves being with her family, the march of the seasons, cooking and gardening. She's been parsing romance from reality for most of her life.

www.ingramcontent.com/pod-product-compliance
Lightning Source LLC
Chambersburg PA
CBHW021340250626
47155CB00002B/720